MIDDLE GROUND

This book is a work of fiction, inspired by the experiences of the author's sojourn in Africa from 1973 to 1980 and those that followed her return to the United States. It was shaped by a Garveyite view of the world. The characters portrayed are products of the author's imagination, and any resemblance to anyone living or dead is purely coincidental. Actual places and events are used fictitiously.

Published in the United States by
Beckham Publications Group, Inc.
P.O. Box 4066, Silver Spring, MD 20914
ISBN: 0-931761-17-4
10 9 8 7 6 5 4 3 2 1

MIDDLE GROUND

Rosalind Kilkenny McLymont

Silver Spring

For Ivy,

the little girl with book dreams.

I didn't let go.

ACKNOWLEDGMENTS

I am deeply grateful to my English composition teachers who recognized, publicly acknowledged and helped nurture my talent: Mr. Duncan, fifth grade, and Mrs. Marcellino, eleventh grade; Calvin Holder and Ann Massay, who read the nucleus of *Middle Ground* in 1976 and made me realize I needed to grow some more; Gary Pierre-Pierre, who told me about Kinshasa of the 1990s; Chris Dupin, who made sure I got the maritime language right; Rachid King, who explained the lyrics of Tabu Ley's songs; Mitzi Rosemin Pierre, who gave me precious snippets of student life at Howard University; Jack Scovil, who affirmed my belief that I was industry-worthy; Barry Beckham and his team, who nipped and tucked the manuscript in the right places; Aziz Adetimirin, who believed enough to keep pushing; my late parents, Alfred and Ruby Kilkenny, and my brothers, Louis and Orin, the wind beneath my wings; Fritz McLymont, my husband, critic, sounding board, copyeditor and standard bearer, who knew exactly when he needed to do a disappearing act; my children, Nafisa, Sifa and Djady, and my stepson, Kahlil, who endured my many moods.

CHAPTER ONE

Shayna sighed, rolled over on her stomach, and pulled the sheet halfway up her back. With eyes pressed shut, she buried her head into the pillow and breathed deep, savoring the total disconnect of the moment. One hand hung down the side of the bed, fingers almost touching the floor. It was a low-platform bed with a single thick mattress, the kind of bed she favored since her introduction to futons in college.

A minute went by and she sighed again; the disconnect was over. *Time to deal with it*, she thought, *wonder what it is this time*?

She focused on the sensations that were sweeping through her body, sensations she knew well. They told her that something big was going to happen today. She had felt the telltale tingling soon after she woke up. The tingling came and went in a warm rush through her body. It would start in the pit of her stomach first then spread up and out, enveloping her heart, her face, her head, and then spreading through her limbs to the very tips of her fingers and her toes. For one sweet moment, it would hold her entire body in its grasp then she would feel it receding, pulling back into a final tiny tingle in her stomach before it was gone.

It lasted no more than ten seconds.

Shayna had implicit faith in these "gut alerts," as she called them. She was eight the first time she could recall this experience. She was tingly all morning. At breakfast, she told her mother that she felt funny—"all prickly and tingly and warmish," she said. Her mother felt all around her neck, made her stick out her tongue, pulled down under her eyes, then announced that she didn't have a fever and wasn't sick.

"You're probably overexcited about that jump rope competition today," her mother said, as she gave her a quick hug.

Shayna didn't think so, but she didn't argue. That afternoon, her best friend Pixie collapsed and died while they were doing their double Dutch face-off against those snotty girls from St. Phillipa's two streets over. Heart attack, the nuns whispered, thinking none of the children could hear them.

The tingling stopped the moment it sank in that Pixie was dead.

That's when Shayna began to believe in her gut alerts. Lying in her bed the very night Pixie died, scared of this terrible thing that hearts could do to little children, she pressed her hand over her own heart and begged it not to attack her and take her away forever like Pixie's heart did to her.

"I'll be good," she whispered into the darkness. "I won't bother those St. Phillipa girls like I did with Pixie."

And then she realized that she was not tingling any more. She lay stiff and still for a long time, waiting for the rush to start again, but it did not. She fell asleep waiting. It wasn't long—the next day, actually—before she figured out that there was a connection between the strange tingling she had felt all day and Pixie's sudden death. From then on she began to pay attention to her gut alerts.

"What are you telling me now?" she wondered aloud now, as she felt another gathering in the pit of her stomach. Her mind raced back in time, searching yet again for reassurance that she was not crazy. There were times when she truly thought she was. But her gut alerts never lied. They heralded good news and bad, but it was always big news. *Really* big ... like the day she met Reginald Sears, her first love. She was eighteen then. *What a self-absorbed idiot he turned out to be*, she thought, rolling her eyes. And that day during her senior year at college, when she learned she'd been accepted for a coveted internship at the *American Business Journal.* That Alicia Warren was soooo jealous! Remembering the look on Alicia's face when she heard the news made her giggle even now.

She stopped giggling as her mind took her to another gut alert day: the day the Apollo space shuttle blew up after takeoff, killing all the astronauts on board. The first black crewmember on an American space mission died in that explosion. He was a close friend of her family. She had known him all her life.

And there was her mother's first ambassadorial appointment, which meant Shayna would have to go to boarding school. It would be her first separation from her mother.

All these events were foreshadowed by her gut alerts. She was not crazy.

Reassured, Shayna rolled over on her back again and sighed. She stared at the ceiling, moving one hand gently back and forth across her chest, now and then drawing a circle around her heart with her fingers. *I suppose this is what spiritually connected folks call a quickening*, she thought, as more rushes came and went.

Mentally she began to scan the "BIGDEAL" file she kept at work on her computer's hard drive. Suddenly, the phone rang. Her heart thudding, she reached for it before it rang again.

"Hello?" Her voice was filled with apprehension.

"Don't sound so worried, baby. It's only me."

Shayna sighed with relief. She grinned widely.

"Mommy!" she cried, snuggling into the phone. "And how is America's number one emissary?"

"Couldn't be better. This is just a quick call to wish you good luck, baby. It's today, isn't it?"

"What's today?"

"I don't believe you! How could you forget? Are you all right?" Janice McWright sounded genuinely concerned.

"Yes, I'm all right, Mommy. But what's supposed to happen today? I know something is supposed to happen because I've been getting gut alerts all morning."

"I knew it! You won the Pulitzer Prize, baby! You won it! Today's the day they make the announcements. That's what your gut alerts are all about!" Janice's voice rose with excitement.

"Of course, the Pulitzer! God, I forgot all about that! Oh Mommy, do you think that's what it is? Could I have won?"

"Well, what else could it be, Shayna McWright? What can be bigger than that? You just refuse to accept how good you are. Oh, Shayna, I'm so proud of you. But I have to run now, baby. I'll call you later. Love you," she said and hung up.

Shayna hung up the phone. With an ocean between them, she cherished these unexpected, hurried phone calls from her mother. They always left her feeling that everything was right with the world. She glanced at the clock: six a.m. Her mother would be well into her day now. Shayna's heart swelled with pride as she thought of her mother: Janice McWright, the United States' first black ambassador to Belgium ... *Belgium*! Not an African country or some island in the Caribbean where they always parked blacks in the Foreign Service. This was Europe, the political capital of Western Europe at that!

There had been articles galore about Janice McWright when she got the appointment a year ago. *The Wall Street Journal*, *New York Times Magazine*, the *Economist*, *Time*, *Business Week*, *Newsweek*, and of course, *Ebony* and *Black Enterprise*. Even her own *American Business Journal* ran a profile of her. All of them had declared her the perfect choice. This month's *Essence* carried a four-page spread about the single mother, tragically widowed early in her marriage to Dillon McWright, Atlanta's glamour-boy, founder of McWright Enterprises:

a high-profile architecture firm that had designed some of the most famous buildings in cities across the southeast.

"Janice McWright is a woman of gorgeous looks and regal bearing. She's a grad from Spelman, black America's elite women's college in Atlanta, Georgetown post-grad. She's the author of three critically acclaimed books on American foreign policy, with a star reporter for a daughter. Her brilliant foreign service career is capped by this ambassadorship. God has blessed our people with this jewel."

The *Essence* writer had been shameless in her adoration.

But Janice McWright had her detractors. Shayna frowned as she recalled the harsh criticism her mother received from the Caribbean-American community and from Caribbean ambassadors in Washington when that ridiculous fight broke out between the United States and the European Union over bananas. "*Bananas*, for God's sake," she raged. "How could countries be independent for 30-odd years and still depend so totally on sales of *raw bananas* to keep their economies going? Couldn't they do other things with the damn bananas? Couldn't they build a *real* banana industry and produce everything you could possibly make from the damn plant and the damn fruit and sell all that to the whole world, for chrissake!"

Janice McWright was all over "Nightline." She defiantly told Ted Koppel and the American people that the European Union was discriminating against American banana producers by giving Caribbean fruit preferential access to its market. That was a violation of the free trade rules the Europeans themselves signed off on in Geneva under the General Agreement on Tariffs and Trade, she argued.

Yes. Janice McWright was the stuff that made black folks beam with pride. *Well, the black folks I know,* Shayna thought with a shrug.

The phone rang again and she grabbed it, thinking it was her mother again.

"Mommy?"

"'Fraid not, sugar. It's your man." His voice was deep and seductive.

Shayna lay back in the bed and purred. "Hmmm. Hello there, man of mine. What gives so early?"

"Let's not go there. Called to say I'm rooting for you, my sweet. Today's the day, isn't it?"

Shayna let out an exasperated sigh. "Am I the only one who forgot all about the Pulitzer? Mommy called just a few minutes ago with the same thing."

"Hey! We're the ones who love you. You may not love yourself enough to remember such things, but we're here and we remember."

Shayna chuckled. She decided not to tell him about the gut alerts and what her mother had said about them. She would not want him to feel sorry for her if she did not win the prize.

"I love you too, Hilton," she said seriously.

"Aha! So you *do* remember that. And you *do* remember that we're meeting for dinner today, don't you?"

"Yes, Hilton, at Londel's."

He ignored her "yes, master" tone. "Okay. Are you naked?"

"Why do you want to know?"

"So my imagination can run wild."

"Don't you have to be at your office by seven?"

Hilton groaned. "You're cold."

"Warm me up tonight."

"You got it… later."

Shayna hung up the phone just as her alarm went off: 6:15. She stretched and lay back against the pillows. It was fifteen minutes earlier than her "get-out-of-bed-right-now" time, fifteen precious minutes she used as personal, alone time before she took on the day's assault. Sometimes she prayed during those fifteen minutes. "Maybe *you* wouldn't call it prayer," she said wryly to her mother once when they were talking about religion and God and all that mind, body, spirit stuff.

"Lord, this is your day, your life; you choose, you decide." That was it. That was all her mind could muster to the great "IT" most mornings, before other thoughts invaded.

Sometimes she would revel in the sweetness of her last date with Hilton. They had been dating for three years now. Marriage definitely wasn't in the works and that was just fine with her. She liked her life. Hilton liked his. She liked her Battery Park City apartment with its Hudson River view. He liked his brownstone with its original oak woodwork on Striver's Row in Harlem. Her career was just taking off in journalism. His was just taking off in finance. He was a Harvard MBA on the fast track to senior management at Citibank. She had her gym and yoga. He had his squash and karate. They did lots of nice "couple" things with other couples at very nice places around New York City. And they made crazy love on silk designer sheets at his place, or at hers, or at some back-to-nature resort during their many weekend getaways.

Yes, she and Hilton Pierce III, were perfect just the way they were.

Surprisingly, their mothers were okay with that, too—at least that's the way it seemed to everybody. Each had broached the subject of marriage to her child just once and had never brought it up since. Comparing notes later, they found out that Shayna and Hilton's responses were almost identical.

"Why are you rushing me, Mother? You're the one who's told me time and time again to get my career going before I even think of marriage. Well, that's what I'm doing. Taking your advice and getting my career going. We'll let you know when we start to think of marriage, *if* we ever get to that point."

And that was that.

"They don't have to bring it up again. They're praying real hard, so they figure it's a done deal. They just know we're no match for God," Shayna said to Hilton with a chuckle on one of those lazy days when they were talking about nothing and everything, wondering why their mothers were so blasé about the freeze from their children on the subject of marriage.

Other times Shayna would spend her last fifteen minutes in bed homing in on a feature she was struggling to find the rhythm for. She was now a staff reporter at the *American Business Journal*. The paper was an upstart daily that blasted its way to the upper ranks of America's journalism hierarchy in the 1980s with its coverage of the flight of America's big corporations to cheaper and less union-influenced production sites overseas and the resulting decline of the country's smokestack communities.

Shayna's beat was market access: America's fight to freely sell American goods in foreign countries, particularly in developing countries that were protective of their own emerging industries. "We'll pry them open with a crowbar if we have to," the U.S. trade representative vowed—or something to that effect.

But Shayna soon realized that not every country was eager to buy processed American food and cigarettes and cars with the steering wheel on the wrong side. Some wanted to manufacture the products they consumed on their own and they fought hard to keep cheaper American and European imports from knocking out their fledgling industries.

Shayna's beat was rife with stories of battles that pitted these forces against each other. When she wrote them, she always showed how American consumers, taxpayers, and Wall Street investors ended up holding the short or long end of the stick, depending on which of the two forces won.

Every now and then when she traveled, she would do a "think" piece, or an offbeat "color" feature for the front page. For these she had won a few minor journalism prizes—not that she was not grateful for them, but she was aiming for *the big one*: the Pulitzer. She was obsessed with winning a Pulitzer Prize. It was journalism's most revered prize, a journalist's highest honor. She *knew* she could do it.

Even so, there were times when she just could not get her story together. "A story has to sing," her editor drilled into her when she interned for the paper.

"Having all the facts is fine. Putting in that nut graph to tell the readers what it all means to them is fine too. But you've got to tie all that up with a rhythm, one that sucks the readers in and keeps them sucked in all the way to the end," the editor said.

When she didn't feel like thinking about Hilton, their mothers or work, and when she was really tired, she would allow herself to succumb to fifteen minutes of that deep, delicious, second sleep. The kind you awake from feeling as if you had slept for hours, but also feeling a little guilty because you knew you stole that sleep from something important you should have been thinking about or doing.

This morning, Shayna surrendered her fifteen minutes to the rushing inside her. In spite of her mother's conviction that she had won the Pulitzer, she was haunted by an unsettling thought that this particular gut alert had to do with something much bigger. Maybe it was because she had learned to read the subtle differences in her gut alerts, so that she could almost tell when the news would be good or bad. She shivered. *Cat walked on my grave*, she thought automatically. Aloud she said, "Do yourself a favor and get out of bed right now, Shayna." Without hesitating, she took her own advice and jumped out of bed. Even if it was bad news, it would be all right in the end, she told herself firmly. Her mother taught her that.

"Things happen for a reason and they happen at the right time, Shayna," said her mother, consoling her when she cried her heart out about some disappointment or the other. "Every disappointment is an opportunity, baby. Every disappointment is an opportunity. All you have to do is look for that opportunity and seize it. Look for the lesson and learn it." Her mother had always emphasized the word "learn."

Shayna stood for a moment in front of her antique mirror with beveled edges and hugged herself. She thought how lucky she was to have a mother like Janice McWright.

Hilton was wrong. She loved herself a lot. Looking straight into the eyes that stared back at her from the mirror, she whispered, "Love you, Shayna. Love you, Mommy." Just before noon, in her tiny cubicle in the newsroom at the posh Wall Street headquarters of the *American Business Journal*, surrounded by pictures thumb-tacked to the wall of herself and her mother, her mother and the nation's chief executive, herself and Hilton, herself and very important people, herself in very important places, herself receiving important awards, Shayna went to pieces.

She had read the gut alerts right. They had nothing to do with the Pulitzer Prize.

CHAPTER TWO

Buju Banton's "Untold Stories" was blasting from the CD player. Merry and Jamillah sang at the top of their lungs, hands and head turned heavenward, their faces suffused in rapture.

"When Momma spen' her las' an' sen' you a class,
Nevah you evah play.
It's a competitive world for low-budget people,
Spendin' de dime while earnin' a nickel,
Wit' no regard for who it may tickle.
My cup is full to the brim.
I could go on and on.
The full has never been told."

They sang every word. Both agreed it was Buju's most beautiful song.

"Listen to this! Oh God, listen to this, y'all!" Caught up in Buju's melodic ballad, Merry and Jamillah heard neither the smashing sound against the kitchen floor nor Amina's frantic scream. They were stepping around the room, dancing to the song Rastafarian style: hopping on one foot, then the other; arms dropping down limp, shoulders and waist swinging to one side, then to the other, their arms following limply; one foot going forward in a cross step, toes turning out, knees bending; then the other foot pulling forward the same way, then pulling back; arms swinging up, heads turning up, then dipping forward, dipping backward. They dipped in place then swung their arms down.

Amina leapt across the den, grabbed the remote control from the coffee table and snapped on the television. Flipping rapidly through the channels, she stopped at CNN and turned the volume up loud, drowning out Buju.

"Rahtid! A wuh g'waan?" Merry exploded. She was a Jamaican and spoke her native patois with pride.

"That's what's going on," Amina said, pointing to the TV. Merry and Jamillah turned to look. A reporter in a helicopter was describing the scene below. As the reporter's words sank in, Merry edged sideways toward the mahogany room divider, her eyes riveted on the television screen. She reached out, fumbled for a button and pressed off the CD player. They stood transfixed as the reporter continued her description of the horror on the ground.

It was the scene of a fatal crash involving a car and a tractor-trailer. The car—what was left of it—was a blackened mass of twisted metal pressed up against the front of the truck. The entire cab of the truck itself was charred. The car must have slammed into the truck head-on and exploded, either on impact or shortly after. Broken glass and bits of shiny metal that escaped the inferno were strewn in a wide radius around the vehicles. Off to the side in the grass, two bodies were covered with white sheets. Several ambulances and police cars were on the scene, their red and blue lights swirling. Walkie-talkies crackled. Fire trucks continued to douse the vehicles. Traffic was backed up in both directions as far as the eye could see.

The cameraman in the helicopter panned the scene, zeroing in for a few seconds on a stretcher carrying a severely burnt man. Medics were placing the stretcher into one of the ambulances. The man was still alive, his face twisted in agony. Jamillah, Merry and Amina groaned in unison. Then a headshot of Janice McWright appeared in the upper left-hand corner of the TV screen. Jamillah gasped and her hands flew to her mouth.

"Shhhh!" snapped Amina. She turned down the TV volume now that Buju had been silenced. Now you could also hear the radio in the kitchen. Amina always kept it on News 88.

Jamillah sank down slowly on the sofa, her hands still clamped over her open mouth. Amina stood like a stone, one hand clutching the knife she had been using in the kitchen. The other clutched the remote control.

Merry sat down hard next to Jamillah. She sat ramrod straight, her mouth slightly open, her hands clasped tight in her lap.

"... apparently, Ambassador McWright and her driver were killed instantly," CNN anchor Robin Rayburn was saying. "We don't know yet how this terrible accident occurred, but it looks like Ambassador McWright's car somehow veered into the path of the tractor-trailer. How and why that happened we do not know yet. You can see that her car is on the right side of the road facing the tractor-trailer. Unlike in the United States, vehicles drive on the left side of the road in Europe. Let's go live to Sophie St. Cyr who is on the scene - Sophie? Are you there, Sophie?"

"Mi God! Mi God! Is dead she dead? Is dead Ms. McWright dead? Mi kyan believe it!" said Merry.

"Robin, it's an absolutely gruesome scene down here. Ambassador McWright and her driver have been confirmed dead, both killed instantly in a head-on collision with a tractor-trailer on this busy expressway. Ambassador McWright apparently was on her way to Brussels National Airport.

The bodies have not yet been removed from the scene. The truck driver suffered third-degree burns when the car exploded on impact. A witness told me there was a second explosion, but he saw the driver jump out of the tractor-trailer before that explosion. Miraculously, no other vehicles were involved in this horrible crash.

"As you can see," she said, making a wide sweep with her free hand that the camera followed, "those immediately behind the Ambassador's car and the tractor-trailer swerved off the road to avoid a pile-up." The camera zoomed in on several cars plunged deep into the grassy banks that fell away from the road.

A grim-faced man in uniform stood next to Sophie St. Cyr when the camera reverted its focus.

"Police Commissioner Pieter Brel is with me now. Commissioner Brel, do we have any idea what really happened here?"

Commissioner Brel was a strapping, six-foot-five native of the Flanders region in the north.

"We have accounts from a number of eyewitnesses, of course. We are putting those accounts together, plus what our experts find, to come up with a picture more detailed than the obvious," he said, his speech laden with the Dutch-French accent common among the Flemish.

"Do you think foul play was involved?" she asked, her eyes fixed on the commissioner with one of her famous "take-no-prisoners" looks. St. Cyr was French by birth, though she spoke fluent English with a distinct British accent. She had a reputation of being the first to ask the question every other reporter wanted to ask but took a fraction of a second too long to do so.

Commissioner Brel looked into the camera. When he spoke, his voice was firm and matter of fact. It wasn't the first time he encountered "Attila the Mouth," as Sophie St. Cyr was known at police headquarters. Many a public servant had been clubbed by her leading questions and provocative innuendoes. Among her peers, she was disliked as much as she was respected.

"It would be most unwise for anyone to jump to such alarmist conclusions. As far as we can tell at this moment, this was a terrible, terrible accident. We will continue our investigation, of course, and will inform the public of our findings in due course," he said.

"Do you know where Ambassador McWright was going at the time of the accident?"

"No I do not," said the commissioner tersely. "I'm afraid I must get back to the investigation now."

Merry, Jamillah and Amina watched the rest of Sophie St. Cyr's report in silence. The scene was teeming with police, ambulances, fire trucks, emergency personnel, and medics. The ambulance carrying the truck driver sped away, its siren blaring. The bodies that were covered with white sheets, no doubt those of Ambassador McWright and her driver, were placed into separate ambulances.

"Mi God," Merry breathed again.

News Anchor Robin Rayburn cut in from Atlanta. "Let's go live to the White House where the President is about to make a statement," she said.

The camera cut to the President. He sat behind his desk in the Oval Office, his handsome face pale and drawn. His jaws were clenched so tight that the muscles at his temples jerked up and down.

"Fellow Americans, this is truly a sad day for our country," he began in his soft raspy drawl. "At precisely nine a.m. Eastern Standard Time today, Ambassador Janice McWright, our country's highest ranking representative in Brussels and one of our most skilled and most loved diplomats, was killed in a car crash on a highway in Brussels, Belgium. Her driver, Paul Vergogne, a trusted Belgian citizen who served at the embassy for over a decade, was also killed. We offer our deepest sympathy to both their families." The president's voice quivered. Amina turned to her friends. They stared at each other in horror.

Normally, the death of an American ambassador, whatever the cause, would not affect them this much. Lord knows America's ambassadors had played their part—directly and indirectly-in shaping and upholding policies that often resulted in hardship for millions of men, women, and children in developing countries. The three friends agreed on this point in umpteen late-night "reasonings" at Spelman.

They would reel off examples of such policy repercussions for the benefit of any newcomers to these sessions, describing U.S. actions in these countries. Then they would launch into a passionate discourse on the "economic lynching" of the Third World at the hands of big businesses in wealthy nations and the governments that backed them, aided, and abetted by the World Bank, the International Monetary Fund, the World Trade Organization and "all those lackey leaders that are still giving up their souls and their people and the resources of their countries in exchange for power and a few beads in a bank account in Europe or America."

Jamillah had written these words in one of her columns for a short-lived campus publication that dealt with world politics.

The chickens would come home to roost, they always argued. They pointed to the bombing of the U.S. Embassy in Beirut in 1983 and, a few months later, the bombing of the U.S. Marine barracks in the same city. Then came the hits on ordinary Americans. Lockerbie and Oklahoma City weren't blips of lunacy, they declared. And more hits on Americans outside: Saudi Arabia, Kenya, and Tanzania; the last two shocked the hell out of everybody because it was Africa, Sub-Saharan Africa. Such things just didn't happen there.

Not that Amina, Jamillah and Merry condoned these acts. Older and much more dispassionate in their reasoning they no longer accepted the politics of extremism. After all, with everybody traveling here and there and everywhere these days, any one of them, or a family member, or a friend could be a victim of such extremism at any time. But it would be intellectually dishonest to dismiss the role America's own actions played in feeding the extreme fringe, they told each other and whomever else reasoned with them.

"My mother always says 'if you don't like mud, don't go to crab dance.' America is a super power and it dances with crabs—maybe not all the time, but often enough. It must get muddy," Amina said during one of their sessions.

But this death was different. They *knew* the deceased and, as far as they could tell, it was a tragic accident. They had spoken with Janice McWright several times at Spelman and genuinely liked her. They knew her daughter Shayna well, for all her snootiness. It was hard to be detached and scholarly about this particular incident.

"The death of Janice McWright is a great loss for America, for my family, and for me in particular. Aside from being my choice for ambassador to one of the most important posts in Europe, she was a close, personal friend. We will miss her skill, her gentleness, her friendship." The president's voice quivered. The agony he was trying to hold in check was genuine. Those in the inner circles in Washington knew how hard the loss of Janice McWright would be for him. She was one of his most trusted political allies, a formidable campaigner for his policies at home and an equally effective spokesperson abroad. Public opinion polls taken right after the president's broadcast would show him enjoying his highest approval rating ever.

"Anybody know where she is?" Jamillah asked suddenly. She did not have to say Shayna's name.

Merry snapped at her instantly. "Oh come on, Jamillah! How would *we* know? You know Shayna: Babylon princess dat! She got *no* time for West In-di-uns. She was one of them that believe in that nonsense about black Americans on top, West Indians right under them and Africans on the bottom, remembah?"

Merry tended to mix Jamaican patois with straight English when she got excited.

Jamillah groaned. "For chrissake, Merry! Haven't we grown past that? I doubt Shayna still subscribes to such nonsense."

"And this is hardly the time to bring it up anyway," Amina chided.

"Well, I ask again, how would *we* know where Shayna is? She made a point of not socializing with the likes of us," Merry countered stubbornly.

The deep, but often unspoken, social divide at Spelman and at other black colleges had outraged all three of them. They had publicly railed against it-—to any group or individual that would listen. Once, during their sophomore year, Merry let loose a colorful tongue lashing on Shayna, with whom she shared several classes. Shayna had just pledged to a sorority whose members turned up their nose at anyone with a hint of a foreign accent. They'd hardly spoken to each other after that, not even when they ended up in the same work group for one course project or another, as was often the case.

Merry admired Janice McWright nonetheless, though she had rained fire and brimstone on her for her "brainwashed, illogic position on the banana issue." On the day of Janice McWright's interview on "Nightline," she called Amina fuming and conferenced in Jamillah.

"You show me a banana plantation in America! Show me how American companies get hurt because they can't sell to the one measly percent of the European market that Caribbean growers control! Show me! This isn't an American fight! This is one company's fight! Big lobby money mek it America fight! Nuh de same Chiquita control de res' o' de market anyway? Dis nuh free trade. Dis a bully trade. Strong man set rule, strong man win all de time! Bwoy, Miz McWright dead wrong on dis one!"

Jamillah and Amina agreed with her wholeheartedly.

Amina knew where to find Shayna. "Shayna is a reporter at the *"American Business Journal*," and a damn good one too," she said.

"How you know?" Merry's voice was rough and disbelieving.

Then she slapped her forehead. "Stupid me! The *American Business Journal* is your bible isn't it, Miss New York Stock Exchange?"

It sounded so silly that she herself giggled. So did Amina and Jamillah.

They were all about the same age, in their late twenties. They argued fiercely and often, and loved each other just as passionately. They'd shared a townhouse off campus for three of their four years at Spelman.

Merry, short for Meredith, was a gynecologist at Brookdale Hospital in Brooklyn. She had come to the United States from Jamaica when she was nine. She was one of those pretty, "no-nation" people—Amina's term—that were so common in the Caribbean. They were a racial hodge-podge that mixed African, European, East Indian, Syrian and Chinese blood in all possible combinations.

Of the three friends, Merry was the only one married. She was expecting her first child; Jamillah and Amina kept reminding her to say "our," since she wasn't a single mom-to-be. Her husband, Phillip, also Jamaican, ran his own importing company that dealt mainly in gourmet tropical foods. He was a frequent overseas traveler, buying his products from suppliers in Africa, Asia, Latin America, and the Caribbean. Merry adored him and he adored her.

Jamillah, a mergers and acquisitions analyst at Goldman Sachs, was a native New Yorker. Her parents and grandparents on her father's side hailed from South Carolina. Jamillah was dark and "comely," as Amina loved to say. She was engaged to a corporate lawyer who was born in the Dominican Republic, but who spent most of his life in the United States.

Despite the stark differences in their backgrounds, they enjoyed sharing each other's cultures. They delighted in the similarities. Much of the food, the earthy outlook on life, the sense of humor, the way children were viewed and disciplined, the social reach of church. Jamillah was as comfortable in the Caribbean as Merry and Amina were at Jamillah's grandparents' farm in South Carolina. Neither Merry nor Jamillah believed Amina when she told them that she was from Africa. Even today, few people found it hard to believe at first.

"Gitouttaheah!" Jamillah burst out incredulously when they first met during a football season victory party at Hampton University in Virginia. They were freshmen at Spelman at the time. A few carloads of them headed up to Hampton to help their friends celebrate their team's winning the championship.

Amina scowled at Jamillah's outburst. She was sick of Americans, black and white, and their stupid ideas about what Africans should look like.

"Sorry to disappoint you by the way I look, Jamillah. I've learned to wear clothes since I came to America. And as you can see, I've removed the bones from my ear lobes and nostrils," she responded coolly. Then, for some inexplicable reason, she and Jamillah burst out laughing at the same time.

Amina was born in Zaire, known today as the Democratic Republic of Congo. Congo was its name before Mobutu Sese Seko came to power. People referred to it as "Congo-Kinshasa" to distinguish it from Congo-Brazzaville across the river. "Zaire" was done away with as soon as Mobutu was overthrown by General Laurent-Desire Kabila.

Amina grumbled when Kabila brought back the original Congolese flag. She still kept the "tricolore enflamée" hanging in her den—not that she admired anything about Mobutu's despotic regime. It was just a great-looking flag. Against a background of green and encircled in golden sunlight, a hand held aloft a torch with a blazing red flame. The current flag, a blue triangle with five white stars in one corner, seemed unimaginative in comparison. It reminded her of the flag of the European Union.

Amina's father was Congolese, her mother was from the West Indies—Guyana, to be exact—the South American nation with the Caribbean culture. The family, there were four children, moved from Zaire to the United States when she was eleven. Her parents were now divorced, but she returned to Congo with her father, sister, and brothers once during high school and twice on her own during summers off from college.

Now a pediatric psychotherapist, she spent at least one month every year at the hospital in Kinshasa where she was born, working for free in the pediatric ward. Her pay, she told Jamillah and Merry, was the reconnection with the other half of her spirit. She re-learned Lingala and perfected her French, and kept in close contact with her father's family, especially one particular great-uncle who was her grandfather's twin brother.

Jamillah and Merry spent two weeks with her in Kinshasa last year.

Amina was taller than her two best friends by a good three inches. And while there was something distinctly "un-American" about her facial features, most people never placed her as an African. She dated occasionally, but there was no "significant other" in her life. She was passionate about her work with immigrant children. She found that many of them were traumatized by their new environment, but their parents were too stressed themselves, and their teachers too lazy, to see it.

She made a ton of money in the stock market and bought an old three-story brownstone in Brooklyn Heights. She converted the street level apartment to a private clinic and worked there with a small staff. She herself lived on the two upper floors. A sizable fortune in paintings by black artists from all over the world hung on the walls on every floor.

Merry and Jamillah were all at her house today. It was one of those rare days when they decided to take off and just hang out with each other.

"Seriously, we should do something—send a card, a wreath, basket of fruit, something," Amina said. "I mean, it's not as if we don't know Shayna. Even though she was conceited, she did work with us for two years on that community outreach project in Atlanta."

"Yes," Jamillah said firmly, as she glared at Merry.

Merry shook her dreadlocks. "Of course we'll do something. Jamillah, don't look at me like that. You of all people *know* I don't care about that American, West Indian, African hierarchy any more, it's BS. That's all it is. There's always bickering in families about who's better than whom, especially when everybody is so ambitious and achievement oriented and under the same pressure to succeed. Nuh true?"

They were silent for a while, and then all three were speaking at the same time.

"As a matter of fact, my cousin..."

"I remember my aunt..."

"Even my brother..."

They looked at each other and burst out laughing.

"God I love us," Jamillah said finally, wiping her eyes.

"... Ironically, the news reached Ambassador McWright's daughter Shayna, a reporter at the *American Business Journal*, just minutes after she received the news that she won this year's Pulitzer prize for beat reporting," the CNN anchor was saying.

"Shhhh! Shhhh!"

"A spokesperson for the *American Business Journal* said Ms. McWright is understandably distraught and has gone into seclusion. He declined to comment any further." Behind her was a shot of the Wall Street headquarters of the *American Business Journal*. Camera crews and reporters were milling about, hoping to catch a glimpse of Shayna.

"Maybe we could call the newspaper and get her home address and number,"

"Yeah, right, Amina. What would we say? That we're close friends? Relatives? So how come we don't know where she lives or what her home number is?" Merry said impatiently.

"Her sorority sisters will put an iron ring around her for sure. Can't say I'd blame them," said Jamillah. "Hey! How about calling them up? Pretend we're one of them."

"They'll check us out for sure. Don't they have secret codes and things?" Amina sounded doubtful.

"Who do we know that belongs to that sorority? They won't deny one of their own," Jamillah insisted.

"So what do we do after we get the address? Just send her something, right? We're not planning to go over there, right? I mean, we really weren't close," said Merry.

"No, Merry. We won't go over there, unless she invites us," Jamillah said.

"Freda is one," Merry said.

"Freda who?" Amina and Jamillah asked in unison.

"Freda Michaelson, don't you remember her? She was a year behind us: nerdy but really nice. She's a gynecologist at Brookdale too. I see her all the time," said Merry. "She must have known Shayna. I'll talk to her tomorrow."

"So what'll we get?" Amina asked.

"A fruit basket?" Jamillah said.

"She won't have an appetite. The fruit will just rot, or she'll give it away," Merry said.

"You don't know that," Jamillah said stubbornly.

"Would you be thinking about food if it was you?" Merry retorted.

"Yeah, I guess you're right," Jamillah conceded.

"Flowers?" Amina sounded as if she herself didn't like the idea.

"She'll be drowning in flowers. They'll remind her of wreaths and funeral homes and she'll be sick of the smell," Jamillah said with exasperation.

They fell silent, each wracking her brain to come up with an appropriate gift. After a while, Amina said, "I have an idea. Let's get her a real old-fashioned brown teddy bear: a good-sized one, dark brown, with big brown eyes; one you want to cuddle and hug. We'll get a nice, blank card, write our own words inside, sign it, hang it with a fancy ribbon around the teddy bear's neck, wrap it up nice in a box with a big bow, and send it."

They thought about that for a while.

"You know, that is not a bad idea," Merry said slowly. "*I'd* want something to hug and cry into."

"Me too. It's a wonderful idea," Jamillah said. "But we shouldn't write anything long and sappy."

Merry started to wring her hands excitedly said, "How about this? How about this? 'For the days when you wish you could hold her, and when you want to cry but you don't want anyone to see your tears.' ... just that, with our names."

Jamillah and Amina stared at her in disbelief.

"Well?" Merry said sheepishly.

"That's beautiful, Merry," Amina said.

Jamillah leaned over and hugged Merry. "It's precious," she said softly. "We'll put our phone numbers on the card, too, just in case."

They fell silent again. CNN was reporting from the scene in Brussels again. They listened for a while then Amina broke in.

"Okay, so that's settled: Merry, checks out Freda, buys the card, and writes the note. I'll check out FAO Schwartz for a Gund teddy bear. Gunds are the best. FAO is bound to have one."

"Lemme know when you're going. I'll come with you," said Jamillah.

"I'll come too," said Merry.

"No way. I ain't goin' into no FAO Schwartz with no mother-to-be. They'd probably have to close the damn store on us," said Amina.

"Oh shut up!" said Merry.

CHAPTER THREE

Shayna did not know where she was or what time it was. She didn't want to know. Knowing would mean thinking and she didn't want to think. She moaned repeatedly. "Pasi! Pasi! Oh, oh, oh!" She rocked herself and said the words over and over again in a monotonous, low singsong voice.

"It's okay, Shayna. It's okay, baby," said the voice of whomever was hugging her. The voice had an ache in it. From time to time, the hands that went with the voice stroked her hair and held her face. Then those very arms would hold her tight again. Familiar hands. Familiar arms. Familiar scent. She kept her eyes shut tight. "Pasi! Pasi! Oh, oh, oh!" she moaned. "Pasi! Pasi! Oh, oh, oh!"

This was her comfort song. As far back as she could remember, this was the song she sang when she was scared or hurt. She would hug herself, rocking back and forth, softly singing the words: Just, "Pasi, pasi. Oh, oh, oh!" over and over again. She didn't know where it came from—never even wondered about it—or what "pasi" meant, if indeed it meant anything. She never asked her mother. It was just there, as much a part of her as her eyes and her nose. She hadn't sung it since the day they buried Pixie. She moaned the comfort song now until the heaving from her sobs subsided. The arms that kept holding her and the familiar scent that came with the arms were comforting. They were Hilton's.

He dashed over to the newspaper by taxi as soon as the news flashed across the top of his computer screen. With the help of the editor and the publisher, he hustled Shayna out of the building, minutes before the first mob of reporters and camera crews descended on the place. The publisher's private limousine had been waiting for them.

When the limo dropped them off at his home in Harlem, Shayna was almost lifeless. She could not get out of the car on her own strength. Hilton picked her up and carried her into his apartment straight to the bedroom. He laid her on the bed, pulled the cover over her legs, and went into the kitchen to get her a glass of brandy and a cup of hot chamomile tea sweetened with honey, the way she liked it.

Shayna refused both. He cradled her head with one arm and tried to coax her to take at least a few sips of the tea, but to no avail. She shook her head impatiently and kept her lips in a tight line.

Hilton did not force her. "Ok, baby. You can have it later," he said. He rocked her gently and she cried until she fell asleep. That was hours ago.

The phone rang. Hilton's eyes flew open. *I must have dozed off,* he thought, looking down anxiously at Shayna. Her eyes were closed but he could tell she was not asleep. He eased her head gently onto the pillows and walked quickly into the living room, closing the bedroom door behind him as quietly as he could.

"Hilton Pierce," he said crisply into his cordless phone. He kept it out of the bedroom deliberately.

"This is John Ramsey at the State Department, Mr. Pierce. I know this is a bad time, but may I speak with Ms. McWright?"

He'd left his phone number with Shayna's editor and publisher.

"I'm afraid she's asleep, sir. Is there anything I can help you with?"

"Well," Ramsey hesitated. "We'll need to keep her under watch, Mr. Pierce. You understand, I'm sure. The FBI has already posted two men outside your building."

Hilton walked over to the window. In a street lined with BMWs, Mercedes Benzes, Volvos and Saabs, the shiny black Lincoln stood out like a visiting cousin from the country.

"Yes, I see them, Mr. Ramsey," he said.

"We'll need Ms. McWright to travel to Brussels to identify her mother's body," John Ramsey said matter-of-factly. "She *is* the closest relative."

Janice McWright was an only child. Her parents died years ago and her aunts, uncles, and cousins were scattered around the country. Christmas cards, a telephone call at Thanksgiving or Easter, or New Year's Day—sometimes on a birthday or Mother's Day—was the extent of her family get-togethers. "Aloof," the family called Janice. Proud as they were of her, the relatives kept their distance, except Aunt Fifi who called at least once a month.

"How soon?" Hilton asked.

"Right away, I'm afraid."

"I don't know ..."

"Mr. Pierce, it's not an option. You can accompany her, of course."

"Right."

Ramsey filled him in on the logistics. Shayna and Hilton would be accompanied by the Secret Service on a flight to Washington. They would leave from there on an Air Force plane that very night for Brussels with the Secretary of State and the head of the Senate Foreign Relations Committee—both very close friends of Janice McWright. A doctor would be with them at all times.

The agents outside Hilton's apartment would take them to Shayna's apartment for her to pick up whatever she would need, and then they would take them to Kennedy Airport for the flight to Washington. Two other agents would meet them at the airport and accompany them on the flight.

"There's sure to be reporters at her apartment, Mr. Ramsey," Hilton said. "Can you keep them away?"

"This is America, Mr. Pierce. The press is ferocious about protecting the people's right to know. But he will try our best to keep them at bay." His voice was laden with sarcasm.

After he finished speaking with Ramsey, Hilton dialed his office. His secretary answered.

"Hey, Sally. Put me through to Greg." Greg Thorton was his boss. Thorton came on the line immediately.

"Glad you called, Hilton," he said. "We know what's happening. Sorry, man … here's the deal. Take a couple of weeks off and we'll count it against your vacation time."

"Thanks, Greg. That's what I was calling about."

"She'll have to go to Brussels for sure. That won't be an easy trip," Greg said.

"Yeah. I'll go with her, of course. We should be back in the country in a day or two, but she will need me around for a while," Hilton replied.

"Like I said, take the two weeks. We'll cover for you here," Greg said quickly.

"That's cool, man. I appreciate that. I'll keep you posted," Hilton said.

He hung up the phone and went back into the bedroom. Shayna was sitting up, staring into space, her face filled with despair. Hilton sat down beside her and took her in his arms. She leaned against him and began to sob. He said nothing. He held her until her crying subsided.

"We have to leave for Brussels tonight," he said gently.

"I know," said Shayna tearfully.

"They're taking us to the airport from your place in a couple of hours." He held her away from him and looked into her eyes with a smile. "We'll run over there now and pack a few things, okay?"

Shayna nodded. She sighed and leaned back against the headboard.

"I'll just throw something together and we'll go," Hilton continued, trying to sound businesslike. He got up and pulled a leather garment bag from a closet. In five minutes, suit, shirt, tie, underwear, robe, toiletries, and a pair of socks were neatly packed. He changed into a casual shirt and slacks and pulled on a sport jacket.

"Hilton."

He sat down beside her again. "What, baby?"

"I don't know what to do. I don't know how to handle this. I don't know how to make..." Her voice broke.

"It's okay. Don't worry. I'm here. It'll all be taken care of," he said cradling her. "Come on," he said gently, lifting her from the bed. "We have to leave."

The phone rang again. Hilton ran outside and grabbed it. "This is Hilton," he said, moving out of Shayna's earshot.

In the bedroom, Shayna looked around listlessly. She spotted her pocketbook on the dresser, picked it up, and went into the bathroom. She stared at herself in the mirror. Her face was tearstained and puffy, her eyes red. The tears started flowing again. Gripping the washbasin with both hands, she bowed her head and wailed silently. "Mommy, oh, Mommy! Please don't let this be true. Please call and tell me it was all a mistake."

Finally she raised her head and looked into the mirror again. It's true, her eyes told her sadly. Stiffly, she turned on the cold water tap and let it run for a while. She stared at the stream of water. With the same robot-like movements, she cupped her hands under the tap and stared at the pool of water in the basin. She splashed the cold water on her face. She wet her face again, and then dried herself with one of Hilton's royal blue, monogrammed guest towels. She took a powder compact from her purse, opened it, and patted her face with the puff.

She applied some lipstick, ran her fingers through her hair, straightened and brushed her skirt, and went back into the bedroom. She picked up her jacket from an armchair and put it on. She went back into the bathroom to retrieve her purse, glanced in the mirror once more, and walked into the living room. Hilton was just getting off the telephone.

"That was Paul. I filled him in on where we'll be," he said. Paul Trichet was his best friend. "You look refreshed. Ready?" He came close to her and put his arms around her.

Shayna looked at him and forced a smile. "Yes, I'm ready," she said, barely above a whisper.

The moment Hilton and Shayna walked through the front door, the agent in the driver's seat of the black Lincoln sprang out of the car. He opened the curbside back door and stood beside it, watching Shayna and Hilton approach. The other agent came out from the passenger's seat and remained at his side of the car. He kept looking around until Hilton and Shayna were in the car and his partner was back behind the wheel, then he got in. Aside from a curt nod to Hilton and Shayna when they reached the car, neither agent said a word.

"Jesus! Straight out of the movies, dark glasses and all," Hilton muttered to himself. He resented the fact that all these strangers had such easy access to him and to Shayna. He could understand in Shayna's case. But he was a private person, damn it. And here they were, at his home, with his phone number, everything. He realized he was being foolish and sighed. *Be reasonable*, *Hilton*, he said to himself. *The situation warrants it. You should be glad to know these guys can move so fast.* He sighed again and resigned himself to government control for the next, who knew how long.

In no time they were speeding down the West Side Highway toward Battery Park City. It was only when they had the highway at the 125th Street entrance that the two agents introduced themselves as Frank Thomas and Robert Jenkins. Agent Thomas, the driver, needed no directions to Shayna's apartment.

Hilton kept his arm around Shayna. She leaned against him all the way with eyes closed. Sometimes, a sob would escape her throat and her body would heave. At those moments, Hilton held her tighter.

The sun was a fiery red ball ringed with silver. It hung low in the western sky. Hilton looked out onto the still, shimmering Hudson River. A few yachts were moored at the boat basin between the 96th Street and 79th Street exits. On the other side of the river, New Jersey was bathed in the sun's fiery glow.

The ride along the river was one he knew well, but it was one he appreciated every time he drove along the highway. Traffic in this direction was lighter than on the uptown side heading toward the George Washington Bridge. People were already heading home to the suburbs north and west.

Ah, river, Hilton sighed inwardly, *all is always well with you, isn't it? So balanced you are. You just roll right on through, doing your thing. You touch this side, you touch that side and keep on moving, nothing holding you back. Not even a world turned upside down. I envy you.*

To everyone but himself, Hilton was in complete control. He was one of those individuals with the remarkable ability to put on an Oscar-winning performance for the audience while his guts were ripping apart inside. He had no doubt he would get through the next few days, weeks even, with a straight back. Being there for Shayna, doing the right things, saying the right things to the right people. Besides, there would be help. Some of Shayna's relatives were bound to come around. There was a death in the family, after all.

It's as if death walks in and sets up this huge screen for those left behind to look at, he thought, *and the screen shows only scenes of happier times, with loved ones whom we shared so much with so many years ago and whom we cast aside because of some stupid quarrel. Seeing all this flash by on that life screen makes us want to be near them again. To embrace them, even for a moment, because we couldn't stand the guilt if another should go and we hadn't taken the time to make things right again.*

They'll be there, Hilton thought, not without some relief. *Family blood flows river deep. They'll be there.*

For a moment, the enormity of the situation overwhelmed him. It wasn't as if he didn't want to be involved in what lay ahead. He loved Shayna. He felt honored, in fact, to be at her side at a time like this, when she needed his strength. His skin crawled as he recalled how she ran to him when he burst into the publisher's office. She clung to him, pleading with him to tell her it was not true, sobbing that she had spoken with her mother just a few hours ago and now they were telling her she was dead. He managed to soothe her and take her away from the office. But he'd known right away what would be coming when all this was over. Everyone, *everyone*, would be looking to him to take care of Shayna in the *right* way. But that wasn't in the plan right now. It just wasn't in the plan.

Hilton thought of what it would be like to be married to Shayna. Sure he'd thought of it before, but he'd always pushed it away ... not the right time yet. He wanted to be in the right spot at the bank before marrying Shayna—or anyone for that matter. That was a good three years away.

Still, he thought with a smile, *we do make one hell of a couple, no doubt about that. . Maybe it's time*, he thought with resignation. *Within a year or so should be good enough. Besides, it might even help speed up my career at the bank. That old boy clique on the top floor certainly wouldn't frown on such a famous wife.*

Instantly he felt ashamed and disgusted with himself. *Jesus, Hilton,* he thought, *what kind of creature are you to think such thoughts at a time like this?*

The car swung onto Shayna's street. A small crowd of reporters and camera crews had gathered in front of her building. Jenkins turned to Hilton. "We'll go into the underground parking lot from the side street. You can go up to Ms. McWright's apartment from the entrance there, Mr. Pierce," he said.

"That's good," Hilton said, wondering if there was anything Uncle Sam didn't know about each and every citizen in the country.

The car drove past Shayna's building and turned left at the corner. Its tinted windows hid its occupants from the reporters. A few feet down the road it turned into a hidden entrance that sloped downward to an underground garage. The driver stopped at the attendant's booth, rolled down the window and showed his ID. On reading the ID, the attendant drew himself up stiffly and saluted. Agent Thomas suppressed a smile and touched his forehead, the way a senior officer might casually acknowledge a subordinate.

The attendant waved the car on. He had been waiting anxiously for this moment. He'd been put on alert hours ago, under threat of dismissal, prosecution, and deportation if he divulged anything to anyone. As the car drove into the garage, he stood in the middle of the entranceway facing the road, his hands folded across his chest and legs spread menacingly apart. He had been given orders to prevent all other cars from entering until the black Lincoln exited the garage.

The attendant scowled in an attempt to look menacing. His orders were the type he knew how to keep. He was a policeman in India before coming to the United States.

The Lincoln came to a stop in front of the elevator that went from the garage to the lobby of the apartment building. Agent Thomas got out and opened the door. Hilton got out first and helped Shayna out. Jenkins was already standing at the elevator, scanning the deserted garage. He accompanied Hilton and Shayna up to Shayna's apartment. Minutes later, Hilton was helping Shayna pack. Agent Thomas stayed in the car. Agent Jenkins walked up and down the hallway outside the apartment.

"Want to clear your messages?" Hilton asked. The tiny red light on her phone was blinking furiously. They were in the bedroom.

"I suppose I should," said Shayna. She sank down on the bed and picked up the phone to listen to her voicemail. Tears streamed down her face as she listened to message after message of condolences.

The buzzer at the front door rang. Hilton went to get it. He peered through the peephole and opened the door when he saw Agent Jenkins.

"Two ladies in the lobby say they are relatives of Ms. McWright. Said they flew in from Atlanta as soon as they heard the news. They said to tell Ms. McWright it's Aunt Fiona and Camille."

"Please let them come up," said Shayna, walking into the living room with an overnight bag in her hand.

Hilton turned to her, his eyes questioning. "It's all right, Hilton. I'm glad they're here," Shayna said.

Aunt Fiona—Fifi, the family called her—bustled in, with her daughter Camille in tow. They looked and smelled as if they'd just stepped out of the House of Chanel. They probably had. Fiona and Camille owned and managed a prosperous upscale boutique in Atlanta where they sold hats—they preferred the French term "chapeaux"—in Atlanta. They were both designers and their chapeaux were bought by wealthy ladies all over the world, even as far away as Japan.

The two women rushed over to Shayna. They hugged and rocked each other and sobbed.

Of all her mother's relatives, these were the only two Shayna really knew. Fiona Grainger was her mother's aunt. She had never married. It was well known in the family that Camille was the child of the CEO of a certain Fortune 500 company, though no one ever mentioned any names. Fiona and he had fallen in love since graduate school at Columbia University in New York. As far as anyone knew, their affair never ended, although he had long married someone else and had four children.

"They couldn't marry, of course. Aunt Fiona's parents absolutely forbade it. So did his. You know how it is, baby. He was a descendant of Plymouth Rock people and she was the descendant of a slave. So they just stayed together as lovers. All these years," Shayna's mom had told her.

"Does Camille know him?" Shayna asked.

"Yes. Apparently he dotes on her and she on him. She never talks about him, though. She knows the deal."

"You think his wife knows?"

"Of course she does. But you know how it is with some women. He can do what he likes as long as he keeps it away from the children and doesn't mention divorce. I bet it's like that."

"Could you live like that, Mommy? Like Aunt Fiona or the wife?"

Janice looked off into the distance and sighed.

"I don't know, baby. I honestly don't know. Women like Aunt Fiona and the wife, you've got to admire them in a way. I don't know if I have their kind of strength."

"Ahem!" It was Agent Jenkins bringing her back to the present. "My apologies, Ms. McWright. It's almost time to go."

"Yes," Shayna said, turning from her great aunt and cousin.

She introduced them to Hilton.

"Thank you for the support you're giving to my niece's child," Aunt Fifi said. She had already sized up Hilton. She was good at that, like most women her age. Good breeding was written all over the young man. He was appropriately deferential; that easy upright stance, confident eyes, tastefully tailored, expensive clothes worn with laced-up leather shoes—his whole attire bespoke the upper floors of a good blueblood firm. And he's here, *with* Shayna. Not on the other end of the phone, Fiona thought appreciatively.

"Aunt Fifi, Camille, we're going to Brussels tonight. You'll stay here, won't you?" Shayna said, her eyes wide and anxious.

"Don't worry, child. That's what we came to do. We'll stay here, manage all the phone calls, the rest of the family, and everything else. Don't you worry about a thing," Aunt Fifi said in a take-charge tone that was so much like Janice.

"I'll deal with the press, Shayna. I can handle them," said Camille.

Shayna hugged them again. "I'm so glad you're here," she whispered.

She and Hilton said their good-byes and left.

Shayna slept all the way to Washington. She vaguely remembered the transfer to the Air Force plane for the flight to Brussels. She knew she had spoken to Donald Parris, the secretary of state, and to Senator Blythe. And there was a woman doctor. She could not recall what she said to any of them.

She slept during the entire flight to Brussels—or so it seemed to everyone else on the plane, including Hilton. The truth is, she had been awake for most of the trip, but she kept her eyes closed, contemplating the enormity, the finality of what lay ahead of her.

Why? Why? Why? Why her? Why my mother? she thought. *She wasn't old. She wasn't sick. She wasn't useless, taking up space. She was beautiful and vibrant. She contributed. She made a difference.*

All at once, images of her mother in action flashed into her head. Shayna saw her, heard her voice: imperious ... stern ... playful ...

disdainful … cajoling … angry … encouraging … sure, always so sure … and laughing. Oh, how she laughed.

"What a ride I've had, baby. What a ride I've had," she said laughing, the last time they saw each other.

It was in Brussels. Only neither dreamed it would be their last time together. Shayna flew there to surprise her mother for her birthday. They went to dinner at Janice's favorite place, Saint-Emilion, in the heart of the European Quarter on Rue Jacques de Lalaing. The restaurant was in a turn-of-the-century mansion, with high ceilings and breathtaking molding. During the day it was a popular spot for serious business lunches. In the evening it became a discreet, almost intimate setting.

The chef knew it was Janice's birthday—he made a point of finding out such details about the restaurant's illustrious *patrons*—and for the occasion, he prepared her favorite dishes, from appetizer to dessert. *How sweet that last dinner had been!* Shayna recalled. Her mother flirted shamelessly with a big handsome Belgian at an adjoining table. He'd flirted back and then insisted on paying their bill, which turned out to be on the house anyway—the restaurant's birthday gift to "Madame L'Ambassadrice." Shayna couldn't help smiling at the memory. *Wonder if she ever saw that man again. She must have had lovers, the sneak.*

Before she knew it, sunlight was pressing against the shades on the airplane windows and they were about to touch down. Shayna sighed and turned to Hilton. He was still asleep. She touched him lightly on his face. *I'm so grateful for you*, she thought. She got up, eased past him and headed for the restroom. *I'm ready*, she thought as she prepared to leave the plane.

I am Janice McWright's daughter and I'm ready.

"That's right, baby," her mother's voice whispered back reassuringly.

CHAPTER FOUR

The funeral service for Janice Grainger McWright a week later aired live on all the major television networks and cable stations. It was a state funeral, held at the massive Basilica of the National Shrine of the Immaculate Conception in Washington, D.C., the largest Catholic Church in the Western Hemisphere and the eighth largest in the world.

Janice McWright was known here. She had found solace and guidance within these walls. Often, while she was still working in Washington—"paying her dues," as she described it—she would slip away to the chapel of Mother of Perpetual Help in the Basilica's Great Upper Church. There she would pour out her troubles to Mary, the Mother of Jesus Christ—she who had been called "Our Lady of St. Matthew," then "Our Lady of Never-Failing Hope," and finally, "Our Mother of Perpetual Help."

Or, Janice would come to the chapel simply to give thanks for another battle won.

Throughout the years, whenever she came back to Washington, no matter how short a stay, she would go to the chapel. And every month, no matter in which corner of the globe she was, she faithfully sent her check to the Mother of Perpetual Help Charity for Orphans.

Everybody who was anybody in America's diplomatic world was in the Great Upper Church now for her funeral. Washington's political brass turned out in full force, led by the president and the first lady. Corporate America's brass was there too. For wherever Janice McWright was posted, she worked tirelessly to get a bigger share of the local market for American products and services.

Black America's political, social, academic and clerical elite were there, as were heads of state and senior officials from countries where she had served throughout her career. Aides, colleagues, sorority sisters, old friends, all packed into the cathedral to honor a woman who made diplomatic history in America.

It was a somber yet celebratory affair. Four choirs, including the Girls Choir of Harlem, of which Janice had been a *patron* for years, performed her favorite hymns. The president spoke of "the nobility" of her service to her country and exhorted fellow Americans to hold her stewardship as a national standard. Aunt Fiona, a bastion of strength, read the eulogy. Her voice never wavered. Then Camille sang "Ave Maria" in an astounding soprano and tore it all apart. The archbishop blew his nose hard into a lily-white handkerchief before he rose to deliver the sermon and give communion.

Loudspeakers had been set up outside to carry the entire service to the hundreds gathered in front the cathedral. They were former classmates and colleagues, students, fans, casual acquaintances, people whose lives Janice McWright touched, however fleetingly. Police barricades held the bystanders at bay.

A collective moan went up, followed by total silence, as the six pallbearers stepped through the cathedral's massive doors with the flag-draped coffin. Many in the crowd crossed themselves as the coffin was slid into the hearse. Soon, the long, somber cortège of black limousines was moving out, heading for the airport. The body was being flown to Atlanta for burial in the private cemetery on the Grainger estate. Only family and a few very close friends would attend.

Shayna was distraught as she stared at her mother's coffin. The coffin was poised to be lowered into the grave. Shayna's body shook violently. From behind her dark glasses, tears poured in steady rivulets down her cheeks. Her body shook uncontrollably. And there was a hollow where her heart should have been. *I'm so scared, mommy. So scared. I feel so alone. How do I deal with this? What do I do now? How do I make this all right in the end? Please help me, mommy.*

Father James from the church where Janice worshipped as a child was intoning the burial mass in Latin. They were lowering the coffin now, and the keening that had been held in check for so long finally broke free. It rolled over the crowd and soared up to meet the huge cotton-ball clouds that seemed to stand still in the pale blue sky. A lone voice burst into "When Peace Like a River," the anthem for every black person's funeral. Without it, there would be no closure. Others immediately joined in the song, women carrying the melody, men in a deep descant. Their voices rose together in resounding triumph on the final line of the chorus: "It is well! It is well with my soul!"

Hilton kept one arm firmly around Shayna's shoulders. Shayna leaned into him. Aunt Fifi was on the other side of her, holding her hand tight. The family was huge. There were Graingers from her mother's side and McWrights from her father's side. Some of them Shayna vaguely remembered; others she had never seen. But they were family and their presence was comforting.

At last it was over and they were moving away from the graveside. The women embraced each other and walked toward their limousines holding hands, saying little. Some of the men blew their noses loudly. Others greeted those they had not seen in a while with hearty hugs and shook their heads sadly. "Well, now! Janice has gone," they said to each other. Then they moved on together, leaving unsaid the words that each one knew the other was thinking: that God in all His wisdom had spoken and who were they to question His ways.

Shayna stood alone looking down at her mother's shiny silver coffin resting in the freshly dug grave. She held a single red rose in her hand. She removed her sunglasses and no longer bothered to wipe away the tears. Hilton and Aunt Fiona were standing beside their limousine, watching her anxiously. She assured them that she would be all right and they left her reluctantly.

In her mind Shayna spoke to her mother. *I will love you forever, Mommy. I will never forget you. Speak to me always as I will always speak to you. I will hear you and I know you will hear me. I will see you in all the beautiful things of this earth as I know you will see me from where you are.* Shayna looked up at the sky. *I promise you ... I promise you that I will be well.* She looked down into the grave again and threw the rose on the coffin. Tears streaming down her face, she whispered the words: "bye, bye, Mommy." Then she turned and walked slowly toward Hilton and Aunt Fiona.

#

"Of course she doesn't know. Her mother never told her and don't you ever put the good Lord out of your thoughts and say anything to her or anyone about it, or so help me, I will make your life miserable, Gillian Grainger."

"Calm down, Aunt Fifi. Now why in the world would I want to hurt little Shayna more than she's hurting already? Can't burst the African baby's bubble, can we?"

"You're drunk, Gillian. Now I know you never forgave Janice because Dillon married her instead of you. But that has nothing to do with Shayna. Shayna is one of us, you hear me? One of us!"

They were alone in the library of the massive Grainger family house, standing on either side of the fireplace, glaring at each other. The house stood on the 100-acre estate. Theodophilus Grainger, Janice's great-great grandfather who was born into slavery, bought the property after emancipation and built the house with money he made from caring white men's horses, fitting them with the finest shoes and leather trappings. He rented out small lots to other freed slaves who paid him sometimes in cash, sometimes in produce. He started breeding horses and soon became one of the wealthiest black men in Atlanta.

The house and estate had always been occupied and managed by a Grainger. Grainger Stables thrived to this day. As generations went by, the family home became known as The Historic Grainger Mansion. It welcomed the elite of America.

It was here that Aunt Fifi, the matriarch of the family, and Camille lived. Family and friends gathered at the house after the funeral. Many of them planned to stay on, some for a week. It was that balmy mood that only family and close friends can create after the burial of a loved one. There was much talk and laughter about the old days, stories of Janice as a child—and so much good food.

Gillian Grainger Bolin was a cousin of Janice McWright. She was a pretty woman, but the bitterness in her heart had seeped into her face and marred her good looks. She married a rich old man—some say she was drunk when she married him; others say slyly that it was he who was drunk—who dropped dead of a heart attack less than a year after the wedding. He left her millions. The story goes that Gillian had been dating Dillon McWright, Janice's husband, and took him to a family picnic at the mansion one summer. Dillon fell in love with Janice the moment he set eyes on her. They were married in a year.

After that day, Gillian took to drinking. They say she ran off to South Carolina and married the first man she met. She never had children. And she never forgave Janice.

"Whether you like it or not, Aunt Fifi, Shayna is not one of us. She has no Grainger blood and she's certainly not Dillon's child. My God! Who the hell does she look like? Dark like that!" Gillian's voice was becoming shrill.

"Be quiet, Gillian! I'm warning you!"

"I will not be quiet. I'm tired of all of you. It's always Janice and Shayna, Janice and Shayna! And neither of them ever gave this family the time of day! Well Janice is gone now and that African baby she brought back to America as her daughter had better not get any ideas about this house!"

Aunt Fifi's hand smashed across her face. Gillian staggered back, holding her face.

"Why in God's name did you come here, you sickening witch? Why?" Aunt Fifi's voice was cold steel.

"Yes, why?" said Shayna. She stood just inside the heavy carved wooden door, her voice as steely as Aunt Fifi's.

Aunt Fifi's hand flew to her mouth as she swung around to face Shayna. Gillian looked startled at first, and then slowly a sneer spread over her face. "This is the *Grainger* family home, Shayna dear. I have a right to be here," she said sweetly.

"What does she mean, Aunt Fifi?" Shayna demanded. She strode toward the two women, her eyes fixed on Gillian.

"Pay her no mind, Shayna. She's drunk as usual." Aunt Fifi swung back to face Gillian. "Leave this house, Gillian. *Now!*"

"No. Let her stay, Aunt Fifi. Stay, Cousin Gillian. Tell me why you hate my mother and me so much. I want to know." Shayna's voice was calm, but her glare was deadly. Instinctively, Gillian stepped back.

Shayna continued walking toward her. She stopped just inches from her face.

"Let me hear it, Gillian!" she demanded.

"For God's Sake, Gillian. NO!" pleaded Aunt Fifi.

Gillian took her glass from the mantelpiece and downed most of its contents. "If she wants the truth, Aunt Fifi, I'm going to give it to her," she said, her words slurring slightly. "You were adopted or something in Congo when your mother—Janice, rather— served there as consul general. Your father—that is, Dillon—was killed in a freak accident in Kinshasa almost as soon as they got there. Janice stayed on in Kinshasa to finish her assignment. I suppose she didn't want to return to America to be pitied. When she finally turned up here she had you with her. I knew you weren't hers or Dillon's. Janice could not have children. Dillon told me so long ago. We remained friends after he married Janice."

She lingered long enough on the word "friends" to ensure that they understood the true nature of her relationship with Dillon.

"Besides, you didn't look like anybody. Didn't you ever wonder about that, Shayna? A smart girl like you?"

Aunt Fifi was beside herself. She looked at Gillian with pure hatred, but refrained from hitting her again. Gillian ignored her and continued.

"You were deposited as an infant, dear, at the American Embassy with a note pinned to your dress begging Janice, it named her specifically, to take you to America and raise you as her own daughter if your father did not want you. The note said your father was an American Peace Corps worker. The name of your father checked out, but when Janice tried to look for him, he had already left the country.

Janice apparently got hold of him in America and he admitted that he lived with a local woman while he was in the country, but he denied having a child with her. Janice herself tracked down the woman he said he lived with. The woman admitted she was the one who left you at the Embassy. She insisted you were fathered by the American. She told Janice he ordered her to get an abortion and then walked out. She had the baby anyway. He didn't know.

Janice contacted the man again, but he insisted again that he had no children with any African woman and that he wanted nothing to do with the woman or her child, or Janice McWright for that matter. He threatened to take action if she didn't stop harassing him. The Zairian woman kept on insisting her daughter *was* American. She said it was too dangerous to keep the child in Zaire. There was talk of war. Her daughter could be killed. Then she disappeared without a trace. So Janice adopted the little girl, you. I'm sure you helped ease the pain of Dillon's death and of her inability to bear children."

Gillian spoke in the ugly voice of someone who waited for years to lash out on Shayna. "Janice erased all traces of your real birth, it seems. So here you are in America, brought up as a privileged Grainger, when in fact you are—who knows what! Janice never even told anyone the name of the man your birth mother said was your father."

Gillian finished with a dramatic sweep of her hand. She drained her glass. Aunt Fifi was wringing her hands, sobbing.

"Shayna, baby, your mother herself told me that story the last time she was here. We didn't know Gillian was in the house. She eavesdropped on the whole conversation."

She threw a damning look at Gillian. "No one else knows," she continued to Shayna. "Everyone accepts you as Janice's child." She gritted her teeth and planted her eyes menacingly on Gillian's face.

"Gillian doesn't. And if *she* doesn't, maybe there are others who feel the same way," Shayna said. She kept her eyes fixed on Gillian's face all the while Gillian recounted Janice's story. Even now, as she spoke to Aunt Fifi, her gaze never wavered from Gillian's face.

"No, baby. That's not true! Don't believe that! Please don't!" Aunt Fifi said imploringly.

Shayna's expression was blank. Gillian stared back at her insolently. She tossed her head defiantly and pursed her lips. Shayna's eyes did not flinch. Gillian began to fidget under Shayna's gaze, smoothing her beautifully tailored skirt, picking up and putting down her glass, patting her hair. She had long slender fingers, manicured nails painted blood red, a huge diamond ring on each hand.

Finally, Shayna spoke. Her voice was filled with pity. "All these years you hated my mother and me. All these years your hatred for us consumed you, you poor miserable wretch. It's written all over your face. God, how pitiful you are! And to think we never even gave you a second thought. All these years you allowed our existence to control your life and my mother never even mentioned you once. *Not once!* I never even knew of you until this day."

Shayna paused. Gillian stood ramrod straight, defiant.

"No, you haven't hurt me, Gillian. You have no power to hurt me. *I'm* the one with the power over you. You made me see that my mother—yes, *my mother Janice McWright*—you've made me see that she was even more beautiful a person than I knew her to be. And a far, far better human being than you can ever dream of being."

Aunt Fifi moved toward Shayna, her arms outstretched. "Shayna..."

Shayna stepped into her embrace. They held each other for a long moment and then Shayna pulled away and looked at Aunt Fifi tenderly. "Whomever I may be born of, Aunt Fifi, I was Janice McWright's daughter until the day she died and I will be her daughter until the day *I* die," she said. She kissed Aunt Fifi lightly on her cheek and eased out of her arms.

"I'll be all right, Aunt Fifi. And you will always hear from me," she said. She walked out of the room. She did not look at Gillian.

Shayna's face was set as she strode from the library. She climbed the stairs, running her hand absently along the beautifully finished mahogany banister. At the top of the stairs, she turned for a moment and took in the loveliness of her surroundings. Aunt Fifi and Camille had done wonders restoring the original woodwork. And they had highlighted so many touches that bespoke the generations that had lived here—all of it tastefully blending into a single Grainger mosaic that Shayna cherished.

Gillian's words suddenly stabbed at her. *I'm not really part of this*. Shayna sighed. None of this is of my blood. I am just my mother's adopted child. She turned and walked down the long hallway into her room. She locked the door behind her, sank down on the bed and buried her head in her hands. Oh Mommy! Mommy! You should have told me! You should have told me! Why didn't you tell me?

She cried until her head ached. She hugged herself and rocked back and forth, moaning her comfort song. *Pasi! Pasi! Oh-Oh-Oh! Pasi! Pasi! Oh-Oh-Oh!*

She awoke to a gentle but insistent knocking on the door and Hilton's worried voice. "Shayna! Shayna! Are you okay? Shayna! It's me! Hilton! Are you okay?"

Shayna pulled herself up from the bed. It was dark. She must have slept for hours. She walked over to the door and unlocked it. Hilton pushed it open and stepped in anxiously. The moment he saw Shayna's face, he pulled her into his arms and held her tight. Neither said anything for a long moment. Hilton was horrified by the way Shayna looked. It's as if she had gone to pieces all over again. She had been almost stoic during the service in Washington and at the burial here in Atlanta. *She's more fragile than she looks,* he thought, rocking her gently, trying to suppress his worry.

Shayna was the first to speak. "Hilton, we have to leave here tomorrow," she said.

"But why? You need to rest here for a while. Aunt Fifi expects you to stay here for a week."

"Oh, Hilton! Please don't argue with me. There is so much to tell you. I really don't belong here. They're not my family."

Her mind's gone, Hilton thought in alarm. "What are you talking about, Shayna? You're not making any sense!" Fear for her sanity made his voice sharp. He caught himself and drew her to him again. "It's all right. You just need to rest. Let's just stay here with Aunt Fifi and Camille and the family. It'll be okay. You'll see after a few days." This time his voice was more gentle, almost pleading.

Shayna sighed impatiently. "My mind isn't gone, Hilton. I know what I'm saying."

She pulled away from him and walked over to the closet. She took out her suitcase, threw it on the bed and began to toss her clothing into it. Her movements became more resolute as she continued packing.

Hilton watched her, bemused. "I don't understand, Shayna. What's going on?"

Shayna stopped packing and stared at him. When she spoke, her voice held no emotion. "It turns out, Hilton, that I am adopted. My mother—Janice McWright is not my natural mother. She adopted me in Africa—Congo-Kinshasa, to be exact. My real mother is Congolese and my natural father, according to my Congolese mother, was an American Peace Corps worker she lived with and who wanted nothing to do with me."

Hilton was flabbergasted. "That's the bullshittingest story I have ever heard. I bet you got that from that drunken woman named Gillian who's been shooting daggers at you with her eyes ever since we got here! She looked like she couldn't wait to drive one into your heart. What's she so pissed at you about, anyway?"

Shayna stopped packing and looked up at him with pure love and gratitude. This man has been by her side throughout this entire ordeal—comforting her, shielding her, loving her, watching over her. She had taken it all for granted. Now she was asking him to jump through yet another hoop without much of an explanation…and with an attitude at that. Christ! She was being so selfish.

She sank down on the bed. She had no more tears to shed. Not today. "Hilton, it's true. Yes, Gillian told me. She hated my mother and I because Dillon McWright dumped her for my mom. But Aunt Fifi confirmed the adoption story. Gillian as much as threatened me about making any claims to the Grainger family assets."

"That bitch!" Hilton spat. "You don't need any of it anyway! What does Aunt Fifi say?"

Shayna smiled. "Dear Aunt Fifi. She slapped Gillian and chased her out."

"So that explains why Gillian stormed out of here without so much as a goodbye to anyone. We were on the verandah and folks simply dismissed it as one of Gillian's drunken tantrums. Then Aunt Fifi came out and told me to go find you."

"Hilton, I have to find my real mother."

"She gave you up willingly, Shayna. Why not let the past be?"

"She wanted me to have a better life in America. And look whom she left me with. Not just anybody at the consulate: the consul general herself, someone who would have the means to find my father, or at least to take care of me. That doesn't sound like someone who was washing her hands of me. That's what my real father did, it seems. Not her."

Suddenly, Hilton smiled broadly.

"What's so funny?" Shayna asked.

"I can hear the reporter's mind clicking. You had me worried there for a while," Hilton said. "Seriously, Shayna. This is crazy. Okay, so you're adopted. Millions of children are adopted. Why go on some wild goose chase? Where in the world will you begin to look for a woman in a country you know nothing about? And a country that's at war with itself, Shayna. *At war!* She could be dead for all you know. Shayna, I beg you! Let it be."

"I know you're afraid I'll be hurt, Hilton," Shayna said softly.

"In more ways than one, baby. You know nothing about that country or those people."

Shayna said nothing.

Hilton continued. "I don't want to lose you, Shayna. I'm afraid of losing you."

Shayna still said nothing. She was staring beyond him, at nothing in particular.

"I want to marry you, Shayna."

Shayna drew her breath sharply. Hilton knew instinctively what she was thinking.

"This isn't pity, Shayna. I love you and I want to marry you. It's as simple as that," he said.

"But you want to marry the Shayna you know. The Shayna who has roots you can relate to. But those roots are all an illusion, Hilton. I can't marry you until I know who I am. It would not be fair to you—not knowing what my real origins are. Besides, what would I tell my children about me? I would not want to keep the truth from them, Hilton. Another Gillian is bound to come along sooner or later."

Hilton said nothing. He knew she was right. In the Pierce family, one's social origins were important. "You always gotta know what's in the blood, son, so when they say your child takes after his mother's father or brother or uncle, it'll be a compliment, not a curse," his father had told him once when he could not say anything about the family of a girl he brought home. Not that he was planning to marry the girl. He was just in the eleventh grade then, for God's sake. He said as much to his father, to which his father replied that any company he kept had to be worthy of an association with the Pierces.

"Hilton, even if there was none of this adoption business I would not want to marry you now. We both know that was not in the plan yet, that you're asking because it's what folks would expect. 'Poor Shayna. She's an orphan now. She needs protecting and comforting. Why don't you marry her, Hilton?' That's it, isn't it, Hilton? That's the pressure you feel, isn't it?"

Hilton said nothing. Finally, he drew a deep breath and exhaled slowly.

"Yes, I did feel that pressure, Shayna. I wouldn't lie to you. But as I watched you these last few days, I came to appreciate the magnificent woman you are. I liked being beside you, watching out for you, taking responsibility for you. I was proud of the way you handled yourself among all the people who came and went—from Brussels to D.C. to Atlanta. Then I'd catch you looking for me and when your eyes found mine, you would light up and look relieved. I gave you something you needed and I like that. I said to myself we are good together. We've grown closer, Shayna. This sad situation has tested us and we've stood our ground together. I want you in my life as my wife. The only pressure I feel now is the pressure of knowing I might lose you in some crazy search for your natural mother and your blood roots."

Amina felt the fight drain away from her body. Her shoulders slumped. "I love you, Hilton. And yes, I will marry you—if you still want me after I find out who I am. That's all I can say now."

CHAPTER FIVE

Shayna and Hilton flew back to New York the next morning. They hardly spoke to each other. They simply held each other's hand tight during the entire flight. That they loved each other was a comfort to both. But neither knew what the next phase of their lives would bring. Both were afraid, but neither wanted to show it.

Hilton stayed with Shayna that night. They talked for a long time. He would go straight from her house to work the next day then from there back to his own apartment. Shayna would ask for a leave of absence. Six months, perhaps a year. She did not know yet.

The moment Hilton left the next morning, Shayna prepared a hot bath aromatized with lavender oil and sank into it with relief. A Sarah Vaughn CD played softly from the small cassette and CD combo she kept in the bathroom. Shayna smiled as "Send in the Clowns" came on, remembering her mother's unexpected karaoke rendition of the song at a July Fourth party in Belgium. It was Janice's favorite song by her favorite singer, and one she had never been able to resist singing. Her own beautiful, soulful voice surprised and silenced everyone at the party. The silence continued even after the song was over. Then the French ambassador began to applaud, walking over to embrace Janice with an exuberant cry of "Magnifique! Merveilleux!" Janice bowed graciously. Everyone in the room cheered. Press cameras flashed wildly. Turning to face the room Janice, sighed with feigned regret.

"Ladies and gentlemen, if it were in my power, I would make sure the caption under that picture in tomorrow's papers in *no* way suggests that France has embraced America's arguments on the issue of subsidies," she said.

The room erupted with laughter and more applause. Washington and Paris had long been at loggerheads over France's practice of subsidizing its exports, which, Washington argued, gave French exporters an unfair advantage in global markets.

"Not to worry, Janice. The press would never commit such a gaffe. They all know how fickle the "embrasse" of a Frenchman is," the French ambassador retorted with equally good humor, provoking even more laughter and applause. By deliberately using the French pronunciation of "embrace," he had given the word its French meaning: "kiss."

An hour later, Shayna emerged from her bath, feeling refreshed and far less despairing than she had felt in over a week. She put on a robe, went into the living room, and called her editor. He spoke to her warmly for a few minutes, and then put her through to the publisher. Those had been his instructions. As Shayna waited for the publisher to pick up, she thought how touching it had been to see so many of her colleagues from the paper and the various journalism groups she belonged to at the service in Washington.

"Shayna! How good to hear from you. Didn't expect to so soon." Colson Carter, III's voice boomed through her thoughts. Unlike many of her fellow reporters, Shayna liked Colson Carter. He was one of those people who saw you as a human being first and everything else afterward. How he dealt with the "everything else afterwards" depended on the importance you yourself attached to whatever it was you perceived yourself to be. He was caring when any of his workers suffered personal tragedy, generous when praise and reward were due, cold and brutal when it came to beating the competition.

The story goes that when he was passed over for the chief editor's position at the *Wall Street Courier,* one of the country's most respected business dailies, he resigned on the spot. He launched *American Business Journal* six months later with money from a trust fund his grandfather had set up for him. His grandfather had owned one of the most successful boat building yards on the East Coast.

"Sir, I'd like to thank you for all you have done for me..." Shayna always felt awkward using Carter's first name. He didn't let her finish the sentence.

"Nonsense, Shayna. We did nothing. Now you listen to me and I don't want an argument. I want you to take some time off with full pay. Take as long as you like. You've been with us since you were a college kid and you've done us proud. The only thing I ask is that you show up at Columbia in May to receive your Pulitzer."

Shayna's her heart swelled at the reminder that she had won the most coveted prize in American journalism, the one she worked and prayed so hard for. She had even used "pulitzer" as the password to her computer when she joined the paper.

"You didn't forget about your Pulitzer, did you? Though that would be understandable under the circumstances," Carter was saying.

"No, I hadn't forgotten, sir. It's just that...just that I keep wondering if my mother had heard the news before she died."

"She never doubted you would win, Shayna. I saw her in

Brussels last year and when I told her we were submitting your work, do you know what she asked me? She wanted to know what date they were going gave out the prizes so she could clear her calendar to be there."

Shayna's eyes stung, but she could not help smiling. She remembered how exuberant Janice was about her gut alerts.

"That's so like her. Thank you for sharing that with me. Thank you for the offer and yes, I will be there to receive my Pulitzer," she said to Carter.

"And I want you to know that I thank you from the bottom of my heart for bringing such a great honor to *American Business Journal*: the first Pulitzer in our relatively young life. I am exceedingly proud, Shayna."

"Thank you, sir."

"Now how are you really, Shayna? Are you getting any sleep?"

"Well, I can't say it's easy, but I'm doing much better now."

"Take the time off. Grieve to your heart's content, and then renew your spirit. Travel. Go somewhere you've never been before. It will help more than you know."

"You know, I think I'll do just that. I don't think I can stand just sitting around here."

"Good girl. Be sure to expense it."

He hung up before she could protest.

Shayna looked around her apartment for the first time in a week. Aunt Fifi and Camille had arranged all the cards in a neat pile on the hallway table. Flowers were in vases. Gourmet baskets were on the kitchen table. Other gifts were arranged on the sofa in the living room. Shayna was grateful that she would be kept busy for several days reading her mail and responding to all the well wishers. She did not plan to leave her apartment. A few reporters were still staking out the building.

She checked her phone messages first. The message bank was full. God knows how many people must have tried to leave word, she sighed. She began to listen to the messages, jotting down names and numbers on the pad she kept beside the phone and deleting the same information from the message bank. She deleted all the calls from magazines and radio stations seeking interviews. *No need to write anything down about those. The most aggressive ones will call again anyway*, she told herself. She saved a few of the messages from colleagues and people she interviewed for her articles and who later became friends. She would return those calls within a week.

She attacked the pile of cards and telegrams next, reading well into the afternoon. They evoked laughter and tears. Some contained checks, some cash. Aunt Fifi and Camille bought several boxes of thank-you cards and had already addressed envelopes to those who sent cards with a return address. They had even placed a stamp on each envelope, bless them. All she had to do was write her own message in the card, stuff, and mail. She would do that over the next few days, she decided.

She continued reading for another hour or so, then took a break to stretch and watch the news. The crash that killed her mother was still the top story on both the network and cable channels. American and Belgian investigators were still combing the wreckage for clues. So much had been incinerated that they had little to go on. The autopsy report on the driver showed no alcohol in his system. Analysts were solicited to give their views on how the loss of Janice McWright would affect America's lobbying strength in Europe. They picked apart all the people whose names were being bandied about as her successor. They tossed and turned the idea of assassination, and which group might be crazy enough to do such a thing and why.

They belabored the question of why Janice McWright was on her way to the airport when she was killed. Her official schedule for the day showed no trips out of the country. Some suggested a secret, high-level meeting on one of the many issues creating tension of late between the United States and the European Union. One of the more sleazy talking heads suggested a secret rendezvous with a lover. He pointed out that the accident *did* happen on a Friday, the beginning of the weekend, and that Janice McWright had been seen a lot lately in the company of a certain French industrialist.

A prominent African-American activist posited that "the real rulers of America" had her killed because she was becoming too powerful. It was the same thing they did to Ron Brown, the first African-American secretary of commerce, the activist declared. "It happens all the time in America. Whenever a black person is getting too popular, too influential, they kill him," the activist said heatedly.

Shayna sucked her teeth in disgust. She never bought into all those conspiracy theories. She flipped through a few more channels and finally settled on CNBC. Business news was on. The Dow Jones Industrial Average had fallen thirty percent in the last week, with Blue Chip stocks showing their biggest one-year collective drop in history. Immediately after the crash, when talk of assassination seemed to be gaining momentum, Fortune 500 companies that operated overseas began to take antiterrorist precautions for their personnel as well as property. Analysts said this would add enormously to their expenditures. At some of the overseas plants owned by American companies, local workers stopped showing up to work, afraid terrorists would strike at any time. As if that wasn't enough, foreign buyers cut back their purchases of American goods, fearing their shipments might be sabotaged, or that they themselves might be punished for doing business with America.

All this was wreaking havoc on Wall Street.

Shayna felt the familiar goosebumps of excitement. *I would have been writing some great stories had I been there*, she thought. She switched to the BBC News, listened for a while, and then clicked to the news from France. Shayna spoke fluent French and Spanish and had a decent command of Mandarin. Her mother insisted on her learning these languages since she was in high school. "Makes you better prepared for the world outside America, which is only about ninety-five percent of the world," Janice McWright said. From then on, Shayna made every effort to perfect her accent whenever she traveled to countries where those languages were spoken.

French television was reporting on the ongoing investigation into the crash. A picture of her mother appeared in the upper-right-hand corner of the screen. Shayna walked over the screen and touched her mother's face. *Mommy, this is real, isn't it? I'm never going to hear you talking to me the same way again, am I? See you, touch your beautiful face, laugh with you on the phone, argue with you, and hear the jingle of the bracelets you always wore. Your TCs, you called them.* Twenty-four carats, solid gold: the bracelets were a fiftieth birthday gift from a close Guyanese friend she met during her first overseas posting.

Shayna smiled through the tears. There were no wrenching sobs, this time, just hot tears rolling down her cheeks. They pooled at her chin before dropping onto her robe. The French reporter switched to another story. Shayna dragged the back of her hand across her eyes and turned from the television. She reached for the gift baskets. They were mostly from organizations and companies, her sorority, the newsroom, her building's tenant board. *I could hold a great party with all this*, she thought wryly as she dug into the cheeses and meats she especially liked. She made a separate list of all who sent baskets. She would have to hunt for addresses for some of them.

The phone rang.

"I thought of you all day. Are you okay?"

Her heart raced at the sound of Hilton's voice. She missed him already. She wanted to feel his comforting arms around her.

"I'm okay," she said bravely. "Busy reading cards, returning calls, snacking from the baskets. You should have taken one. I can't eat all this. I'll have to give some away."

"I'd love to have one. I'll come for it."

But she noticed that he didn't offer to come that very night, as he surely would have done before.

"The newspaper gave me a year off with pay," she continued in a rush. "They told me to travel if I want to and expense it. That means they would like me to write while I travel. They didn't say that, of course. All the publisher wants me to do is show up at the Pulitzer awards ceremony."

"My God! The Pulitzer! You won a Pulitzer! And I didn't even congratulate you. I'm so sorry, baby."

Shayna laughed. "It's okay. With all that was happening, it was the last thing on my mind. You were so wonderful with me, Hilton."

Hilton hesitated. "Shayna, do you think you can go out for a small dinner? Just you, me, and our usual little clique tomorrow night. They're dying to see you."

"Oh Hilton, I don't think so. I'd just like to be alone right now."

He didn't push it. "Have you decided what you are going to do?" He sounded anxious.

"Not yet. I need to get these thank-yous out of the way, pay some bills, put a few things in order with my mother's lawyers. They're sending all her stuff over from Belgium to her townhouse in Manhattan. I'll have to go through it some time. I don't know when I'll do anything, as far as my real mother is concerned."

"I'm here whenever you need me, Shayna," Hilton said.

"Thank you, Hilton. That means a lot to me."

"I love you, Shayna."

"I love you, Hilton."

Then they hung up.

It was after nine. Shayna had not eaten a proper meal all day. She wasn't very hungry. She poked around again in the gourmet baskets and extracted a box of chamomile tea leaves, pumpernickel raisin bread, smoked sable and truffle butter. *Nice*, she thought. "These baskets really work," she said aloud.

She brewed a small pot of tea, made a sandwich, and settled herself on the couch again. She would watch some mindless television and then go to bed. Tomorrow she would tackle the gifts piled up on the other side of the couch. She looked at the pile of geometric shapes. *What lovely wrapping*, she thought. One box, bigger than all the others, caught her eye. She recognized the store's logo. She reached for it with a smile and tore off the wrapping. *When did Hilton find time to get to FAO Schwartz?* she wondered. The shaggy brown bear stared up at her with huge brown eyes. Shayna ooohed with delight and hugged it tightly. The ribbon around its neck was red with black polka dots and was tied in a snazzy bow. Shayna opened the card. Tears sprang to her eyes as she read the words.

> *For the days when you wish you could hold her*
> *And when you want to cry*
> *But you don't want anyone to see your tears*
> *Our prayers are with you, Shayna.*
>
> Amina, Jamillah & Meredith

Their phone numbers were written under their names. Shayna's hand flew to her mouth. She looked at the card for a long time. She thought back to the days when these three challenged her mercilessly on so many issues, especially that Meredith. Their arguments were always razor sharp. How many times had they left her intellectually battered! *They ate me up, though I didn't want to admit it*, she thought with a smile. It seemed so long ago. They had not seen or spoken to each other in years. *It's all water under the bridge now*, Shayna said to herself. *At least I hope so. The funny thing is, they got along so well with my mother. I know they thought the world of her. And my mother was so impressed by them. She always asked about them.* Shayna grinned. *And they're still so smart.* A smart gift from three of the smartest women I have ever known.

Somewhere along the way she heard how successful they had all become. Wait 'till they learn that I'm African—at least half, for sure. Me, of all people! Merry will get a good laugh. I can hear her. "Chickin nuh come 'ome a roos?" Shayna said aloud, imitating Merry's rich Jamaican speech. She imagined Merry, chortling over the news, and it made her laugh out loud. "Yah, mon! Dem ah boun' fi come 'ome a roos'!"

Shayna fell over on the couch laughing at her perfect imitation. The Jamaican accent was so easy to pick up these days, with it plastered all over the television and radio. Even *white* people were talking Jamaican. Brad Pitt really took off in the movie *Meet Joe Black.*

God! Merry will really get a kick out of this! Shayna laughed until tears streamed down her face. She looked at the phone numbers again.

Wonder if it's too late to call. It's almost midnight. I'll call each of them tomorrow beginning with Amina. She's the real cool one—half African, half West Indian, wasn't she?

Then it hit her.

"Holy Mother of God in heaven! Amina is Congolese! She's from Congo-Kinshasa!" Shayna shouted the last sentence. She sprang up from the couch and stood still for a moment, trembling. She looked at the clock: five minutes to ten. She grabbed the phone, but chickened out just as her finger was about to dial. She sat back on the couch shaking her knees together nervously. She looked at the phone and looked away quickly. Over and over again she kept looking at phone and looking away. The clock in the kitchen chimed ten. Shayna grabbed the phone with one hand, grabbed the card with the other, read Amina's number out loud in a rush and dialed it at a speed she would not have thought possible for anyone.

Amina answered on the first ring.

"Hello."

Shayna recognized that sultry voice anywhere.

"A-Amina?"

"Ye-es?" Amina did not recognize Shayna's voice immediately.

"I hope I didn't wake you. This is Shayna."

"Shayna? *Shayna!* Oh no! You didn't wake me at all. I was just finishing a report on a case." Amina said hurriedly. "Shayna! I'm so sorry about your mother's death. We could not believe it. Jamillah and Merry were over at my house that day when it happened. We watched it on the news. Oh, Shayna, we admired her so!"

"I know you did, Amina. Listen, I'm sorry I called you so late. I got back last night from Atlanta and just opened your gift. I can't thank you enough. It's so perfect. The three of you were always so on the money with everything."

"Well, look who's talking, Miss Pulitzer Prize winner!"

"Oh that! Would you believe I forgot all about that 'till today?" Shayna chuckled.

"It's so good to hear laughter in your voice, Shayna."

"If anyone had told me a week ago that I would be laughing within a week, I would not have believed them. The mind adapts quickly, I suppose."

They were silent for a moment. Amina waited for Shayna to speak.

"Amina, can we have lunch sometime?"

"Of course. When's good for you?"

"How about tomorrow?"

"Hmmm. If it's tomorrow, it'll have to be dinner. I have patients all day."

"Dinner is just fine. I know you must think I'm rushing this, but I do have something urgent to discuss with you."

"Don't worry about it, Shayna. I'd be glad to help in any way I can."

"I'm counting on that, Amina, really counting on it. I'll tell you all about it tomorrow. I won't keep you away from your work any longer. I plan to call Jamillah and Merry to thank them for the teddy bear too. I've named him Mr. Pasi."

"Mr. Pasi! That's a strange name for you to come up with. What made you use that name?"

"I don't know. It's my baby word. As long as I could remember, I would sing this song to myself when I'm scared or hurt."

She hummed it for Amina.

"Oh! That's Abeti Masikini's song "Pasi, Pasi." She's Zairian-Congolese. It was a hit in the 1970s. But how would you know that song?"

The silence was long. Too long.

"Shayna, are you there? Are you okay?"

"I'm okay, Amina, bless you. You just said something that—I'll tell you all about it tomorrow. I'll leave you now. Goodnight, Amina, and thanks."

"Night, Shayna. I'm glad you called. Sleep well."

Amina mulled over Shayna's call for several minutes. It was a strange call. What could Shayna possibly have to tell her that was so urgent and that required a meeting in person? Amina dialed Jamillah and hooked them both into a conference call with Merry. She knew they would not be asleep. They all usually went to bed around 1 a.m.

"Shayna just called," she announced excitedly to Jamillah and Merry.

"Huh, all the way from Atlanta? How come? The funeral was only two days ago."

"That's what puzzled me too. But I didn't ask what happened. Shayna said she came back to New York last night. And hear this! She wants to meet me tomorrow. Says she has something urgent to discuss with me. Hear that? Urgent."

"Urgent? What could be so urgent that she has to rush back to New York before the mud dried on her mother's grave and call you at almost midnight?" Jamillah demanded. "And how could she possibly want to discuss it with *you*? She hasn't talked to you in *years*. Not to you or any of us. We haven't been in touch with her at all."

"I haven't the foggiest. But I'm meeting her for dinner tomorrow. Remember, she never had any real close friends. She was always aloof. Anyway, she says she'll call you guys later today. She loved the teddy bear. Wants to thank you, too."

"Hol' up! Hol' up yah!" Merry had been silent all along. Now she was ready to have her say. "Afta all these years, Shayna call you at midnight to thank you for a teddy bear, and then ask you to meet her for dinner to discuss somet'ing urgent. An' all dis right afta she berry her mudda? Dat nuh mek sense. Yuh tink she tun fool wid grief?"

"Merry! She's not crazy. How can you say such a thing?"

"Well tink about it. It mek sense to unnu?"

Their silence on the line was deafening.

"Nooooo. Not really," Jamillah said hesitantly.

"Not really," agreed Amina.

"See! Amina, you sure you'll be okay? Jamillah and I had better come with you," said Merry.

"Yeah, right! Like you and that belly can do something!" Amina laughed.

"She's just dying to hear firsthand what Shayna has to say," Jamillah chimed in.

"Well, aren't you, Jamillah?" said Merry.

"Of course! But I'm being cool about it, unlike you," said Jamillah.

"For God's sake, Merry! When Shayna calls you tomorrow, please don't try to wrangle an invitation to dinner. If she asks you to come, that's one thing. Other than that, say nothing. Promise?" said Amina.

"What kind of social klutz do you take me for, Amina?"

Jamillah giggled. "We know you, Merry."

Amina chuckled. Jamillah laughed outright.

"What if I make a subtle suggestion that we meet soon for dinner?" Merry asked.

"Don't you dare!" Amina threatened.

"Okay! Okay!" Merry said hastily. "But if we're not going to be at the dinner, you'd better talk to us as soon as you get home. I'm going to bed now, ladies. Got surgery tomorrow. 'Night all."

"Me, too. Night y'all," Jamillah said with a yawn.

"Night. I'll call you guys ASAP tomorrow," said Amina.

CHAPTER SIX

Amina recognized her immediately. She had seen Shayna on television during the coverage of the funeral. But she had also seen her just a month before on one of those CNN roundtables with leading business journalists. The topic was the long-term fallout from the currency crisis that had lassoed Southeast Asia's economic bull run. Shayna heatedly defended her position that South Korea would be the first to come back and would do so fast and furious.

"There's going to be a shift in the economic dynamics of the region as a result of this crisis and South Korea is going to emerge an even bigger player. Pay attention to that humongous project in the city of Inchon that Seoul is putting billions of dollars behind. They're putting in place a state-of-the-art logistics infrastructure that strengthens the country's air, sea, road, and rail links that they're calling Eurasia. And they're also building their own version of Silicon Valley. You'll note that the Koreans went to Europe first to entice investors to the project. American companies need to start staking out some turf in that project now if they want to get a worthwhile piece of the commercial action later. And believe me, that action is going to be *big,*" she told them.

"Yeah, right! All North Korea has to do is rattle its sabers and that's the end of that," one skeptic scoffed.

"He's right! How far do you think this Eurasia concept will go if South Korea's trains can't pass through the north?" another said.

"Those two will never come to blows again. Asians are subtly circling the wagons. It's all about commerce now..."

Always the debutante, Amina smiled, as she took in Shayna's perfect makeup, immaculately groomed hair, tailored white linen dress, pearls, brown and white clutch bag, and matching pumps. *Anyone else in that outfit would seem overdressed in these surroundings*, Amina thought; nonetheless, she thought that a pair of gloves would set Shayna's outfit off just right.

Shayna spotted her, waved and began to walk toward the table. Amina rose to meet her. Amina arrived at the restaurant about ten minutes before. She suggested meeting at The Baobab, a "root-sy" little restaurant in "Little Africa," the three-block stretch of 116th Street in Harlem that Senegalese and Guinean merchants revitalized into a thriving commercial strip. The wide street was lined with clothing and tailor shops, grocery stores, restaurants, money transfer services, taxi dispatchers, electronic appliance stores, and music stores. You could eat off the sidewalks, they were so clean. The Senegalese and Guineans lived in the area as well. They were mostly Muslims and worshipped at the mosque at 116th and Lenox Avenue.

The community bustled with men, women and children. The young women were tall and shapely and slender and wore tight jeans. They looked like models, with smooth, black skin and gleaming smiles. The married women were big and regal in traditional cloths. They walked comfortably along the street as if they were back home, laughing and chatting in Wolof. Some sat in groups on chairs and boxes on the sidewalk or on the steps of an apartment building. Every now and then, strains of the rolling rhythm guitar of Congolese music and the high-pitched quarter-notes of the more Arab-influenced Senegalese songs seeped into the air as someone opened and closed the door of a record store.

Little Africa sprang up fast around the outdoor mart the city erected further east to appease the Senegalese merchants the mayor chased from the sidewalks of 125th Street. It was a place that was going places. Amina figured Shayna could relax here without worrying about being recognized. Little Africa, and certainly The Baobab, was still off the beaten track for Shayna's kind of "beautiful people" and the press. The Baobab thrived in the eat-in and take-out business. Its clientele ranged from diplomats and very rich merchants to the humblest taxi drivers. To the unpracticed eye, however, they all would seem to be poor, struggling immigrants. The menu was strictly Senegalese. It boasted the best *thiebou djen* in New York. *Thiebou djen* was a popular dish of fried rice with fish and vegetables.

"Hello, Amina," Shayna said nervously as she hugged Amina. "You look great! I'm so glad you could meet me."

"Shayna! And you look wonderful, as usual. I'm so glad you asked me to meet you. It's really been a long time, hasn't it?"

They sat down and a young waitress appeared from nowhere. She arranged their place settings while asking in barely accented English if they would like anything to drink. Amina made a gesture with her hand and the waitress immediately disappeared. Discretion was sacred here. Amina leaned across the table and touched Shayna's hands.

"How many years has it been? Let's see. Last time we saw each other was when your mother…" Amina stopped abruptly. "Oh Shayna, I'm so sorry." She squeezed Shayna's hands. Shayna's lips quivered and a tear rolled out of one eye.

Amina said, "God what a klutz I am. All day long I kept warning myself not to say anything that might bring up the hurt and what do I do? The first words out of my mouth! I'm so sorry, Shayna."

"Oh, Amina. It's okay, really. It's just that it's still so fresh." Her voice shook. She withdrew her hands from Amina's, snapped open her purse and took out a white, lace-trimmed handkerchief. She patted her eyes and cheeks delicately. "I've got to get used to this. I will," she said.

"You know, I was thinking as you were walking over to the table that a pair of white kid gloves would look great with that outfit," Amina said, wanting desperately to lighten the mood.

Shayna suddenly giggled, snapped open her purse again and took out a pair of white crocheted kid gloves.

"I thought the same thing when I looked at myself in the mirror. So I rummaged through this drawer I have filled with all sorts of dainty, lacy things and found these. Of course I wasn't going to carry them in the open. But somehow, just knowing I had them made me feel sort of properly dressed." She giggled again. "Silly, isn't it?"

"We-ell…"

"Oh go ahead and laugh, Amina. Merry would."

They both laughed.

"Shayna, don't think I am laughing at you. I'm laughing at *us.* We're women now, but we still have so much of the little girl in us. The little girl who wants to dress up like Mommy."

"That's why Mr. Pasi is so precious to me. Thank you again for him, Amina," Shayna said gratefully.

"The words on the card were Merry's, you know."

"Merry's? *Meredith's?*"

"Oh yes! Rough-tough, fire-mouth Merry. She's expecting a baby."

Shayna shook her head and grinned with genuine pleasure. "I spoke to her and Jamillah today. I told them I was meeting you for dinner and asked if they wanted to join us. I know how close you guys are so I thought I might as well tell all of you at the same time."

"So are they coming? I haven't spoken to either of them all day."

"No. They both said they'd really love to but they've got work to do for tomorrow."

"We'll all get together soon enough. Don't worry."

Amina sat back in her chair. The waitress, deftly reading the cue, came over again. Amina ordered grilled tilapia with Moroccan couscous and vegetables. She warned the waitress to go easy on the salt. Shayna ordered lamb stew with white rice and fried plantains. The restaurant's warm, homey atmosphere made her realize how hungry she was for some real, home-cooked food. You didn't count calories in a place like this.

Amina said, "Have you ever drunk sorrel? It would help neutralize the salt if your food is too salty for you. It's very sweet, but you can always add water to it."

"I've had sorrel once before. It's not bad. But did I hear you order baobab juice? Is that really something from the tree?"

"Uh huh. It's almost like a lassi. You know, that yogurt drink East Indians have."

"I'll take the sorrel, but I'll taste your baobab juice."

The waitress wrote down their orders and left.

"This place has such a cozy atmosphere, Amina. Just what I needed. I didn't know such a community existed in New York," Shayna said, looking around appreciatively.

"A lot of people don't. At least not yet. I've watched it grow over the years. Great things are happening in Harlem. It's a good place to invest. I'm thinking of opening a clinic here."

"I know. My boyfriend lives on Strivers' Row. He's planning to buy one of those brownstone shells and fix it up."

"Smart man. Those shells cost a fortune these days. Lots of whites are gobbling them up—white South Africans especially, I hear."

They paused as the waitress returned with their drinks. They twisted off the caps on the plastic bottles and poured the contents into their glasses.

"Here's to friendship," Amina said, raising her glass.

"To friendship," Shayna repeated.

When Shayna put down her glass, she looked directly into Amina's eyes. "You must think I've lost it, Amina, calling you up like that, asking to meet so urgently after we hadn't seen each other for so many years."

"No. I don't think you've lost it. I figured you just needed to talk to somebody neutral."

The words tumbled from Shayna as if she wanted to get them out before she changed her mind and held them back. "Janice McWright was not my real mother. My real mother is Congolese—from Congo-Kinshasa. I was born there. My real father was a Peace Corps worker who doesn't want any part of me, doesn't even acknowledge me. My mother—my birth mother, that is—asked my mother—I mean, Janice, my *mother,* mother, to take me and bring me to America."

Amina almost knocked over her glass. She sat back in her chair and stared at Shayna in disbelief.

"I have to find her, Amina. I have to find her. I need to know who she is so I can know who I really am. Thinking of you after I saw the teddy bear made me remember you were born in Congo-Kinshasa. I thought somehow you could help me. I have no idea where to begin." Her eyes, huge and pleading, were fixed on Amina's.

"So that's where 'Mr. Pasi' came from," Amina breathed.

"I didn't know what that word was until you said what you said on the phone. It's from my comfort song. All I know is that ever since I could remember, whenever I'm frightened or hurt, I would sort of chant this thing, *"Pasi, pasi, oh, oh, oh"* over and over again."

"It *must* be from Abeti Masikini's song. They play it every now and then still. It came out in Zaire in the mid-seventies."

Amina sang the first two lines in Lingala.

Pasi! Pasi! Motema na ngai o
Pasi! Pasi! Nakufi, nazua-e!

By the second line, Shayna was humming along. She did not know the words, just the tune. The "oh" she kept repeating was she retained from the "o" sounds in the first line.

"*Pasi* in Lingala means 'problem.' It's got one 'S,' by the way. Abeti is singing about a problem that she is carrying in her heart," Amina explained.

They fell silent, looking at each other.

"How did you find out?" Amina asked.

Shayna recounted what had happened in Atlanta.

"Talk about turning your world upside down!" Amina said sympathetically. "As if you needed to take this on at a time like this."

"All of a sudden, I feel as if I'm living in a world I no longer know. I don't know how to move forward."

"You'll figure it out. But for sure you'll have to go to Kinshasa to do some digging."

"I know," Shayna sighed. "God! I feel so overwhelmed!"

"Just pretend it's a story you're investigating," Amina said.

Shayna looked at her, then looked away. They sat in silence, as Shayna reflected on Amina's words; Amina just let her be.

"Hmph!" Shayna said after a while, placing her elbow on the table and propping her face in her hand. "Hmph!" she said again. Then she smiled, a small smile, and moved her head up and down slowly, as if something was beginning to make sense. "You know, you're so right," she said slowly, turning back to Amina. "It makes perfect sense to approach it like that. I should have thought of that. I guess my head is not as clear as I thought it was."

"You're only human, Shayna. You would have gotten 'round to it sooner or later. In Kinshasa, you'll stay at my place. I bought an apartment since I spend so much time there every year."

"You do?"

"Yes. I do volunteer work at the clinic where I was born."

"You're amazing!"

"Not really. Self-love and self-preservation have a lot to do with it. Sometimes I think I get more out of it than I give."

"I wonder if I'll remember anything."

"You'll remember smells, though you probably won't be able to associate them with anything. You'll just know that they're familiar smells."

"I still can't believe I'm African."

"How do you feel about that?"

"I don't know...incomplete. Suddenly, I'm one big mystery to myself. All my life, I've rolled along in this neat, pretty package, everything so tidy, so privileged. And now, now the wrapping paper is off and I can't seem to find who I am. I get angry sometimes, resentful. Good God, Amina! Why me? What kind of test is this that wipes the only mother you ever knew off the face of the earth and throws another one at you who may not give a damn about you? And she's from a place I've pretty much dismissed for most of my life?"

She sighed heavily and looked at Amina, her eyes filling with tears. "Amina, I was a real ass at Spelman, wasn't I? I mean, I was like a goddamn standard bearer for that hierarchy crap. No wonder you guys couldn't stand me. It all seems so stupid now, so meaningless. I'm a pretty sorry case, aren't I?" she said, wiping away a tear with her handkerchief.

"Hey! Hey! Hey! Don't beat up on yourself. College is where people get caught up in all kinds of crap. We all did. Merry, Jamillah and me, we were pretty well packaged ourselves, just in a different wrapping from yours. None of us cared to see the middle ground. I guess what really matters is that you learn to recognize the crap for what it is and shove it aside. That's what life is all about, I suppose: journeying into your true self, shedding crap. Merry, Jamillah, and I, we're still shedding crap," Amina said.

Suddenly, she started to giggle. "Christ! Listen to me! I *sound* like crap." She laughed outright. Shayna joined in.

"Well, it must be profound crap because it makes perfect sense to me," Shayna said, laughing so much she could barely get the words out.

"But seriously, Shayna. You've got a whole new world to discover inside you now," Amina said, when she managed to stop laughing.

"And I'd like to think that I've learned—am learning—to, how did you say it? Recognize the crap for what it is and shove it aside," Shayna said. The corners of her mouth twitched, but she did not laugh again.

"Well, you're doing just that. You're here, aren't you? Looking for your truth," Amina said.

The waitress arrived with their order just then.

"God, this looks so good. I'm starved," Shayna said.

#

Pineapple, the man said to himself as his eyes took in the pale yellow linen pantsuit she was wearing. He'd noticed her the moment she walked in. *What a striking woman*, he thought, *such unusual features, all sorts of racial mixes there. And the exquisite cut and softness of her clothes for all its casualness.* She walked with such grace, half-smiling, exuding such warmth. There was something very continental about her...*African* continental. He couldn't put his finger on it. It was more in her attitude than in her looks. She was definitely Western. *But there's that something.*

She's a river child, the man thought. That's how he described the people of the African Diaspora in a poem he wrote years ago, during his travels with his father. When he traveled, he delighted in reading the faces of these people, "trying to divine which waters they sprung from," was the way he explained it in his writings.

"My African blood rolls around the earth like a curious river, always finding the middle ground that allows it to pass by," he wrote in the poem. "Ah, this River! It meanders all through Europe, Asia, the Middle East, the Americas, converging with the waters of those places in interludes that spawn rivulets as beautiful in their uniqueness as the purest drop of African blood." Much like the uniqueness of the woman before him now. He had watched her covertly as she chatted easily with the owner of the restaurant while she waited for her companion. He heard her speak to him in French. He caught her accent. It sounded Parisian, but wasn't there something African about it, too?

Then the other one came in: stunning too, but in a different way. *This one carries her beauty on the outside*, he thought. *She has not yet found her inner beauty like the other one.* His eyes went back to the first one and his heart pounded. He studied her face as she spoke. He took in the range of emotions that flowed through her conversation with her female companion. He saw her reach for the other one's hands. He saw sadness, laughter, disbelief, resignation, excitement, hope. He caught a word here, a word there, enough to tell him, finally, that the first one was Caribbean, the second one American. *And yet...*

He was staring at her when she suddenly looked his way, catching his unmistakable gaze. He did not blink; neither did she. The intensity of her stare jolted him, though no one could tell from his cool return. Their gaze remain fixed on each other.

CHAPTER SEVEN

At thirty-five, Crispin Abeli reigned over Musana Holdings Plc., a multibillion dollar business empire that reached into Africa, Asia, Europe, Latin America, and the Caribbean. Musana Holdings was a true pan-African company, with operations in every region of the continent. It was listed on the French Bourse and on the New York Stock Exchange. Crispin was known in business circles worldwide as Africa's wonder boy. Son of a famous United Nations diplomat, he attended elementary and high school in Belgium, earned his undergraduate degree from the London School of Economics, and a master's from Massachusetts Institute of Technology's Sloan School of Management. One week after he graduated from MIT—second in his class behind a Chinese student (his best friend)—he flew back to his country to turn his father's small import-export company that his uncle Yafari was managing into a global company. *It will be the likes of which no one has ever seen in Africa or in the hands of an African,* he promised himself on the plane.

He loathed living in the United States. He described the country as "technologically awesome, but socially primitive." Before he left Boston, he told his inner circle of friends that he had had enough of seeing and reading about black entrepreneurs getting shafted by what he considered a well-orchestrated, corporate, financial, and government assault through minority set-asides. In fact, he was tired of the whole culture of race and the depraved psychologies it bred among blacks and whites alike. Most of all, he was fed up of the portrayal of Africa as a giant charity case—a continent that existed on the largesse of "donor" countries and "aid" groups and "debt forgivers" and "foreign investors" who had to be kept happy with incentives so outrageous that they practically turned the continent into a prostitute. U.S. and European policies toward Africa were shaped by the same culture and politics of race that ran amuck in their own countries, Crispin fumed. He swore that he would never buy into this global "minority" politic. He was going to build a business empire that, for generations to come, would benefit those of his flesh and blood first: his country, his continent, his race.

"It's all about making deals," he told his inner circle of friends. And he learned about making deals from the very best, beginning with his father, a master dealer at the UN, then from the leaders of the Fortune 100 companies he worked as an intern. At these companies, he was always placed on the executive floor, invariably as an assistant to some senior VP or to the chief executive himself. The corporate brass liked this handsome, sophisticated, sharp-minded African who spoke beautiful English and fluent French, dressed like the real Saville Row, and whose father was a UN diplomat. They pegged him for a future political leader or business tycoon in Africa. Cultivating him was a strategic corporate move.

Crispin understood all this and played into it. He was there to learn, not to convert anybody. And learn he did. From the moment he landed back in Congo, he began to strike bold deals with like-minded classmates he grew close to in London and Boston and who went back to their respective homes in other parts of Africa, Asia, Latin America, the Middle East, and the Caribbean. Every Friday evening in Boston, he and these other minority graduate students had gotten together, usually at someone's apartment off campus, to exchange ideas on how their countries could survive as prosperous independent entities in the face of what the lone Brazilian in the group termed "rampaging economic enslavement in the guise of open markets and free trade."

They were all from entrepreneurial families. And they were all fiercely nationalist. They spoke of themselves as the 1990s counterpart to the Third World nationalists of the 1950s who studied in Europe and America and went on to wrest their countries from colonial rule. As new entrepreneurs, they bought and sold raw commodities, consumer goods, capital equipment. They invested in each other's food-processing plants, transportation companies, and telecommunications companies. They used every legitimate trick in the London and Boston books to finance their trading and investment deals—barter, forfaiting, factoring, leasing, even personal credit cards. They played the stock and currency markets in New York, London, Paris, Hong Kong, Tokyo. And they kept up their subscriptions to the *Economist*, *CFO*, *The Economist Intelligence Unit*'s country and regional reports, *The Journal of Commerce*, *The Wall Street Journal,* and *The Financial Times*.

In less than ten years, the Abeli family's Musana Import-Export S.A. became Musana Holdings Plc. The Musana Commercial Bank in which Crispin's friends had invested was known as the small businessman's bank. It gave favorable terms on loans to small entrepreneurs, including farmers, with sound business plans and capable management in place. There were branches of the MCB throughout the country and in neighboring Congo Brazzaville, Rwanda, Burundi, and Uganda. It was one of the best performing banks on the continent with not a single loan default on record. Rather, loans were repaid in advance.

The Musana discount superstore chain opened stores in every French-speaking country in West and North Africa. Negotiations were underway for the first store in South Africa. After that, it would be easy to sweep the English-speaking countries. The stores were known for good quality and low prices. European and American closeouts sat side by side on the shelves with products manufactured in Africa, Asia, and the Middle East. A few Caribbean products were beginning to appear. Shoppers of all income brackets frequented the stores, paying with cash or credit card. There was a price line for every pocket.

Crispin helped finance the construction of hospitals, technical schools, and low-income housing developments. He steered clear of politics, although the ruling party's top brass kept hounding him to take up a cabinet position in the government. He was generous in his support of government projects he considered beneficial to the country, and quietly advised on business-enhancing policies. But he remained stubbornly uncommitted. No one could finger him as anyone's "boy," neither did he seek to have anyone as his "boy."

"I'm a businessman, nothing else," he always said. "Building business is my only business."

But there was more to his business than building Musana Holdings. Crispin believed that the salvation of his country, of all of Africa for that matter, lay in fostering responsible and sustainable private enterprise—not the kind of enterprise in which government officials and workers played fast and loose with the national treasury down the line; and certainly not the kind that hustled for the moment. The enterprise he dreamed of would be steeped in the spirit of the pre-colonial African traders. The traders of those days had vision. They used solid planning and meticulous management to keep their families and societies prosperous for generations. These were the values Crispin sought to instill in those who passed through the training and apprenticeship division that was a fixture at every Musana company.

With his workers, he was compassionate, but firm. A staunch believer in the notion that prevention is better than cure, he refused to subscribe to medical insurance plans. Instead, he contracted with naturopathic doctors and made annual preventive whole-health consultations mandatory for employees at every Musana company, from top management down, immediate families included. As a result, the high instance of sick leave that plagued most large companies was virtually unheard of at Musana companies.

"Crispin Abeli," one French magazine wrote, "epitomizes the pragmatic business romanticist, if there was such a creature."

His mother pleaded with him to get married, to take a wife and have children on whom he could lavish his wealth.

"I'd like to, believe me. I'm still searching for the right woman," he told her.

"What do you mean the *right* woman? Look at all these beautiful daughters of well-to-do families that are available. They have traveled, they are educated, sophisticated. What more do you want? They are all *right* women, Crispin Abeli. You do date some of them."

"Yes, Mother, I know they are *right,* as you and everyone else see them. But the ones I may have considered are already married and the ones who are left have no passion about anything beyond themselves. They look right, speak right, act right, but what do they *do*? What do they *believe* in except looking and speaking and acting *right* all the time—until they snare a man! They're trappers. I want a woman who is as passionate about *something* as I am about what I do...something worthy. That's the kind of woman who would understand me. She would understand what it means to teach our children the importance of commitment and dedication."

"Ah! Your head is in the stars. Where is there such a woman these days, my son? Your father married the last one when he married me." She chuckled.

"You are shameless," he said with a smile. "You can laugh all you want, but I know she is there somewhere. I just don't know where. I'll find her, though. Most people may not believe it, but this Crispin Abeli has no intention of remaining a bachelor or childless."

"Well, I suppose if you can imagine her, she must exist. After all, I gave birth to a man like you, so someone must have given birth to a woman who suits you. But I don't see you really looking. You lock yourself in that office downtown and you leave only for meetings, to travel or to go to your empty home, a beautiful home, but such an empty home." She sighed. "Is it that you are looking for a foreign woman?"

"Would you be unhappy if I married someone who is not from our country?"

"Not *un*happy. But if you *must* marry a foreign woman, at least she should be a black woman. Your first choice should be another African, then a Caribbean next; Americans are last."

Crispin laughed. His mother's mouth twitched as she tried to suppress a smile. She gave up and started laughing herself. She had often described to her children her experience with the social hierarchy at Howard University when she studied nutrition there. As an African, she was on the bottom of that hierarchy, she recounted with amusement. She and other African students joked about it when they got together, and chastised their African-American and Caribbean friends for being so petty and brainwashed.

Aziza Musana was head nutritionist at the city's biggest public hospital when Crispin's father met her. He was visiting the hospital as part of the delegation of government officials that made their annual rounds of the country's health and educational institutions. Before the week was out, he had gone to her father to discuss marriage. She remained his only wife and their children were his only children. Even in this day, that was unusual for a man of his social stature.

Crispin was at his parents' home for lunch the day his mother chided him about marriage.

His parents lived in an audaciously exclusive enclave of a once-wealthy suburb that had been swallowed by the city's refugee spillover. The refugees trundled into Kinshasa every day, hundreds of thousands of villagers fleeing rebel action, or the threat of it, in the remote towns and villages. Crispin was the only child of his parents still living in the country. His brothers and sisters lived in other parts of Africa, the Middle East, and Europe. All were married with families of their own. All were involved in managing the scattered and vast Musana empire.

His father, now retired from the United Nations, had dined with Crispin and his mother and was now locked in the library with the somewhat traumatized minister of foreign affairs who stopped by a few minutes ago. Local and foreign officials, and even businessmen, were frequent visitors to the home. They sought the elder Abeli's counsel on matters to do with global politics, or they stopped by just to enjoy the company of "the most revered African diplomat," as the *Economist* magazine once called him.

Crispin was proud of his father. The elder Abeli would have made secretary general of the U.N. had it not been for his open criticism of the United States and its bully tactics in international affairs. "People like me, we go to the United States only to study, not to live," he once told his children. "You study in its universities, in its corporations, in its streets, at its social gatherings, in its churches, and from its television programs, so that when the time comes, you can deal with Americans in their own language to get what you need for the good of your own people or for your own well being."

He had nothing against the American people. They loved their country just the way it was and did whatever it took to keep it that way. That's the way it should be, he argued. He too loved his own country, with all its political and social disasters and industrial underdevelopment. He loved it as much as Americans did theirs. His American friends understood and respected that. Not that it mattered. Nobody was trying to get anybody to give up what they had.

Crispin himself lived in the Gombe residential district of the city, in an imposing villa behind a high brick wall on the bank of the Congo River, that colossal, dark highway of water that straddles the center of Africa and penetrates deep into its treasure trove of timber, farmland, gold, diamonds, copper, and cobalt. Gombe was the same old story—another once-exclusive residential area prostituted by the wit and brawn of survival, as rebels hacked away at the city's lifeline to the fruits and vegetables and livestock in the hinterland. In the daytime, hawkers of every basic item lined the promenade along the river in a makeshift survivors' market. Their supplies were replenished by daring river runners crossing back and forth between the two Congos. At night, the hawkers disappeared, leaving behind the debris of another day's struggle for survival. At night, the river became lack and silent, except for the occasional splish-splash of a shadowy vessel hauling goods for the city's underbelly.

The colors of the oleanders and the fragrance of jasmine on the wind redeemed it all. Driving back from his parents' home that day, Crispin took in everything about the city and its people—the good, the bad, the ugly, the indifferent. The country began to bleed long ago from decades of corruption and mismanagement. When Kabila rode into the capital, signaling the end of Mobutu Sese Seko's three-decade reign, people prostrated themselves in the streets, shouting in jubilation that deliverance from evil had come. The euphoria didn't last. Civil war broke out as armed rebels, fed up with Kabila's policies and his inability to relieve the nation's crippling poverty, launched an assault on the eastern region and began pushing toward Kinshasa. The war became a multinational fray, dragging in eight countries. The rebels were backed by Kabila's former allies, Rwanda and Uganda, who helped him overthrow Mobutu. Zimbabwe, Namibia, Angola, Chad, and Sudan jumped in on the side of the government, bolstering

Kabila's troops with guns and soldiers. Burundi dove in on its own to fight Burundian rebels based in eastern Congo.

Soon the Rwanda and Uganda-backed rebels were gaining on Kinshasa. Kabila beat them back with help from Angola and Zimbabwe. For a brief moment, the people of Kinshasa were jubilant again. But Kabila's hard-nosed position against negotiating with the rebels and his clampdown on all opposition plunged the country deeper into conflict. Kabila's popularity plummeted as the cost of war soared. Footloose soldiers who had not seen a paycheck in months terrorized civilians. Gangs of urchins roamed the streets, turned away by families that no longer could afford to feed them. Out of the confusion sprang a new breed of entrepreneurs known as *bacheques*, flamboyant wheelers and dealers who could broker any deal, find any product or service for a price.

And yet, most of the time in Kinshasa, it was as if all was well, as if what was going on beyond the capital was nothing more than a rumor. People worked and loved and laughed and cried. They went to market, danced at weddings, gave life to babies, buried their dead. Children went to school and took exams. Merchants made money. Laborers labored. Politicians politicked, blaming food shortages and shoddy municipal services on criminals, the rebels, neighboring countries, or the Western Powers—whichever group was the most convenient scapegoat at the time. Human decency held it all together. It's always there in the darkest days, that decency, embodied in that critical mass of people who keep things on middle ground from falling apart. You find them in every nation. They reason and cajole and enforce, keeping the criminal and the corrupt from crossing that final line.

"Countries bleed, but they don't die," Crispin said aloud as he turned off the Boulevard. He was almost home. He grabbed the phone on the fourth ring. Mizele, his housekeeper, was at yet another wake. That was his usual excuse to get a day off—a relative had died. "At this rate, you'll kill off your whole family before the new millennium," Crispin said with amusement when Mizele asked for the time off.

"Mais non, patron. C'est vrai, je vous assure. Mon oncle est mort d'un accident d'auto," Mizele answered, his eyes filled with hurt.

"But Mizele, *mon cher,* wasn't there an uncle of yours who died in a car crash last month?"

"Yes, *patron.* But that was my uncle on my mother's side. This is my uncle on my father's side who just died. I don't know why we have such bad luck in my family, *patron.* Someone must have put a fetish on us," Mizele said, his face filled with sorrow.

Unlike most house servants, Mizele spoke very good French. He was putting himself through technical school, studying computer programming. Crispin figured out long ago that Mizele used French when he was lying, though he had never let on to Mizele. Crispin knew that it was easier for Mizele to lie to a European than to one of his own people. So when he needed to pull a fast one, his mind simply switched Crispin the Congolese to Crispin the child from Europe and America.

"Hâlo."

"Crispin! Where the hell have you been? I've been trying to reach you for hours. What's the matter? Your finances crumbling along with that crazy country of yours? Can't afford hired help?"

Crispin laughed. Eliezer Ten Pow was the eldest son in one of Hong Kong's ocean shipping dynasties. He was about to become chairman of the company, now that his father finally agreed to retire after his nearly a fifty-year reign at the helm. He was one of Crispin's closest friends and most trusted business associates. They met at school in London. Eliezer introduced Crispin to tai chi and he practiced it every day since.

"ET! Good to hear from you, man. I was at my folks in Mbinza. How's the family?" Crispin said, using the nickname that had stuck after his name was printed on the class registers as "ET Pow."

"All fine! You're going to be an uncle again."

"You're messing with that rhino horn stuff too much, ET! You'll kill that poor girl."

"I should send you some, Crispin. Maybe it'll make you hurry up and take a wife—make me some nephews."

"In due course, ET, in due course. And you can keep your pulverized rhino horn. We've got some snake stuff that not even you would want to fool around with."

"Think we can make a market for it in China?"

"Too late. It's already there. Some of your compatriots took it back two years ago after they finished building that rail line for us. In their gratitude, they left us with quite a few children of the Yangtze River."

"Strategy, my friend! Strategy! We were preparing the ground for future relations between our countries. Seriously, though, I'm afraid I'll have to drag you to New York."

"New York? What's up?"

"My father wants me to receive an award on his behalf. It's the annual shipping industry get-together. I'd like you to be my guest."

"I'd be delighted. Now, tell me why you *really* want me to go to New York. What or whom are we going after?"

"Brazil. There's a nice little shipping line up for grabs in Sao Paulo. Glaucio called me about it. He says you, Dennis, he, and I should join and buy it. He'll meet us in New York to run it down. Dennis will be there too."

Dennis Ramon, CEO of CariRam Enterprises in Grenada, was the new don in the Caribbean region's food processing industry. A year ago, he had beaten Jamaica's Grace Kennedy, the region's long-reigning monarch, in a bid for a massive citrus operation in Cuba.

"Who're we up against?" Crispin asked.

"Some American, European and Japanese boys."

"Together or separate?

"Separate consortia."

"Could be rough. You know how much those guys want to control Brazil. I'm game, though. When do I head for the Big Apple?"

"This weekend. I say, what do you make of Janice McWright's death?"

"Tragic indeed. She couldn't see the world's forest for the American trees, but she was a decent human being. America has lost a good advocate on the Europe scene. It will have an impact. The Europeans don't like the secretary of state at all."

"Yeah. I suppose your father is going to the funeral."

"Yes. And no, I will not accompany him. He knew her. I didn't."

"All the same, looks like you'll be in the good old U-S-of-A around the same time; might as well go to the funeral with dad. Give him my regards. Ciao, fella."

"Take care."

CHAPTER EIGHT

Crispin's eyes remained fixed on Amina's.

She was used to men staring at her. She could even tell where they were from by the way they stared. Africans stared in a lordly "I-will-have-you-if-I-want-you, woman!" way. West Indian men stared with a tease in their eyes. Theirs was an "It-would-be-so-nice-to-play-with-you" stare. Southern European men stared that way, too, especially Italians. African-American men, she found, did not speak with the eyes the way Africans and West Indians did. They either smiled outright and nodded, or tightened their lips and looked away quickly, as if they wouldn't be caught dead staring at a beautiful woman.

This man's stare was unlike any she experienced. No imperiousness, no tease, no smile, no nod, no uptightness. But his eyes seemed to impale hers in a confrontation with her most private self. He was stripping her down to her very soul, as if he needed to see her pure and true.

Amina felt her own eyes flicker and her heart quicken as the eyes of this stranger fixated on her. His stare went deep into her. She reached deeper, faster than his eyes, into that reserve of strength that lays dormant in every human until it receives the ultimate command. Silently, Amina commanded. Her eyes hardened into a final thrust, pushing against this man's invasion.

He stood his ground, cool and deep.

Amina lost. The defiance ebbed from her eyes. Now she was truly seeing him. She caught her breath at what she saw. It was as if all the passion of his soul had inflamed his eyes. This man wanted her in a way that was beyond lust. She felt the stirring between her legs. Involuntarily, her lips parted. Her breathing quickened. How could a stranger touch her so intimately, from a distance? She saw a smile flicker in his eyes.

"Amina!" Shayna was whispering. *"Amina!"*

Amina caught herself and looked away abruptly from the stranger…their dance transpired over an interlude of seconds, the depth of a lifetime.

"That was *obscene!*" Shayna said, leaning across the table, barely able to hide the amusement behind her look of shock.

"What was obscene?"

"The way you looked at that man. Wow! Do you know him?"

"I know who he is. No, I don't know him. Let's get out of here." Amina signaled to the waiter and reached for her purse.

"Whoa! Why, you're totally flustered. He really got to you."

"Let's get out of here, Shayna!"

Shayna ignored her. "And what do you mean you know who he is and you don't know him? You're not making sense, Amina. I'll take care of that." Shayna grabbed the check before Amina could pick it up.

"Oh come on, Shayna, my treat."

Shayna ignored her. "Well? How do you know who he is?"

"Well *you* know who he is, don't you? Anybody who reads a decent newspaper would know him. Take a good look at that table again."

Shayna swung around to face the man who had made such an impression on Amina. He was now deep in conversation with the three men at his table. One of the three was Chinese; one was clearly Latin; the other, with a well-groomed, dreadlocked ponytail, was definitely West Indian. They were all casually dressed, but their clothing spelled very exclusive tailors in very expensive capitals.

"My sweet Lord. That's Crispin Abeli!"

Amina groaned. "For Christ sake, Shayna, don't gawk. And keep your voice down. Come on. Let's go."

"Are you kidding? I can't leave now. Don't you see who's with him? This is like finding a pot of gold, Amina. Journalists have a hell of a time getting near to those guys. And here I'm sitting just a few tables away from them—*all together*. I want an interview."

"I'm out of here."

"Not yet! I won't take long. I promise." Shayna's attention was riveted on the group of men.

"Bye!"

"Okay! Okay! I'm coming! I'm coming!" Shayna sighed. "Amina, I'll never forget that you made me blow a chance for an interview with Crispin Abeli, Eliezer Ten Pow, Glaucio Texeira and Dennis Ramon. The Third World's golden boys all together in the same room! They *must* be working on some deal and it's *got* to be big. God I wish I had a camera! How can anybody walk out on this!"

"No problem for me."

"Yeah! *You're* not a reporter."

"And *you're* supposed to be in mourning!" Amina regretted the words instantly. "I'm so sorry, Shayna. That was uncalled for." She reached for Shayna's hand.

"It's okay. I'll forgive you that one. You must be really upset," Shayna said. She paid the bill and Amina led them out of the restaurant hurriedly.

"I'd love to know what they're doing in New York. Abeli's supposed to hate America. I know his father was at my mother's funeral," Shayna mused as they walked east on 116th Street to where they had both parked.

"I haven't the slightest idea," Amina said nonchalantly. The thought that Crispin Abeli might have picked up her reaction to him annoyed her. She lengthened her stride.

"Hey, don't take it out on me because you and one of the world's richest and most gorgeous men made love with your eyes *en pleine publique,*" Shayna laughed, quickening her steps to keep up with Amina's long stride.

"You're crazy!"

"You know I'm not. He touched you and you liked it."

"You're enjoying this, aren't you?"

"Sure am. This is the stuff of high romance, passion. It isn't over, you know. The way he looked at you, I *know* he's going to find you one day. So I guess I'll eventually get my interview." She sighed.

"*Nothing* happened in there, Shayna. So you can just drop those crazy ideas you're pumping into your head."

Shayna giggled and held up her hands. "Hey! I'm not being judgmental here.

"God! I must have looked stupid!" Amina said irritably. "What could have possessed me? Don't you dare say it, Shayna!"

That was too much for both of them. They burst out laughing.

"Okay. I won't say he possessed you," Shayna said, struggling to keep a straight face. "But I'm serious, Amina. That was some high voltage in there. The two of you are bound to meet again. You're in his city for three months of the year, for chrissakes. That man has so much money he could hire the whole damn FBI to find out who you are and where you are."

Amina said nothing.

Shayna continued, "Wanna bet he'll find you in Kinshasa when you go back this time?"

Amina remained silent.

"Okay. I'll drop it. So where do we go from here?"

"To Kinshasa, of course. When do you want to go?"

When next are *you* going? I've got loads of time off from work."

"I usually leave the end of May, early June."

"I'll be ready," Shayna said determinedly.

BOOK TWO

Congo-Kinshasa
The 1970s

CHAPTER NINE

Suke could not resist the call of the song. She scrambled to her feet, picked up her four-month-old nephew, and bound him to her back with the cloth she spread on the ground for them to sit on, and then ran across the yard to join the other girls. She broke into the ring just as they reached the part where they had to wriggle their hips.

Suke wriggled her hips, going down low and coming up again in perfect unison with the other girls in the ring. The baby gurgled with pleasure. The girls clapped and stepped and wriggled their hips again, all the while singing:

> "Eee yo lay eee yay ay
> Eee yo lay eee yay!"
> (clap! clap!)
> "Eee yo lay eee yay ay
> Eee yo lay eee yay!"
> (clap! clap!)

Suddenly, the other girls froze. Suke kept going until she realized that she was the only one still singing and dancing. She stopped and looked around, puzzled. Everyone was looking at her.

"What's wrong? Why is everybody looking at me?"

She said it more as a challenge than as a question.

"Go away, Suke! You can't play with us," one of the girls standing next to her said.

"Why? What have I done?" Suke demanded, planting her hands on her hips. She was genuinely surprised, but wanted to make it clear that she was ready to defend her right to play with the group.

"You're married. You can't play anymore."

"*Married? Me*? You're lying, Nzinga! You're lying! I'm not married!"

The other girls giggled.

"Oh, you're so stupid. Go away! Go ask you sister! She'll tell you," Nzinga said, giving Suke a shove.

Suke stamped her foot and shoved her back. The baby began to wail. Suke paid no attention to him. "I'm not married. And I'm not going away. I am playing!" she said angrily, giving Nzinga another shove.

Baby on her back or not, Suke was a hell of a fighter and everyone knew it, none better than Nzinga who tangled with her many times before and had come out the worse for it. Nzinga decided against getting physical. Instead, she planted her hands on her hips and sang out in a loud, mocking voice.

"Suke wants to play-o
Suke go away-o
Make your babies Suke-o
Suke, Suke, Mama-o"

She clapped her hands and wriggled her hips, exaggerating the wriggle so much that the other girls burst out laughing. Suke's eyes filled with tears. She knew when truth was staring her in the face. This was not the usual argument she had with Nzinga. She was used to fighting over who danced better than whom and who stole this or that from whom and who said this or that about whom. But this talk of being married and making babies was much too grown up for little girls. This was the kind of talk that Nzinga, precocious as she was, would never engage in for play, especially with grownups in hearing distance.

Not wanting anyone to see her cry, Suke turned and ran to her sister Yolita, who was cooking on a wood fire beside the doorway of her house. Yolita's house was one of the six or so adjoining brick flats lined up in a row behind a modest villa in a multifamily compound. It was a typical arrangement in the "cîtés," those sprawling, bustling communities on the outskirts of Kinshasa that were home to most of Kinshasa's five million residents. Family members or friends migrating from their villages to the big city sought accommodation in the cîté with those who had come before and had managed to acquire their own home.

Suke came to live with Yolita when Yolita's first child was born. Yolita needed help with the children so she sent for her. Like everyone else in the compound, Yolita and Suke belonged to the extended family of the man who lived in the villa in front. The man was a supervisor in the central post office downtown and lived in the villa with his wife—a "city-bred bitch," as the other women in the compound called her behind her back—and their four children.

Most of the women in the compound kept their households going with money they earned from the small businesses they themselves set up and ran. Many bought items wholesale from manufacturers or distributors and either sold them in the market themselves or sold them semi-wholesale to neighborhood shops and beer joints. These women sold basic commodities like soft drinks, beer, tomato paste, sardines, cooking oil, beans, rice, vegetables, soap, cloth, and baby items. Others raised chickens and sold their eggs and, occasionally, a chicken or two.

No matter what business they were in, every one of the women in the compound could dress to the nines when the occasion called for it. At such times they would step out in expensive superwax super wax cotton prints done up in the latest styles by local tailors, with the latest fashion in shoes, matching pocketbooks, and gold jewelry—nothing less than 18-carat. Their men worked as low-level civil servants downtown, as factory workers, or as overseers for those ubiquitous government projects with seemingly limitless budgets.

It was a typical compound, with the usual lusty bickering and bantering, screams of children, and the occasional wife beating. Goats bleated, roosters caw-caw-caw cawed, laying hens clucked, fighting dogs snarled and yelped. Overriding it all was a comfortable feeling of kinship and security.

Suke held the baby securely under its bottom as she ran to Yolita. "Big Sister! Big Sister!" she wailed. It was impolite to call an older sister by her given name.

"Imbecile! Stop all that noise!" Yolita's husband growled. He was watching his wife cook. He had just been fired for the third time in as many months—for drinking on the job—and spent most of the time watching television sprawled on an old couch in the tiny living room, wrapped from waist to calves in a cloth. To anyone who inquired about his progress in finding a new job, his answer was the same: he was putting together a business plan in his head. He was through working for people who had a smaller brain that his.

Yolita resented his rebuke of her little sister. At least Suke earned her keep. All *he* did was lose jobs and sit around all day.

"Don't be such a brute," she snapped back at him.

She paused to look up at Suke. The other women in the compound stopped what they were doing to watch them.

"Come, Suke," Yolita said gently. "Why are you crying?"

"They chased me away," Suke said, pointing to the girls who had already resumed their game. "They don't want me to play with them. They said I was married and that I couldn't play anymore."

"So what if you are married!" Yolita's husband said irritably.

"Yolita, stop wasting time with her and hurry with the food. I'm hungry!"

It wasn't even near lunchtime. Yolita cut her eyes at him.

"Suke," she said, putting her hands on her little sister's waist and drawing her close. "Do you remember Citoyen Madiata, the man who came here yesterday and brought those two goats, the cases of beer for everyone, and those clothes for you?"

"Yes, Big Sister. And he gave lots of money to brother-in-law."

"Heh! Heh! Hehhh!"

The snicker came from Micheline's house two doors down. Micheline was the compound's resident prima Donna: beautiful, unmarried, and the mother of two small children who refused to work. She lived on the money she got from her children's father, who was a big shot in the army. Micheline said he was very close to the president and was very rich. The compound took the part about his being close to the president with a grain of salt. They had only Micheline's word to go on and that wasn't always worth much.

Still, once a month, the black Mercedes Benz with darkened windows—the kind army big shots drove—would pull up in front of the compound and Micheline, waiting out front all dolled up and doused in Charlie, would climb in. The car would drive off with a screech. It returned with Micheline hours later.

The very next day, Micheline would start spending. She'd buy new clothes, Ambi skin bleach, jewelry, shoes, and makeup for herself; new clothes, shoes, and toys for her children; baskets of fruit, vegetables, ground provisions, cooking oil, cans of *Pilchards* sardines, tomato paste, dried salt fish, frozen chickens, and beef for her refrigerator; beer for everyone; little gifts and Fanta soft drinks for all the children in the compound. This was the time to catch her for a loan. She would dole them out grandly to all who requested one, at no interest.

All this largesse usually lasted three weeks. As the third week drew to a close, Micheline would steadily turn crabby. She would snap at the children, drop snide remarks about who owed her money, and roll her ample hips and cut her eyes when she walked past the women. The women would sigh and look at each other knowingly. The whole compound was familiar with "Micheline's mood" that came on in the week or so before "Benz Day." They ignored it. Micheline was a good soul, basically. She shared her wealth. You can't forget such things.

"Heh! Heh!" The mocking sound came again from close behind the curtain over Micheline's door. It was louder, in case no one had heard the first time. Benz Day was about five days away.

Yolita's eyes shot daggers at Micheline's house. She opened her mouth to aim a few choice comments in that direction, but at that very instant, Suke moved closer to her and laid her head against her bosom. Yolita's face softened and she smiled. She put her arms around Suke.

"That man is your husband, Suke. You will go to live with him in four years, when you are fourteen," she said.

Suke's eyes opened wide. Tears welled up and spilled over, but she made no sound. She turned to look at her friends. Nzinga was in the center of the ring now, rocking her hips this way and that while the others clapped and sang.

Suke looked at them for a long time. Yolita held her, waiting anxiously for her to say something.

"It's true what Nzinga said? That I'll make babies? Like you?"

Yolita's eyes brimmed with tears. "Yes," she said in a low voice.

Suke was looking at Yolita again. "That's all there is to being married?

Yolita sighed and looked away. She felt old for her nineteen years. "That's mostly all there is, yes," she said.

The baby on Suke's back began to fret. "Hush," said Suke soothingly, bouncing him up and down with her hands under his bottom. "Hush."

She turned from her sister and looked at her friends again for a long time. Then she looked past the doorway to her brother-in-law who was now cutting his toenails with a knife. Suke's face was blank. Still bouncing the baby, she began to walk toward the old mango tree in the far corner of the compound. She walked slowly, with her head down, bouncing the baby absently on her back.

CHAPTER TEN

"Suke! Suukaaay!"

Madiata was drunk.

Suke, bring us food! We're hungry."

It was midnight. Suke was exhausted. She had been awake all night trying to pacify her daughter who was teething. The child had finally fallen asleep at her breast and she herself had dozed off.

"Sukaaaayyy!"

A fist pounded on the bedroom door. The infant jumped and started screaming again. Suke laid her down on the bed and jumped from the bed, gathering her cloth more securely around her. She opened the door just a crack.

"Yes?" She kept her eyes downcast. She was frightened. He might hit her.

He pushed the door open wider and stuck his face in. "Quiet your child and bring us food!"

"Yes, sir," she said timidly, backing away from the door.

He pulled it shut and went back to his guests.

Suke picked up the baby and tied her to her back. The child stopped crying immediately. Suke opened the door again and headed to the kitchen. She switched on the light, lit the burner under a pot of leftover cassava-leaf stew, and filled another pot with water and placed it on the second burner. She half-filled a basin with water, dropped a bar of soap into it, draped a towel over her hand, and went into the living room so that her husband and his guests could wash their hands. When they finished, she took the basin outside, emptied it, washed the towel with the soap, and hung it on the line to dry.

Then she sat down on a low stool in the kitchen to wait for the water to boil. When it boiled, she would add cassava flour and stir it with a long wooden spoon until it became a thick, heavy meal. Then she would remove the pot from the fire, clamp it firmly between the soles of her feet and beat the meal until it formed a smooth, sticky fufu. She already had the wooden spoon in her hand.

The baby fell asleep again. She herself must have dozed off, for the next thing she knew Madiata was pinching her.

"Wake up, woman! What kind of hostess are you! How can you sleep when my guests and I are hungry?"

Suke jumped and pulled her hand away with a cry, rubbing the reddened spot where he had pinched her. The baby screamed.

"The water is boiling. Make the fufu quick!" Madiata said irritably. He stumbled back toward the living room, collided with the doorway and swore loudly.

There were three guests, two men and a woman. The two men worked for Suke's husband, who was head of the local sanitation bureau. The woman with them had come to the house before. Suke knew she was Madiata's mistress. She had a vulgar laugh and kept her arms around Madiata's shoulders.

Suke kept her eyes lowered as she served them. She was seventeen now, taller than the average young woman. Her body was firm even though she had borne two children, her breasts high and full. Her skin was that reddish brown commonly found among the people from her province. Women with that color did not have to use bleach, although some still did.

Suke wore her hair threaded in one of the latest styles. It enhanced the shape of her face. From years of carrying water and firewood and baskets of this and that on her head, she walked with a smooth, easy uprightness—even when she wore high heels—that made her stand out among the graceless, plodding city girls in the neighborhood where she now lived.

Suke had grown into a truly beautiful young woman. Young men going to and from school or work whistled at her if she happened to be at the gate when they passed. They called out to her that she was "kitoko mingi. [Very beautiful]." Suke would pretend to ignore them, but their whistles and comments about how pretty she was pleased her and made her feel good about herself. There were no praises or compliments for her in her home.

The eyes of Madiata's mistress raked over Suke. The woman's laugh grew louder, more affected. She ran her hands possessively over Madiata and pressed her body hard against his, keeping her eyes on Suke all the time. She was much older than Suke. "Where are we going after we eat, sweetheart," she purred, loud enough for Suke to hear.

Suke kept her eyes lowered and finished serving them, then went to sit on a mat in a corner of the room where she had laid her baby. She would have to remove the dishes when Madiata and his guests finished eating. She sat in the proper traditional way--legs together and stretched straight in front, back upright. She gazed tenderly at her daughter, crooning softly to her as she slept.

"We're going nowhere," Madiata said loudly to his mistress, his mouth full.

"You mean we'll stay here, with all these people?" Her eyes knifed into Suke. "Oh no, sweetheart. Let's go somewhere private."

"Nowhere, woman! It's midnight. I'm tired." He pushed her hands away.

"Awwww, come on. Let's go to my place."

"I said no! Suke, get rid of these things and bring us beer!"

Suke obeyed, her face showing no emotion.

"Why do you keep that idiot girl?" the woman sulked.

"I paid a lot for her bride price. She is my wife."

The woman made a slow sucking sound with her teeth. She did it so slowly that it sounded more obscene than a spoken curse. "Besides," she said scornfully, "What can she do for you, eh? Wife my behind!"

"She had two children for me."

"Ah!" the woman said with a dismissive flick of her wrist. "Any she-dog can produce."

"Quite so, my dear," Madiata chuckled, dipping the last piece of fufu into the stew and holding it poised in front of his mouth. "But it is what I did with her to make her produce that is more interesting."

He placed the fufu in his mouth with a flourish and turned to the woman with a wide grin.

His mistress fixed her eyes on him as her face contorted. Her mouth twisted, her eyes narrowed, her nostrils flared. Her long fingers curled. She was a predator about to strike.

"You know," her voice clawed, "I bet you had to rape her to get them!"

He slapped her. She shrieked with laughter, throwing back her head and opening her mouth wide. "Oh yes!" she cried derisively. "You had to rape her to get those babies!"

Two quick slaps knocked her head hard from side to side.

Suke did not wait around. She gathered up her sleeping child and hurried into the bedroom. She placed the baby in her crib and covered her. Trembling with fear, she returned to the living room to clear away the dishes. She wanted to finish quickly, before she was left alone with Madiata.

By the time she returned to the living room Madiata was shoving the woman toward the door, thrusting her out with one hand under her chin. He was shouting at all of them.

"Get out! Get out all of you pigs! You, woman, don't let me see you again! Do you hear me? Never again! Out!" He shouted at the top of his voice.

The men scrambled through the door. Madiata shoved the woman behind them and slammed the door. The woman's raucous laughter and high heels echoed loudly in the street. Madiata yanked the door open again, hurled a few filthy words at her and slammed the door again. He slammed it so hard that Suke jumped and dropped a plate. She bent to pick up the pieces, but she was trembling so violently that Madiata, seeing her, became more enraged.

As she crept past him, he grabbed her and threw her on the couch. Suke closed her eyes and waited, motionless ...

Suke was never accepted by her husband's household, which consisted of his mother, a younger sister with her husband and their three children, and an arrogant younger brother with leering eyes. Madiata was paying for his education at one of the better technical colleges in downtown Kinshasa. Suke kept far from him.

Madiata bought the land and built up the compound mostly with money he siphoned away from the budget for sanitation cleanup projects and with the monthly payoff he received from the owner of a local food processing operation who dumped his factory's waste in an open pit on public land. The payoff was hefty enough to make Madiata turn a blind eye to the illegal dumping.

The house where Suke and her in-laws lived was Madiata's second home. His first, located several miles away in a more upscale community, was where his first wife, their five children, and one of the wife's aunts lived. Suke's mother-in-law and sister-in-law resented everything about Suke. They were far more disposed to the first wife, a calculating woman who invested her husband's ill gotten gains in all kinds of property that she put in her own name, but who sent them money and food and cloth once a month.

"That way they'll keep their distance and leave me and my marriage in peace," she told her aunt.

When she found out about Suke, she almost killed Madiata.

She cursed him and insulted him mercilessly and threatened to kill Suke. Madiata bought her a brand new, white Mercedes Benz and she shut up after that. Nothing more was said about Suke. Suke herself had nothing to bribe anyone with. Madiata's mother controlled the household finances. She did all the shopping and gave Suke only a tiny allowance. Suke remained deferential to the older women in the house and spoke to them only when they spoke to her.

One day she overheard her mother-in-law warning Madiata about her, "That Suke! Hah! See how the young men call at her? She'll give you no end of trouble when she grows wings and learns to fly. See how arrogantly she walks already!"

"Wait 'till she starts demanding expensive clothes and jewelry like all these city girls. You never should have given so much for her bride price," complained the sister, who sat at home all day giving orders and growing fatter and fatter.

At first the women interpreted Suke's silence and impassive expression as surliness.

"You'd think some people would appreciate the good home and food and clothes their husband gives them. Ingratitude is worse than witchcraft!" a visiting in-law said loudly after listening to the complaints about Suke.

Suke's relentless silence and straight back drove them mad. The family added "haughty" to their litany of complaints. To quell his family's increasing resentment of Suke, Madiata would scold or beat her in front of them—to no avail. Suke kept up her stony silence, giving polite responses when necessary. It wasn't that she meant to be rude. She just did not know what to say to them. They clearly did not like her, so why should she bother them, she reasoned.

Finally, the mother-in-law and sister-in-law concluded that Suke was retarded. She *had* to be, with that kind of silence. The very thought of it was maddening.

"A costly bride price paid to a foreigner for an imbecile!" grumbled the sister, though she dared not say it to her brother's face.

"If he wanted to marry a suckling, he could at least have gotten one from his own village. Just because she has a pretty face he gets fire in his balls. Mark my words! That same pretty face is going to throw spit on his flames!" the mother said.

No one except Madiata and Yolita's husband—not even Yolita herself—knew that Suke had been given in marriage to settle Yolita's husband's debts. He borrowed money from Madiata to set himself up in the taxi business shortly after he lost his second job as a bus driver. He spent the money that Madiata loaned him on an old Peugeot 504 that one of his mechanic friends fixed up. The mechanic swore the car was as strong as an elephant and would run for at least five years, by which time it would have earned far more than what was spent on it.

The Peugeot broke down less than a month later. Yolita's husband had already blown whatever little money he made from the first taxi runs and there was nothing left to repair the car. His payments to

Madiata ceased. Madiata threatened to have him thrown in jail. Then one day, Madiata's eyes fell on Suke. He approached Yolita's husband with a proposal. Give him Suke, he said, and he would write off the debt. Yolita's husband was relieved. He did not think twice about the offer. He persuaded Yolita that the marriage would be good for Suke.

"See how attractive she is? She needs to be protected by someone like him. He has money and position," he told her.

Yolita acquiesced because she did not want Suke to experience the financial battering she herself was coping with. Madiata's offer was formally accepted. For the public's benefit, he put on a big show when he came to give the bride price, showing up one Sunday afternoon when he knew everybody in the compound would be around. He presented Yolita's husband with a thick wad of notes, two lengths of superwax super wax for Yolita and five for Suke, a goat, and beer for the whole family compound. The deal was that Yolita's husband would return the money when they went into the house.

Madiata was thirty years older than Suke. When she moved into his house, he bought her lengths of cloth imported from Senegal, gold jewelry, high-fashion shoes and handbags, and the expensive Charlie perfume. Charlie was all the rage in the *cîté* in those days. But Suke rarely went out. She wore her expensive clothing when she served the high-level party officials Madiata sometimes brought home, when she went to the market on Saturdays, and when she took her children to the clinic for their checkups.

Madiata discouraged visits from her sister and her family, although Suke herself was free to visit them whenever she wished. On the advice of his mother, Madiata also discouraged her from having friends.

"Too much socializing ruins a marriage," his mother said to him when Suke seemed to grow too friendly with two girls her age further down the street.

Suke's children fared far better than she did. The mother-in-law lavished affection and gifts on them and protected them from her other jealous grandchildren. That was just fine with Suke. As the children grew older, her mother-in-law took greater control of their upbringing. Suke did not protest. She could not even if she wanted to. Tribal law dictated that they belonged to her husband and his family, not to her. Her children will always know that she was their mother and that she loved them, she would make sure of that.

Shortly after the scene between Madiata and his mistress, Madiata was fired from his sanitation job and assigned to the local prison as deputy chief warden. Less than three months later, he was demoted to a low-level supervisory position at the customs department. Before the year was out, he had been phased out of public service altogether. Everyone knew the hand behind Madiata's downfall was his ex-mistress. Her new lover was a commandant in the National Security Force. It wasn't hard to put two and two together.

But the ex-mistress was not satisfied with ousting Madiata from the civil service. She got him implicated in a sensational case sweeping the country: the trial of a dozen activists who allegedly were caught disseminating anti-government propaganda and spreading counterfeit money throughout the country. The trial had become a national soap opera. It was aired daily on television and broadcast simultaneously on the radio. The lawyers for the defendants and the state prosecutors treated the nation to the finest oratory. But most people saw the trial for what it was—a concocted affair to distract the population from the hardships wrought by an economy in freefall.

Madiata was not arrested, but he was put under close surveillance. The government house where his first wife lived was seized. She tried to thwart the seizure by twice "forgetting" an envelope with money in the office of the housing commissioner. When she realized that that kind of memory lapse would get her nowhere with the commissioner, she threw the tenants out of one of her many properties in a less exclusive district and moved in with her children and aunt.

Jobless, shunned by his friends and even many of his family, Madiata was forced to crawl to his first wife for support. She took him into her new home but treated him with contempt, declaring loud and often that "lover boys who stuck their thing into a honeycomb sooner or later will feel the sting of the bee."

Somehow, Suke's house was unaffected. But it was not long before the household began to feel the financial pinch. The cost of living soared as mismanagement, theft, and poor earnings from plummeting commodity prices on the world market took their toll on the national economy. Loud quarreling and hoarding became commonplace in Madiata's second household.

It wasn't long before Suke became the scapegoat for all the misfortunes befalling Madiata. Madiata beat her and insulted her so often that even his mother had to warn him that he risked killing "the idiot. Was that worth going to jail for?" she demanded.

Madiata was a confirmed drunk now and Suke's impassive face seemed to mock his failing manhood.

Suke knew she would leave. She did not spend any time

pondering this. She didn't even recall consciously making the decision to leave. She just knew she would. She knew it even before the mess with the ex-mistress, just as she knew now that the day of her departure was drawing near. Her mind and her spirit lived in the freedom of her departure and that was the strength behind her silence.

The day she left she did not have to run. She calmly packed a cloth bundle with her clothing and the jewelry Madiata gave her and walked out of the compound. Her mother-in-law and sister-in-law saw her go. They said nothing. They did not try to stop her. Madiata was not at home. Her children were playing happily with their cousins. She could not take them with her. She'd have no case in any court, formal or otherwise. She was eighteen years old.

She did not expect a warm welcome at Yolita's house and she did not get one. Everyone in the compound heard of Madiata's troubles. Yolita and her household more or less expected her, but she was another mouth to feed in these unforgiving times. Besides, if Madiata chose to, he could raise a stink about being owed a bride price, or at least part of it, since Suke was the one who "abandoned the marriage bed."

Yolita's husband would have to find some kind of money to appease him. Nevertheless, they took Suke in. Yolita did not have the heart to send her little sister back to such a cruel situation, especially if everything she heard about it was true.

Suke's expensive clothing and jewelry did not last very long. She sold them to provide food for herself and Yolita's family. That kept the resentment of her presence at bay for a while. Her jobless brother-in-law spent a good part of the money Suke gave to Yolita. He flashed the money around to impress the local dons, hoping they would partner with him on a new taxi venture. He had a sharp suit made by the best tailor in Big Market and walked around in it everyday. He invited friends over and fed them beer and chicken stew and fufu.

It was this very brother-in-law and his friends who made Suke aware that her good looks could be put to use. Daily they made remarks within earshot about girls half as beautiful as Suke whose families were not suffering at all during "the crisis" because they were making big money downtown with big businessmen and government ministers and diplomats.

"They can't come *near* Suke when it comes to looks."

"Some of them even have long breasts from nursing children."

And they would laugh.

One night, when all of Suke's money had been spent and no taxi deal materialized, Yolita's two youngest children went to bed crying of hunger. It had been the same the night before. But this night Yolita had yelled at them to be quiet, shouting that crying would not bring food to them. Then she herself burst into tears. Her husband was sitting outside clad in his usual cloth from waist to calves, smoking marijuana.

Suke brought out some sweets she had been saving for the children, broke them into little pieces, and pushed the pieces into each mouth one at a time, telling them they were not to cry because everything would be all right soon. She spoke to them softly until they fell asleep, then she tiptoed across the room and sat down on the floor next to Yolita, gathering her into her arms and rocking her back and forth. Yolita clung to her, sobbing quietly into her bosom.

Suke stayed with Yolita until she stopped crying. Then she got up, went into the bedroom and took out one of Yolita's European dresses from the makeshift wardrobe. Every woman had at least two such dresses, one of which had to be black. Suke put on the black one with the full ankle-length skirt and tight halter top. She clasped one of Yolita's fake gold necklaces around her neck—the real gold one had been sold long ago—and applied some lipstick and eye makeup. She grabbed the old Charlie bottle on the dresser and dabbed behind her ears, wrists and knees with whatever was left. She strapped her only surviving pair of high-heeled, black patent leather sandals to her feet and walked out of the compound.

She did not stay around her own neighborhood. She squeezed herself into a taxi and headed for downtown Kinshasa, to the hotel discos where Europeans, Americans, Lebanese, and rich Senegalese wined and dined and danced and played.

CHAPTER ELEVEN

Bryan Parkins did not particularly like hanging out with his fellow Peace Corps workers in Kinshasa. He would not be caught dead with hippies back in the States, so why should he hang out with them now? In Africa, of all places.

He called them hippies because that was what they looked like when he first saw them, though they swore up and down that they were not hippies.

"That's almost racist, man, lumping us all together like that because we look a certain way!" one of them argued hotly. "You of all people should know how stupid that is."

"Well, you sure look like hippies to me," Bryan drawled.

That was their first meeting. It had taken place at the American School in Kinshasa at a briefing for the Peace Corps' newest arrivals. Bryan arrived half an hour early, a habit he developed in the service after wise words from an intelligence officer: "Get the lay of the land before the other guys. It messes with the mind of anyone coming in after you. They'll be so busy wondering what you saw or did before they got there, they won't be able to focus on the business at hand; gives you the upper hand psychologically." Bryan had never forgotten those words.

With an inscrutable demeanor, he watched the three young men file into the briefing room. He took in their long hair, their clean but raggedy blue jeans trimmed around the ankles with broad bands of multicolored cloth bearing Native American motifs; the embroidered muslin tops with long sleeves and round neck opening into a "V" down the chest; the necklaces with "peace" pendants. How could they not be hippies?

Cut that hair, give them a good bath, dress them up in a suit and they'd coast on Wall Street. No questions asked, he said to himself.

Bryan pretty much kept to himself in the days after that meeting. Then he left for the eastern province where he was to serve for the next three years as head site engineer for the new road that was to run right into Kinshasa. He soon forgot about the hippies.

But now, three months later, he was back in Kinshasa with them for an important gathering of all the Peace Corps workers in the country, and from the neighboring countries to the south and east.

Two senior State Department officials were in town and would be speaking to them. Washington, it seemed, picked up intelligence about rebel activity along the southern border of the country. Over the next five days, there would be a wrenching country assessment, with private, individual debriefings during which each Peace Corps volunteer would be grilled on the contents of his or her daily journal. All Peace Corps volunteers were required to keep such journals.

Curious about the way they gathered information, Bryan paid close attention to everything the State Department officials said and did, making mental notes of what he himself would have done differently. He shared these notes with no one. Instead, he stored them away in his mind, telling himself that they would become useful one day.

At last the five days of intense briefing and scrutiny were over. It was Saturday night and everyone needed to unwind. Bryan allowed the hippies to persuade him into accompanying them to a popular bar in Matonge, the swinging cîté about twenty minutes from downtown Kinshasa. He was not disappointed. The band was a popular one. It warmed things up with a spicy charanga set then swung into the titillating local rhythms that influenced so much of the music in the African Diaspora. The dance floor was jammed, hips riding the beats in easy undulating movements.

The hippies were having a whale of a time. Bryan sat at a table and watched them dance, shaking his head in amusement from time to time. One of the hippies caught his eye and waved, a wide grin on his face. Bryan raised his bottle of beer in acknowledgement.

"Would you like to dance?"

It was a woman's voice. The words were spoken in heavily accented English.

The band slowed the tempo to Tabu Ley's Mongali Yena, a song about an older woman complaining that her young lover was so ungrateful and grudging with his love, even though she lavished him with expensive gifts and cooked him the finest meals.

Bryan turned towards the voice. Suke smiled at him and held out her hand. He instantly liked the way she seemed to lift her lips off her small, even white teeth. He even liked the little gap between the upper two that sat front and center. He smiled back.

"Dance?" she repeated and held out her hand to him.

Bryan put down his beer and stood up, still smiling. He took her hand and followed her to the dance floor. *Nice*, he said to himself, surveying her from the back. *Thank you, Jesus*, he added, emphasizing his gratitude with a quick lift of the eyes heavenward. One of the other hippies saw them approach the floor and grinned. He shot Bryan a wink and thumbs-up sign. Bryan ignored him.

"So how did you know I was American?" Bryan asked in French after a while. His French was passable.

"You look American. Just like your brothers over there." She used her chin and lips to point out the hippies.

Bryan stopped dancing. "Brothers! *Brothers*? Me? Them?" He stabbed at his chest with his thumb to emphasize the 'me,' then jerked the thumb toward the hippies.

Suke was puzzled. "Did I say something wrong? You're all Americans, aren't you?"

"Yes, but I'm *Black*. They're *White.*"

"Of course, but you're *American*! Different colors, same tribe, isn't it?" Her eyes widened inquisitively.

Bryan frowned at her. Where had he heard something like that before? Something about culture being stronger than color? He shrugged and put his hands on her waist. Tonight was not the night to deal with such issues.

"Let's just dance," he said.

They spent the night together … and the next.

On Monday morning, Bryan said to her, "Come away with me."

"Yes," Suke said.

Brian and Suke caught a small plane from Ndjili Airport to Bukavu the next day. Bryan paid for Suke's ticket. Considering that she was going to live with him, he was surprised that all she carried was a single suitcase and a large colorful basket, the kind chic young women used when they went to the market or, for those who could afford it, to the supermarket downtown.

"I've brought only what matters most to me. The rest I left with those who need them more than I do," Suke said in response to his raised eyebrows.

She was referring to Yasmin, her closest friend. Suke borrowed the suitcase from her. Suke met Yasmin about a year ago, on the very night that Suke walked out of Yolita's house. Suke was standing on a half-lit corner a block away from the trendy cinema on the main Boulevard, looking as if she were waiting for someone, when a sleek black Mercedes Benz drove past. A few feet away, the car slowed down, came to a stop, and then backed up to the curb beside Suke. The driver rolled down the tinted window and leaned across the passenger seat.

"*Bonsoir, citoyenne. Vous attendez quelqu'un? On peut vous déposer quelque part*?"

He was a not-too-handsome, handsomely dressed man in his fifties. Suke sized up his voice and face in two seconds flat. Senegalese, she thought. She approached the car.

"Good evening. No, I'm not waiting for anyone in particular. And yes, I wouldn't mind a lift." She made her voice soft and pleasant.

The man opened the door. Suke shoved aside a rush of panic and climbed in. She climbed in the "mama-benzi" way, the way well-to-do women who drove or were driven in a Mercedes Benz did. She seated her bottom first then daintily swung both legs into the car at the same time.

The man held out his hand. "I am Abdou. My friends in the back are Yasmin and Maurice. Suke shook his hand, introduced herself and exchanged pleasantries with the couple in the back.

"If you are not in a hurry, perhaps you can join us for a drink," Abdou said.

"I'd be delighted," Suke replied.

Abdou's hands were all over her as soon as they entered the nightclub. It was a popular disco at the Intercontinental Hotel. Out of the corner of her eye, she saw Yasmin stoically pretending to enjoy Maurice's groping. Yasmin caught her eye. She winked at her and nodded to the ladies' room.

"God, I hate it when they paw at you like that," Yasmin said as soon as the door closed behind Suke.

Suke shrugged and said nothing. The women appraised each other candidly.

"That dress looks really good on you," Yasmin said.

"Thanks. I like your shoes." Suke replied.

"I bought them in Paris."

"You sound like you lived in Paris."

Yasmin, Suke found out, returned from Paris a month ago. She was eighteen and had lived in France for five years with her father's brother, a diplomat, and his family. She had just finished high school but was not yet ready to start university. She wasn't sure what she wanted to study. "In that case, you should spend some time back home. Maybe you will be able to decide on a career there," her uncle said. "You can always come back when you are ready."

Yasmin flew home, armed with a recommendation from the ambassador, a diploma from a classy girl's school in France, a fat allowance from her uncle and her very good looks. She would get a job in Kinshasa for a year or so, probably in one of the ministries, she thought contentedly. And it would be nice to see her mother and her father and all her other brothers and sisters and cousins. She sighed.

She would have to stay in the village for at least two weeks.

By the end of the first week, she felt she was suffocating. It had been a week of welcomes village style. Family and friends she had outgrown, the curious, the hawkeyed matchmakers—they came unannounced all day and into the night. They brought eggs and chickens and baskets of ground provisions as gifts. It seemed as if her mother and older sisters never stopped cooking. She was grateful for the love and the bonding and the celebration of her return, but it was overwhelming. And her money was running out, what with all the "little somethings for beer" that a daughter from Europe was expected to hand out.

"I have this job in the city," she lied when she could stand it no longer.

They understood. She had been away too long.

In Kinshasa, Yasmin installed herself in an inexpensive but exclusive Catholic-run hostel for unmarried career-oriented young women. The inhabitants, who were rigidly screened, came from all over the country. A few came from other African countries. At the hostel she found out that the president's brother had launched a new airline and was hiring. She got a job as an administrative assistant as soon as she produced her letter of recommendation. She had been on the job less than a month when she became the mistress of one of the divisional managers and a cousin of the head of the military. He set her up in a plush apartment, with all sorts of rules about where she could go and whom she could associate with. They lived the good life.

A year later, he began to gravitate toward someone else and Yasmin decided she was too young and had too much going for her to be locked away like an old toy.

"One day when I get out of this kind of life, I'm going to go to Paris, or maybe Brussels. I'm going to start my own business and travel to those countries," Suke said to Yasmin.

"Really? What kind of business?" Yasmin was genuinely curious. There was something about Suke that made her believe she was going to do exactly what she said she would do.

"Trading. I can buy things in Europe and sell them here for a huge profit."

"What kind of things?"

"Oh, all sorts of things; whatever people want and can't get: good blouses and underwear for women, shoes, handbags, perfume, jewelry; accessories for the house like sheets and towels and toasters; and even parts for cars. It's hard to find good quality things in Kinshasa these days."

"Hmmm. But can't you borrow the money you need to get started instead of putting up with *that* kind of thing?" She flicked her hand toward the door in a gesture of disgust.

Suke shrugged. "It's the fastest way and the most independent way. I give myself two years at most."

"How come you're so determined for someone who's—what, my age?" Yasmin was starting to like Suke more and more.

They talked and talked until a woman came in and told them that two anxious Senegalese men were asking for them. The woman was laughing as she delivered the message.

"If you don't want them, I can take care of them for you, you know," the woman offered. Suke and Yasmin got up and sighed in unison. They looked at each other and broke into giggles, covering their mouth like little girls as they pushed open the door and headed toward the men.

The Senegalese were history after that night, but the friendship between Yasmin and Suke grew deeper. Yasmin taught Suke how to apply makeup, how to speak French with a Parisian accent, how to use contraceptives. She made Suke get rid of "that stinking Charlie" and gave her one of her own bottles of Givenchy. Suke was Yasmin's alibi, which probably saved Yasmin from being beaten when her lover came to the apartment and did not find her there.

"I was bored so I went to stay with Suke. What do you expect? That I would sit here and watch the four walls while you are out playing? I'm not one of these little Kinshasa wenches who would swallow all your crap just to live in an apartment like this, you know." And she would pout, make her lips tremble and then burst into tears. It worked every time. He would hold her in his arms, apologizing for being such a bastard and leaving her alone like that, telling her how much she meant to him no matter what she heard or saw. He would make love to her tenderly then, and leave her a thick wad of notes.

"You and Suke amuse yourselves," he would say magnanimously.

When he left Yasmin would squat on her bed and count the money, laughing uncontrollably.

"Our day is coming, Suke my sister," she would sing softly as she stuffed the money into the tip of a pair of her most outrageous shoes.

She was going into business with Suke. They talked it over for hours when she told Suke of her decision. It made perfect sense. She knew Paris, where to go for the best deals, how to handle Parisians.

Suke worked the best hotels in town. She was strict about keeping foreign-only clientele.

"None of these Zairian men will ever wash their mouth on me, *ever*," she told Yasmin.

Yasmin would join her sometimes and they would double date. Suke moved into Yasmin's studio in the Catholic hostel. Yasmin decided not to give it up, just in case. She told the nuns that Suke was her cousin who had just come from Paris, would they mind if she stayed there in such a wholesome, nurturing environment while she got her feet on the ground? Of course she could stay there, the nuns said. Suke insisted on paying the rent herself, which she could afford to do now, even after putting aside money for "the business" and giving something to Yolita.

The night before Suke left with Bryan, she and Yasmin clung to each other and cried.

"I'm happy for you, Suke. I will miss you and I'll worry about you. But I am happy because you are happy."

"I've never felt like this about anyone, Yasmin. Is this what they call love? I don't even know. All I know is that I want to be with him. I'm scared to go but I want to be with him."

They did not talk about their business plans. Suke talked only about one day marrying Bryan and moving to America. Yasmin listened, squeezing her hand.

"Oh Yasmin, I will dream of it until it comes true," Suke said.

"Dream hard, Suke. And promise me you'll always be true to yourself."

Bryan looked at the woman beside him. He found himself thinking of the lyrics to "Play Me," a Neil Diamond song that one of the White boys in his unit in 'Nam played so much that he'd finally come to like it and know the words by heart.

> "She was morning
> And I was nighttime.
> So I one day woke up
> To find her lying beside my bed;
> So I softly said, 'come take me.
> For I have been lonely
> In need of someone…'"

Suke's eyes were closed. Bryan knew she was not asleep. He ran his finger gently along her nose and over her lips. He traced tiny circles on her chin. Suke opened her eyes and smiled at him. He squeezed her hand. She squeezed his back. He couldn't wait to get her back to his little villa overlooking Lake Kivu.

CHAPTER TWELVE

Bukavu, capital of the Kivu region, is like the palm of a hand, with its heel sitting on land and the fingers spread out into the majestic Lake Kivu on which Humphrey Bogart seduced Katharine Hepburn in "The African Queen." The lake separates the Congo from Rwanda. This is the East African side of the Congo, with its temperate climate, softly spoken Kiswahili and one-hour time lag behind Kinshasa in the west.

The lake shimmers like silver in the day and darkens like ebony at night. It is stocked with tilapia and giant catfish that fishermen catch each night to sell the next day. Cattle thrive on the land. Plantations of coffee, tea, papaya, pineapple, banana, yam, and cassava flourish in the rich volcanic soil. And there is an abundance of minerals.

Rich and resplendent in nature, Kivu should have been the country's breadbasket and the high-earning tourist destination it was when the Belgians ruled. But Kivu was like a woman scorned.

It continued to pay a heavy price for its loyalty to Patrice Lumumba, the country's first prime minister, who was overthrown and assassinated more than twenty years earlier.

Neglect was written all over downtown Bukavu. The roads, municipal buildings, public schools, and hospital were in disrepair. On Avenue Royale, the Residence Hotel stood like a faded beauty, clinging to its past grandeur. Families and laundry spilled out of the apartment buildings along the lakefront. The stateliness of these buildings was still visible under the broken windowpanes and walls blackened by the soot of coal fires.

The Europeans who lived in this old resort town were an assortment of leftover colonials, recently arrived neo-colonials fleeing poverty in Europe, civil servants and other professionals, and a small diplomatic corps.

The United States and a few other countries maintained consular offices in the town. The streets bustled. People were always going somewhere. A sizable mixed-race population spoke volumes of what went on in private between Europeans and Africans.

But not even the most heart-rending neglect could mar the innate beauty of this city, with its awesome view of the lake everywhere you turned. Residential neighborhoods remained intact for the most part, with their charming villas and well-tended gardens. Here and there, the crumbling walls of an abandoned house stood valiantly against the thick creepers that clawed their way out of overgrown gardens.

It was in one of these neighborhoods that Bryan lived, in a fully furnished, cozy two-bedroom cottage with a fireplace. A split-level garden overlooked the lake. Stone steps led from the lower level down to the lake, flattening out into a jetty. Suke developed a routine of waiting here at dawn on Saturday mornings to buy tilapia from the fishing boats heading to market with the night's catch. The first time she waited, she swung her bucket and called out as they rowed by. Three canoes swung toward the jetty and began to race each other to get there first.

By the third Saturday, Suke made it clear that she would buy only from a certain fisherman. From then on, his was the only canoe that would break away from the group to serve her. She would buy enough tilapia for a week, and cook it in various assortments: in a thick tomato sauce, in a peanut sauce with ground provisions, with cassava or sweet potato leaves, or just plain grilled over coals.

Once a week, she would take a taxi to the bustling market at Uvira. "It's better if I went alone," she insisted to Bryan. "If they see you with me they will try to make me pay American prices. Then I'll have to waste time haggling and haggling. You stay home and rest."

Yes, Suke threw herself into making a comfortable, loving home with Bryan. She made Bryan let go of the house helper and hire a gardener instead. "This house is too small for two of us. I can take care of it myself," she argued. With the gardener's help, she revived the wilted herb garden and planted corn, cabbage, onions, tomatoes, and carrots. She wished Yasmin could see how happy she was, how loving and caring Bryan was.

Once, about two months after she had arrived in Bukavu, she telephoned Yasmin's apartment. A recording said the phone was disconnected. Suke did not worry about it. Either Yasmin got angry and did something to it, or she got her man angry and he did something to it, she told herself. Yasmin had a hot temper and a mouth to go with it.

Most days Bryan worked from dawn to dusk.

"That's just the way it is, honey. When the rainy season hits, there's not much we can do on the road so we have to get in as much work as possible now," he told her in his now familiar those-are-the-facts voice.

Not that Suke complained. She simply said once that he worked too hard and that he was always tired. She never mentioned his work again after that day. On weekends, Bryan simply wanted to laze around the house, make love to Suke, work out with his weights in the garden, and sit on the jetty and stare at the lake.

Suke became friends with Dominique, a pretty 16-year-old refugee from Rwanda with huge doe eyes. She lived next door with a middle-aged Frenchman who was a marketing manager for a multinational pharmaceutical company. The Frenchman had a wife and children back in France. Dominique knew all about them, but "they are there and I am here and the twain shall never meet," she told Suke with a laugh.

She was still in high school. She was driven to the local "athenée" every day in a limousine that waited all day for her until school was out. People said she was a little crazy, but in school, she was sharp as a tack and stayed at the top of all her classes. Before Suke came, she would try to seduce Bryan whenever the Frenchman was away on one of his trips, sidling up close to him when she caught him outside and doing all sorts of coquettish things with her eyes. It was all fun to her. The more Bryan made it clear that he was not interested, the more she laughed and teased.

The day after Suke arrived, she showed up at the back door with a basket of fruit and vegetables and introduced herself. Standing in the middle of the kitchen, she looked Suke up and down, smiling broadly with appreciation.

Hmm! But that old Bryan did well, *dit*. "Welcome! I'm Dominique from next door," she embraced Suke warmly. "Bryan wouldn't let me touch him. So now that you're here, I'll leave him in peace and let you have the honor," she said with a laugh.

Suke couldn't help laughing with her, much to Bryan's disgust. Dominique came over regularly after that to keep Suke company. When her Frenchman was away, she'd bring her homework and stay until Bryan got home. Bryan still did not trust her, a fact she was fully aware of, but which seemed to amuse her immensely. Sometimes, when he came into the room where they were chatting, she would nudge Suke then bat her eyes and blow kisses at him. Then she and Suke would collapse in giggles. Bryan would suck his teeth and ignore them.

Other times, she would get very serious and ask him go over a new math concept with her. The first time she asked him, Bryan did not even look up from the newspaper he was reading. He thought it was another of her games. But Suke persuaded him to help her.

"She's not playing, Bryan. Honestly. Dominique never plays when it comes to her schoolwork," she said.

When he finally acquiesced, Bryan was surprised and impressed by the intelligent questions she asked. He really had to think hard to come up with an answer to some of them. After that, Dominique every so often would draw both him and Suke into a lively discussion of the country's economic and political situation. She liked to read the local and French newspapers and listen to the international news on her short-wave radio, she told them. Bryan enjoyed those conversations. He decided Dominique wasn't so bad after all. He would just have to put up with her teasing. Besides, she was good company for Suke.

Bryan himself had made a few friends among the engineering team on his road project and with a couple of Americans at the American Cultural Center. Everyone greeted Suke warmly when Bryan introduced her at a barbecue at the home of one of the Americans one Sunday.

"Well, it's a pleasure to meet you. We're so glad Bryan is not alone anymore," the host's wife said to Suke, as she led her inside to meet the other wives and girlfriends.

Except for the host's wife, Suke was not comfortable with these women at first. She could tell they were sizing her up all the time. Her natural grace, enhanced by Yasmin's lessons, made her stand out from the rest. As the evening wore on, the women finally began warming up to her. She conversed easily with them about her impressions of Bukavu. By the time the party was over, she received several invitations to lunch and tea. She, in turn, invited some of the women to lunch at her own home.

Later that night, Bryan pulled her tight against him.

"You were great," he said, nuzzling her neck.

"With what?' she asked, pressing her head into his chest.

"You outclassed a lot of those women," he said.

Suke wished she could tell Yasmin how happy she was.

#

"What does that sign over there say, Suke? My Swahili is not that good."

They had been driving along a muddy path for twenty minutes looking for a farm that was supposed to have the best hatching eggs and day-old chicks in Bukavu. Suke persuaded Bryan to raise their own chickens. The fresh fowls in the market were old and tough and the price of frozen chickens was way too high, she argued. And they did not even taste that good. They'd be much better off raising their own chickens. And they wouldn't have to worry about fresh eggs either.

Bryan did not put up much of a fight. He gave Suke a generous allowance every month for the home and her personal needs. He was amazed at what she was able to do with the money *and* save at the same time. She opened a bank account in town, she told him. "Fine with me, it's all yours," he'd said. If it made economic sense to raise their own chickens, then they'd raise their own chickens, he reasoned.

"What sign?"

"That one over there on that big tree."

Suke followed his finger. "I see the sign, but I can't read it."

"I'll get closer." Bryan pulled the car closer to the sign. "There. What does it say?"

"I don't know."

"What do you mean you don't know? You speak Swahili. I've heard you."

"I speak Swahili but I cannot read the sign, Bryan," Suke said, annoyed.

Bryan was puzzled. "Are these letters different from the letters in your own language?" he asked her.

"Bryan, I cannot read the sign because I don't know how to read. Do you understand that?"

"What do you mean you don't know how to read? Didn't you go to school?"

"No."

"You never went to school?" Bryan was staring at her incredulously.

"Yes."

"Yes you went to school, or yes you never went to school?" Bryan demanded impatiently. He could never get used to the way Africans answered negative questions.

"Yes, I never went to school," Suke responded irritably.

"But that's against the law!" Bryan shouted.

"Whose law, America's? This is Zaire, Bryan!" she shouted back.

Bryan took a deep breath. He was angry, but not with Suke. He lowered his voice. "But why didn't you go to school? How could you *not* go to school? I don't understand."

"There was no money. It takes money to go to school, you know. Besides, someone had to help take care of the little ones. That's the way it is in Africa. And then I got married." She resented the way he made the ways of her country seem inferior.

"*Married?*"

"That is what I said. I got married. I was ten." She studied the shock in his face with satisfaction. They were all alike, these foreigners who wanted to be in Africa but refused to accept its ways. What do they know about life anyway?

Bryan sat motionless, staring blankly ahead of him. His hands gripped the steering wheel so hard that his knuckles turned several shades lighter than their normal color. He could not believe what Suke was saying. A woman this beautiful, this sophisticated, this smart; a woman who spoke French with a Parisian accent; this woman could not read ... which meant she could not write either. And as if that weren't enough, somebody married her off when she was ten years old. *Ten years old, for chrissake.*

He shook his head as the anger welled up inside him. Of all the contradictions he had seen since he arrived in the country, this was the most unforgiving. He could pretend he did not see the crates of food imported from South Africa, even as the president dazzled the world with his eloquent condemnation of apartheid. He could say it wasn't his business that the government was a kleptocracy, where the diversion of funds began at the very top and trickled down to every government office in every district in every town.

He could even ignore the fact that down-and-out Europeans could come into the country and live high and mighty, with elderly manservants they referred to as their "boys." And how many times did he bite his tongue when he saw soldiers roughing up the old women who were selling along the roadside? If the women could not produce a vendor's permit, the soldiers would kick away their peppers and tomatoes, or grind them into the ground with the heel of heir boots.

But this! This was personal. This young woman that he was living with had never gone to school and as far as her country was concerned, that was all right!

"This place is screwed up," he said aloud. "God-damned screwed up!" he shouted, crashing his fist against the steering wheel. Suke uttered a frightened cry and jumped out of the car. She slammed the door as hard as she could and stormed off down the path.

Bryan stared after her in surprise. He stuck his head out the window and called after her.

"Suke! Don't walk away from me! You don't understand! It's not you! I'm not mad at you!"

Suke ignored him. Bryan started the car impatiently, forgetting he had left it in first gear. The car sprang forward and jerked to a stop. Bryan hit the steering wheel again with his fist, cursing the car and swearing that these goddamn stick-shifts were the worst invention in the world. He put the gear in neutral, started the car again and caught up with Suke.

"Where the hell are you going, Suke? Come on, get back into the car!"

"I'm going to find chickens!"

"So get back into the car and we'll find them together!"

She marched on, paying him no mind.

"Suke, I'm not angry with you. Please get back into the car. Let me explain."

It was useless. She strode forward with determination. Bryan coasted beside her, saying nothing.

A few minutes later, she stopped, sniffed the air and turned on to a narrower path. It was too narrow for Bryan to drive alongside her, so he pulled back behind her. He watched her with stormy eyes. Her shoulders were hunched in anger. *What a damn shame*, he thought. *What a damn shame*.

They drove home in silence, a crate of noisy day-old chickens on the backseat and a tray of eggs was on the floor.

She came to him after dinner, as he lay on the couch listening to his jazz tapes. She sat at his feet and told him all of it, about her marriage, her children, her sister and brother-in-law, her decision to go into the street. Bryan listened in silence. He did not speak even after she finished.

"Teach me to read and write, Bryan," she said finally.

"It will have to be in English. I can't read or write French that well."

"English is fine. Dominique can teach me in French."

He reached for her hand. "Let's start now."

#

"You know what would make everything perfect, Dominique? A baby. I would love to have a baby for Bryan."

They were sitting on the back steps eating fufu and "sombe," a stew made of cassava leaves. They ate with their right hand, breaking off a small piece of fufu at a time, rolling it into a ball with the tips of their fingers and dipping it into the stew. Their fingers never touched their mouth as they ate.

"So why don't you?"

"He doesn't want me to. The Peace Corps is strict about that, he said."

"The Peace Corps can go to hell. It's your life, not theirs."

"Why don't *you* have a baby?"

"Oh no, not me! Not till I'm married and that won't be until after I get this Frenchman to send me to medical school in France. I'll marry someone my own age and have babies."

"You want to be a doctor?"

"Do you think that all I want out of life is to be this old Frenchman's mistress? At my age? Don't be silly, Suke."

Suke sighed. "Before I met Bryan, my friend Yasmin and I planned to go into business together. We were going to travel back and forth to Europe, buying all kinds of things to sell in Kinshasa."

"So you've abandoned those plans?"

"I suppose so. I'm with Bryan now."

"And you think he's going to marry you and take you back to America when his tour is over?"

Suke did not answer. When they first came to Bukavu nearly three years ago, she would have answered "yes" without hesitation. Now she was not sure. Every time she talked about being his wife and having his children, his lips would tighten and he'd say nothing. Sometimes he would look at her hard and walk out of the room. She had long since stopped talking about it, even in jest.

"Suke, Suke. We're just their comfort women. They never marry us, you know," Dominique said, putting an arm around Suke's shoulder. "The best thing is to get whatever you can out of it, whatever can serve you in the future when they leave."

"You think you know everything, don't you," Suke said irritably, pushing away Dominique's arm. Dominique promptly put it back. Suke let it stay.

"In Rwanda, I saw my big sisters go after men like Bryan: Europeans, Africans, Black Americans, it didn't matter as long as they were foreigners with good jobs. They had the same dream as you, that the men would marry them and take them away from Rwanda and all its wars. One of them went mad after the man she was living with returned to Germany. She was my favorite sister. I swore that would never happen to me."

"Yasmin told me to dream hard and to be true to myself."

"Maybe she was talking about your first dream, about making it in business."

They ate in silence for a while.

"I'm pregnant now, Dominique."

Dominique stopped eating and stared at her. "Does Bryan know?"

"No. And I'm afraid to tell him."

"You must tell him. Then you'll know exactly where you stand."

"I know." Suke sighed again.

#

Bryan was livid. "Get rid of it!"

"No!"

Bryan laughed. "You can't tell me no. If I say you have to get rid of it, then you have to get rid of it."

"I don't care what you say. I want our baby!"

"So you did this on purpose. Well, get this! I'm not marrying you, Suke. I'm going back to America when my tour is over next month."

Suke sank down on the floor and covered her face. She began to moan, rocking herself back and forth. Bryan stood over her, furious. His breathing was hard and heaving.

"I thought you loved me, Bryan. I thought we would marry," Suke wailed.

Bryan dropped to one knee in front of her and shook her roughly by the shoulders. "Marriage was never part of the deal. You know that."

"No I didn't. No I didn't. You said you loved me." Suke said, clutching at his shirt. Bryan pulled himself away and stood up.

"Get rid of that baby, Suke!" he said. His teeth were clenched so tight that the muscles at his temples rolled up and down under his skin. Suke had never seen such rage in him, not even on that day when they went to buy the chickens and she told him she could not read.

"Why can't you marry me?" Suke screamed at him. "Why?"

"Because I've decided to go back to my wife and children."

Suke covered her ears and swung her head from side to side. It was over for good with his wife, he had told her. She had moved out and taken their children with her. They had a boy four years old and a girl just turning two.

"Can you imagine? She said I needed psychiatric help, something about demons I'd brought home from Vietnam," Bryan had said bitterly. "*She* was the one with the demons, all wrapped up in herself, never wanting to please me. I think she had someone on the side even though she swore she didn't. She must have."

He signed up with the Peace Corps a month after she left him. He promised himself that he would make her pay for taking his children away from him.

"No! No! No!" Suke screamed. She wanted to die right there, right then. She curled herself up on the floor, drawing her feet up against her chest in a fetal position. "Kill me. Kill me now. Please kill me, Bryan," she begged, her body convulsing violently.

Bryan looked at her coldly. Their relationship was only temporary. What made her think there could be more? She should have understood that, a girl like her. He wasn't her ticket out of this sorry country. He turned and walked out of the room.

#

Suke awoke in the same spot on the floor. Sunlight streamed through the windows and bathed her face. She jumped up and ran into the bedroom calling Bryan's name. He was not there. *He's gone to work*, she told herself. He felt bad and didn't want to wake me. When he comes home tonight it will be all right. She would make herself extra pretty and cook his favorite meal for when he came home.

But Bryan did not come home that night, nor the next. Suke sat at the window all day long, wearing his favorite dress.

"He's not coming back, Suke," Dominique said in her matter-of-fact tone.

"Yes he is. He probably had to make one of those emergency trips up country where there are no telephones. I want him to see me as soon as he drives in," Suke replied calmly.

"Suke! Listen to me!' Dominique planted herself in front of Suke and gripped her by the shoulders. She swung Suke away from the window to face her. "Listen to me," she said firmly, holding Suke's face in her hands. "Look at me, Suke. Bryan wants you to go back to Kinshasa. I went to his work site after school today to find out what the hell he was doing. He sent this letter."

Suke grabbed the envelope from her and tore it open. The letter was in simple English. It would not be hard for her to read after all the lessons with both Bryan and Dominique. She read the letter slowly, saying the words in a whisper. Her head dipped as she pronounced each word, in the manner of someone who was not very comfortable with the language.

Dear Suke,

I have to end it this way. If I stay in the house, you will continue to hope for what I cannot give you. I care for you in my own way, but I cannot do what you want me to do. It was never my plan to stay or to take you with me to America. This money will pay for the doctor and for your ticket back to Kinshasa.

Bryan

A cry tore from Suke's body. She read the letter, over and over again, one hand covering her mouth in disbelief. After a while, she looked up and stared into space. Her lips were folded into a thin line. She stood up, threw the letter and the money to the floor and walked into the bedroom. Dominique picked up the letter and followed Suke as she read it.

"*Eh bien*! *C'est la vie*!" she said when she finished.

"Oui. C'est la vie," Suke said without emotion.

Suke pulled her suitcase from under the bed and began to toss her clothes into in. Dominique sat on the bed and watched her.

"It's time to make your dream with Yasmin come true, Suke."

"Yes, I know."

"What will you do about the baby?"

"Let us not speak about the baby, Dominique."

"I'll take you to the airport."

"Thanks. I'd like that."

CHAPTER THIRTEEN

Suke went straight to Yasmin's apartment after she landed at the airport in Kinshasa. Anni, Yasmin's live-in housekeeper, greeted her at the door with sad eyes. Hadn't Miss Suke heard the news? Miss Yasmin died a week ago.

"She committed suicide. She drank poison. They took her body back to her village..."

Suke's legs buckled before Anni could finish the sentence. Calling for help, Anni caught her just before her head smashed against the doorjamb. Two other housekeepers from neighboring apartments ran to her aid. They lifted Suke's limp body and laid her on a couch in the living room.

When Suke regained consciousness, she saw the three women bending over her, their eyes deep and dark with sympathy. They were fanning her and making those mournful little sounds women made when they grieved with someone who had lost a loved one.

Suke struggled to get up, but three pairs of hands sprang forward in unison and held her down.

"Don't get up, Miss Suke. Rest a while."

"Here, drink this," one of the women said, reaching for a glass of water on the side table and holding it out to Suke. Suke knocked the glass angrily from the woman's hand. She was still struggling to get up.

"Where is Yasmin?" she demanded, looking around wildly and glaring at the women. "I want to see her! Now!" She flailed her arms like a crazed animal, but they managed to keep her pinned to the couch. They were all bigger and much stronger than Suke.

"Where is she? Tell me where she is! Where did you go, Yasmin! Yasminaa! It's me, Suke! I've come. I've come for our dream, Yasmin! Yasmiiiiiinnnn!" Suke's voice trailed off and she collapsed against the back of the couch.

The women held on to her firmly, and then softened their grip as she broke into anguished sobs. Her grief ravaged her body before their eyes. For the second time that day, she found herself curled in a fetal position. She wailed miserably. The women stroked her, as mourning sounds rumbled in their throats. It's good that she's crying, their eyes seemed to say to each other.

Suke cried for the wretchedness of her young life. She cried for Yasmin and the dream they shared. She cried for Bryan, whom she loved and lost. She cried for the baby in her womb, the two she had borne, the mother she never knew. *Haven't you given me enough? Oh God! Haven't I suffered enough?* screamed her tormented mind into the emptiness she felt around her. She tossed from side to side, her body wracked by sobs. It was as if she wanted her tears to wipe the slate clean, to settle whatever account she needed to settle with whomever it was in the Great Unknown that had sent her so much hurt.

When she stopped crying hours later, she told herself that the account was settled. The hurt was gone and it would never come back to her. She would not let it.

"Stay here for now, Miss Suke," Anni said. The other housekeepers had long gone. *Their tongues are already wagging with this new gossip*, for sure, Anni thought with disgust. She would give them a fine piece of her mind when she saw them again.

"*Patron* is traveling, but he wouldn't mind if you stayed. He said that if you came looking for Miss Yasmin, you should stay as long as you liked," Anni said gently to Suke.

Suke was too drained to say anything. She lay on the couch, one arm flung over her eyes, the other hanging listlessly, touching the floor. She shook her head to indicate she would stay.

"Will you eat something now, then? Some fufu?"

Suke sighed. "Yes." Her voice was steady, but small and empty.

Anni went into the kitchen and returned several minutes later with a plate of fufu and fish stew, and a cup filled with a warm brown liquid.

"This tea will make you feel better," she said, handing Suke the cup and placing the plate on the table beside the couch. "I put your suitcase into the other bedroom where you will sleep. You know the one."

"Yes, thank you."

Anni turned to leave the room.

"Were you there?"

Suke's voice was so low that Anni at first thought she imagined hearing her speak.

"Were you there, Anni?"

Anni stood still for a moment, and then turned around to face Suke. "No, Miss Suke. Miss Yasmin sent me away that day. She told me I could take the day off to visit my family. But I was the one who found her. I should not have gone. I wish I had not gone."

"It's okay. How could you have known?" Suke comforted her, sipping the bittersweet tea. It was a blend of traditional herbs that Suke could not name, but which she accepted without question as a tonic that would do her good. People like Anni could be trusted with such things.

"When I came home that night, her bedroom door was open and the light was on, so I stopped to greet her and to see if she needed anything. She was lying across her bed the way she did when she went out and came in tired or a little drunk. She did not answer me when I greeted her, so I went in to wake her up. She didn't like to fall asleep like that in her dress-up clothes. She always told me to make sure she got up and changed if ever I found her like that. But when I shook her and called her name she would not wake up. I kept trying.

I was afraid because I thought she might be sick. I knew she could not have passed out from drinking too much beer because she never drank like that. You know that, Miss Suke. So I bent over to look into her face and that's when I saw her eyes wide open and staring. I waved my hand right over her face but she did not blink. I put my hand to her mouth but there was no air. So I knew she was dead. Oh Miss Suke, I hollered so loud. I called *patron* right away. When he came, we searched around and he found the empty glass on the floor under her bed. He said it smelled like poison."

Anni's voice shook at times but she did not cry. She must have told the story a thousand times.

"*Patron* did the same things I did to see if she was alive. He cried like a baby, holding her in his arms. He said it was his fault for leaving her alone so much with you gone. I didn't say anything then, Miss Suke, but I'll say it now. He was wrong to try to lock her away alone like that. After you left, he didn't want her to go anywhere, even though he hardly came around. He may not have poured the poison down her throat, but for sure he helped lead her to it. He'll suffer, that man.

She had no other friends, you know, Miss Suke. She said no one could take your place. She talked about you with so much love. She said you were happy and she did not want to intrude. That's why she did not go to visit you. *Patron* called a doctor and the police. Then, then they came and took her away."

She sighed, her hands clasped in front of her, while her head hung to one side.

Neither spoke for a while. Then Suke asked calmly, "Why do you think she did it? Did something bad happen to her? Was she unhappy?"

"You know Miss Yasmin, Miss Suke. If she was unhappy she never let you see it. She was her usual self all along. Up until I left that day."

"Thank you for telling me, Anni. "You can go to bed now. I'll clean up out here."

"It's okay, Miss Suke. I don't mind."

"No, I need to be busy for a while. Go to bed."

"Good night, Miss Suke."

Suke sat up on the couch and covered her face with her hands. She began to massage her forehead, then her temples. *So much to do, so much to think about*, she said to herself, *but not now. I don't want to think just now.* She picked up the plate and began to eat slowly, forcing herself to keep her mind empty.

When she finished eating, she carried the plate and cup into the kitchen. She glanced at the table where she and Yasmin had sat so many times and looked quickly away. This is where they had laughed about their escapades with various men, gossiped about which girls had run out of Ambi and how black and ugly they looked, dreamed about how rich and powerful they were going to be one day. She forced herself not to think of those days.

She washed and put away the dishes, wiped down the counter, and left the kitchen. She went straight to her room, took off all her clothes, folded them into a neat pile—which she placed on the bed—and headed into the bathroom. She sat on the edge of the tub and ran the water, testing it for the right temperature as she poured a generous amount of bubble bath into it. She kept it warm. She didn't trust hot baths.

"Don't you think sitting in hot water is bad for women?" she had asked Yasmin.

"Why should it be? In Europe, women take hot baths all the time. Doesn't seem to bother them."

"Europeans are different. It just seems to me that all that hot water could do something to women down there," Suke said.

"Oh Suke that's just village talk. Keep the water warm then," Yasmin replied impatiently.

Suke trailed her hand absently in the warm water, watching the bubble bath rise into a frothy, rose-scented spread. She lowered herself slowly into the water. Yasmin taught her to bathe this way, especially at night.

"Showers are for ordinary people who don't love themselves," Yasmin said.

Suke bathed this way all the time in Bukavu. Sometimes, Bryan would get into the tub with her and they would play around and make love. Her heart lurched at the thought of Bryan, but she shoved him out of her mind. She spent close to an hour in the bath, letting out the water when it cooled and replacing it with warm, sudsy water.

She slept soundly when she finally climbed into bed, wrapped in a cloth that covered her body all the way down to her calves. She didn't even hear Anni open the door and listen for the sound of her breathing.

#

Suke awoke early the next morning, but stayed in bed until almost noon. Anni knocked on her door around nine and called out that she had prepared breakfast. Suke told her she would be out later for it. *Now I can start to think*, she said to herself when Anni left. She would not go back into the street. She would have the baby, not to remind her of Bryan, but to remind her that she had known love and joy. She would not go back to Yolita either. Between what she had put away before, and what she saved from Bryan's allowance, she should have enough money to get her started in business. But how and where to start? She needed a sponsor, someone who could introduce her to the right people and teach her how to make money, but who? Whom could she trust?

Hours later, she still had no answer. She got up and went into Yasmin's room. She closed the door behind her and stood there looking around. The room was neat and clean, as usual. It was a pretty room, comfortable and feminine. The mahogany four-poster bed stood in the middle of the floor.

"I don't like my bed against any wall. Don't ask me why. I just don't," Yasmin told her once.

Yasmin's perfume filled the room. Suke walked over to the wardrobe and opened it. Yasmin's clothes were packed tight on the rack running across the width of the wardrobe. There were dresses she had bought in Paris and countless, locally made outfits of ankle-length, tight-fitting skirts and matching bodices in all the latest styles. These had been made by Suke's own tailor in the cîté. Rows and rows of shoes and sandals took up the floor of the wardrobe.

Suke almost laughed out loud as her eyes fell on the bright yellow and pink sling-back shoes with thick four-inch heels that Yasmin brought from Paris. The shoes raised many eyebrows in Kinshasa, even among the girls who thought they had seen everything.

"I know they're outrageous, but I like them," Yasmin said defiantly when she first showed them to Suke. She bought them on a whim, she said, from a bohemian boutique on the Rive Gauche in Paris.

"What's Bohemian?" Suke asked.

"People who aren't afraid to live by their own rules."

Suke had laughed and laughed. "Is that what you are? Bohemian? For sure no one else in Kinshasa would be bold enough to wear something like that." Surprisingly, the shoes always looked classy with the outfits Yasmin wore.

Suke touched the dresses one by one, giggling each time she came to one that reminded her of a particularly funny incident. She felt much lighter by the time she had gone through the clothes and the shoes. The room was so alive with Yasmin she gave in to the urge to talk to her. "You, Yasmin, you're a bad girl to make me cry so much," she scolded, her voice barely above a whisper. "You should have looked for me. Whatever it was, we would have talked it away."

Suke kept walking around the room touching this and that, talking softly to Yasmin. She told Yasmin about the baby, about her life with Bryan, and how it had ended. She told her that she was ready now to make the dream real, but that she needed a sponsor. "Do you know one, Yasmin?" Yes, she vowed to her, she would keep her promise and always be true to herself from now on.

She found the letter on the dresser, in a pale blue envelope with her name written on it in Yasmin's handwriting. "How did you know I would learn to read?" Suke lay on her back on Yasmin's bed and opened the letter. It was written in French.

> "My Darling Suke,
>
> *I know you are angry with me for doing what I have done, but it is better this way, believe me. I found out that I have this terrible new disease for which there is no cure. The doctor said it was some sort of virus that was attacking my immune system. I got it from having sex with someone who has it, he said. I do not know who it is. What does it matter now, anyway? Just promise me that you will be careful with those men out there. Some of them are walking around with this disease.*
>
> *The doctor said I would die in a few months and that it would be a very painful death, as the virus slowly eats away my body. You know me, Suke. I am*

too vain. I cannot sit by and watch myself rot like that. And you know I cannot stand pain. So I decided to go out before I begin to decay. You would have been proud of me. I made sure I was all dressed up when they found me, with my make-up perfect and my nails done. I almost put on the yellow and pink shoes, but I thought those bitches at the hospital would steal them off my feet.

Dearest Suke, don't cry too much. It would have been awful if I had stayed around.

The apartment is yours. I bought it the same year you left and put your name next to mine on the title, which I hid under the floor of the wardrobe. Be sure to find it. I thought we would use the apartment for our office someday.

Forgive me, dear Suke, but I did not think Bryan would stay with you. I said nothing when you were leaving because you would not have listened to me anyway. And I didn't want to spoil your happiness. Anyway, you-know-who thinks he is still renting the apartment. Whenever he paid the rent, the landlord would take out the ten percent I agreed to give him to keep his mouth shut and bring the rest to me. I considered it just compensation for having to sleep with him even though he was sleeping elsewhere most of the time.

I know. I'm naughty. But we had so much fun together, didn't we, Suke?

So! If it is over with Bryan, you must go back to our dream. There is a roll of bills in each foot of the yellow and pink shoes. (I hope you find that funny. I wanted to make you laugh.) That and the apartment are my investment in our business. I will always be your silent partner. (That was meant to be funny too, but maybe you won't get the joke now.)

One more thing: now that I am gone, you will need someone to show you the ropes. Not that I knew it all, but at least I had connections we could use. Go to Musana Import-Export in Lemba and ask for Yafari Abeli. He is my mother's cousin. Tell him who you are. He will know what to do.

No more tears, Suke. I love you. Wherever I am, I will be protecting you.

Your Yasmin.

P.S. I knew living with Bryan would force you to learn to read."

Suke pressed the letter to her bosom and held it there; for how long, she did not know. Yasmin had said goodbye. A tear rolled out of one eye and Suke wiped it away roughly before it reached halfway down her cheek.

"No more tears, Yasmin. I promise," she said.

CHAPTER FOURTEEN

Musana Import-Export was a general wholesale-retail store the size of a small supermarket. It imported from Europe all the necessary supplies for the home and all the basic equipment and machinery used for light industry, especially auto repair. Yafari Abeli managed the store for his brother, a diplomat who lived in Europe with his family. His brother was several years his junior. He was the son of his father's third wife.

Yafari was a gray-haired man. He was tall and big. He wore well-tailored jackets of the best cotton prints, trousers of fine tropical wool, and expensive leather shoes. Typical of the men of his class, his girth was a public statement that he lived well, ate well, and was well connected. His children were teenagers. All of them were attending school in Belgium.

Yafari was a kind man, but he never showed his emotions. He was not cold, just private. His workers called him Papa Yafari. He was expecting Suke. He asked her no questions about herself or her background and Suke volunteered no information. The look in her eyes and the expression that came over her face when she mentioned Yasmin's name told Yafari all he wanted to know.

He did not discuss Yasmin's death with her either. All he knew was that the young woman before him, with her deep eyes and that determined set to her mouth, was starting life down a new road. The best way to go down that road was the only way to go down that road—forward, without looking back ever. Yafari Abeli would not be the one to cause Suke to look back.

Suke was as green as a banana shoot when it came to the business of import and export. But that did not bother Yafari at all. She learned fast and Yafari increased her responsibilities and access to confidential information as fast as she learned. He trusted her implicitly. He started her at the very bottom, in office administration. He made her answer the phone, deliver messages from one department to another or to associates outside. He ordered her to separate and stack documents into neat files. From administration he moved her into inventory, where she checked orders when they came in from the suppliers and verified shipments before they went out to the buyers.

Suke soon became familiar with the names of all the company's suppliers and customers. She developed her own system that told her which supplies were running low and which customers would need to be re-stocked soon. When she reported back to Yafari, he would have her call the suppliers and customers directly to place an order or pitch a sale, depending on what was needed. He liked the way she spoke French with a slight Parisian accent.

From inventory, Yafari moved her to logistics to deal directly with transportation and customs service. She arranged shipment schedules with the company's customs broker and assembled all the information for customs documentation. In no time, she knew all the permits and certificates that were needed, which agencies to get them from, and how to negotiate with the bureaucrats in those agencies so that she got them when she wanted them.

Suke took to accounting like a fish to water. She learned to handle the numbers and balance the books with such poise that Yafari one day hugged her in front of everybody after a particularly grueling audit. She stood her ground with the company's bankers, questioning every fee, every charge to the account.

She learned about the movement of currency exchange rates and how to work with those rates to the company's advantage. And in every area of Musana's external dealings, she found out whose palm needed to be greased and how much grease it took. Not that Musana wasn't doing well before Suke came; it just seemed to do well with fewer headaches for everybody after she got there.

Yafari could not have been more pleased with his protégé. He never had to explain anything twice. He paid her well and let her use a company car with a driver. But he insisted that she learn to drive. He began to take her with him on his monthly trips upcountry to check on operations and meet with the manager at the branch store. Yafari's associates around Kinshasa began to talk about the serious, sharp young woman who worked for him, wishing they had someone like her to organize their own businesses.

If anyone resented Suke's rapid ascent in Musana they said nothing. Mama Yafari, Yafari's wife and closest adviser, had put the word out that Suke was her niece.

Mama Yafari was a fat, good-natured woman who watched over Musana like a hawk. Like most women of her generation, she was the de facto human resources administrator of the business. Workers came to her with their complaints and she dealt with them summarily but fairly. She settled disputes between the workers in the same way and coached many a marriage back onto solid ground.

Though she came from a family that was well off, she had gone no further than high school. She married Yafari when she was eighteen. She ran her household with the same good-natured but firm hand. She brooked no insolence, not from her children, her household staff, the workers at Musana or their families.

No worker would dream of crossing Mama Yafari, no matter how much they resented Suke.

Suke kept her relations with her fellow workers on a cordial, strictly business level. She gave respect ungrudgingly to whomever it was due, being especially deferential to the older men and women who had been with the company from the start. She shunned all social life, except for dinner at Papa and Mama Yafari, and a rare visit to Yolita, who finally threw out her good-for-nothing husband and now made a living as a hairdresser.

As her pregnancy progressed, she grew more exhausted when she got home from work. She would take a long bath as soon as she got home, have dinner, watch the eight-o'-clock news, then go to bed. Sometimes, she would watch a show after the news with Anni, who stayed on as her housekeeper. But most times, she simply went straight to bed. She got up at six every morning and was on her way to work by seven to avoid the traffic nightmares for which Kinshasa was notorious.

Driving, even being driven in Kinshasa was not an experience Suke looked forward to. It was as if the sole intent of those in control of the other vehicles—cars, buses, trucks, and sundry ingenuous creations of wood and metal on wheels—was to move from point A to point B in the shortest possible time, obeying a minimal set of rules and observing no courtesies whatsoever. The result was an alarmingly high incidence of fatal accidents and bottlenecks that lasted for hours.

Often, the traffic police, at the most notorious junctions, would give up in frustration and simply stand by the side of the road to watch the chaos. They closed their ears to the blaring horns and the curses hurled at them. Other times, especially toward the end of the month, the same traffic police would make things worse by pulling over ramshackle taxis for real and concocted violations, letting them go only after the driver had surreptitiously stuffed a few bills into the pocket of one of the policemen.

On the day Suke's baby was born Yafari went to the hospital with his wife. Suke told them that she was going to name the baby Yasmin, but Mama Yafari made her change her mind.

"Give her a name that has no past and carries no sorrow, one whose meaning will come only from the life she will create for herself," she said. "Name her Shayna." The name just came to her, she said. No, she had never heard it before. It's just a name that popped into her head right there and then. A name free and clear for a life that's free and clear. They never asked Suke who the father was.

By the time Shayna was a year and a half, Suke felt she learned almost all she needed to know about running a business and about importing and exporting. All that was left for her to experience were the dealings in Europe itself. But she would not dream of asking Papa Yafari to send her there. That would make her seem ungrateful. Already he had allowed her to do far more than she ever expected. And Mama Yafari, how kind she was to her! She could not thank them enough. She would have to learn how to do business in Europe on her own.

#

One Sunday afternoon, Yafari and his wife were sitting on the verandah of their home in Mbinza. Yafari had fallen asleep in his chair, lulled by the heat, the quiet, and a sumptuous lunch. He woke a few minutes later thinking of Suke.

"Suke will be leaving us soon," he said to his wife in a heavy voice.

"But we expected this. It was Yasmin's plan," she replied, fanning herself. She too had fallen asleep, but she woke up long before her husband and was unwinding the threads in her hair. Jeannette, her neighbor's maid, would be coming over soon to re-thread it.

Yafari sighed deeply. "Yes, I know." He had come to depend on Suke more than he realized.

"Has she said anything about leaving?"

"No. But I know there is little more I can teach her now."

"Ahaaaaah," Mama Yafari said, making the singsong sound that meant 'is that so?' "The time went by so quickly."

"There is only one thing left for her to learn and that is how to deal with the Europeans on their own territory," Yafari continued as if his wife had not spoken. "Strange, she has never asked about that."

"Suke will never ask you for more that you have given her. She has good manners."

"That's true."

"You can always send her to Europe with your head buyer the next time he goes."

"Yes. That's what I planned to do. She won't need more than three such trips."

"She still hardly smiles," Mama Yafari said pensively. "She keeps herself so aloof."

"I don't blame her, too many parasites around. They would waste her time and suck her blood dry."

She will be such a young *mama-benzi*," Mama Yafari said, shaking her head and smiling. Then she burst out laughing. "Eh! Suke, a mama-benzi! Waaah! That girl is something else!"

CHAPTER FIFTEEN

Word of an invasion of Shaba, the southern province bordered by Tanzania, Angola, and Zambia—and long a hotbed of insurrection—spread rapidly through Kinshasa on the waves of the "radio trottoir," the city's reliable grapevine that carried all the news the government tried to keep from the public. The rebels attacked from Angola, the grapevine said, and Mobutu's best friends—Belgium, France and Morocco—had sent troops to the rescue, flown in on American planes.

Known as Katanga until its name was changed in 1971, Shaba was the capital of the country's mining industry, with rich deposits of copper, cobalt, uranium, cadmium, tin, gold, silver, and other minerals. Copper mining was a centuries-old practice here, long before the Belgians colonized the region in the 1880s.

The province was rebellious from the start. One month after the country gained its independence from Belgium in 1960, backed by Belgian interests afraid of losing their liberal access to its vast mineral resources under the Lumumba's decidedly nationalist regime, it seceded with Moise Tshombe as its president. That the secession came so soon after independence was perhaps a bigger shock to Kinshasa than the secession itself, for Tshombe made it clear at the independence negotiations in Brussels that his vision for the new Congo was a loose federation of independent states and not the centrally governed republic that Lumumba advocated.

A bloody face-off ensued between the central government in Kinshasa and the Katangese army commanded by Belgian officers and reinforced by Belgian mercenaries. Lumumba appealed to the United Nations, which sent a small force into Katanga, ostensibly to keep the peace and oversee the withdrawal of the Belgian troops. But repeated clashes between the U.N. force and the Katangese army kept reunification at bay. Each side blamed the other for the most horrific atrocities against civilians. The rest of the country, meanwhile, was in turmoil because of the power struggle between Lumumba, the prime minister, and Joseph Kasavubu, the president. Kasavubu eventually succeeded in ousting Lumumba with the help of then Colonel Joseph Mobutu, who placed Lumumba under house arrest. Lumumba escaped, but he was recaptured and flown to Katanga on Mobutu's orders, where he was murdered.

Around Africa, and in the Caribbean, Europe, South America, and North America, the African Diaspora mourned his death. Lumumba had been their hope for the Congo, the jewel of the pan-African movement that was sweeping the continent.

U.N. forces eventually routed Tshombe's forces in 1963 and reunited Katanga with the rest of the country, but the province remained volatile. A U.N. investigation later charged Tshombe with complicity in Lumumba's murder.

News of the new invasion frightened Suke. Orchestrated by well-armed Tshombe loyalists and white mercenaries who seemed to flock to the region, it was the most serious rebel action since the 1960s. It shook the regime in Kinshasa so badly, the "radio trottoir" reported, that the ministers of government were sending their immediate families, mistresses, and whatever money and valuables they could out of the country by the planeload.

In the cîté, bets were placed that the government would close the airport once these families were safely out of the way, which is precisely what occurred. The government began to clamp down on the population in Kinshasa, imposing a curfew from eight at night to dawn and curtailing foreign travel. The merchants howled, but, as everyone expected, they quickly found ways to circumvent all the new regulations. The "radio trottoir" blared that the reason for the clampdown was the fear that rebel leaders would sneak into the capital and organize underground to overthrow the government.

Many well-to-do Shabans, and anyone reported to be or suspected of being anti-government, were detained as part of the government's campaign to terrorize the population out of any thought of subversion. The new breed of market dons became a convenient target. Made up mostly of young traders who learned commerce from their parents and were vendors in the main markets, this moneyed class did not hide its contempt for politics and politicians. They were a literate group, their parents having insisted on educating them at least through high school. They were distrusted by government leaders and admired by the masses.

Shaba gave the government a good excuse to harass these nouveaux-riches. They were dragged from their homes or businesses at all hours of the day and night and taken to military headquarters. Some were released the same day after questioning; others were forced to spend a night, some even a week, in the most humiliating conditions in the military lockup. One or two were never seen or heard from again.

To legitimize its actions, the government, which never admitted to the invasion of Shaba, announced that it had proof that some of the market dons were financing rebel activity throughout the country with money they deposited into rebel bank accounts in Europe. Everyone knew, of course, that this was a lie. The market dons were interested in one thing only: making money. They wanted no part of government, rebel or otherwise.

Suke had two strikes against her. Though she had none of the telltale trappings—the big house in the cîté, the Mercedes-Benz, the rapid weight gain to show she could afford to buy food in abundance—she was considered nouveau riche by virtue of the business she owned. And she was from Shaba. Her family had moved to Kinshasa before she was born.

The situation in Kinshasa worried Suke more than she allowed anyone to see. Already some of the business owners she knew had been detained. She feared most for Shayna. *What would become of her if anything happened to me*, she kept asking herself.

She left Musana a year ago and set up her own company, ShaYaSu International, in a small warehouse in the cîté. For most of that first year, she supplied wholesalers around Kinshasa with bulk food items and hardware that she traveled to Uvira to buy from traders who sneaked across the lake, or came in by road at night from Uganda, Rwanda, and Tanzania. She spent no time in Bukavu on these trips. She arrived by plane in the morning, took a taxi to Uvira where she made all her purchases by noon, loaded the purchases onto a truck that belonged to a fleet owned by one of Musana's delivery agents, and headed back to the airport on the same truck for the late flight back to Kinshasa.

Her shipment would arrive in Kinshasa on the next morning's cargo flight and another truck from the same delivery agent would transport it to her warehouse.

Toward the end of the year, she began to travel to France, Belgium, and Germany where she had made connections during her trips for Musana. Her business was doing well; she had just begun to see profits. Then the invasion came and all hell seemed to break loose.

"I can't travel anymore, not even to Uvira. I'm too afraid to leave Shayna with all the madness that's going on here," she said to Papa Yafari.

He had sent his car to bring her to his office and she had come right away, asking the driver no questions. After a few general comments on the situation in the country and the impact on each of their businesses, Suke blurted out her fear of leaving Shayna alone.

"I think both of you should leave the country, Suke," Papa Yafari said gravely.

Something about his tone startled her. She leaned forward in her chair opposite his and looked at him more closely. He looked directly back at her. Her heart lurched at what she saw in his eyes. Papa Yafari was worried.

"Why do you say it like that, Papa Yafari? Is there something you know?" Suke said. The fear in her voice was unmistakable.

"Yes, there is. And I say again that you and your daughter should get out of the country, at least until Kinshasa settles down. Go to Europe. You know people there now," he said, without breaking his gaze.

His voice was so stern that Suke began to wring her hands. "They're talking about me, aren't they? My name has been mentioned," she said frantically.

"Your mother heard—and I'm not even sure it's true, but that's what she heard—that a certain general was wondering about ShaYaSu." The 'mother' he was referring to was Mama Yafari.

"Wondering? What kind of wondering?"

"He was asking who you were and who your friends were and where you came from."

Suke slapped both hands to her forehead and made a moaning sound.

"Your mother and I will help you, of course."

"But Papa Yafari, I can't leave my business now! You know that."

"Then send Shayna away."

"Where? To whom?"

"To the safest place, to America," he said with an even keel.

"But I don't know…" she stopped abruptly. Papa Yafari saw the flicker of pain in her eyes before she averted them from his. "I don't know anyone in America," she continued quietly.

"Her father is there. America is Shayna's home too, Suke," Papa Yafari said.

The silence between them was warm and tender, like the silence that occurs from time to time in a girl's first conversation as a woman with her father. Suke did not ask how he knew, but she was certain that he had not gone around prying into her background, just as she was certain that what he knew had never passed his lips before, not even to tell Mama Yafari.

"I can't prove it," she said quietly.

"What do you mean you can't prove it?"

"He does not know about her. He did not want me to have her."

Papa Yafari's shoulders slumped and his chin fell to his chest. It was as if someone pushed a tube into his heart and drained out every ounce of joy. Suke had never seen him display such emotion.

"What does her birth certificate say?" Papa Yafari asked, lifting his chin slowly.

"She has no birth certificate. I did not apply for one."

"Suke, you must find a way to leave. This general, apparently he wants to talk to you."

Suke stamped her feet and pushed herself up tall and stiff. She folded her arms across her chest and shifted impatiently from one foot to the other, turning her head from side to side. Her breathing was heavy. Finally, she stood still and faced Papa Yafari.

"Papa Yafari," she said defiantly, "I have nothing to hide. I work hard, I built my business myself, I run it fairly and squarely. I take care of my child. I wish no one ill. Let this general come. With a whole battalion if he wants. I..." She stuck out her chest and hit it with the palm of her hand in rapid-fire slaps, "...will have something to say to him too. I refuse, *refuse*, to run and leave my business to those dogs after all I went through. Not me! Not this Suke! Hah!"

"What about Shayna?"

The blaze in Suke's eyes died instantly. Her voice fell to just above a whisper. "Don't worry, Papa Yafari. She will be all right. I will put her in good hands."

#

Suke stood across the street from the American Embassy and studied the uniformed young man in the guard shelter just inside the tall wrought-iron gates. She knew that a new guard would come on duty in half an hour. The only people entering the gates so early in the morning were locals who tended the grounds or worked in the other buildings in the compound.

The other buildings included an apartment complex that housed some of the American staff at the Embassy. A small army of Zairians was employed in the complex as domestic help. The ambassador's residence stood several hundred yards behind the Embassy, half hidden behind a thick hedge of flowering hibiscus. Suke looked up at the sun. In less than an hour, the American staff and a higher level of local employees—secretaries, consular aides, and various other departmental assistants—would begin to arrive.

The Embassy would open to the public shortly after that. Suke made up her mind to slip in with the menial workers. She spent the previous three days observing the movements at the main gate from early in the morning. The menial workers seemed to arrive all at once and were admitted without scrutiny. One or two of the women would be accompanied by a young child. Suke thought it would be easy to pass as a new maid.

On the second day of her observation, she struck up a conversation with one of the women she had seen enter the compound the day before. She asked the woman about the possibility of being hired in the apartments as a maid. The woman must have caught a telltale inflection in Suke's speech for she responded immediately in Suke's native language, telling her that the Americans were always coming and going and were always looking for good people, "clean like you," to take care of their children. In fact, there was a new family right now on the second floor of the building she herself worked in and they were looking for someone.

The girl who worked for the family that previously occupied the apartment had gotten married and had gone to live in the country with her husband, the woman explained. Suke should try there, she said. They wanted someone right away. No, she didn't know their name, but she could knock on their door today and let them know that Suke would be coming tomorrow.

Suke tightened her grip on Shayna's hand and looked down at her. Shayna was looking around curiously, one finger in her mouth. She was not used to being on the road this early. *This may be the last time we ever see each other, my darling daughter*, Suke thought. *Will you remember me and how much I love you?*

She looked across at the guard again, picked up Shayna, took a deep breath and crossed the street to join the group of workers approaching the embassy gate. The woman she had spoken to was not among them. She kept her head bowed as she passed through the gate with the others. She wore a cloth draped over her head, covering her down to the waist. She held Shayna tight against her, on the side away from the guard. The guard, a young white man with a baby face, barely glanced at the group before waving them through. Once inside the gate, Suke started off toward the apartment complex, trailing the others who were headed in that direction.

Out of the corner of her eye, she saw one of the gardeners looking at her as he watered a patch of roses. She picked up her pace slightly, looking neither left nor right. Shayna was quiet, she noticed. *She's probably asleep.* The child had not uttered a word since they left the car.

Normally, Suke would have asked her why she was so quiet and would have coaxed her into conversation. But now she was grateful for her silence. She didn't think she could bear Shayna's innocent, trusting chatter. She looked back quickly when she reached the apartment building, but the gardener was nowhere in sight. No one else was watching her. The other workers said nothing to her. Aside from a casual "see you later" as they went off in different directions, no one said anything to anyone once they passed through the Embassy gates. Some of them said good morning to Suke, but did not pay her any attention after that.

Instead of going into the building, Suke moved toward the rows of cars parked under it. Looking around, she saw that there was a separate street entrance for the apartments, but it was closed and padlocked. There were no sign of a guard or local watchman, although there was a guardhouse beside that gate as well. A lawn stretched wide and green behind the building, with several benches, a gazebo, and a play area with a sandpit, swings and slides.

Suke carried Shayna to one of the benches out of view from the apartments and sat down. They could wait here until it was almost time for the Embassy to open, she thought. She set Shayna down beside her on the bench, cupped the child's face in her hands and turned it up toward her own. Shayna's eyes were heavy with sleep.

"Shayna Yasmin, you're going to stay with a very nice lady here for a while. Maman has to go away to take care of some very important things and it will take a while to finish it. So you will stay with this lady. She will take good care of you."

Shayna looked into her mother's eyes and shook her head up and down. Then she laid her head in Suke's lap and went to sleep. Suke smiled and stroked her daughter's hair. She could feel the sting in her eyes. *Don't cry*, she warned herself harshly. After a few minutes, she removed the cloth from her head, folded it into a pillow and placed it gently under Shayna's head. She lifted the child's feet onto the bench, stroked her head again for a few minutes then eased her off her lap, letting her head rest on the makeshift pillow on the bench. Shayna did not stir. Suke deliberately woke her at four that morning and kept her awake until then.

Suke stood up and unwrapped the cloth she was wearing as a skirt, transforming her outfit into an ankle-length dress. She folded the cloth in two and covered Shayna with it up to her shoulders.

She removed a pair of high-heeled sandals from the shoulder bag that she'd hidden under her head cloth and exchanged them with the cheap flat rubber sandals she had been wearing all along. She sat back down the bench. She would wait a few minutes longer, until the Embassy staff and early-bird visitors began to arrive. By then the new guard would be at the gate. If anyone came by before she left, she could easily explain that she was early for an appointment.

Her heart pounded faster as each moment drew her closer to the time she must separate from her daughter. To keep her mind occupied, she drew a mental picture of Shayna laughing and playing with other little children in a garden just like the one they were in now, only it was in America. Suke fixed her mind on that image.

Finally, it was time. She checked to see that the note was securely pinned inside of the bodice of Shayna's dress. She addressed it to "Mme. Janice McWright, Consul General, Embassy of The United States of America. Private and Urgent!" The idea to place Shayna in the care of Janice McWright instantly came to her that day when Papa Yafari held up Shayna's life before her and challenged her to let her live it in the fullness of her birthright.

The first time she heard of Janice McWright was at a get-together at the home of the honorary consul general in Bukavu. Suke and Bryan were chatting with a three other couples, including the consul-general and his wife, when the conversation turned to Janice McWright and the tragic death of her husband in a car crash in Kinshasa. There were comments about what a charming, intelligent, and dignified woman Janice McWright was; how she raised the standards of the American Embassy in a country that was so tied to the French and the Belgians, but which was so important to America; about how terrible it was for someone to become a widow at such a young age.

"The last time she visited us here she told me she was hoping to start a family soon," the consul general's wife said. "I think in a way she hoped that having a family would rein in Dillon. Not to speak ill of the dead, but we all know what a playboy he was."

Shortly after that, Suke saw Janice McWright on television giving a speech on behalf of the ambassador at the opening of a modern children's hospital on the outskirts of Kinshasa. The hospital was a project of the U.S. Agency for International Development. Suke was moved by Janice McWright's compassion for the children of a country that was not her own. And she was impressed that the consul general could give such a speech even as she coped with her own grief.

"I hope she has children of her own one day. She will be such a good mother," Suke said to Bryan.

Satisfied that the note was securely pinned to Shayna's dress,

Suke stood up, took out a pair of sunglasses from the handbag and put them on. She bent down, pressed her palm against Shayna's forehead, and then kissed her daughter for the last time.

Suke walked out of the American Embassy compound without even a glance at the guard. The sun was well up, now. Outside the gate, she stood calmly at the curb for a moment, looked left, then right, and then left again, as if she were expecting a car. She looked at her watch, checked to the left and right once more, and then headed down the street to the left. She did not stop walking until she reached the next corner. She stood there staring into the horizon, narrowing her eyes to keep out the glare of the sun.

She inhaled deeply, hoisting her shoulders as she inhaled and dropping them heavily as she exhaled. She started across the street. Halfway across, she hesitated. It was just a tiny break in her stride in which she turned her head slightly as if she would look back. But she did not look back. She faced full forward again, lifted her chin and moved on.

She felt the stinging in her eyes again, but this time she did not warn the tears away. She strode forward, her mind fixed on what lay ahead of her. There was no need for her to worry about Shayna. In her heart, she knew what Janice McWright would do.

On the other side of the street, she disappeared into the early morning crowd. Kinshasa's five million people had begun their daily sameness of living, oblivious to the drama of yet another mother parting ways from her child.

BOOK THREE

CHAPTER SIXTEEN

Crispin's thoughts took him back to the restaurant in Harlem, as he drove toward the marble and copper-trimmed building that housed the Musana Holdings headquarters. One of sub-Saharan Africa's architectural marvels, the building was erected in the early 1970s as a center for international commerce. But the volume of foreign tenants it hoped to attract never materialized. Bad press about the country's increasingly autocratic regime, economic mismanagement, and smoldering social disenchantment kept most investors away. The local business elite refused to go near it, claiming they could not afford its rent, at a time when the cost to pay for overseas supplies rose every day.

The real reason, everyone knew, was that no business owner in his right mind wanted to get involved in what it would take to get a lease on the place—the kind of connections they'd need and the payoffs they'd have to make. By the late seventies, the building had become the proverbial white elephant. The government was paying through its nose to keep the lights on, the toilets flushing, and a legion of 'round-the-clock security guards to protect it from pillagers.

Musana Holdings acquired the building under the new government's privatization program and financed its refurbishment entirely on its own. The building was still called the Commercial Center, but Musana occupied the entire top two floors and rented the remaining space to foreign embassies and multinational corporations that returned to the country after Mobutu's overthrow. The ground floor housed various shops, banks, restaurants, and two business centers.

It was almost one-thirty in the afternoon. The street was teeming with students. Cocky teenage boys walked with an easy swagger. They wore dark-blue trousers with knife-edged seams, starched white shirts with the collars turned up, and black leather shoes. On the other side of the street, sassy teenage girls eyed them coyly. The girls wore pleated navy-blue tunics with white blouses. Their waists were belted tight.

Crispin could tell from the colors of the uniforms that these were students of the elite Jesuit and Franciscan high schools nearby. Crispin himself received his elementary and secondary education at the Jesuit school.

He was returning from lunch with the Brazilian ambassador. The ambassador heard from a reputable source in Sao Paulo that Musana Holdings might be joining a consortium the Texeira family was putting together to bid on an old shipping line that the government had been trying to sell off for months. The ambassador, an industrialist who still held his partnership in one of Brazil's largest auto manufacturing plants, vowed that he would do whatever he could to seal Musana's participation in the Texeira consortium. Not only that, he would make sure that they won the bid. He was determined to make sure the shipping line remained in Brazilian hands.

Like many of his fellow Brazilians in high circles, he saw Brazil as the rightful leader of a slowly emerging, potentially formidable front against the rich industrialized nations. Brazil would lead this front against the wealthy nations' campaign to create a global economy based on free, but not necessarily fair, trade. Developing countries like Brazil considered this campaign high-handed and unfair. Why should they be forced to play on equal footing with nations that had grown fat from the very practices they now wanted to outlaw in the name of free trade? Poor countries wanted to grow fat, too. There was ample room for compromise.

Ambassador d'Andrade had visions of the shipping line plying the ocean lanes from South America, through the Caribbean Basin to West and South Africa, and then on to Asia and back. Under the shrewd guidance of a Texeira-Musana team, such a shipping line could put Brazil solidly at the helm of a south-south trade that was bound to come into its own in less than a decade. Launching the service now would only speed the growth of that trade.

At present, direct service between the Americas and West Africa was virtually non-existent. The more established lines argued—and rightfully so—that there wasn't enough freight on the return from Africa to justify such service. Most carriers leaving the Americas with freight destined for Africa offloaded at a European port, where the cargo was transferred to one of the myriad of lines that had been serving Africa direct from Europe since colonial times.

Adding an Asia leg to a direct Americas-Africa service, as the Texeira-Musana consortium was certain to do, would ensure enough cargo on that haul back. Already exports from Asia to West Africa, South America, and the Caribbean were skyrocketing. Merchants in these countries declared that even with transportation costs factored in, it still was cheaper to buy from Asia than from Europe and the United States.

Figuring out the trend wasn't rocket science, Ambassador d'Andrade said to his African and South American colleagues in Kinshasa. Anyone with the limpest finger on the pulse of global commerce could tell that sooner or later, there would be enough to haul back from Africa to the Americas. Investors from India were positioning themselves on the continent already, particularly in garment production, to take advantage of the Africa Growth and Opportunity Act that freed up access to U.S. markets for a range of made-in-Africa goods. Any fool could see that European, American, and other Asian manufacturers eventually would shift production from expensive Asia to Africa for the same reason. In Sao Paulo, the industrial and commercial capital of Brazil, the talk was all about how the spillover production from these factories would head for Latin America and Caribbean markets.

Crispin, Glaucio, ET, and Dennis shared the ambassador's vision. They agreed in New York to move forward on the bid for the shipping line and Crispin relayed that decision to Ambassador d'Andrade during their lunch today. Ambassador d'Andrade could not contain his glee. He rose from his seat, reached across the table and shook Crispin's hand. "A very wise, decision, Crispin; a very wise decision indeed. You have made me a very happy man today. You and your group will not regret it, I assure you," he boomed.

The moment he got back to his office, Ambassador d'Andrade put a call through to Sao Paulo. He stood up when the man on the other end picked up. "Meu irmão," he said, "do you know that joke they have about our country? That Brazil has a bright future and always will? Well, soon we will see who has the last laugh."

On the ride back to his office, Crispin mentally reviewed the discussion in New York and made a few quick notes on the most strategic moves the new consortium needed to make. *The first move should be some sort of alliance with a major shipping name*, he thought. That would silence anyone who might want to make an issue of the consortium's relative inexperience in ocean shipping. He would send an e-mail to the others to come up with some names, he decided.

His thoughts drifted to his silent encounter with the woman in the pale yellow suit. He pretended not to notice her hurried exit from the restaurant. When he himself was leaving, he approached the owner, hoping to find out who she was. The owner, blank-faced, politely responded that she was a private guest at the restaurant just as he was.

"A regular guest?"

"'Regular' is an irrelevant term, *patron*."

Crispin knew when to quit.

He thought of her every day since. As he drove along Boulevard Trente Juin, he saw again the color and fit of her suit, her smile, the liquid brown eyes that stared back at him, flickering for the quickest instant. He saw her lips part almost imperceptibly. Crispin felt aroused. The CD was playing Roberta Flack's "The First Time" and he recalled what it was like seeing her for the first time. His fingers tightened around the steering wheel and he took a deep breath. Still following the lyrics of the song, he pictured himself kissing her mouth, lying with her.

He caught himself seconds before he collided with the woman and the boy. Time seemed to move in slow motion. He knew he was a part of the scene unfolding before him, and yet he seemed to be totally detached from it. He was seeing everything from a distance. He heard voices shouting. They seemed far away at first. Then time speeded up and they grew louder.

"Attention! Attention, Mama!"

"Mama! What are you doing? Be careful with the child!"

The voices were urgent, some of them even angry, as the people in the street shouted to the woman to be careful with her child. Crispin saw the woman. He could not tell if she was an old woman or a young woman grown old too fast. She was wrapped in a shabby "pagne" and she carried a deformed teenage boy on her back. Out of nowhere, a European man had run right in front of them and snapped a picture, catching the woman full in her face. He must have been a journalist. There were no tourists in Kinshasa these days. And the international aid workers knew better than to take casual photos in a city under siege.

The woman swung her face away from the camera and the child on her back, frightened by the flash and his mother's sudden movement, began to wail: loud, jumbled, animal-like sounds.

The woman stumbled into the street, holding on to the child. She did not see the car. Crispin braked hard, but it was too late. The woman's anguished eyes fell on his as the car rammed her. She fell backward, smashing the boy to the ground.

Crispin was out of the car in a flash. A crowd was gathering fast. The European photographer quickly vanished. Vanishing from the scene of an accident you caused was the smartest thing to do in Africa. All foreign journalists were warned about this. If your car hit someone, or a goat or a cow, the worst thing you could do was stick around to offer help or compensation. Things could get nasty. Going to the nearest police station to make a report was just as bad. The best thing to do was to go home, call your embassy and arrange to go to the police with an embassy official.

The crowd around Crispin's car was more curious than unruly.

"Are they dead? Are they dead?"

"Isn't it Monsieur Abeli's car?"

"It's Monsieur Abeli himself!"

"Surely they're dead!"

"There's no blood."

"He wasn't going fast."

"The European has disappeared, the coward!"

Crispin was kneeling beside the woman. She was moaning. The boy's limbs were twisted grotesquely underneath her. He made no sound. His eyes were closed.

"Are you in bad pain, Mama?" Crispin asked gently.

The woman groaned. Crispin was afraid to move her. He reached under her and felt for the boy's pulse. It was faint, but it was there.

"Is he dead, Monsieur Abeli?"

"No, thank God."

A sigh of relief rippled through the crowd. Now they could scold the woman about her reckless behavior.

"How could you take such risks with this poor child, eh, Mama?" a man said.

"Hhhhmmm!" the crowd agreed in unison.

Don't you know you shouldn't run into the street like that?"

"Hhhhhmmmm!"

"Eh, Maaama?"

Crispin pulled his cellular phone from the inside pocket of his jacket, dialed the operator, and asked to be put through to Clinique Ngaliema. Once through, he identified himself and asked for an ambulance to be sent immediately. He gave the location and clicked off.

By now the woman was struggling to get up. "My son! My son!" she moaned weakly.

A few other people were kneeling beside her. An old man held her head.

"He's alive, Mama. Don't worry."

"Don't let her move," someone said.

"Back away, you stupid people! Give them air. Back away!"

Ten minutes went by and no ambulance came. The crowd had doubled. The boy was whimpering now. Saliva drooled from one side of his mouth. The man was still cradling the woman's head. The woman reached out to her son and stroked his face weakly.

Crispin decided to take a chance. There was no telling when an ambulance would show up. And the boy did not look good.

"Help me put them in my car. I'll drive them to the hospital," he said to the man holding the woman's head.

"It may not be so wise to move them, *patron*," the man said.

"I know. But we can't just leave them here until God knows when."

Others came forward to help. They lifted the woman carefully and laid her down on the back seat of the car. A woman smoothed her shabby cloth over her legs. Another group of helpers gathered up the boy carefully and strapped him into the front passenger seat. Crispin reclined the seat as far back as it could go.

"Lay still, *mon petit*," one of the men said to the boy. The boy did not seem able to move anyway. His eyes were still closed.

"Do you want me to come with you, *patron*?" the man asked.

"No, that is not necessary. I can manage from here. I appreciate your kindness." Crispin thanked the other helpers and drove off slowly … still no sign of an ambulance.

The moment Crispin pulled up at the emergency entrance, four orderlies and a security guard rushed to the car. Crispin and his car were well known at the clinic, which was a principal beneficiary of the Musana Foundation's annual charity budget.

"Get stretchers! Quick!"

In no time, the woman and her son were being wheeled into the emergency room. A doctor came over immediately.

"Crispin! What's this all about?"

"Hello, Dr. Charles. Just the person I want to see." He shook hands with the surgeon and recounted what happened.

"OK, I'll take it from here. You can take off. We'll keep you posted," Dr. Charles said.

"No, I'll wait here."

"I understand how you feel, Crispin, but there's really nothing you can do here."

"I don't mind."

"Very well. You can sit in my office if you wish. I'll come to you once I examine them both, in about half an hour."

Crispin called his office and spoke briefly to his secretary. He did not feel like being cooped up in Dr. Charles' office. He wandered into the waiting room and slumped into a chair in the quietest corner he could find. He cupped his hands over his face and then ran his fingers over his head, sighing. *I could have killed them both,* he thought. He closed his eyes and went over the accident. *Nothing you could have done,* he told himself firmly. *Just thank God you weren't tearing ass up the road this time.*

He sighed again and opened his eyes. Several pairs of eyes were on him. Most people in Kinshasa knew Crispin Abeli by sight. He smiled at no one in particular. Smiles flashed back. He looked at his watch, stood up, and ambled down the corridor. He walked toward the sound of crying babies. *Must be vaccination day,* he thought.

He stood in the entrance of a huge room crowded with young mothers, babies and small children. He leaned against the doorway, contemplating the children's strong, healthy bodies. These were the lucky ones. Their families had money to pay for medicine.

He thought of the boy he struck. *What future does he have,* he mused. *Even when there is no war, what can our country offer him? And all the others like him?*

And then he saw her.

She was stooped in front of a chair, talking gently to the little boy seated in the chair. The boy was scowling, with his arms folded defiantly across his chest. A tall woman wearing expensive cloth and heavy gold jewelry stood beside the boy's chair, looking down at him anxiously.

Crispin froze. He squeezed his eyes shut and opened them again. She was wearing a doctor's robe over brown silk trousers, and brown and white saddle shoes. Her long braids were pulled back in a chignon that was coming undone. Small white pearl studs adorned her ears. She was smiling at the boy as she spoke to him. Crispin's heart raced. *It can't be the same woman. Not in Kinshasa!* Just then, Amina stood up and turned to speak to the tall woman. Crispin began to move toward them.

"There you are, Crispin! They told me you had come this way."

Reluctantly, Crispin stopped and turned to Dr. Charles.

Dr. Charles migrated to the Congo as a little boy. He came with his parents in the 1960s, when professionals were fleeing "Papa Doc" Duvalier's war against the intelligentsia in Haiti. Many of these professionals settled in Canada and the United States, creating enclaves in places like Nyack, New York. Others took up residence in Francophone Africa, where they contributed desperately needed skills to countries just emerging from colonialism. Dr. Charles' own mother, who used to be a teacher back in Haiti, opened a private kindergarten.

His father was a lawyer. He and another Haitian joined with a French-trained Congolese lawyer and launched a practice to serve wealthy private clients. Haitians were held in such high esteem that to be told you were "like a Haitian" was considered a compliment.

Like most Haitian children growing up in post-colonial Africa, Dr. Charles attended French schools. His schoolmates were mostly other foreign children whose parents were diplomats, technical assistants or executives with multinational corporations. The children of the Congolese elite who remained in the country also attended these schools.

Dr. Charles spoke Lingala like a native. He learned it from his Congolese friends and the small army of hired help around his parents' home. He did all his university studies in Belgium and returned to the Congo as soon as he was a fully qualified surgeon. He joined the staff at the clinic within a week of his return and never left. He trained many of the local doctors, and even non-locals who came to the country for a stint in tropical medicine.

About six month ago, he began to threaten that he would cross the river and offer his services to a country where "the health of the citizenry was not being sacrificed so that greedy politicians could be satiated." It was a brazen reference to government officials who siphoned off funds that poured in from overseas to improve the country's medical services. No one took Dr. Charles' threats seriously. Everyone knew he would never leave the Congo. Politicians were told of his accusations, but not one of them dared touch him. Doing so would only provoke more outrage against the government, at home and abroad.

"Come! We can talk in my office." Dr. Charles grabbed Crispin's elbow and began to lead him away. Crispin turned back to see if Amina was still there. She was gone. There was no sight of the woman or the boy either.

"Is something wrong?" Dr. Charles asked, following Crispin's eyes.

"Oh, er, no. I just saw—er, I thought I—thought I recognized someone. I just…" He trailed off as he looked over his shoulder one last time.

Dr. Charles looked at him quizzically. "This accident must have shaken you up more than you imagined, Crispin," he said with concern.

"No, No. I'm all right. It's nothing. I'm fine."

The doctor guided Crispin into his office and offered him a chair. He went straight to the point.

"The boy is in bad shape. He regained consciousness and then blacked out again. Not a coma, though. His previous condition, of course, exacerbated the effect of the blow to the head. We'll have to keep him in for a while."

"I'll pay for all his treatment, of course. But tell me this, Dr. Charles. Could anything have been done while he was a baby to address his deformity?"

"Probably. But it would have produced very limited results. Quite a few children his age were born that way in a number of African countries. Apparently their mothers had been given various experimental drugs early in their pregnancy. It's all been hushed up by the ministries of health, of course. The most we can do for these children is try to make them comfortable, see that they are well-fed and clothed. But as you know, Crispin, whatever facilities we had for that sort of care no longer exist. The children's hospital the Americans built nearly thirty years ago is so run down that no one wants to serve there. And our enlightened government cannot afford to, or I should say chooses not to, make the welfare of children a priority. So children like that boy are condemned to a life of utter neglect. Their families can do but so much."

Crispin was silent.

"So what do you want to do, Crispin?"

"That's an easy question to answer, don't you think? We'll refurbish the American hospital. But do we have anyone here who can run it?"

"There's one woman I know who would be perfect. Unfortunately, she lives in America. She only comes here to practice for two or three months every year."

"Oh?"

"Yes. Her name is Amina Milenga. She was born right here at this clinic. Her mother is a Black American. No, Caribbean. Her father is Congolese. She's a pediatric psychotherapist. She's wonderful with the children. The parents love her too. So committed."

"Oh!"

"Yes. She first came to the clinic to offer her services about three years ago. We told her we couldn't pay her much, but she said she was not doing it for money."

"Oh."

"Yes. She's got her own practice in New York, a thriving one, too. I visited once. Crispin, please don't say 'oh' again."

"Ah! Is she the doctor I saw in the children's center where you found me just now?"

"It must have been. She's the only doctor we have there today."

Crispin pursed his lips. "Can't we persuade her to take the position? She wouldn't necessarily have to be here every day of the year, or even every month, would she?"

"Noooo, I suppose she wouldn't have to."

"Is she married? Family of her own?"

"She doesn't talk about her family or her personal life. Someone said she's one of the Milenga clan. You know them, the agriculture barons from Kivu: very politically connected. We know she's not married. Not because she hasn't been asked, I can assure you. Many of our doctors are heartbroken. A very prominent figure in our society has also proposed, from what I hear. Seems she's just not interested."

"Maybe she has someone in America."

"And he has never set foot in this country to see her during her stay here? What kind of man would that be? No. My guess is that she's unattached, Crispin. Either that or she's exceedingly discreet. Such a beautiful woman. Perhaps you would like to meet her? Talk to her yourself?"

Crispin did not see the glint in Dr. Charles' eyes. But he heard the tease in his voice. His thoughts were racing. *So that's who she is. I wonder if she has thought of me since that day.*

"I can introduce you," he heard Dr. Charles say.

"Oh, er, er, yes. Er, would you? Perhaps I can talk her into heading a children's hospital here." He was trying hard to sound businesslike.

Dr. Charles smiled and looked at his watch. "It's a deal. But I'm afraid not today, though. I have to be in surgery in a few minutes. Perhaps tomorrow?"

"I planned to come to see the boy anyway."

"Good. Tomorrow, then. Say hello to your parents for me when next you speak to them."

They shook hands and Crispin left the office. He was tempted to walk back to the room where he had seen Amina. She may be there again. He started off in that direction.

"Oh, Crispin." Dr. Charles had come out of his office. "The boy's room is in the other direction. I just realized I have to get to a meeting and I have to go that way. Let me take you to him."

#

Amina closed the door of her small office on the second floor and leaned against it. She closed her eyes, took a deep breath, and exhaled slowly. She had seen him. She had heard Dr. Charles call his name and had looked up quickly. She could not believe it. Did he find out who she was and followed her? *Don't flatter yourself, Amina.* The man is in his own country and at a hospital where he is the largest benefactor.

She practically dragged Mrs. Kitambo and her son out of the room when he turned to speak to Dr. Charles. She walked over to the window overlooking the garden and main entrance and stood before it, hugging herself. She was attracted to Crispin Abeli. There was no denying that. She could not get him out of her mind since that day at The Baobab.

In the three years she had been coming to Kinshasa, she had seen him only once or twice on local television. He shied away from the press. She paid little attention to him when she saw him on television. She had never been curious about his private life, anyway, although she *did* read his profile in a magazine featuring the new industrial dons of the Third World. After reading it, she concluded that a man that rich, that good-looking, and with that much brain was either conceited, eccentric, or impossible to talk to about ordinary matters like love and children's health and the day-to-day survival of people who literally performed miracles with next to nothing. It was a totally illogical conclusion, she knew, but that was the way she felt and she was not ashamed to say so…at least not to herself. Or to Jamillah or Merry, of course.

True, like everyone else in Kinshasa, she was proud of his accomplishments. He was, after all, one of them. She liked the way he stood up for Africa without romanticizing it, or without making excuses for the crimes of its leaders. And like every other woman, she had wondered fleetingly what it would be like to be romanced by such a man.

She saw him in person only once before The Baobab, at a dinner in New York years ago. She was with a group of doctors and one of them pointed Crispin out to her. She barely glanced at him. She was deeply involved with Michael at the time. No. Crispin Abeli had no place in her head until that day in New York when he glued his eyes to hers and plundered her soul.

The blood rushed hot into her face as she recalled the moment. She didn't want to be attracted to him. She didn't want to be attracted to *anybody*, for that matter. Not now. Not for a long, long time—maybe never again. Not after Michael. Dating was fine. And there was nothing wrong with having sex every now and again when she really wanted it. That was a purely physical thing. The heart did not have to be involved.

She was engaged to Michael for two wonderful years. They were planning to marry once she finished her board exams. Then suddenly, he was given a big career opportunity. He would have to travel to Costa Rica to help set up a research operation for the pharmaceutical company he worked for. They were both torn up over it, but she urged him to go. Whatever happened, it would be for the best, they philosophized.

It sure did, Amina thought, still hugging herself. She stared at the people moving about in the garden below. About six months after Michael left, she received a long letter from him saying it would be better if they saw other people. No, he was not seeing anyone else, he'd said. They had known each other since college. This was their first time apart and he was discovering a lot of things about himself. He was sure it was the same with her. They should each get to know themselves better, perhaps meet other people. Maybe later they would get back together again. And if they did, it would be a much deeper relationship, wouldn't it? Having learned so much more about themselves and all?

She was shaken, but she wrote back stoically that he was right. Yes, she was discovering a lot about herself, now that she was alone. *Maybe I should have fought a little harder*, Amina thought now. "Fat lot that would have done," she said aloud with disgust.

She found out about his new ladylove in the people section of one of the monthly news magazines she subscribed to. There he was, at a nightclub in Rio with Sandra Marshall falling all over him. She was the new darling of the fashion runways. The caption on the photo said they had been dating for several months. She clipped the photo, caption and all, and mailed it to Michael with a one-line note: "All the best, Amina." And that was the way it ended for good. There were no phone calls. No letters. No e-mails. No visits.

Once she saw them together at a fancy charity ball in D.C. She stayed at the ball for as long as propriety dictated, carefully avoiding them. Then she ducked out and cabbed it back to her hotel. She fought back tears all the way to the hotel. They gushed out the moment she got off the elevator and started down the empty hallway to her room. She cried for days. It was a hurt she never wanted to experience again. Jamillah and Merry helped her through it. Jamillah told her later that Merry called Michael in Costa Rica and cursed him out in the worst way. It made her laugh. But Jamillah made her swear she would not let Merry know she knew about it. To this day, Merry did not know that she knew. Sometimes she thought she would never get over him. She still felt a pang when anyone mentioned his name.

So what was all this nervousness over a man who had looked at her in a way that still made her blush? Of all the men she could allow—yes, allow—herself to be unnerved by, she had to pick this one. She must be crazy—or horny. She almost laughed out loud. Well, it had been a long time since she had slept with a man. Amina rolled her eyes at the memory of that last encounter. She described it to Merry and Jamillah as a "sexual aberrance." The guy was married. He was nervous. It had not been worth it.

She watched the silver Mercedes Benz drive through the gates of the hospital and turn left. She sighed, turned away from the window and sat down behind her desk. She picked up the folder in front of her and began to record her notes on little Etienne Kitambo. A few minutes later she put down her pen and stared straight at nothing in particular. Chrispin Abeli was still on her mind.

CHAPTER SEVENTEEN

"At the American Embassy yesterday I met an old gardener who'd been there when my mother served as consul general. The ambassador said he was the only person they could find from that time. His great niece works at the American Cultural Center and she brought him in." said Shayna with little emotion.

She should have been more excited, Amina thought sadly. "Well? Was he of any help? Did he know anything?" Amina forced herself to sound excited. But she, too, was beginning to think they were going nowhere fast with the hunt for Shayna's mother.

They were relaxing after an early dinner in her three-bedroom, split-level condo in a high rise just off the main Boulevard in Kinshasa. Amina was rarely home this early. Children were the biggest tragedy of the seemingly endless civil war. Her cases often kept her at the clinic until well after dark. On those occasions, a military Jeep would follow her car to make sure she arrived home safely. The escort was Dr. Charles' idea. He arranged the whole thing.

Amina and Shayna arrived in Kinshasa over a month ago. Shayna went to the American Embassy the very next day for a meeting she arranged with the ambassador while she was still in New York. During the meeting, the ambassador promised to do whatever he could to help, but he was not overly optimistic. He just did not want to raise any false hopes, he told Shayna. This country was in the throes of political and ethnic turmoil. Thousands had been killed, he told her bluntly. But he promised to talk to his staff and to the employees at the Cultural Center and at the American School. He even offered to have an attaché accompany her to the municipal court to see if they could dig up any formal adoption papers. Shayna's hopes soared at the idea.

Barely able to contain her excitement, she had gone to the court with the attaché the next day. But instead of being dealt with in the businesslike manner she expected, she and the attaché were passed along from bureau to bureau. At each stop, they were kept waiting for what seemed like hours before they were allowed to see the person connected to the bureau. They had to recount repeatedly the reason for their visit.

Eventually, an officious-looking woman beckoned them into a large, musty smelling office with oversized, early twentieth-century mahogany furniture. She sat them down in front of her desk and looked directly at Shayna for a long moment, twiddling her thumbs. Finally, she told them there were no adoption records anywhere in the court. Shayna had had enough by then. She stood up abruptly, said 'thank you' coldly to the woman and stalked out of the room. The attaché was right behind her.

Neither of them saw the shock on the woman's face.

"I guess that's that," Shayna said when they were back in their car. The attaché was taking her back to Amina's apartment.

"That's that," he said. "You'll need real high-ups to break through that wall. And I'm afraid not even the ambassador would be of any help there. America has fallen out of favor here since we voiced our displeasure about some of the government's activities."

Shayna went to the embassy nearly every day since, hoping to find someone or something that would link her to her birth mother, or at least her whereabouts. In the evenings, when she discussed her day with Amina, Amina advised her to keep talking to the Congolese staff, especially the ones who did the most menial jobs. If anyone knew anything, they would be the ones. Not the Americans.

The ambassador gave her free rein and urged the entire staff to be as helpful as they could. It all led nowhere. Shayna grew morose as the days went by with not even a whisper to cling to. What she saw in the streets compounded her feelings of hopelessness: the decaying buildings; the hungry, desperate look on the faces of women and children begging; the ubiquitous lines for food; the near riotous scramble for the decrepit minivans that were the only means of transportation for the millions who clogged the city by day; gun-toting soldiers pushing and shoving the civilians. Despite her brutal candor, nothing Amina said back in New York about life in Kinshasa prepared her for this.

"I hate this depressing city!" she cried out one night to Amina. That it was her birthplace was an abstract fact, she said angrily. She was as disassociated from it as it was from her. Shayna knew it was different with Amina. But for her, nothing about Kinshasa made it personal. Not even the thought that somewhere within it was her mother, and maybe brothers, sisters, grandparents, aunts and uncles, and cousins—her history. Not even the thought that one of the people with whom she made eye contact—as she went back and forth between the Embassy and Amina's home—could be her mother or her brother or her sister gave her comfort. Why was she here? She asked herself the question over and over everyday. Why put herself through all this to find someone who coldly gave her up when she was a mere infant? Perhaps Hilton was right. Perhaps I should just go back home and let things be.

But she knew she would not let things be. She *had* to know.

No matter how long it took. No matter how painful the quest.

"He said he didn't get a good look at the face of the woman he thought was the one who left me there. When he saw her, he didn't know who she was or what she was doing there. It was only afterward that he thought she might be the one who abandoned the child. He says he remembered seeing a child with the woman. He had never seen her before and never saw her since."

"But would he recognize her if he saw her now?"

"I asked him that. He said he was not sure. He gave my mother, Janice, the best description he could at the time, he said. But it was so long ago and it wasn't even much then. He said she covered herself with a cloth from her head down, like those women from the East or the north. He doesn't think he could describe her at all now."

"But what made him link her to you that day?"

"He said something about the way she walked behind everyone else. He said it was very early in the morning, too early for the regular staff to be around. No one told him to look out for a new maid to show her where to go. And she kept my head pressed down into her all the time, as if she didn't want anyone to see my face."

Amina frowned.

"Your mother eventually managed to track her down, didn't she? And she formally adopted you, right?"

"Yes. Apparently one of the maids in the staff residence mentioned that a woman in the street had asked her about working as a maid, but she had never shown up. She was able to give a good description and even identified her tribe. Other workers who had seen her the next day backed up her description."

"There was some sort of note, you said."

"Yes, that's what Gillian and Aunt Fifi said."

"So where is it now?"

"No one knows. Aunt Fifi thinks my mother may have destroyed it. But I don't think so. Not the Janice McWright I know."

"So where could it be?"

Shayna sighed. They'd gone over this in New York. But she and Amina both knew that repeating the facts over and over again could dislodge some vital piece of information from Shayna's memory—something Janice may have said.

"It wasn't among any of her papers, not even in her bank vault. Believe me, I searched and searched. It's somewhere. I just don't know where."

"And you're sure you've never seen your birth certificate?"

"Never. I've always had a passport that gave the United States as my birthplace. As consul-general, my mother could have easily fixed that."

"What about her contact with the man who is supposed to be your father. Any clues about his whereabouts?"

"None. Aunt Fifi said she never gave any hint of who he was or where he lived. She wiped him out of her mind when he denied that I was his and made it clear that he wanted nothing to do with me."

"There *must* be formal adoption papers somewhere in Kinshasa. You're sure your Aunt Fifi doesn't know of such papers?" Amina said after a long silence.

"Positive. I asked her. Besides, I *did* go to the court, remember?" She said the word "court" with a sneer.

"There must be adoption papers somewhere in this city," Amina said, ignoring Shayna's sarcasm. She slapped her hands together. "There must be adoption papers somewhere in this city," she repeated.

"That's the third time you've said that, Amina."

"But there must be. That's one thing European colonies knew how to do—keep records. Go into any ministry or any government office and you'll see stacks and stacks of files, all brown and dog-eared and with that sweetish, pipe tobacco smell. Sometimes, they have them hanging from those old metal pins that I swear date back to the time the Belgians first landed."

"I know. I saw them and smelled them," Shayna said.

Amina snapped her fingers. "I know! Gaston can help us," she said.

"Gaston?"

"My cousin. He knows where every skeleton is buried in this town. He's the son of the uncle we had dinner with the night after we arrived. He got back from Europe yesterday."

"So where is he now? When can we speak to him?" Shayna was beginning to show interest.

"I'll call him right now." Amina picked up the phone, dialed, waited a few seconds, and then spoke in French.

Even from across the room Shayna could hear the shout of delight on the other end of the line.

"For God's sake, Gaston, you'll burst my eardrum. What did you go to Europe for this time?" Amina bantered with Gaston for a few minutes. Finally she said, "Gaston, I'm looking for information on the birth mother of a friend of mine who was formally adopted by Americans. This was more than twenty-five years ago. Would there be records anywhere in our God-forsaken judicial system?"

Shayna saw Amina frown as she listened to Gaston's response.

"Absolutely nothing?" Amina said. She listened for a while then said, "Yes, she was. Devout, I think." She paused again to listen to Gaston.

"You're right! We never thought of that," Amina said excitedly.

"What's he saying? What's he saying?" Shayna was almost beside herself with impatience. Amina gestured to her to be patient.

"So how do we get in there? Should we make an appointment first? Whom do we ask to speak to?" she asked Gaston. She listened again for what seemed an eternity to Shayna. Shayna was pacing the floor, her hands clasped tightly in front of her. Finally, Amina hung up. Shayna stopped pacing.

"Well?"

"Gaston is tied up for the next few days, but he will pick you up on Friday at ten o'clock. He'll take you to the Franciscan convent first. He thinks the child—you may have been baptized or formally blessed in their cathedral before you left the country. That's where all the expatriate Catholics worship. Janice was Catholic—I told him she was. Gaston doesn't think she would have left the country with such a little child without going through some sort of religious rite. This was an African baby. Janice would have known that the local staff at the embassy and in her own house would predict all sorts of bad luck if she did not have the child formally blessed in some way."

Shayna listened in silence. "What good would that do?" she said dejectedly when Amina stopped speaking. "All that would show is Janice's name and signature on the baptism certificate."

"It will also show the name of the attending priest and maybe the name of a witness. What if your mother, Janice that is, told the priest about your real mother? Maybe she left a copy of the adoption papers there. Don't you have to show a birth certificate or something to the priest?"

"I'm not sure," Shayna said slowly. "I'm really not sure."

"Come on, Shayna. It's worth a try." Amina poked her playfully in the side.

Shayna sighed. "Yeah, I suppose so."

"That's better," Amina said with relief.

The damn priest is probably dead though," Shayna giggled.

"Now watch out for Gaston. He's the biggest playboy from here to Brussels."

"Amina, do I look or sound like I can be bothered by any Don Juan right now?"

"Don't say I didn't warn you."

The phone rang. Amina reached lazily for it. She raised an eyebrow as the caller identified himself.

"It's for you, Shayna," she said, handing her the phone.

Shayna was on the phone for about fifteen minutes. After she hung up she turned excitedly to Amina.

"The paper wants me to interview Crispin Abeli. Apparently he's part of a consortium gunning to buy a Brazilian shipping line. If they get it, and if what our editors suspect is true, Crispin and his group would be ushering in a new era in global shipping!"

"Are you sure you're ready to take on an assignment?"

"Well it's a whole lot better than moping around waiting for a break in the case of my missing Congolese mother," Shayna replied testily.

"Heeyyyy. I'm on your side, remember?"

Shayna plopped down beside Amina and put her arms around her. "I'm sorry, Amina. Of course I know you're on my side. I'm just so frustrated."

"I know," Amina said, hugging her back. "Go for it, then."

"I just hope he's in the country."

"Yes, he is. I saw him at the clinic today."

"You did? And what did you speak about, pray tell!"

"We didn't speak. We didn't meet at all."

"Meaning you scooted out of his sight."

"I did not."

"Yeah right! You're hopeless, Amina. Anyway, you've got to come with me when I go to interview him."

"What'll you do? Pass me off as your photographer?" She groaned the moment the words were out of her mouth.

Shayna pounced on the idea. "What a brilliant idea! You're great with a camera! Weren't you a photographer for that snooty magazine in Atlanta all those years we were at Spelman?"

"Sorry. I don't do newspapers."

"This is your start, then. Amina, you've got to come," Shayna pleaded.

"Besides, you don't even have an interview lined up. Crispin

Abeli doesn't give interviews, remember?" Amina said stubbornly.

"Oh I'll get one."

"And just how do you plan to do that? You probably won't get past his first secretary, much less his second."

"You really don't think I'd call his office, do you?"

"Where else will you call? His home?"

"Precisely. Only *I* won't call. The Brazilian ambassador will. He'll set it all up."

"The Brazilian ambassador." Amina repeated the words slowly, looking at Shayna sideways as if she had lost her mind.

"Yes. I just found out who he is. He's actually someone I know pretty well. I interviewed him a couple of times long before he became an ambassador. Back then he was a big-time industrialist that was always asked by the government to accompany the Brazilian delegation to the IMF-World Bank meetings in Washington.

In a casual conversation with him at a reception, I discovered that he had a lot more passion and insight about the consequences of free trade than anyone else on any of the Third World teams. So I began to quote him. After that, all the other news organizations started quoting him too. He even started appearing on all the big-time TV shows. He sent me a nice letter thanking me for being the first to give the world the true perspective of Brazil and the rest of the developing world on free trade. Said he owed me one many times over. With all the great press he got, he was a shoe-in for an ambassadorship. He's supposed to be slated for a European posting after this one."

"And how is His Excellency going to orchestrate this this newspaper interview at the home of Crispin Abeli?"

"We'll soon find out. I'm calling him right now. I got his home number from my editor."

It was arranged within an hour. Shayna should meet Crispin at his home the next afternoon at five. He would give her no more than twenty minutes.

"Told you," Shayna gloated, catching Amina by the waist and dancing around the room after Ambassador d'Andrade called her back with the news.

"You were kidding about my accompanying you, weren't you, Shayna?" Amina said in a small voice.

Shayna stopped dancing abruptly. "No I was not, Amina. You are coming with me!" she said firmly.

She softened when she saw Amina's expression. "Amina, please, I can't go alone. I've got the address, but I don't know my way around this town."

"I can easily arrange for a driver to take you there directly. He would wait for you and bring you back."

"Why are you so afraid of him? Just what do you think he will do to you?" Shayna's voice rose slightly in exasperation.

Amina did not answer. Shayna did not let up.

"So what if you have feelings for him? So what if he figures that out? You think he's going to use you and abuse you and trample you into dust? Come on, Amina! If your back ain't bent, ain't nobody gonna ride it. And your back doesn't look bent to me."

Amina threw up her hands. "This discussion is utterly ridiculous. Why are we talking about people riding other people's back? And what feelings can I possibly have for Crispin Abeli when I don't know the man?"

"Lustful feelings. The kind you exhibited in the restaurant."

"Let's just forget the restaurant, okay? I am not lusting after Crispin Abeli, Shayna McWright."

"Prove it!"

CHAPTER EIGHTEEN

"This is the lowest level of blackmail, Shayna McWright," Amina grumbled as she wound down the car window to talk to the approaching watchman.

"Mr. Abeli, please. He's expecting Shayna McWright," Amina said in Lingala when the watchman bent down to her window. The watchman's eyes took in Amina, Shayna and the entire interior of the car in one quick sweep, and then came to rest on Amina's again.

"I'm sorry, Madame. *Patron* is not at home," he said officiously.

Amina turned to Shayna with a triumphant smile. "Apparently he's not at home. Let's go."

"That's a crock. Ask him if he's sure. Ask him if he'll be back soon."

"Is he expected back shortly?"

"Oh yes, miss. Any time now. In fact, he told me to expect you. You can wait inside."

"I got that much," Shayna said smugly before Amina could translate.

Amina cocked an eyebrow at her. "You're quick," she said. "All right, come on." She sighed in resignation.

"He's only a man, Amina. A gorgeous, gloriously rich man who excites the hell out of you," Shayna teased.

"I'll turn this car right around if you don't stop."

"Okay! Okay! I won't talk about it anymore…not today, at least," Shayna muttered.

"I heard that."

They drove into the compound. The watchman directed the car to a spot in the shade.

"Shayna, you'll do all the talking, okay? I'm just your chauffeur and photographer for the day, got it?

Amina kept up her fussing as they were admitted to the house. Shayna ignored her. "Oh this is nice!" she exclaimed, taking in the architecture, the layout, the furnishings. "Now this bespeaks a man of great depth."

"Would you care to wait on the verandah, miss?" Mizele spoke his finest French. He was eager to impress these two beautiful, obviously American women, especially the one who spoke to him in Lingala. He led them across the living room and through the French doors to a wide marble verandah. The verandah overlooked a meticulously manicured lawn, rimmed by clusters of flowering plants. A stone walkway led from the verandah stairs to a swimming pool at far end of the lawn.

"My God, how beautiful! Amina, look at those exotic flowers!" Shayna said.

"It *is* lovely," Amina said in a low voice. "And peaceful."

Amina ran her fingers along one of the pink marble columns and leaned against it. It was as if some force was propelling them together: first, The Baobab, then the clinic, now here she was in his home, in his garden, in his intimate space. His eyes flashed across her mind and she shivered. *For God's sake, get a grip, Amina,* she scolded herself silently. *You're going way overboard. Men like Crispin Abeli have the world at their feet and all its women to choose from. They don't think twice about the ordinary women they see in homely little restaurants in Harlem, even if they look at them that way.* She took a deep breath and followed Shayna along the stone path toward the pool.

"I could take off my clothes and jump right in," Shayna said as Amina caught up with her. She turned to Amina and squeezed her hand.

"Amina, thanks for doing this. I know I conned you into coming but I had to. The truth is, I need you with me because I feel so vulnerable. I have this fear that someone might look at me one day and recognize me and say something, and I wouldn't know what to do or say. So I don't want to be alone too much, in case that happens."

"Oh, Shayna. Never mind me. I'm okay, really." Amina squeezed Shayna's hand in return.

"You sure?"

"I'm sure." Amina looked around. "You're right. This really is a beautiful place." She walked over to the bar next to the pool house and sat on a stool, elbows on the counter. Throwing her head back, she closed her eyes and took several deep breaths of the jasmine scent that hung in the air. She had seen the jasmine trees in the courtyard. There was another one at the bottom of the lawn.

Shayna stood beside the pool looking at the water.

"Something to drink, miss?" Mizele had come up quietly and slipped behind the bar.

"Oh, yes, please. A Primus. Want anything to drink, Shayna? I'm having a Primus."

"I'll have one too," Shayna said, approaching the bar. "Your *patron* won't be long, will he?" Shayna said to Mizele in broken Lingala.

"No, Miss." Mizele smiled appreciatively at her effort. He served them and left. They sipped the cold beer.

"Wow! It's hard to believe we're in Africa. Not just in Africa. In the Congo, a country that's supposed to be sinking into economic hell," Shayna said as she looked around the bar.

"You know, Amina, it's hard for me to accept that I'm part of this country—actually linked to it by birth and by blood—not by some romantic fixation on Africa as the Motherland," she continued. "I can't believe that these people and these singular things that shape their lives, that I am of all this. It seems so unreal.

I mean, we're talking about me. *Me*, Shayna McWright! Janice McWright's daughter. This can't possibly be where I began. The only reason I should be here is to get a story, like I'm doing now. That's the me that I'm relating to in this country, the objective journalist chasing leads in Africa, the wretched continent. I'll write one hell of a story and the nightmare will be all over. I'll have my life back. Shayna McWright, Black American elite."

Amina remained silent, allowing Shayna to vent. She often wondered how Shayna felt, really felt, about being Congolese. But she never asked. *Shayna would talk about it when she was ready*, she told herself.

"Sometimes I feel disloyal to Janice just by being here. I mean, she never told me about all this, so she obviously didn't want me to know. She buried it. So why shouldn't I? Hilton said I should. Maybe he was right. It's so confusing." She raised her eyes from the frothy amber swirls in her glass and looked at Amina with a half smile. "So you see, if someone says to me one day: 'you came back,' or 'you look so much like your mother,' meaning my Congolese mother, I don't know how I would handle it. I just don't know."

"Being Congolese doesn't change who you are, Shayna. There are no initiations to go through, no testifying to do. And you don't have to prove anything to anybody—Congolese or American.

Just be yourself. Sure, you've got a whole new world to explore. But that's only if you choose to do so. And if you choose to do so, it should be on your timetable, nobody else's."

"You love this country, don't you?"

"Yes, I do. I also love my mother's country, although I relate to it in a different way because I've never lived there. None of that makes me any less Guyanese than my mother. And I'm no less Congolese than my father is just because I left here as a child. I accept that I have been shaped by three cultures: Congolese, Guyanese, and American. And they aren't fighting each other inside me. They're just there in one big mix. Actually, I think the mixed product is pretty magnificent."

"Thank you, Amina," she said.

Amina smiled at her. She stood up and stretched. "Mr. Abeli should be here soon. It's almost 5:30."

"Look at those Chinese swords on the wall. I guess he collects them," Shayna said, gazing at the wall behind the bar.

Amina's eyes followed the direction of Shayna's gaze. "Why, those are tai chi swords," she said in delight. She got up and walked over to the wall to examine the swords more closely.

Shayna was surprised. "Tai chi? I thought that was just a slow dance people in China do in the park early in the morning. A form of exercise. Where do swords come in?"

"Most people know very little about tai chi. It's actually a martial art. If you speed up the moves, you've got full self-defense, my girl." Amina was examining the swords closely.

"And how did you come to know so much about it?"

"I have been practicing tai chi for years. Every day, in fact. You haven't seen me because I do it early in the morning in my room or downstairs when you're still asleep."

Amina reached up and gently removed one of the straight swords. A red tassel was tied to the hilt. "Nice," she said, drawing the sword out of its scabbard and turning it this way and that.

"So you really know how to use that?"

"Uh-huh," Amina said, executing a few moves. "Let's see if he has any music. I'll show you. I can use the practice."

She went behind the bar and thumbed through the stack of CDs, finally selecting one. "Here's one I know. Temple music. Now let's see if I can operate this high-tech player." She fiddled with the player for a few minutes. "We're all set. Hit this button when I say ready."

She took off her sandals, moved aside the tables and chairs and took up the starting position. She nodded to Shayna. The music opened with five gongs. Amina began to execute the forty-two moves of the straight sword form. She was light and agile, moving low and slow like a cat. Her eyes were riveted on an imaginary foe off the tip of the long blade. You could almost feel the energy move around her. The sword became an extension of her arm as she swung, circled and thrust. Shayna was mesmerized by Amina's gracefulness and the effect created by the haunting music of the monks.

Crispin was mesmerized too as he watched from the verandah. He walked slowly and without a sound toward them as Amina finished the form, bringing the sword back to her side in the same position as when she had begun.

"My God, Amina! That was beautiful. You are really good!" Shayna said applauding.

"Yes, you really are."

Amina and Shayna swung around at the sound of Crispin's voice.

"Sorry. I didn't mean to startle you," he said, seeing the expression on Amina's face. "I apologize for not being here when you arrived. Something came up and I had to run out," he said, smiling at both of them. He extended his hand to Shayna. "I'm Crispin Abeli."

"Shayna McWright. Pleased to meet you. We didn't mind the wait, actually," Shayna said, shaking his hand.

"I can see that," he said. He turned to Amina and bowed. "Osu!" he said, acknowledging her martial arts skill with the traditional Japanese expression.

"Osu!" Amina replied, returning the bow.

"I'm honored to meet you, Dr. Milenga. I see you are a student of tai chi. What a delightful surprise," he said, fixing his eyes intently on her.

"I—please, call me Amina. I hope you don't mind my troubling your swords. It's a beautiful collection," Amina said nervously.

"And I'm Crispin. No. I don't mind you using my swords." Once again, he had her trapped in his gaze.

"Er, for the record, Mr. Abeli, I dragged Amina here against her will to be my photographer," Shayna said quickly, determined to avoid a repeat of the scene at The Baobab.

"Photographer? Is there no end to your surprises, Dr. Amina?"

"I'm just an amateur, really. I hope I won't disappoint you."

"Highly unlikely. Shall we go inside? It's very hot out here. Much cooler inside."

#

Crispin ended the interview precisely twenty minutes after it had begun, without admitting that he was involved in a consortium to buy the Brazilian shipping line. True, he conceded that the sale of the Brazilian shipping line was an extremely exciting development in global transportation. But he didn't dwell on the subject. Instead, he deftly switched the conversation to the modernization of the Port of Matadi, Congo's only seaport on the Atlantic Ocean. He talked about the need for a twenty-first century overhaul of sub-Saharan Africa's seaports in general, not only the physical structures, but also the administrative policies and processes as well.

He gave his views of the future of the Panama Canal, which came under Panamanian control on January 1, 2000. The U.S. should have ceded the waterway to the Panamanians long ago, he argued. "The Panamanians will do a hell of a job with the canal and they'll gain a lot economically in the process. They'll open up the canal to all sorts of innovative investment. Shipping—no, transportation is what determines the economic wellbeing of a country," he said.

"Do your business associates share the view that the sale of the Brazilian shipping line is an exciting development?" Shayna threw the question out when he paused to sip the drink Mizele brought him.

Crispin took it in cool stride. "I have many business associates. I can hardly speak for them."

Shayna reeled off the names of the men she had seen him with at The Baobab. "Did the shipping line come up in your discussions when you met with these men last month at The Baobab?"

Crispin put down his glass slowly and smiled. "Ah!

The Baobab," he said, a look of pleasure crossing his face.

The clicking of Amina's camera stopped abruptly. Crispin and Shayna turned to look at her at the same time. Amina fumbled with the camera.

"Sorry," she said. "Just a minor adjustment here. Please continue."

"I hope I will get to see all of those pictures, Amina. You've used up an entire roll already. Do you find me *that* fascinating?" Crispin said playfully.

"It's up to Shayna whether you see the pictures or not. It's her film, or rather, her newspaper's film," Amina said crisply, ignoring his last question. She pointed the camera at him and started clicking again.

Crispin gave a little laugh and turned back to Shayna. "I'm not sure my business associates would appreciate my disclosing to a journalist what we did or did not discuss in a private meeting, Shayna."

"Well, the word in New York is that you've all formed a consortium to buy the shipping line. Is that true?"

"No comment."

"Ambassador d'Andrade won't comment on that question either. Is he sworn to secrecy?"

"I have no control over what Ambassador d'Andrade says or does not say."

"Do you think there should be direct shipping from South America—say Brazil, for example—to Africa?"

"Of course!"

"Is that what you would do if you owned that Brazilian line?"

"I would not want to answer a question like that without having studied the line and a host of relevant conditions."

"You're saying that you haven't done so."

"Is that a statement or a question?"

"Do you think a non-European, non-Japanese or non-American consortium would stand a chance in the bidding?"

"Why wouldn't it?"

"Would you like to see such a consortium in the bidding?"

"Wouldn't everyone? Isn't 'diversity' all the rage these days?"

The cat-and-mouse interview continued until Crispin looked at his watch and called time. Shayna was disappointed but not crushed. Crispin's skill in dodging reporters' questions was legend. She certainly had enough to build a decent front page story, dressed up with Amina's exclusive pictures.

Crispin insisted that they stay for dinner. Amina objected immediately. It would be very late by the time they finished. It would not be wise for two women to be driving home alone that late at night, she said.

"You're very kind, but Amina is right," Shayna said. "We really should be going. We've already taken up more of your time than you planned to give us."

"Well then, will you be my guests on Sunday evening? Musana Holdings is hosting a dinner for an investment delegation from the United Arab Emirates. It will be at the clubhouse at the top of the Centre du Commerce International."

Amina and Shayna looked at each other. *Yes,* Shayna's wide open eyes declared. *Sure, why not*, Amina's said in return.

"We'd love to," Shayna said to Crispin.

#

"I pulled it off, Amina!' Shayna was ecstatic all the way home.

"Pulled what off? He didn't give away anything."

"He sure did. Maybe not exactly what I wanted, but I got enough. He was so intent on staying away from the Brazilian story that he gave me more information than he's ever given any reporter anywhere. Besides, I'll be watching to see how much time he spends with the Dubai shipping guy on that UAR delegation Sunday. Dubai's got one of the busiest port and shipping operations in the world."

"What makes you so sure someone from Dubai will be there?

"Crispin's got close friends in Dubai. He went to school with one of the younger sheikhs. They're Crispin's kind of people: sharp, visionary, thinkers outside the box—very comfortable with their "Arabness." They've gone way beyond oil, into tourism, trade, all kinds of manufacturing. Now they've surprised the whole shipping world with their preparations to accommodate the new generation of big container ships. Nobody expected that part of the world to be servicing those ships."

"You know a lot about Crispin, don't you."

"Yep. From covering my beat at the newspaper."

"So you think he's in on the Brazilian deal and may be getting some kind of help from the sheikhs?"

"You bet he's in on it! It makes perfect sense with his philosophy. He and that whole gang he was with at The Baobab are in on it. They're tight, those guys."

"The bidding's going on now, isn't it?"

"As we speak. They should announce the winner next month."

"Think he'll get it?"

"It's hard to say. Everybody wants it bad. It's a pretty nasty fight, I hear. The Third World is circling the wagons and the First World is pretty worried. Lots of stuff going on under the table. But they say Crispin Abeli always gets what he wants. I know the Brazilians genuinely like him."

"He's very likeable, no doubt about that."

"Yeah. You were eating him up with that camera. And boy does he have the hots for you!"

"You really think so?"

"Didn't you see the way he looked at you *again*? And how about that look on his face when he said 'Ah, The Baobab.'" Her imitation of Crispin was near perfect. "Stopped you dead in your tracks, didn't he?"

Amina laughed. "I must have looked like a real fool fumbling with the camera. But yeah, I like him."

"See! He doesn't bite after all. And isn't there just a teensy weensy bit of lust in there somewhere?"

"There is some, yes. A lot, actually."

"Whew! All of a sudden this Kinshasa is wicked!"

#

Crispin rocked back and forth in his favorite rocking chair, looking at his watch impatiently every few minutes. Finally, he picked up the phone and dialed. She picked up on the third ring.

"Bonsoir! Qui est à l'appareil?"

"Hello, Amina. Crispin here. I hope I didn't disturb you."

"Crispin! Oh!" It was the last voice she expected to hear.

"I wanted to be sure you arrived home safely."

"Oh yes. Yes, we arrived safely, thank you. No, you didn't disturb me. It's—it's very considerate of you to call."

"It's the least I could do. You seemed anxious about getting home."

"I hope I was not rude. I did not mean to be."

"No, you weren't rude, Amina."

She liked the way he said her name.

"I'm looking forward to seeing you on Sunday," he said.

"Yes, so are we. Thank you again for inviting us."

"I will send my car for you. At six o'clock. Is that okay?"

"Oh no! There's no need. It would be no trouble for us to drive. It's not far from my home."

"But then, if you drive you will want to run away again."

She heard the tease in his voice. It excited her.

"Nobody ran away. And surely you're not suggesting that you would hold us against our will, are you?"

"I would never hold you against your will, Amina."

That statement was way too loaded. Her mouth dared not respond. But her body did. Instantly, she wanted him so much she could almost feel his body against hers.

"It would be no trouble to send my car for you, Amina. May I?" he said when she didn't respond.

Amina swallowed. "Okay, Crispin. You win. Your car, then." Was her voice too husky?

"Good. I'm very glad we met, Amina."

"Yes, Shayna and I were delighted to meet you too. It was good of you to give her the interview. And you have such a lovely home."

"There you go again. Running away." He sounded amused.

"What *is* it with you and this running away?" she said defensively.

"Amina," he said firmly, "I'm saying that I, Crispin Abeli, am glad that I met *you*, Amina Milenga."

She said nothing. He waited.

"Crispin?"

"Yes, Amina?"

"I'm glad I met you, too. Good night."

Her voice was at the depth he knew he reached in her that day at The Baobab. It excited him all over again.

"Good night, Amina."

They would fill each other's dreams again.

CHAPTER NINETEEN

Gaston's once-over was so shameless that Shayna launched into a hip-bobbing runway strut across the living room. At the far end of the room, she turned expertly to show off every angle, then hip-bobbed back. She came to a stop right in front of Gaston, settling into a final pose that said "Well?"

Instead of being embarrassed, Gaston broke into a wide grin and applauded her performance enthusiastically. Shayna gaped at him. Before she could close her mouth, he took her hand and raised it to his lips with an exaggerated bow.

"Gaston Tambwe at your service, mademoiselle McWright." He spoke in English with a heavy French accent.

Shayna couldn't help but laugh. "Shayna," she said, dropping into an equally exaggerated curtsey.

Gaston held out his arm in a perfectly placed crook and Shayna slipped hers into it. He was about her age, she guessed.

He was dressed in an understated but impeccably cut European suit, with a perfectly matched pale-green silk shirt open at the neck. She couldn't identify his cologne. Maybe it was aftershave. Whatever it was, it was very subtle and very masculine and very appealing. He wasn't a knockout in the looks department, but he exuded such virility and strength, and at the same time such joie de vivre, that Shayna at once felt drawn to him. Not so much in a sexual way, but in a way that made her feel secure. The way she felt with Hilton in the days right after her mother's death.

The ride to the convent turned into her first real sightseeing tour since her arrival in Kinshasa. Gaston knew the city inside out and, it seemed, everybody in it. He pointed out every building and residence that would interest an American journalist, adding all the juicy tidbits about their occupants past and present. He repeatedly interrupted his narrative to shout back a greeting to the men, women and children who hailed him. He explained the nuances of the body language and subtle rituals that were being played out in the streets. Every relationship, no matter what kind, stood on ceremony, he said. Shayna marveled that even in the midst of such a political and economic quagmire, ancient social courtesies still stood their ground.

At a busy stretch along Boulevard Trente Juin, Gaston pulled up beside a group of teenage boys sitting beside the road. They were peddling a motley assortment of empty bottles, loose cigarettes, and matches. He signaled to the one who seemed to be the oldest. The boy jumped up immediately and approached the car with a wide smile. He greeted first Gaston and then Shayna, in softly spoken Lingala. Gaston spoke to him for a few minutes, then drove off.

"What was that about?" Shayna asked.

"Oh, I just wanted to make sure that all is well with him, his family, and his friends."

"That all is well?"

"Yes, that no one had died."

"You know him?"

"Yes, his father has worked in my family's textile factory for years."

"He didn't ask you for money and you didn't offer him any. Why?"

"Why should he ask and why should I give? He is working. He is not a beggar. There are other ways to make sure food is in his belly."

"Like what?"

"His father and all the other workers pool their money to buy food in bulk every month from a wholesale distribution center we own. Mostly cassava flour, rice, beans, oil, and salted fish. We give them an extra discount because they are our workers. And to show our gratitude for their business, because we know our competition has been undercutting us, we add some extras like cans of tomato paste and onions. The cigarettes and matches those boys are selling are bought in bulk from us the same way."

Shayna closed her eyes and leaned back in the seat. She had not felt this relaxed in weeks. Finally, they arrived at the Convent.

"Nervous?" Gaston asked as he drove through the gates.

"Yes."

"Don't be. Either they have something for us or they don't. If they do, we move forward. If they don't, we still move forward."

"Move forward with what if the nuns have nothing to tell us?"

"Keep hope alive!" he said, mimicking Jesse Jackson's exhortation to the Black community. The phrase was such a fixture in the civil rights leader's speeches that Africans nicknamed him "Keep Hope Alive."

Shayna shook her head and laughed.

A young Congolese novice admitted them to the Convent and led them to a sitting room, where she asked Gaston to wait with the other visitors. She gestured to Shayna to follow her through heavy wooden doors. When the doors closed behind them, the novice told Shayna in French that she was taking her to see the Reverend Mother. She spoke so quietly that Shayna had to bend toward her to hear what she was saying.

They walked down a hallway to the Reverend Mother's study. The novice knocked softly on the door and opened it slowly. She signaled to Shayna to enter ahead of her.

The room was large, with heavy ebony furniture and faded woolen carpets that looked like they had been there since early colonial days. The Reverend Mother sat behind a desk that faced the door, her back erect. She was an elderly Belgian, with berry-brown skin from decades in the tropics. Her elbows rested on the desk. Her hands were clasped.

As Shayna and the novice came in, she leaned forward slowly and rested her chin on her thumbs, studying Shayna with piercing eyes. Shayna approached the desk nervously. The Reverend Mother's face remained expressionless. She was skilled in the art of wielding power with the slightest of gestures and with silence. The novice crossed herself and genuflected. Shayna automatically went through the same motions. The novice backed silently toward the door, genuflected again and left the room. Shayna stood still, head still slightly bowed, waiting to be addressed. She felt like she was back at elementary school in D.C. She would bear the silence, however long it would be.

"I have waited so long for you to come, Shayna McWright," the Reverend Mother said finally.

#

Amina sat at her desk in the small study in her apartment, listening to Jon Lucien's rendition of "Jinji." She kept a duplicate collection in the apartment of all the music she owned in New York. She decided not to return to the clinic that afternoon. She had gone home for lunch, which she did whenever something was troubling her and she needed to think it through without being distracted.

Crispin Abeli was troubling her today. She kept turning his words over and over in her head: "I, Crispin Abeli, am glad I met you, Amina Milenga." And the way he said "good night." Amina wondered if she was reading too much into all this.

She leaned back in the chair and closed her eyes, savoring the music and the lyrics. She felt the familiar stirring between her legs. She imagined herself making love to Crispin Abeli.

Careful, Amina. The warning sliced through her reverie like a blade of cold steel. She opened her eyes. Yes, she should be careful, she told herself. If what Dr. Charles said was true—and there was no reason for him to speak otherwise—Crispin may be interested in nothing more than her professional expertise. *So what about the scene in the restaurant in Harlem? What was that all about?* she mused.

Amina reached for the CD's remote control player and rewound the disk to the beginning of "*Jinji.*" She closed her eyes again. Her mind whirled with conflicting emotions. She thought she would have seen Crispin today at the hospital when he went to visit the boy. The nurses said he went every day. *He probably came while I was with Dr. Charles*, she told herself. The minister of health was scheduled to visit next week and for the last two days, she had had long meetings with Dr. Charles and the senior hospital administrators, putting together a report on the conditions at the hospital. She herself stopped by the boy's bed every day on her rounds. His mother was always there, feeding him or lying on a mat on the floor beside the bed.

"Not much more we can do for him. We'll have to discharge him soon," Dr. Charles said when he found her there earlier today. The boy was asleep.

"It's a shame he got no help when he was much younger. There should be some sort of facility in Kinshasa to care for children like him. I've seen far too many deformed kids around this city. Many of them would do well with the right therapy," she replied.

"That's exactly what Crispin Abeli said. About a facility, I mean. He wants to refurbish the old American children's hospital, you know."

Amina's skin tingled at the mention of his name. "He does?" she said, gazing at the boy in the bed.

"Yes, he does. If he really does it, that would be one good thing that came out of this accident."

Crispin found me as a result of that accident, Amina thought.

"Of course, we would have to find someone to run such a facility," Dr. Charles was saying.

Amina said nothing. She had a good idea where this was leading.

"Amina, you would be the best person to do it. I told Crispin so."

Her heart slowed. "You told Crispin so?"

"Yes. We talked about it the very day of the accident."

"The very day of the accident?"

"Yes, Amina, my dear, do stop repeating everything I say. Funny you should do that, though. Crispin does the same thing. Did you know that? Of course you don't. You don't know each other." Dr. Charles knitted his brow and shook his head, as if he had just made an amazing discovery. "Anyway, how does the idea sound to you?" he continued.

"You mean the idea of refurbishing the clinic? I think it's a wonderful idea?" Amina said. Her thoughts were far away. *Is that why he's being so nice to me? God, I hope not. I hope it's more than that. I want him to like me for me. Not for some job.*

"Well?"

"I'm sorry, Dr. Charles. What did you say?"

"I said what do you think of the idea of you heading the children's hospital when it's refurbished?"

"But I don't live here. And I have my practice in New York. I can't abandon it. Surely you can find someone else."

"We're talking about the best qualified person, not the one who is most readily available. And you wouldn't have to live here necessarily, Amina. Doesn't someone run your practice for you when you are here in Kinshasa?"

"Tell you what, Dr. Charles. I promise I will think about it. Is that fair enough?"

"That's fair enough. Take your time. Crispin will want to speak to you about it himself. You'll meet him soon, I'm sure."

"Did he say that?"

"Say what?"

"That he wants to speak to me about it?"

"Well, I strongly suggested the idea to him and he didn't dismiss it. He was quite enthusiastic, in fact."

The more Amina thought of that conversation with Dr. Charles, the more she argued to herself that Crispin's interest in her was purely clinical, so to speak. She was just another potential pawn to move somewhere into his empire, she told herself miserably.

Abruptly, she reached for the telephone and dialed the number for the nurses' station in her department. The head nurse herself answered. She was a pleasant, middle-aged woman who joined the staff as a nurse's assistant nearly twenty years ago.

Amina told her she would be out for the rest of the day, but could be beeped or telephoned at home if she was needed. The nurse told her all was quiet, as Amina expected.

It was one of those god-awful nuisance days.

Just before noon, military Jeeps began racing through the streets, scattering man and beast alike in their path. They all seemed to be headed in the same direction: toward the presidential palace. Groups of soldiers trotted behind them, armed to the teeth. Noisy black helicopters circled in the skies, dipping and dropping as if their pilots were trying to outdo each other, menacing the population. The television and radio stations kept blacking out, though no explanation was being given for the heightened military activity. Word soon spread of an imminent attack on the city by the rebels. Everyone fled to their homes.

Normally, Amina would have gone back to the clinic anyway. She had experienced such days before. As far as she and most people she knew were concerned, this was another show of might against the underground opposition's calls for an overthrow of the government. No formal curfew would be announced. None would be needed. The people would simply lock themselves in and leave the roads to the military. Everything would be back to normal by tomorrow morning.

But today, Crispin aside, Amina was worried about Shayna and wanted to be there when she and Gaston got back. Shayna didn't know about the military's shenanigans. She may panic even in Gaston's capable hands. And what if—God forbid—there <u>really</u> was something going on with the rebels?

She jumped when the phone rang.

"Amina! Thank God! Are you OK? Merry's on the line too." Jamillah yelled above the static on the line.

"Heyyyyy! Lord, it's good to hear from you two! How's our baby doing, Merry?"

"Fine and kicking hard. Amina, how are you? How's Shayna? We're hearing all sorts of crazy news about that place. Why don't you two come home?" Merry's voice was filled with worry.

The static stopped suddenly while she was speaking, so the words "come home" came through really loud.

"Oooh my ear! Don't shout, Merry. Shayna's fine. She's chasing down a lead with my cousin," Amina said. "There's nothing unusual going on here except for the military chasing all over the place. And there's nothing strange about that. Why? What are they saying on that side?"

"That rebels are attacking Kinshasa. That there's widespread disenchantment with the government. That people have had it up to their necks with all the human rights abuses. And that the military is out in force in the streets and American citizens are being urged to take safety precautions. It took us hours to get through to you," Jamillah said.

"Christ! They make it seem as if the place is about to blow. Believe me, it's not as bad as all that. Not a thing is going on beyond the usual muscle flexing by the military. It'll all blow over in a few hours."

"Well, just be careful. And have you guys heard the latest on the car crash that killed Shayna's mother?"

"What latest?"

"Sophie St. Cyr broke the news on CNN today that U.S. intelligence is calling it an assassination. Apparently they found that the brakes in the car had been tampered with. And here's another shocker. They're saying a Congolese national may have had something to do with it."

"Oh my God! An *assassination*! And a *Congolese* is involved?" Amina said incredulously.

"Yep! That's what they're saying."

"But where—why—assassination for what? And why a Congolese?"

"They're saying the last person known to have anything to do with the car was this Congolese maintenance worker and he has disappeared. Naturally, that makes him the number one suspect."

"But that just does not make sense. Why would a Congolese—since when do Africans go about assassinating Americans? Or taking on America, period! We're too busy killing off each other. I just can't believe it. Do they even suggest a motive?" Amina's voice was almost shrill.

The static erupted again. For a moment, it was impossible to hear anything else.

"Jamillah? Merry? Are you there?" Amina shouted.

"Hello! Hello! Amina! Are you there?"

Jamillah's voice began to penetrate the static.

"Yes, Yes! I can hear you. Barely, but I can still hear. I was saying I find it hard to believe that a Congolese would have anything to do with the death of Janice McWright. We haven't heard anything like that over here. Not even through the grapevine," Amina said.

"Amina, let's put your beliefs aside. The main thing is, Washington is talking assassination and that means they'll be out for blood. Look at what you've got. The U.S. made it clear they're unhappy with the way Kabila is handling things. They're making all kinds of human rights abuse noises. Now I don't want to say this is the way it is, but wouldn't it be very convenient to implicate Kabila in something like that? All they would have to do is drop a few strong hints to the usual suspects in the press about a state-sponsored hit and let them run with it? Who knows what could go down over there?" Jamillah sounded very convincing, as if she had thought through the whole thing before the phone call.

"Maybe there *is* a connection between the CNN report and what you say is going on over there, Amina. All that stuff about the military running around," Merry said worriedly.

"Calm down, you two. Calm down. The Americans aren't going to do anything here. And *if* they are going to do anything, they'd make sure American citizens are out of harm's way. Especially Janice McWright's daughter."

"I guess you're right," Merry agreed reluctantly.

"Yeah, I guess so," Jamillah said, still sounding doubtful.

"So how are they linking this Congolese to the crash? Who is he supposed to be anyway?"

"All they said is that a Congolese with Belgian citizenship was hired at the Embassy a few months before as some sort of outdoor maintenance man. It *would* be like Janice McWright to okay the hiring of someone from the Congo, wouldn't it? Maybe she even knew this guy or maybe his people, from way back when she was there. She could practice her Lingala..."

"Jamillah would you cut the editorializing and give me just the facts? Sheesh!" Amina broke in.

"Okay, okay. What they said was that one of his duties was to clean the cars of the senior people at the embassy, including the ambassador's. He hasn't been seen since the day of the crash."

Jamillah and Merry waited for Amina to speak.

"That's bad," Amina said finally.

"Sure is," Merry said emphatically.

"Bad for Congo."

"Bad for Congo indeed," Merry repeated.

"So did they say anything else?"

"Just that they're looking for him. You know what *that* means. A dragnet from here to God knows where that will haul in a heap of folks over there."

"Shayna doesn't know this. At least she didn't when I left for the clinic this morning." Amina said.

"Well, she'll know soon enough. How do you think she'll take it?" Merry asked.

"Wish I knew. She's still trying to sort out what being part Congolese will mean for her life."

"Where *is* she, by the way?"

"She's following up a lead on her birth mother. My cousin took her to a convent. He thinks the nuns may know something. He's pretty sure Shayna was baptized before Janice McWright took her to the States."

"Hmmm. Makes sense."

"It's the best we've got so far. It's been brick wall after brick wall."

"This is all so depressing. We'll get all the facts soon enough. Let's change the subject," Merry said.

"Yes, let's," Jamillah agreed. "So have you met him yet, Amina?"

"Him who?"

"Crispin Abeli."

Shayna told them about the restaurant incident when they all went out together before she and Amina left for Kinshasa. They teased Amina mercilessly.

"Amina, you're not saying anything."

"Well, I saw him."

"You mean you saw him like on a date?"

"No, Jamillah! I saw him at the hospital."

"So wuh happen? Wuh you do?" Merry said excitedly, lapsing into her Jamaican patois.

"I ran."

"Yuh do wha?"

"I ran." Amina started to laugh.

"You lie!"

"I'm telling you. I know he saw me, but this other doctor came over and distracted him. I left the room the moment he turned his head."

"Was he there looking for you?"

"Of course not. It was just a coincidence. His car hit a woman and her child and he brought them to the hospital. The boy was in pretty bad shape."

"So, Amina, sweet dear. How long do you think you can run? He *knows* where you are now. And he has good reason to be at the hospital."

"Every day if he wants to," Merry said.

"I know," Amina said.

Jamillah and Merry heard the worry in her voice. They knew the deal. Amina had not yet completely healed after Michael. She has to learn to trust all over again.

"She's got a three-inch-thick wall around her heart that no one's going to tear down without a fight," Jamillah told Shayna.

"But I did meet him after that," Amina said in a rush.

Before Jamillah and Merry could say anything, she told them about Shayna's interview and Crispin's invitation for Sunday. She didn't mention his phone call. She was beginning to think she was reading too much into it. She hadn't even told Shayna about it. Well, not all of it. Only that he called to see if they got home all right.

"You got something sexy to wear on Sunday, right?" Merry demanded.

"Sexy in the Western sense is out of the question, Merry. These are Muslims, remember?"

"Wear one of your Congolese outfits. That's sexy and demure all wrapped up in one," Jamillah said with finality. She continued almost on the same breath. "You sure he ain't lookin' at Shayna, right? Or that *she* ain't lookin' at him, right, Amina? Our girl may have changed for the better in many ways, but we don't know how much she's changed in *that* department. She had a killer rep on campus, remember?"

Amina laughed. "No. I don't think it's like that with Shayna now. She's got a boyfriend who asked her to marry him. She wants to, but not 'till she knows more about her Congolese background."

"Just don't let her get too friendly, anyway. Privenshan bettah dan cure, nuh so it go?" Merry cautioned.

The static was starting again.

"I may lose you for good this time, guys," Amina said as the scratching grew louder.

"We love you, Amina. You and Shayna come home as soon as they tell you..."

The line went dead. Amina kept holding on in case the connection was re-established. She hung up when a high-pitched tone tore into her ear. She went into the living room and turned on the television. World news should be coming on any moment now. She sat down and half-listened to the recap of the local news.

She was more worried than she had let on to Merry and Jamillah. She had a feeling Shayna would be furious and bitter when she found out that a Congolese might have been involved in her mother's death. Shayna was still very much a child of America. Even if she found her birth mother, she didn't have to do a thing about being Congolese.

Maybe she won't find out, Amina mused. *Maybe by the time she hears about this guy, they will have ruled him out anyway. I just can't believe a Congolese would do that. Why should I bother her with what's nothing more that a suspicion at this point?*

Her conscience came out swinging. *Surely you're going to tell her, Amina! You've got to tell her. No I don't. Yes you do. Why? Because if you don't and she finds out that you knew all along she probably will never speak to you again. How do you know that? I just know it. I feel it. How would she know that you knew all along anyway?*

Amina's continued debating with herself until she realized the world news was over. Local news was on now. *No matter. I'll catch whatever I missed in the recap*, she sighed.

The recap carried it in two crisp sentences: "Washington. A State Department spokesman said today that a Congolese national may have been involved in the recent death of the United States ambassador to Belgium. The spokesman declined to name the individual, saying the person was only a suspect and was being sought for questioning."

The phone rang again. Amina stared at it, her heart beating fast. It rang again. She took a deep breath and picked it up.

"Hâlo?" she said, expecting the caller to speak French.

"Dr. Milenga, this is Tom Miller at the U.S. Embassy. May I speak to Miss McWright, please?"

Amina was not surprised by the call. Come to think of it, they should have gotten in touch with Shayna long before the TV broadcast the news to the whole country.

"I'm afraid she's not here," she said coolly.

"Do you know where she is?" Tom Miller's voice was equally cool.

"Yes, I do. Is she in danger, Mr. Miller? Because if she is, this phone call is a little late, isn't it?" Miller's crew-cut embassy voice irritated her and she did not hide it. Where did he get off with his attitude, calling this late in the game?

"It's important that we speak with her as soon as possible, Dr. Milenga. Is there any way we can reach her?" Miller said, ignoring Amina's question.

"She left for the Franciscan Convent around ten this morning. She's with my cousin. She may still be there. I don't know." Amina replied icily.

"Thank you, Dr. Milenga. If she comes home soon, please let her know that we need to speak with her. Thank you." He rang off abruptly.

"Jackass!" Amina said into the dead phone and slammed it down. She was all nerves. They'll want Shayna to leave the country for sure, she mused. They'll probably want all Americans to leave.

"Crap!" she said. "Crap! Crap! Crap!"

CHAPTER TWENTY

Shayna felt her heart stop. It started again, slamming against the walls of her chest. She stood motionless, her eyes wide and staring at the Reverend Mother, her fingers curled into a death-like grip on her purse.

The Reverend Mother drew herself up from her chair and moved from behind her desk. Her face was a mass of wrinkles, like spider webs spun out of control. Her gray habit seemed to cover nothing but bones. She stood in front of the desk, erect and serious, her eyes never leaving Shayna's.

Her movements shook Shayna out of her daze. She blinked and opened her mouth to say something, but nothing came out. She clamped her mouth shut and tried again. Nothing. Her chin began to quiver.

"Your mother Janice told me that one day you would come. I had almost given up hope of being alive when you did. When I heard the news of her death, I knew you would be coming soon."

The nun's strong voice belied her frail appearance. She was Belgian, but she spoke faultless English with a slight British accent.

"Come." She held out her arms and Shayna move closer, tears spilling down her cheeks. She bowed her head to receive the blessing.

"I prayed for her soul. I knew her well. She worshipped here," the Reverend Mother said, holding Shayna with both hands at arm's length and looking deep into her eyes.

Shayna was afraid to speak. Whatever she tried to say would come out in a sob. She knew it. The Reverend Mother guided her to the little sitting area, motioned her to sit on the faded couch, and then sat down beside her.

"How lovely you are, Shayna Yasmin. Janice brought you to me about a month after you were found. She had already adopted you and wanted you to be baptized in our cathedral."

Shayna tried to speak again, but the Reverend Mother held up her hand.

"Let me finish first, my child. Your natural mother also wanted you to be baptized before you left the country. It said so in the note she left on you."

Shayna drew her breath. "You know about the note, Reverend Mother?"

"Yes. Here it is." She withdrew a plastic envelope from the folds of her habit and held it out to Shayna. "Janice wanted it to be kept at the Convent here with a copy of your baptismal certificate. She said to give it all to you when you came."

Shayna took the envelope and held it with trembling hands in her lap. She looked at it for a long moment. Through the cloudy plastic, she could see the folded, aged notepaper with its safety-pin holes. This was it. The link to her history. A piece of paper that bore the touch, the feelings of the faceless woman who had brought her into this world and whom she once knew as "mother." This woman would have held her close, would have loved her, and would have cried for her. The only woman she knew as "mother" also touched this piece of paper. Two women, two mothers, both somewhere in the unknown, yet here in her hands, very much alive.

Shayna raised brimming eyes to the Reverend Mother. The old nun looked back at her steadily. Shayna knew that look so well. It was the call to strength. She had seen it in the eyes of the nuns at school. And how many times had she seen it in Janice's eyes?

She extracted the note slowly from the envelope and unfolded it gently. The paper was so crisp with age that it started to give at the folds. Shayna moved her fingers slowly back and forth over the tiny holes. Then she stopped suddenly, knitting her brow. Something seemed to tug at her memory. What *is* it? What *is* it? But it was gone almost in the same instant. Like those dreams that drift away from you when morning comes, fading before you can catch it in your consciousness.

Her thoughts returned to the room. The Reverend Mother was looking at her thoughtfully. Shayna looked again at the holes in the paper. *It must have been a big diaper pin*, she thought, surprised that she could be so detached at a time like this. The thought of herself in diapers made her smile. She blinked her eyes dry, still smiling, prolonging the moment.

The handwriting was a childlike script. The note itself was written in French, in simple sentences.

> *"I give my baby to you Madame McWright to take to America as your own. Her father is American. He does not know her. He did not want me to have her. Please baptize her at the cathedral in Gombe before you go to America. Her name is Shayna Yasmin."*

Shayna read the note over and over again. "my baby," the woman had called her. And it was she who named her, not Janice McWright.

The Reverend Mother called her by both names. That wasn't unusual in Kinshasa. Your second name was just as important as your first, she learned. Traditionally, the combination identified the specific ancestor after whom you were named. Someone who called you by both names was someone who knew you really well.

Shayna spoke the two names out loud, accenting the "–min" in Yasmin. She liked the name Yasmin. She hated when people pronounced it the wrong way, with the accent on "Yas-" as if they were saying "Jasmine." Aside from the Reverend Mother, she could not recall anyone ever calling her Shayna Yasmin. Not even Janice.

She pressed the note to her bosom and held it there for a long time.

"She didn't give her own name," she said finally, speaking more to herself than to the Reverend Mother.

The Reverend Mother did not speak.

Shayna brought the note up to her nose. Did she imagine the faint fragrance? No. It was there, something she thought she recognized but could not name. Something French. As if anticipating her next question, the Reverend Mother handed her another envelope.

"Your baptismal papers," she said.

Shayna removed the two sheets of paper and studied them. For some reason she had expected more, though she did not know what exactly. Other names, perhaps. People she could track down.

"This was an unusual situation, Shayna. There was no father. Your mother was alone. I, of course, was there and the officiating priest and some of the other nuns. The only other persons there from the American Embassy were the ambassador and his wife as witnesses. And, of course, you know that they have both passed on."

The Reverend Mother seemed adept at anticipating her questions.

"Did you meet her, Reverend Mother?"

"No, my dear. Of course Janice did manage to speak with her, but she did not tell me how or where she found her. I asked her once, but she said it didn't matter and that the woman disappeared without a trace anyway. Even then she did not mention her name. But it would be on the formal adoption papers. I did not see the papers. But I know there is a copy over at…"

A knock on the door interrupted them.

"Come in," the Reverend Mother said.

A pretty middle-aged nun with creamy white skin entered. She crossed herself and genuflected.

"Sister Claire?" the Reverend Mother said.

"Excuse me, Reverend Mother. May I have a word with you?"

"Of course." The Reverend Mother stood up and walked over to Sister Claire, who remained just a few steps inside the door.

Sister Claire spoke to the Reverend Mother quietly in her ear. The Reverend Mother had her back to Shayna so Shayna could not see her expression. After a few minutes, she heard the Reverend Mother say, "Thank you, Sister Claire," and Sister Claire left the room with only the slightest of nods in Shayna's direction. The Reverend Mother crossed the room and stood before Shayna.

"Shayna, you must go to your embassy straight away. There is some news, apparently."

Shayna jumped to her feet.

"News? What news? About my mother?"

"About Janice's death, yes."

Guilt clouded Shayna's face. She had not meant Janice. *How could I be so disloyal to her*, she thought miserably.

"Don't be troubled, Shayna. There can be no disloyalty in a situation such as this," the Reverend Mother said.

Shayna looked at her gratefully. "Do you know what it is?" she asked, grabbing her purse and heading for the door.

"I have no details, no."

Shayna couldn't help but smile. Nuns have this way of letting you save face while telling you that there's no way they're going to give you what you're asking them for. She knew their language well. They spoke it with such grace.

"Thank you for everything, Reverend Mother," Shayna said, and bowed her head for the blessing.

#

Gaston saw the anxiety on Shayna's face, but he asked no questions, not even when she asked if he would mind taking her directly to the American Embassy.

They drove in silence. Shayna's head rested on the back of her seat. Her eyes remained closed.

"They found out something about the car crash that killed my mother in Brussels," she blurted out when they were about a block from the embassy.

Gaston took one hand off the steering wheel, reached for Shayna's and held it tight. He had been in Brussels at the time of the tragedy. He learned from Amina that Shayna was the daughter of the ambassador killed in the crash.

Shayna closed her fingers over Gaston's, grateful for the reassurance of his touch, for his understanding silence. She knew they would always be friends. Gaston knew it, too. They looked at each other at the same time, smiling the way friends do when they realize for the umpteenth time how lucky they were to know each other.

#

"I take it you haven't heard the news, Shayna." Ambassador DeGrasse got to the point immediately after introducing her to Tom Miller, the deputy ambassador. He motioned to them to sit.

They were in DeGrasse's office. Shayna met Tom Miller once before, on her first visit to the Embassy after her arrival in Kinshasa. She disliked him instantly. His voice was irritatingly tight and nasal and officious. And he had this way of looking at you with his steely blue eyes as if you were guilty of treason.

Shayna pegged him right away as "intelligence." She had been to enough American embassies to know how to spot them. One dead giveaway was their lack of deference to the ambassador, though it was barely noticeable to anyone who was not trained to look beyond the surface of things. Miller's lack of deference to DeGrasse was as plain as day to Shayna.

"No, Sir. I haven't. What *is* the news?" She sat erect, steeling herself for whatever was coming.

"Your mother's death may not have been an accident."

Ambassador DeGrasse decided that brutal honesty was the only way to go.

Shayna sat forward sharply, her palms pressing hard on the arms of the chair, as if she would spring up at any moment.

"What? What did you say?"

"Tests showed that the brakes were tampered with," Ambassador DeGrasse said.

Shayna seemed frozen. She squinted at him as if she were registering his words in slow motion, then suddenly slumped back in the chair and covered her face with her hands. *I can't handle this!* her mind screamed. *This is too much...too much for one human being to handle in one day.* For the first time since she arrived in Kinshasa, she yearned for Hilton. Her breathing grew heavy and she shook her head slowly from side to side.

Ambassador DeGrasse felt the fragility of the moment. He stuck to the cold road. Shayna, he knew, had the clinical mind of any good journalist. He would steady her with cold hard facts. Nothing soft. Nothing droopy.

"Here's what we know, Shayna. This guy applied to the embassy for work about three months or so before the tragedy. Said he was looking for work as a maintenance man. He'd worked for years at an American company in Belgium, but had gotten laid off. Had good references, though. The embassy folks checked him out, found him clean and hired him. Likable guy, everybody says. Seems your mother used to practice her Lingala, or what was left of it, with him."

He paused, ostensibly to light his pipe, but really to see what effect his approach was having on Shayna. He looked at her and smiled inwardly. She uncovered her face and was leaning toward him. She knitted her brow impatiently as he sucked and puffed once, twice, a third time. Her breathing quieted.

"He didn't show up for work the day of the crash," he continued, satisfied that Shayna's moment had passed. "But he was there the day before and apparently the last thing he did before leaving was check out your mother's car. Of course, all this came out after they found that the brakes had been messed with, when intelligence started combing through everything for clues. Naturally, they ran double and triple checks on all the non-Americans. They weren't ruling out anything or anyone. That's when everyone realized that our Congolese guy was missing, vanished without a word or a trace, and that he was the last one to touch the car, aside from the chauffeur, of course, who was killed in the crash.

"In all the confusion after the crash, no one had given the maintenance man a second thought. After all the checking and cross checking, his picture finally turned up in a Belgian intelligence file. It was a picture from years ago. He was in the company of a white South African who is said to be the leader of a soldiers-for-hire group that has been training the Congolese rebels in the Shaba region. The maintenance man actually comes from a well-known family of Shaba secessionists. His grandfather was killed during the secession in the 1960s, and then his father and brother were killed in the invasion in the 1970s.

He wasn't on any wanted list or anything. He came to Brussels soon after his father and brother were killed and finished school. Bright, but seemed out of it, his teachers said. Kept pretty much to himself. After school, he bummed around a bit, then got a job as a low-level technician with an American company. He stayed with it until he was laid off when the company fell on hard times.

There was nothing spectacular at all about his life. It was the South African that the Belgians were tailing when that picture was taken here in Brussels. Aside from that, there's nothing more on him. The Belgians kept an eye on him for a while, but he was never seen again with the South Africans or anyone suspect."

Ambassador DeGrasse paused again to puff on his pipe. Shayna uncrossed her ankles then crossed them again. She was fully composed now, her eyes intent on the ambassador's face. Ambassador DeGrasse continued.

"So there you are. Was this guy involved in any way with your mother's death? We can't say for sure, but Washington is calling him a prime suspect. They've put out a net spreading across Europe and into Africa."

Shayna remained silent for a while after he finished. Her head was spinning. She had a million questions, not the least of which was why anyone would want to assassinate her mother.

"Is that the only lead they have?" she asked. "What if this guy had nothing to do with it?"

"We're still looking at a few other things," Tom Miller said curtly.

"Like what?" Shayna said disdainfully. "What's the motive?"

"I'm afraid I can't say," Miller replied with an edge in his voice.

"Oh I bet you can't. Perhaps our superpower intelligence capabilities aren't quite as formidable as we the people are led to believe," she said spiritedly, looking straight at him. The deputy ambassador reddened. His ex-Marine jaw twitched.

"The point is, Shayna, in light of this new evidence, we think you could be in danger in this country," Ambassador DeGrasse said quickly, cutting off the retort that Miller had already opened his mouth to give.

"Why would I be important to this guy or whomever he may be working with, *if* he's working with anybody? If someone was targeting my mother, well, they certainly got her, didn't they? What would they want with me?"

The ambassador looked quickly at Tom Miller, a look that was not lost on Shayna. She turned slowly and deliberately to face the deputy ambassador and kept her eyes on him as Ambassador DeGrasse made an effort to respond to her questions.

"We don't want to take any chances. There could be leftover resentment. Who knows what's in the minds of assassins?" he said lamely.

Shayna swung back to him.

"Leftover resentment? Ambassador DeGrasse, would you mind telling me what you're talking about?"

When a response did not come fast enough she swung back to Tom Miller.

"Would you care to speak, Mr. Miller?" she said with exaggerated politeness.

Tom Miller did not stand on ceremony.

"As you know, Ms. McWright, your mother was consul general here when Shaba was invaded in the 1970s. In fact, she traveled to the region just days before the invasion, purportedly on one of Mobutu's organized tours to assure the Western powers that he had everything under control. There were rumors of rebellion, you see."

"So why would that make her a special target? She wasn't the only one on that tour, was she?"

The question hung in the air.

"Yes, she was, as a matter of fact," Miller said dryly. "The tour was her idea. Mobutu made it a highly publicized affair. The entire thing was broadcast live on national television. Shortly after that, Shaba was invaded from neighboring Zambia. France, Morocco, and the U.S. came to Mobutu's rescue and crushed the invasion. It's possible that your mother became some sort of symbol in the eyes of the rebels. These guys are crazy and they're cowards."

"I would think, Mr. Miller, that anyone who assassinates an ambassador of the United States is neither crazy nor cowardly. Think about it. Perhaps our own intelligence gathering would be better served if we stopped underestimating the minds of those who view America and Americans as their enemy, however reprehensible their reasons," Shayna said frostily.

"Come, come, Shayna, Tom. This is getting us nowhere. Anyway, Shayna, maybe you should think about returning to the United States."

"Is that really necessary, Ambassador DeGrasse? I mean, you're just guessing at all this, aren't you? There's no actual proof that the Congolese guy did it, is there? Besides, don't you think if I were in *real* danger here the enemy would have struck already?"

"The State Department will feel more comfortable if you left. So will the president, I'm sure."

"Your Excellency, I'm not trying to be difficult, but I'm sure you know why I am in this country. I think I am beginning to make some progress on that score. I can't leave now. It's simply out of the question," Shayna said with finality. Ambassador DeGrasse drew a deep breath and sucked calmly on his pipe. "I suppose we can't force you," he said with resignation, avoiding Tom Miller's eyes.

Miller, who had been holding his tongue behind the thin line of his mouth, stood up abruptly. "Have it your way, Ms. McWright. As Ambassador DeGrasse said, we cannot force you to do what you do not wish to do. I assure you, we are not grandstanding. Ambassador McWright was very important to us in Washington, so important that her family also is very important to us. But perhaps we're overdoing it in your case. You are, after all, a private citizen, over 21, in the country of your birth."

That last bit was more than sarcastic. It was nasty. *Too nasty*, Shayna thought. She looked at Miller querulously. This was way too much passion coming from him. Even his eyes were filled with it. She knitted her brow. *Something is not adding up here*, she thought. *There's way too much intensity in this room*. She zeroed in on Miller's words. "Very important to us in Washington. Very important."

When she addressed Miller, it was in a slow, steady voice, devoid of anger. "Mr. Miller, my mother served in this country nearly thirty years ago. Please tell me why she would be assassinated now for something that may have happened back then."

The heat drained away from Miller's face. His shoulders dropped several inches. Shayna was surprised at how much younger he seemed. "Africans have this saying about time being longer than twine. People do not forget certain things, Ms. McWright," Miller said, sitting down again. He spoke almost softly.

"Go on, Mr. Miller. What are these 'certain things?' Was my mother doing more than a consul general's work when she was here?" Shayna kept her voice as gentle as his.

Tom Miller actually smiled. He knew that she already knew what he was going to say. He knew, too, that she knew that he knew this.

"Yes."

"And in Brussels?"

"Yes."

"And it involved Africa…the Congo? Both then and now?"

"Yes."

Shayna pursed her lips and looked past Miller.

"I don't suppose you'd tell me exactly what she was working on at the time she was killed, Mr. Miller," she said slowly, her eyes still on the wall behind Miller.

"That's a correct supposition, Ms. McWright."

"Although I can make an educated guess, given Washington's feelings about the way things have been going in this country lately."

She said this more to herself than to Miller.

He did not respond. He knew she didn't expect him to.

No one spoke for a while. Shayna broke the silence.

"Ambassador DeGrasse, Mr. Miller," she said, looking from the one to the other. "I know that in her heart of hearts my mother believed that our way, that the kind of contract we have in America between the government and the people, is the best way for a society to blossom and prosper. After what I've seen in my own travels, including here, I believe so too. But the Congo..." Shayna took a deep breath. "...the Congo is also my country, in a way. No. Not 'in a way.' It just is. With all its alien ways and its tragic wars, it is a part of me. Believe me, I still don't know what that means for me, but it's something I have to resolve. I just cannot leave now. I need to know. I need to find my birth mother if she's alive, or at least find out something about her family. I'm sure you can understand that."

Tom Miller nodded. He got up from the chair and extended his hand to Shayna. It was over, for now at least. He shook Shayna's hand with a curt "Good day, Ms. McWright" and left the room.

"So you will remain here for how long?" Ambassador DeGrasse asked when they were alone.

"I can't say—another month maybe, not for very long. I'll know when it's time to leave."

#

Tom Miller frowned deeply as he re-read the report from the CIA station chief in Brussels. Someone must have leaked it, or a good part of it, to Sophie St. Cyr. *Attila the Mouth was good, but she wasn't that good*, Miller thought, using the Belgians' nickname for the CNN reporter. She had far too much information. *The leak had to have come from Capitol Hill*, he thought with disgust, *some zealot looking to make a case for his isolationist policies.*

Now that CNN had spread the news all over the world about a possible Congolese connection, he had to move even faster. He either had to find the suspect before the Congolese security police did, or he had to make sure he was with the police when they found him. Miller was the best at drawing a person's psychological profile based on that person's most insignificant habits and movements. From what he read of the suspect, he was sure the man was in the Congo by now. He had to talk to him before he "disappeared" or "died" in police custody.

Something about his alleged connection to Janice McWright's death did not ring right.

Miller put down the report and leaned back in the soft leather chair behind his desk. He swiveled the chair around so he could face the window and clasped his hands behind his head. His gaze reached up above the trees to the clear blue sky. He thought of Shayna McWright. Few people impressed Tom Miller. Shayna McWright did.

#

Shayna cried for a long time at home that night. Amina held her all the while.

CHAPTER TWENTY-ONE

The view from the River Club at the top of the International Commercial Center in Kinshasa was nowhere near the spectacular kaleidoscope one might expect to see at night from such a commanding height above the city.

Below, the lights of Kinshasa were far and few. Small clusters of dull yellow bulbs bravely defied the huge span of blackness. Occasional beams of headlights from a car, or a military Jeep, swung into a street. Red tail lights hurried away from downtown Kinshasa toward the cité. Kerosene lamps flickered where street vendors conducted the usual brisk night trade and where women sold tchikwang and beignets and long French loaves and grilled chicken and thick pieces of blackened meat on sticks.

Night had fallen early. But there was a full moon, and it bathed Kinshasa in a silvery glow. Far off to the left the Congo River glimmered, silent.

How could a city so full of tragedy feel so peaceful? Amina mused, as she gazed through the huge plate-glass window. She was sipping a glass of wine, half-listening to the Emirati trade minister.

The formal part of the evening was over and the guests were chatting animatedly in little groups in the cocktail lounge.

Ice tinkled against fine crystal. Bursts of laughter filled the room.

The trade minister, a tall, elderly sheikh with a lascivious gleam in his eye, was trying to impress upon her how progressive the Emirates were when it came to women. "Our women are very much involved in our society at all levels," he was saying earnestly. "They are educated. They should contribute to our economic growth. We don't want them veiled from head to toe and afraid to open their mouths. This is a new century, Dr. Milenga, a new century."

"It certainly is, Mr. Minister," Amina said agreeably. She wanted to say something about the fact that there was no suffrage in his country, but she thought better of it. No need to compromise the goodwill Crispin is building up with his guests.

The minister beamed.

"One day you must come to our country to spend some time with our women doctors. There is a lot you can discuss together, I am sure," he said.

"That's a very good idea, Mr. Minister. Perhaps you can arrange a tour for me through your ministry of health," Amina said. *Why not? I've never been to the Middle East. Might as well go in style if I'm to go*, she told herself.

A young man from the minister's delegation joined them. He apologized for interrupting, and then addressed the minister in Arabic. The minister excused himself to Amina with a slight bow and went off with the young man to join a group of Congolese.

Lucky devil, Amina sighed. *I was just going in for the kill. Oh well!* She glanced at the group the trade minister was approaching. She recognized some of them: the Congolese minister of industry and commerce, a few wealthy businessmen. Gaston was with them, too.

"Just about all of Kinshasa's movers and shakers are in this room," she whispered to Shayna in a rare moment when they were standing alone together. They were both used to this kind of event and were working the room with skill. Amina made a beeline for the people she knew or recognized from news reports, and she made a point of greeting each of the foreign guests. It was easy to tell who these guests were. They stood out in their long white robes and heavy black moustaches.

Looking around, Amina saw Shayna engaged in an earnest conversation with one of the sheikhs. *The shipping guy, no doubt*, she thought. She's finally closed in on him.

"Shayna is relentless, isn't she?" Crispin's voice said.

He was standing just behind her. So close that she could feel his breath on her neck. She smelled the faint fragrance of his cologne.

"Yes, she is," she replied, laughing, praying that her nervousness did not show. "Will she get anything out of him?"

"She might, if he's is in a talkative mood, which he seems to be," Crispin said, coming to stand beside her.

Amina turned to face him.

"And what will he tell her?"

"Oh, not you too. Is this a team effort?"

Amina chuckled. "I'm sorry. It just slipped out. You don't have to answer," she said.

"Oh I didn't plan to," Crispin replied, liking her quick sense of humor. "I'm sorry I have not been able to spend more time with you. It's been a busy evening," he continued seriously.

"Oh, there's no need to apologize. I can imagine how important this event must be for you. I'm enjoying myself, actually. And so is the delegation, from what I have seen. You should be pleased."

"I am. And I want you to know that I'm grateful for the contribution you're making to the evening's success. You've been circulating, charming everyone. The sheikhs are not an easy lot."

"You've been watching me, Crispin" she said, cocking her head to one side and looking at him with a playful smile.

"Yes, to put it mildly," he said with a twinkle in his eyes. "I find it hard not to look at you when you're in the same room with me. But you know that already."

Amina felt the blood rush into her face. She raised her glass to her lips. Her hand shook.

"I seem to have this habit of making you nervous, Amina. Why?"

"Well, I—I…"

"Yes?" His eyes would not let hers go.

"Crispin, you're…"

"Amina! What a surprise! Crispin, you never told me you knew Dr. Milenga!"

Dominique Yamungu, the country's top oncologist, flung her arms around Amina and kissed her—on one cheek first, then on the other, then on the first again. The two met about three years before at a World Health Organization conference in Geneva and hit it off instantly. Amina was part of the U.S. delegation. Dominique refused to believe she was Congolese until she switched from English to Lingala.

A regal and elegant woman just shy of fifty, Dominique had a private practice in Kinshasa, but she traveled frequently throughout the country, visiting as many hospitals and training as many nurses and interns as she could. She was married to the vice president of the country, whom she met when they were both at university in France.

Amina was genuinely delighted to see her. She had not seen Dominique since her visit to Kinshasa the previous year. She embraced Dominique warmly. "I thought you were in Bukavu, Dominique. Dr. Charles told me that's where you were. Have you been here all evening? I didn't see you," she said when they finally released each other.

"I got back from Bukavu yesterday. I slipped in during the last speech to help wave the flag for Crispin. But I've got to get back to one of my patients. He's really in a bad way. Sorry, Crispin."

She kissed him lightly on both cheeks.

"Please don't apologize, *tantine.* I'm glad you were able to come at all. Amina and I are just getting to know each other, actually," he said smiling at Dominique.

Dominique caught something in his voice when he said Amina's name.

"Ah, ah, ah!" she said in that singsong Congolese way. "Did I interrupt anything? But even if I did, it wouldn't change what is meant to be, would it?"

She squinted at Crispin. "I think, Crispin, you like our Amina," she said with delight. "You should like him back, Amina. He's perfect for you."

"She's right you know, Amina." Crispin said with a straight face.

"Is this a team effort?" Amina laughed, throwing up her hands in mock frustration.

"Crispin! Amina!"

Shayna was walking over to them excitedly.

"Oh, excuse me. I didn't mean to interrupt," she said, glancing uncertainly at Dominique as she reached them. She went on speaking, nonetheless. "Amina, Crispin, do you mind if I go off with those guys I'm talking to? I want to talk to them some more before they leave tomorrow. Don't worry, Crispin. Their lips are sealed when it comes to Brazil. I tried." She said it all in a rush.

Crispin raised his eyes heavenward and pursed his lips. Amina began to laugh.

"Did I say something funny?" Shayna asked.

Dominique introduced herself. "No, my dear. I am Dominique Yamungu, a friend of Crispin's family. These two evidently were on the verge of something hot when I barged in. I was just getting it back on track when you barged in," she said dryly.

Shayna giggled and glanced at Amina. Seeing how uncomfortable Amina looked, she slipped her hands through hers. Before she could say anything, Dominique changed the subject.

"Where's your aunt, by the way, Crispin? She said she would be here," she said.

"She came, but she left almost immediately. She was fine when she arrived, then all of a sudden, she seemed upset, really shaken. But she wouldn't tell me what was wrong. She just said she had to go."

"Hmmm. I'll call her on my way back to the hospital." She looked at her watch. "I've got to run, children. Good to meet you, Shay..." She stopped abruptly. Her eyes were riveted on Shayna's face.

"What is it? What is it?" Shayna said anxiously, leaning toward Dominique.

Dominique blinked and shook her head.

"Oh, it's nothing. Just a hot flash. They come on so suddenly sometimes. Dastardly things! Didn't mean to be rude. Amina, I'll see you at the clinic." She kissed them all and left hurriedly, stopping to shake hands with several people as she made her way out.

"For a moment I was sure she recognized me," Shayna said, her eyes still on Dominique. Her voice was filled with disappointment.

"So did I. But what a beautiful woman she is. What energy!" Amina said quickly.

"Yes, she is quite a lady," Crispin said.

Shayna sighed and turned to them. "Seriously, guys. You don't mind my bailing out on you like this, right? Gaston is coming with me. He'll see me home," she said flatly.

"I don't mind. At least you won't be hounding *me* about my business deals," Crispin said.

Shayna laughed. "Oh come now, Crispin. Surely I'm not that obnoxious."

"No, Shayna. You're not obnoxious at all—insistent, but not obnoxious."

"Whew! That's a relief. It was really good of you to invite us, Crispin. I had a wonderful time," Shayna said, extending her hand to him. "And with the story I'm getting out of the sheikhs, you couldn't top this evening."

Crispin took her hand and raised it gallantly to his lips.

"It was my pleasure. Enjoy the rest of the evening. I'll take Amina home myself," he said.

Shayna looked at Amina, her eyebrows arched.

"Amina." She pressed her cheek against Amina's and whispered into her ear. "Baby, that man is coming at your wall with a sledgehammer. You don't stand a chance."

#

Dominique was shouting angrily into her cell phone.

"How dare you run away from her? How dare you! What gives you the right to deny her your identity?"

"Don't be stupid, Dominique. What was I supposed to do? Go up to her in front of all those people and say 'hello, I'm your mother. I abandoned you when you were two years old?' You're out of your mind!"

"*You're* the one who's out of your mind. You should be shot. I should order you shot. You're dead anyway. You have no heart. Your money has eaten it."

Dominique fell sideways as her car swerved suddenly to avoid a Jeep that had swung into the oncoming lane to pass the car ahead of it.

The Jeep swung back into its own lane, narrowly missing a head-on collision with Dominique's car. As it shot past, the driver grinned and waved at Dominique's driver.

Dominique straightened herself and lowered her window. She stuck her head out. "Imbecile!" she yelled after the Jeep. "I hope you die!" She retreated back into the car and closed the window. As she raised the cell phone to her ear again, she glanced into the rearview mirror and saw Raymond, her driver, looking at her disapprovingly. She made an impatient gesture with her free hand, mouthing to him to keep his eyes on the road. She pressed the cell phone to her ear, turned her body away from Raymond and hunched over as if to keep him from hearing her conversation.

The voice on the other end of the line was no less furious than hers. "So! Madame wife of the vice president will have me shot, eh? That would be a neat way of settling everything, wouldn't it? And what will you tell her then? 'She was my dearest friend. I am so sorry she died before you could know her.' Oh I could just see you with your fake tears. You crocodile!"

Dominique chortled. She threw herself back against the seat of the car and laughed so hard that she had to hold her sides. A peal of laughter came through the phone. "You're so silly, Suke— crocodile indeed!" Dominique said, gasping for breath.

"You get me so mad sometimes, Dominique. I don't know how we've remained friends all these years. Where are you, anyway? Why aren't you still at the River Club?"

"I'm on my way back to the hospital. Old Tshimanga will pass tonight."

"It's time. He has really suffered, the poor man."

"Poor man my foot. That old geezer was ferreting right down to the wire. His wife is two months pregnant. She's twenty-five."

"At least he's leaving her wealthy. She'll forget about him in no time."

They giggled.

"So what are you going to do, Suke?"

"Nothing, absolutely nothing."

"You don't know what you're saying, Suke. You're still in shock."

"My God! I never thought I'd see her here, in Kinshasa. What could she be doing here?"

"Well, why else would she be here? You think she's on vacation in a miserable country like this?"

"She's a journalist, remember? She could be on assignment, covering the situation here."

"So soon after her Janice McWright died? I don't think so. You really think she knows nothing? You don't think she came here to look for you?"

"She can't know. That was the deal we made. Mrs. McWright swore she would never tell her."

"Suppose she told her family, then, and Shayna found out somehow? You know how ugly family can get at funerals. Even in America it happens, I'm sure."

"Well, nobody has any proof. Her birth certificate and adoption papers are all here in Kinshasa, with the Jesuit priests who baptized her. That was what was decided, Mrs. McWright and me. There is nothing to show in America."

"I think she came to Kinshasa with Amina Milenga. You know her, the Congolese doctor whose mother is American. The one who spends time at Ngaliema every year."

"Yes, I've heard of her. People say she's nice. Is that the one who was with her tonight?"

"Yes. And I think our Crispin has it really bad for her. I swear to God he would have shamed himself in front of those Arabs if I had not butted in. Anyway, Shayna is staying with her. I know her well. I can ask her about Shayna."

"There's no need to ask her anything. As far as I'm concerned, I do not exist for Shayna. Let's leave it at that."

"You're making a mistake, Suke."

"I said let's leave it at that, Dominique. I mean it."

"Okay, Suke. I'm too tired to argue anymore. You have anything to eat at your house?"

"Of course, Sombe, your favorite."

"Good. I'll come and spend the night with you when I leave the hospital. My house is too empty. The children went back to France for school and Renee is traveling with the president."

"I'll tell the guard to look out for you."

"Okay. See you in a..."

"Dominique?"

"Yes, sweetheart?"

"Do you really think she could be looking for me?"

#

Crispin dismissed the limousine that brought Amina and Shayna to the River Club and drove Amina home in his own car. He was silent as they drove along the darkened boulevard. Every now and then, Amina would steal a look at him out of the corner of her eyes. His eyes were fixed on the road, but he seemed deep in thought. She wondered what he was thinking.

Without realizing it, she sighed aloud. Her own thoughts were in turmoil. She was alone with Crispin and had no idea what she was going to do when they got to her house, or what *he* was going to do, for that matter. She did not like feeling so uncertain. *What if he tries to kiss me?* she asked herself. *Kiss him back.* The answer came back immediately. She knew there and then that she'd do just that. She liked him, a lot. More than liking him, she wanted him. But she didn't want him to think she was an easy lay. She still believed that most African men thought American women were easy.

She, Merry, and Jamillah had pronounced emphatically on that point at Spelman. They'd seen and heard of too many cases of college boyfriends suddenly confessing after graduation that they were married or engaged to someone back home, or they had to go home to marry somebody that their parents had chosen for them. It was always one of their own women. Every African man they confronted about it denied it, of course.

But the three of them persisted, telling the men that they got their stupid ideas about American women from those stupid movies and TV shows they watched. They railed that black women, decent black women—which was most black women—were quite conservative and didn't just jump into bed with a stranger. Some of the men argued back impudently that Hollywood and TV took their cues from real life, that nothing they produced was ever one-hundred percent fiction.

Like many of the positions she, Merry and Jamillah took at Spelman, it all seemed so high-handed and trivial now. But she still didn't want Crispin to think she was easy. She knew Crispin wanted her. He made that clear in more than one way. Of course, she had seen him looking at her at the River Club when he thought she was not seeing him. *What if he tries to make love to me tonight*?

She sighed aloud again as her thoughts battled each other. One side was telling her to relax, to go with the flow. *Let the vibes take you along, Amina. Enjoy it. You only walk this way once.* The other side, much more cautious, demanded a plan. *You'd better take control, girl. Decide how far you want things to go and don't move an inch past that point.*

Amina sighed again.

"Now I'm really worried. That's the third or fourth time you've sighed like that. Is anything wrong?"

Crispin's voice broke the silence so suddenly that Amina jumped.

"Oh!" she exclaimed.

"My Lord! I'm sorry. I didn't realize I would startle you. I just wanted to know if you're all right. You're sighing as if you have the world on your shoulders." His voice was filled with concern.

"Sorry. I wasn't aware that I was sighing. I was just thinking."

"Troubling thoughts, it seems. Care to share them?" He looked at her quickly and then turned his attention back to the road.

"It's nothing, really," Amina said.

"Really?"

"Really."

Crispin looked at her doubtfully. Amina kept her eyes straight ahead.

"I'm okay," she said. "Really."

"What did you think of the delegation?" he asked, abruptly changing the subject.

Amina answered as if she had been mulling that very question all along.

"I sensed that they are willing to invest in the Congo, but only if you advise them what investments to make and when. They trust you implicitly—your confidence in the country, your assessment of what makes sense and what does not. That's the only basis on which they will move," she said.

Crispin was impressed by her answer, but he remained silent, waiting for her to finish.

"That's a heavy burden they are placing on you. The government is counting on their investment," Amina continued.

"What do you think they should do?"

"They should help us rebuild our transportation infrastructure. Help modernize the port at Matadi, for one thing. The country is not going to be at war forever. We need to start preparing for the twenty-first century."

"So you think they should come in immediately?"

"Why wait? Sure things are very fragile here. But I don't think anyone would mess with the port. Whoever is in power will need it."

Crispin fell silent again. Amina waited for him to speak. If she was surprised by the change in his mood, she did not show it. She liked the fact that he was asking her opinion on matters that were important to him. It made her relax. She would go with the flow from here on.

"Do you think I should buy the Brazilian line?" he asked suddenly.

"Without question. I wish I could get in on the deal myself."

Crispin laughed. "A regular bull, aren't you?"

"Guilty as sin and just as shameless."

"I bet you own some of me too," he said, glancing at her.

Amina avoided the dangerous side of that double entendre.

"Are you asking me if I own stock in Musana Holdings? Or are you telling me that I do?"

"Both, I guess."

"And why would you be interested in what I have in my itsy bitsy stock portfolio? For that matter, why should I even discuss my portfolio with you?"

"Well, I may be able to give you a few tips. You may want to increase your stake in me, for instance."

Either he was talking raunchy, or she was filtering his words through her own raunchy feelings.

"Insider trading is illegal where you're listed, Mr. Abeli. Besides, I think I've been doing pretty well on my own, thank you," she said briskly.

"Doing well with your stock portfolio or doing well with me?"

"We're talking about stocks, Mr. Abeli. Solely about stocks."

"But I'm one of your stocks, aren't I? You own me."

"Do I?"

"I want you to."

"Why?"

"As Dominique said, and as I agreed, I'm perfect for you. You will never lose with me. I'll always be up."

"We're still talking about stocks, right?"

"Right. My stock."

"You called her 'tantine.' Is she your aunt?"

"Nice move," Crispin said admiringly. "No, she isn't my real aunt. But she is like my aunt. I've known her practically all my life. She is a close friend of a woman whom I also call my aunt, though she too, is not a blood relative. You may have heard of her. Sukaina Tshiala.

"You mean the woman who owns ShaYaSu?"

"Yes."

"Hmmmm. I just know her from the newspapers. I've been to one of her stores, but I've never seen her there, of course. So she is Dominique's close friend. Speaking of Dominique, she looked at Shayna in a strange way tonight, don't you think so?"

"You heard her explanation."

"I didn't buy that at all."

"Why not?"

Amina told him the reason why Shayna was in Kinshasa.

"So you think Dominique may have recognized her?"

"Yes. You don't seem surprised that Shayna is part Congolese."

Crispin shrugged. "I guess I'm not. When you were at my house the other day, I kept thinking there was something almost familiar about her. Anyway, such mixes are not at all unusual. Want me to ask Dominique about it?"

"I have a feeling she won't say anything even if she knew."

"I can…"

"Whoops! You're passing my house."

Crispin braked hard, reversed, and turned into her driveway. He parked just beyond the entrance to the building and turned to face her.

"I enjoyed the evening, Crispin," Amina said.

"So did I, Amina. You made it very special for me. And I value your insights immensely."

"Crispin…"

"Yes?"

"It's not very late. Would you care to come up for a cup of tea or a glass of wine?"

"I'd love to."

#

"What would you have done if I hadn't invited you up?" Amina asked as they stepped into the foyer of her apartment. She threw her purse and keys on a triangular-shaped corner table. She'd been dying to ask that question.

"I would have escorted you into the lobby, said goodnight and left," he said.

"You would not have asked to come up?"

"No. I may be direct, Amina, but I am not presumptuous. I firmly believe that it is better to be asked to step up…"

"…than to be asked to step down," she said, completing the saying that her mother had drummed into her since she was a child.

"Who came up with that, anyway?" Crispin said, looking around her living room.

"Can't help you there, I'm afraid. I always thought it was an original of my mother. Please, make yourself comfortable," Amina said.

"Mind if I look around a bit first? You have very interesting artwork."

"They're from all over the Diaspora. Be my guest. You can put on some music if you like. I'll just get out of these high heels." She excused herself and went upstairs.

Crispin had put on a Manu Dibangu CD and was studying a portrait of a gray-haired, light-skinned woman when Amina returned. She had changed into a sarong and matching top.

"That's my grandmother, my mother's mother," she said, coming to stand beside him. "She died before I was born. But my mother speaks of her so often that I feel I know her personally. In a way, I've lived with her all my life, I suppose."

"She is beautiful. She has European blood."

"Yes. Her father was an Englishman."

"Your mother is Caribbean."

"From Guyana. How do you know?"

"Dr. Charles told me."

"Ah, yes. Dr. Charles. He said you wanted to talk to me about something."

"I do? What about?" Crispin turned to face her. He seemed genuinely puzzled.

Amina's heart soared. "*Yes!*" she shouted in her mind. "About—about a children's clinic. Something about you refurbishing the old children's hospital and my heading it once it's ready," she said coolly.

"Oh, that! Yes, I guess I should talk to you about that, shouldn't I?"

"You don't have to if you don't want to."

"Actually, I do want to. But not now."

"May I fix you a drink? Or would you prefer some tea?' she asked, turning toward an ebony sideboard that served as her bar.

"What are you having?"

"A tisane."

"Then that's what I'll have."

"Do you like it warm, cold or at room temperature?"

"Warm, by all means."

There it was again. That raunchy undercurrent in his voice. Or was it in her hearing? Or both? Amina excused herself again and went into the kitchen.

"Mind if I remove my jacket?" Crispin called to her.

"Please."

He was wearing an abacos, the high-collar jacket that buttoned all the way up to the throat. It was similar to the Mao suit that was worn in China during Mao Tse Tung's cultural revolution, or to the Nyerere suit popularized by Tanzania's first president, Julius Nyerere.

In Congo, the abacos became the national dress for men under Mobutu's doctrine of "zairianization." Zairianization was a cultural nationalism that sought to rid the local culture of European influences. European dress and European names were banned. Zairian men and women were to be addressed as "citoyen" and "citoyenne," respectively, French for "citizen." It was the cultural counterpart of what Mobutu termed "Mobutism," which was nothing more than localized socialism. For instance, Mobutu came up with a list of ten shortcomings—les dix fléaux—of the Zairian people that hindered the country's economic advancement. He introduced the practice of "salongo," or community work, which everyone, even the government ministers, had to do.

The abacos, which really stands for "à bas le costume," French for "down with the suit," was still worn as formal dress, even though European suits were back in vogue. As in the days of Mobutu, those who could afford it had theirs made in Paris or Geneva. The only difference between those and what the local tailors made was the cloth itself. You could not find that rich cloth locally.

The pale blue, silk short-sleeved tee shirt Crispin wore underneath his jacket showed off his excellent physique. Amina swallowed hard as she came toward him with their drinks. His fingers touched hers lightly as he took the cup from her. He was sitting on the couch.

"This aroma is truly pleasing. Is this your own private brew?" Crispin asked, as he inhaled in the steam rising from the teacup.

"Yes. I like to experiment with different herbs," Amina said, sitting down at the other end of the couch and tucking her feet under her. "This one is made of herbs from Guyana. What you're smelling is called 'sweet broom.'"

"Well, here's to the future," Crispin said, lifting his cup and leaning toward her to clink hers. "And to our friendship. Cheers."

"Cheers," Amina said, leaning in to him.

The CD had reached Manu Dibangu's original version of "Oa Na Mba." Crispin put down his cup and slid down in the couch, stretching his long legs under the coffee table. He rested his head on the back of the couch and stared up at the ceiling. He hummed a few bars of the song, and then half sang, half spoke the lyrics as Manu Dibangu did.

"That's an old song by Manu. Not many people remember it. Somehow, I'm not surprised you do," he said. Changing the subject abruptly, he asked, "What led you to tai chi, Amina?"

"I was at a point in my life where I felt I needed more peace, more balance—a total wellness, if you wish. I saw this old, really old, Chinese man doing tai chi in a small park near my home in New York and I stood there fascinated. His body was fit for such an old man and he was so lithe and flexible. I'd never seen such peace emanating from anyone. I waited until he'd finished and talked to him about tai chi. He explained to me what it did for the mind and the body. He said he could not remember a day when he did not do tai chi.

His English was not very good, but I was interested enough in what he said to do further research. The more I read about the benefits of tai chi, the more I was convinced that it was the right thing for me. So I found a school and joined. That was about ten years ago."

They talked for hours, asking all sorts of questions about each other. Sometimes Amina would get up to change the CD, sometimes Crispin would. Their teacups were empty, but neither seemed to notice.

Amina asked him about his own introduction to tai chi; about the pressure of building and maintaining the Musana empire; about his parents, brothers, sisters; his feelings about the Congo and what was happening to it; about Africa in general and how he saw it in the global scheme of things.

He asked her about being half-Caribbean and half-Congolese; about choosing pediatric psychotherapy and coming back to the Congo every year, even now, when it was so dangerous; about her work in the States; how she spent her leisure time.

"So you've never married?" he asked.

"Never. And you?"

"Never. Why haven't you married? Surely there was—is someone special in your life."

She did not answer right away. She looked away from him and let her eyes rest on her grandmother's picture. Crispin waited.

"There is no one," she said quietly. "There was, once, but that ended years ago."

"But you still think of him. You still love him, it seems."

Even with her face averted, she could feel the intensity of his gaze.

"Do you, Amina?" he insisted gently when she did not answer.

She turned toward him. He was facing her, one leg folded on the seat of the couch, an arm stretched out along the back.

"No, Crispin, I don't. That is over," she said, looking directly at him. "It's just that the experience has left me—has left me..." She smiled awkwardly and shrugged. The expression on his face was unreadable.

"Has left you afraid to fall in love again?" he said softly. His eyes probed hers.

"Yes."

"And would you like to, to fall in love again?"

"I don't know. Sometimes I think so, yes. I like the sharing, the companionship that comes with love. But sometimes I think not. I don't want to be hurt that way again. I'd rather remain alone than go through that again."

"But how can you tell in advance if you're going to be hurt?"

"You weigh the facts," she said emphatically.

"The facts? You mean past behavior, reputation, current relationships, that sort of thing?"

"Are you making fun of me?"

"No, I'm not," he said. "Do you think you could fall in love with me?"

Amina's eyes widened. "What kind of question is that?"

"A serious one. Do you think you could fall in love with me?"

"How do you expect me to answer that? I don't know you that well. I can't say yes, I can't say no. I—I—how can you ask me that? That's not a fair question," she ended lamely.

"I could fall in love with you, Amina. I have already fallen in love with you."

"But you don't know me. You're playing with me, Crispin. You shouldn't do that," Amina said. She was shaking. Crispin Abeli just declared to her that he was in love with her. She did not know whether to believe him or not, and at the same time, she was afraid of what she herself was feeling.

To her annoyance, tears sprang to her eyes. She was not prepared for this. "Please excuse me," she said, her voice trembling. She jumped up from the couch and ran into the kitchen. The door swung shut behind her. She leaned against the counter in the middle of the floor, her hands pressing on the counter top. She closed her eyes and dropped her head forward, trying to stop her body from trembling and to control the waves of desire that were rolling through her body.

"That man is coming at your wall with a sledgehammer and you don't stand a chance," Shayna said. *Well, Shayna, here I am. Bludgeoned!*

How long she stood like that she did not know. She did not hear the door open, but she felt Crispin's presence in the kitchen. He was approaching her. Now he was standing behind her, very close, saying nothing, not touching her. Then he held her by her upper arms. Amina's body tingled at his touch. She felt his breath warm on her neck. They stood like this for a long moment. It was as if he was waiting for her to grow calm. Then he moved in closer to her, brushing his lips against her neck. Her entire body shuddered and she gasped. The sound made him hold her more tightly. She lifted her head and leaned it back against his shoulder.

His hands moved slowly along the sides of her body, caressing her. She tensed as he wrapped his arms around her waist and squeezed her. He swayed her gently to one side, and then to the other, back and forth, on a slow rhythm. Their bodies were molded to each other. His lips left a trail of warmth on her bare flesh. Amina closed her eyes and succumbed to his rhythm. Her body had never been possessed like this before. Crispin moved his hands down to the pit of her stomach and pressed in gently. The sensation was maddening, causing Amina to catch her breath again and again.

"I want you, Amina," he said softly.

He turned her around by the shoulders and looked deep into her. He drew her into his arms and placed his palms, one on top the other, flat against the small of her back, drawing her tight against him. She adjusted her hips to fit his erection between her legs. The move drove him crazy.

"Ohhhh!" he exhaled and brought his mouth down hard on hers.

She returned his kiss just as hard, locking her arms behind his neck and thrusting her hips into him. She began to shudder. Somehow, Crispin managed to tear himself away from her. Still breathing hard, he held her at arms' length, willing the storm in both of them to abate.

He saw the hurt and the embarrassment in her eyes. She had invested so much.

"Amina. I don't want it to be like this," he said, drawing her back to him. "Not when you're still afraid to love. Not when you don't know if you can trust me. I want all of you, your body. Oh God, how I want your body. But I want your heart and I want your mind, too. I want your trust. And that is what you will always have from me: all of me. When you are ready."

Amina hid her face in his chest. She felt drained. It would have been so much less complicated if he had simply made love to her.

"What if it takes me a long, long time to reach that point?" she murmured.

"How long is long?" he said, holding her tight. "I've waited so long for someone like you to come into my life. Now that I have found you, I can wait until you find me. However long it takes, Amina, I can wait."

CHAPTER TWENTY-TWO

Shayna sat at the bar with Gaston, sipping her fourth beer and swaying to the beat of the music. She was feeling on top of the world. They were in a popular nightclub in Matonge, the swinging cîté, about twenty minutes by car from the Intercontinental Hotel where the UAE delegates were staying.

Matonge was so well known for its high life that the same name had been bestowed on the quartier in Brussels that had become the center of African culture.

It was Gaston's idea to go dancing after he and Shayna left the hotel. It had been a long, intense session with the head of the delegation—who was also the head of the central bank—and the ministers overseeing industry, commerce and transportation. Where the ministers remained cagey and spoke in generalities, Shayna pressed for specifics, figures, and concrete examples. She challenged them on the discrepancies between their statements and the reality as she knew it. At times they seemed angry, insulted even, by her probing. But she managed to mollify them, assuring them in the most deferential language that all she sought was the truth; that the readers of her newspaper—decision makers in the government and private sectors—were interested neither in the standard slant on the Arab world that you found in general interest papers, nor the standard PR from the Arab nations themselves.

What her audience needed to know, she told the sheikhs, was whether or not the UAE was going to become a global player of consequence or not. She herself believed the former, she told them. They had to trust her with the real story. The meeting took place in the suite of the head delegate. Gaston sat away from the group, keeping a protective eye on Shayna. He almost cheered when she ended her speech on wanting the real deal. As if she read his mind, her eyes caught his and he gave her a thumbs up. The interview ended only when Shayna felt she had her story. Gaston could hear the fatigue in her voice as they took leave of the delegates.

"You need to unwind," he said to her in the elevator. "Let's go dancing. I'll take you to Matonge. Have you been there yet?"

"Not for dancing. Amina took me there a couple of times to see some of her friends and to see her tailor who is making some clothes for me," she replied wearily. "You're right. I can really use some relaxation."

A popular band was performing at the nightclub. It was playing its own hits, which everyone seemed to know. Shayna came alive as soon as she and Gaston entered the club. The crowd on the dance floor was building. Within an hour, there would be little room to move.

"Those Emirati sheikhs were something else, weren't they, Gaston?" Shayna said, her words slurring slightly. "But I loosened them up. I got a damned good story."

Gaston grinned and raised his glass of beer in a toast to her. "Yep! You handled them magnificently! Here's to you," he said and took a long swig. "Ahhhhhh! There's nothing better than a cold Primus in a sweltering bar in the cîté!" he declared, bringing a fist down on the counter for emphasis.

"Oh yes there is: your fourth cold Primus in a sweltering bar in the cîté. Here's to the fourth Primus!" Shayna said, raising her own glass.

"Hear! Hear!" Gaston said.

They clinked glasses and drank. Gaston put down his glass and stood up, snapping his fingers and moving to the beat of the music. "Come on, my girl. We came here to dance, so let's dance," he said to Shayna.

"Aha! You're gonna teach your countryman to dance the way she should. Or is it your countrywoman? Oh hell! Let's go." She jumped up, grabbed his hand, and dragged him to the dance floor.

Gaston launched into the latest moves. Shayna followed him without missing a beat, picking up the steps easily. She even threw in a few that she copied on the spot from the other women on the floor. She moved with such ease, it was as if she had danced that way all her life.

They danced until they were dripping with sweat. Gaston looked at his watch and saw that it was after two in the morning. "We should call Amina. She must be worried," he said as they took their seats at the bar.

"I doubt Amina has time to worry about anyone other than herself tonight," Shayna said with a knowing laugh.

Gaston grinned. "Oh yes. I did a double take when I saw the way Crispin was looking at her. To think that someone has finally smitten the heart of Crispin Abeli: the man for whom no woman is good enough. That's how the available women in Kinshasa describe him, you know."

Shayna snorted. "That's just sour grapes. But tell me, Gaston, I know he's never been married, but has he ever been involved with anyone?"

"Crispin? I don't think so, although it's hard to know for sure. He and I are friends, but we aren't that close. He's an obsessively private person. Let's just say I've never seen him seriously involved with anyone, nor heard his name linked with anyone's in that way."

"Well, Amina is a fine match for him. She's beautiful, smart, sophisticated, and compassionate. She loves this country with a passion that matches his, too. And I found out that she knows a hell of a lot about international business and economics, his kind of world. So when they've done with all the lovey-dovey stuff, they can actually talk to each other. They're perfect for each other."

"You know that and I know that and I'm certain Crispin has figured that out already. But pulling Amina out of her fortress won't be easy. You know your friend."

"Just a matter of time before he succeeds, Gaston. You should have seen them the first time they laid eyes on each other. We were in this restaurant in New York. Mama mia! You've never seen heat like that!" Shayna said, wringing her hands and executing a little dance.

Gaston caught her just before she fell.

"Well, my gazelle, Crispin is taking care of Amina as we speak and I have to take care of you, it seems. Come on. It's time to go," he said.

"So soon? Let's do one more beer after this one and one more session on the floor. Come on, Gaston," she pleaded.

"No deal. You've had enough of both."

"No I have not!" she said indignantly. She jumped up and stumbled against a young man who was ordering drinks. "Oops. Excuse me. I'm so clumsy," she said to the young man in perfectly accented Lingala, flashing him a sheepish smile.

"No problem. You can stumble against me any time," the young man replied, giving a split-second once-over. He threw Gaston a look of envy mixed with admiration.

Gaston took Shayna firmly by the arm and began to lead her away. "We're leaving now, Shayna, before you inflict more damage on the good *patrons* of this bar."

"Party pooper," Shayna said, sticking her tongue out at him.

"Help! Help!" she cried, feigning fear and trying to shake him off.

She stretched out her arms to the young man she almost knocked over. "Help me! He's abducting me!" she said.

The young man blew her a kiss and gave Gaston a thumbs-up sign. Gaston put an arm around Shayna's waist and pulled her toward the exit.

"Coward!" Shayna said to the young man.

The tone of her voice and the expression on her face made Gaston burst out laughing. He laughed so hard that he had to lean against the wall to keep him from doubling up.

"Jesus, Gaston. I didn't know I was that funny," Shayna said, laughing all the same.

For some reason that made Gaston laugh even harder. Soon they were both leaning against the wall, consumed by laughter. A passerby called to Gaston.

"*Gaston! Eh, mon cher!* Since when did you start drinking like that? The pretty lady must be a bad influence."

Gaston raised his head and called back to him. "You've got it wrong, Didier. She just did something very funny, that's all," he called back.

"If you say so," Didier said. "See you at the meeting on Monday."

"You bet," Gaston said.

He turned to Shayna and took her hand. "This time, we're really going, Shayna. We're disgracing ourselves."

"Who was that?" Shayna asked.

"The youngest minister in our government," Gaston replied cheerfully.

"Ooookay. We're outta here," Shayna said.

At that hour of the morning, she expected it to be chilly outside. "Oh! It's so warm. I'm in Africa, aren't I? I'm an African in Africa having a good time with a good African man," she sang gaily.

"Consider yourself privileged, my songbird. The car is right over there." He steered her toward the car.

"Mind if I sleep at your place? I'd hate to barge in on Amina and Crispin at this hour. All I need is one of your shirts to sleep in and the bedroom, of course. You can use the couch. I'm sure it's comfortable," she said as they walked toward Gaston's car.

"I have no problem with your spending the night at my house and yes, all the couches are comfortable. But I'll sleep in my own bed, thank you. I have a big house with lots of bedrooms. You can have any one of them."

"Show off," Shayna snorted.

They got into his BMW and drove off. Shayna chattered breezily about how wonderful the evening had been and how she never thought she could have so much fun in Kinshasa. Suddenly, she fell silent.

"Sleeping?" Gaston asked after a while.

"No. No, I'm not," she sighed. "Gaston, what do you really think of me?"

"I think you're an intelligent, strong woman who is not afraid to go after what you want or value, even when there's all kinds of muck and mire in the way and you're scared stiff. You're a woman who is often over-analytical, but who can be as spontaneous as life itself, like tonight. A woman I am proud to have as a friend and as a countryman—no, countrywoman—countryperson…whatever…fellow Congolese. Why do you ask?"

"Lately I don't seem to know who or what "me" is anymore."

"Well, you showed an awful lot of your Congolese "me" tonight—the way you danced, the way you spoke Lingala to that young man you almost wiped off the face of the earth. Your Lingala was so perfect he assumed you were Congolese. Come to think of it, even I thought nothing of it until now. It seemed so natural—as it should be."

Shayna leaned over and kissed him on the cheek.

"You're so kind, Gaston. You should be married and making some woman happy," she said.

"I'm not trying to be kind. I'm just stating things the way I see them. You're putting too much thought into being Congolese. That's not something you can intellectualize about, Shayna. There's no formula. You're Congolese and that's all there is to it. You are also American and that's that. You're making it seem as if there were some sort of—what's the word I want—some sort of competition, or tension, between the two. There's none. You're a perfect balance of both. You just don't see it yet," he said.

"That's exactly what Amina said. It's just that I feel as if I have to be a certain way—act differently, somehow," she said.

"Why? Maybe I should amend what I said about the Congolese part. You're Congolese, but not like regular Congolese. You're Congolese Shayna style. But that's okay. Don't get me wrong. After all, every race has its share of weirdoes," he said with a straight face.

Shayna hit him playfully with her purse and laughed, suddenly feeling much lighter.

"Ouch!" he said, laughing. "Anyway," he continued seriously, "who says I'm not married? I have a wife and two children in Boston."

"You do? In Boston, as in Massachusetts?"

"Oh yes. When things started to fall apart here we decided to move the family out. Europe was out of the question for me. America is where I wanted them."

"Why?"

"In America, my children can learn what it really means to be an African in today's world without hating themselves in the process. The lessons of color and cultural differences are stark in America. Living there makes you really appreciate your roots and recognize your responsibilities to your people. It does not annihilate you. In Europe, especially in France—which is the only place in Europe where I would live—those lessons are more blurred. It is too easy to lose yourself. There isn't a presence forceful enough to keep you culturally intact so that you know exactly who you are and exactly what your responsibilities are.

And then there is Africa. Here in our Congo, for example, when you are as wealthy as I am, especially in times like these, your children tend to grow up with a false sense of privilege and an arrogance that borders on obscenity. They often do not know what it is like to be responsible, to have to toil. I'm not talking about doing the job handed to you in the family business. I'm talking about going out there with nothing but your brain, your brawn, and your God—whatever you perceive that to be—and pitting all that against life's indifference.

But then, in our Congo, our children can be killed at any time, for any reason. Maybe that is why the wealthy ones are so apathetic while the poor ones worry about surviving. So I chose a place in between for my children, where there is enough pressure to keep them balanced, to keep them aware of who they are and what their responsibilities are as a consequence, but where they can also have fun. Besides, those New England schools are so damn good."

"A place in between," she repeated thoughtfully.

"Exactly. I believe life is all about finding that solid ground in the middle," he said.

"Well what do you know? Gaston's theory of middle ground...and all other ground is sinking sand," Shayna said, recalling the line in the chorus of hymn her mother sang when she was particularly frustrated. "I'm impressed. And I thought you were just a rich and shallow playboy," she teased.

Gaston responded seriously. "Not hardly, Shayna. In my line of business, I deal with women all the time. I deal with them both as customers and as business associates. I may take a few of them to dinner, accompany them to a reception or some other formal event if they ask me to; but it's always strictly business for me. Look at us. Did you know that people are already saying, "Gaston has a new lover"? That lover would be you, Ms. McWright. And all because I've been seen more than once with you, dancing, driving around. I've given up trying to protest my reputation, Shayna. The fact is, no one is more important to me than my wife and my children. And they know it. That's good enough for me."

"Your wife is a lucky woman. I hope I get to meet her when I go back to the States."

"When are you going back?"

"I don't know—soon. I miss my home. I miss Hilton. It's been nearly three months and I don't seem to be getting anywhere with this hunt for my birth mother. Maybe I'm too idealistic. Maybe I should just call it off and go home. The embassy wants me to go. They think I may be in danger from some Congolese guy who they think killed my mother."

"Yes. There are all sorts of rumors going around Kinshasa about that news report, which, by the way, has never been repeated either on radio or on television. They say the Congolese government pledged to cooperate fully with Washington to find the man, but also warned Washington to keep its big guns and its big mouth in check because there is no national conspiracy in this town to blow away Americans. Supposedly, we told Washington outright that we won't be a scapegoat for any plan for this country—or Africa, period—that Washington may have had up its sleeve all along."

"Hmmmm! Interesting. I didn't think any country besides Nigeria could be so bold," Shayna said, shaking her head slowly. "Hmmmm! That's really interesting," she said again. She kept shaking her head, half-smiling, as if she discovered an unexpectedly pleasing dimension to Congo.

"You know," she said after a while, "I have this gut feeling that if this guy really did it, it was for a deeply personal reason. Not that I am justifying it. It's just how I feel. I want them to find him so he could tell us what it is. And I want to be there when they question him."

"I agree. I feel it's personal. Notice no other American ambassador or diplomat or executive has been hit."

Shayna switched the subject. She did not want to be clinical about her mother's death.

"Do you honestly think I could find my birth mother, Gaston?"

"I'll be honest with you, Shayna. It's going to be extremely difficult, almost impossible. You can't put anything in the papers and you can't put the word out on the streets. All sorts of charlatans will crawl out of their wormholes."

"So you think I should give up?"

"I didn't say that."

They drove in silence for a while.

"You didn't finish your conversation with the Reverend Mother. Perhaps you should pay her a second visit," Gaston said quietly.

Shayna bolted up. "Is there something you're not telling me, Gaston?" she said sharply.

"No, Shayna. All I know is that you had to run out on your meeting with the Reverend Mother and she may still have more to say. It's as simple as that."

Shayna sighed.

"You're right. Will you take me back?"

"Of course. Here we are. Home, sweet home."

Gaston lived in a Spanish-style villa in Mbinza, on the same street as Crispin's parents. He pointed out their house to Shayna as they passed it, but she was too sleepy to pay attention. She yawned and leaned heavily on Gaston's arm as they walked from the garage to his front door. Her legs seemed ready to give out.

"I think I had too much to drink, Gaston."

"I'm not touching that one."

"Don't!"

"Mama Jeannette! Ma-Jeannetti-ay!" Gaston called out as he closed the door behind them.

An elderly woman hustled into the room, wrapping her "pagne" more securely around her waist.

"I'm coming! I'm coming! No need to shout at the top of your lungs at this hour of the night," she fussed in Lingala.

"Mama Jeannette, this is a friend of Amina's. She's spending the night here. Help her get to bed."

He spoke to the old woman in Lingala, switching back to English when he turned to Shayna.

"Mama Jeannette is my wife's aunt. She'll take you off my hands now. See you in the morning."

He kissed her on the forehead and went upstairs.

"Nite. And thanks, Gaston," Shayna said, yawning sleepily.

Mama Jeannette smiled at Shayna, said something to her in rapid-fire Lingala, and guided her along a corridor on the ground floor to a guestroom. Shayna made a beeline for the bed, flung herself across it, and promptly fell asleep. Mama Jeannette removed her shoes, eased her body around until it was stretched out along the length of the bed and spread a cover over her. She plugged in the scented electric mosquito repellent and turned to leave the room.

Halfway to the door, she turned back and stared at Shayna. She stood there for a long moment, frowning as she studied Shayna's face. Finally, she crossed the room and opened the door. She turned again to take another look at Shayna's face then closed the door softly.

Gaston went into his own room and telephoned Amina.

#

Crispin picked up his phone on the second ring. He was used to receiving calls this late. He was awake anyway. His need for Amina would not let him sleep.

"Crispin," he said into the phone.

He listened for a while then spoke.

"You have brought me good news, your Grace. I am delighted. I will make arrangements to travel with you when you leave today."

He listened for a few minutes more and hung up. He stood there, staring at the floor. He was in his living room, dressed in a robe and pajamas. He crossed the room, slid back one half of the patio doors and stepped outside into the warm, still night. Not a leaf stirred. He looked up at the sky. The moon was behind a cloud. The stars were as diamonds scattered languidly on a blue-black velvet sheet.

"Amina," he said softly. Her name seemed to escape into the night with a will of its own. He leaned against one of the marble columns on the patio and folded his arms. He spoke her name over and over again in his mind, seeing her face, feeling her body against his. He tried to imagine how it would be if she loved him as he loved her. *What if she never loves me? What if it remains just a physical attraction for her? What if she could never gets past her fears?* He pushed away those thoughts. He would give her time as he promised. *Maybe it's good that I am going away*, he told himself. The last thing I would want to do is crowd her.

About half an hour later, he stepped back into the living room and locked the door. He went to the phone and dialed her number. She answered on the first ring, as if she had been waiting for his call.

"Yes?"

"Amina…" He heard her exhale. "Amina, leaving you was so very hard."

"You could have stayed. You didn't have to go," she said.

"I know. But I meant what I said about wanting all of you."

"Crispin, I…"

"It's okay, Amina. I also meant what I said about waiting."

She said nothing. He spoke again.

"Amina, I have to go away tomorrow—later today, actually."

He heard the slight catch in her breath.

"You do?" She spoke in whispery voice. He yearned to hold her, to tell her how much he loved her.

"I didn't know this until a short while ago. I have to go back to the UAE with the delegation to finalize—to sign some papers. Prince Farouk just called me."

"But that's good news, isn't it? It's what you were hoping for. I'm happy for you. Of course you must go," she said with bravado.

"Maybe it's better this way. I don't want to crowd you," he said.

"When will you be back?" she asked quickly.

"In a few days, a week, maybe longer, depending on what happens there. I may have to go to China when I leave, possibly even Brazil."

"Oh. I hope it goes well for you."

"Will you be here when I return?"

"Only if you will be gone for a short while. I planned to leave in just over a week."

It was his turn to be silent. He wondered if she would stay if he asked her to.

Amina waited for him to speak, with bated breath. *I wonder if he will ask me to stay*, she thought. And would I, if he did?

Neither would ever know.

"I pray that you learn to love me, Amina," he said finally.

"I'll miss you, Crispin," she said.

#

The telephone on the nightstand next to Ambassador DeGrasse's bed rang. The ambassador's eyes flew open and he automatically looked at the clock beside the phone: two a.m. He reached for the phone before it finished ringing the second time. Fully alert, he listened to the caller for several minutes.

"Consider it done," was all he said.

He hung up and got out of bed. His wife stirred and rolled over on her side to look at him.

"Everything all right, dear?" she asked, reaching out a hand to him.

He took her hand and kissed it. "Yes, dear. Go back to sleep. I'll just sit in the alcove for a while."

He reached for his robe and felt around under the bed with his feet for his slippers. Tying the band around his robe, he shuffled over to the chocolate-brown leather recliner in the little alcove on the far side of the bedroom. He eased himself into the chair and lit a cigar. The chair faced a window that looked out over a rolling green lawn. This was his most private spot in the residence. It was inviolate. Not even his wife sat there. It was just big enough for his recliner, a little side table, and a small bookshelf. It is where he came when duty called and he was reluctant to answer.

He thought of Shayna McWright and the instructions he was just given. The call came directly from Washington, from the CIA director himself.

"Move her out of there next Sunday and I don't care what she says. Our suspect is being taken in on Monday. Take Dr. Milenga too. We don't want her caught up in anything. Miller knows the plan."

Ambassador DeGrasse sighed. He felt sympathy for Shayna, knowing how badly she wanted to find her mother. Needed to, he corrected himself. More than anyone else he understood that need. An adopted child himself, he recalled his own quest for his birth mother, the years it had taken even with a paper trail, then finding her. He had only a few precious months with her. She'd already been diagnosed with terminal breast cancer.

He did not have the heart to tell Shayna that he did not believe she would ever find her birth mother. Janice McWright erased every link to her adopted daughter's Congolese family, except for the papers that the Jesuit priests had. The Reverend Mother called to tell him about those papers the same day Shayna visited the convent. Shayna had already left and was on her way to the embassy. She left before she had a chance to tell her, the Reverend Mother said. Perhaps he could mention it to her.

But he forgot to mention it to Shayna. Ashamed, he himself went to see Father Elens, head of the brotherhood in the Congo, only to learn from him that the priest who oversaw the records went insane one night years ago and set himself afire in his office. The priest lived, but most of the records were lost in the fire, including all the records from the 1960s and '70s.

Ambassador DeGrasse reached for the bottle of Remy Martin brandy that sat permanently on the small table beside the recliner, and poured himself a shot. He downed it immediately. Usually, one shot was all he needed to relax. Not this time. He took another shot. He suddenly felt old and tired. He was not looking forward to Operation Janice.

In his 30 years with the Foreign Service, serving in Congo was his most frustrating assignment. It wasn't his first assignment in Africa by any means. He served in just about every trouble spot on the continent, as he had in Asia, the Middle East, and more recently, in Eastern Europe. The difference here was the feeling of helplessness. The feeling that the United States wielded no clout whatsoever in the unfolding situation in the Congo; the feeling that he himself belonged to a different era in foreign policy, where things were more cut and dry, more predictable, and where his benign manner was enough to win over the most belligerent adversary.

These days, developing countries like the Congo were led by a proud, much more hard-line group of people who were not at all quick to bow to Western pressure. These leaders were largely children of the post-colonial era and, therefore, much more exposed to the ways of the West. They had witnessed too many undelivered promises, too many shifting goal posts and double standards on trade rules and aid for economic development. They learned from the West that charity really should begin at home; that, as the song says, love of self is the greatest love of all and it is this that gives power to the powerful.

So they began to design their own strategies and form alliances to fit those strategies, knowing that even if they fucked things up for their countries, it was their own homegrown fuck-up. There was pride in that. Hell, can you blame them? That kind of pride was as American as apple pie. If you're going to hell anyway, why not ride in a chariot of your own making than be hauled there in somebody else's ass-drawn pine box? *Nobody said it better than Sinatra*, he thought. Quietly, so as not to wake his wife, he hummed a few bars of "My Way." He was beginning to mellow.

On his fourth glass of brandy, it struck him that he was witnessing right here in Kinshasa the parameters of the new game that would be played out in the next millennium. The swiftness of the collapse of Mobutu's government, with the big Kahuna himself ignominiously fleeing the country, took Washington by surprise. Surprise quickly gave way to annoyance and finger pointing, with Ambassador DeGrasse on the receiving end of the pointing. Then came Kabila who, cheered on by Washington, set off on a good foot toward reconstruction and reform, only to renege on his promises to democratize the political system and clean up the country's administration and finances.

In Ambassador DeGrasse's eyes, that was tantamount to pouring salt on a fresh wound. It was all so unpredictable, so humiliating. That was when they decided to send in Tom Miller, a.k.a. "The Ferret," an upstart with a mere city college education with a knack for ferreting out accurate and timely information in seemingly the most hopeless situations. He was the agency's new golden boy. Now this. Shayna McWright had thumbed her nose at Washington's concerns, not to mention their golden boy, and he had been unable to do anything about it. Ambassador DeGrasse was no fool. He knew that Operation Janice was his final test.

He pondered his options. He could stay on in the service after his tour in Congo ended next year. They would prefer that, he knew. Keep down any noises about trouble on the diplomatic front. They would find a low profile but dignified spot for him in some remote country with no strategic interest to the U.S., or even in Washington itself. On the other hand, he could use his connections to keep himself on the high profile end of things for a few more years. It would ruffle a few feathers, but it could be done. There was always the other option, of course, the one that had nothing to do with Washington at all. He laughed bitterly to himself. *Let's face it, the name DeGrasse is like mud in Washington these days*, he thought.

Washington...his thoughts dwelled on the politics of his nation's capital for a while. Underneath its outreach to "new and emerging markets"—a campaign whose language suggested that a softer eye would be cast in the direction of Asia, Africa, and Latin America—Washington was just as hard line in its foreign policies. Perhaps more so now, as Congress and administration after administration paid attention to the voices on the home front. The Department of Defense was making the case that the world was still dangerous even without a Soviet threat. Labor and environmentalists wanted to curb practices in foreign countries that benefited overseas production and hurt American factories and workers. Multinationals wanted unimpeded access to overseas markets, infrastructure development contracts, and raw materials. Intelligence was pressing the point that the fight for global markets was a real war in which American companies needed the skills and connections of the intelligence community.

Ambassador DeGrasse shared every one of those views. Self-interest was, is, and always should be the order of the day among nations. But it's how that interest accommodated the interests of others that determined whether the world was at peace or at war. Ambassador DeGrasse was not sure what the world was coming to; nor was he sure there was a role for him in whatever way Washington planned to deal with the notion of accommodation, if indeed it planned to do so.

Piddling as it seemed amid all that he reflected on, Operation Janice made him realize how very tired and out-of-place he was. Perhaps it was the way the instructions were delivered to him. He did not know. But he cared about such things.

He stood up, drank the remaining contents in his glass, and placed the glass on the table. He stood at the open window and took a deep breath. He took a second, then a third. He turned from the window, walked over to his bed and looked down at his sleeping wife. He smiled. They shared forty years together and children and grandchildren that made a man's heart swell with joy and gratitude.

He untied his robe, tossed it to the foot of the bed and slipped under the sheets. Lying on his back, his eyes fixed on the ceiling, he made his decision. The end of his tenure in Congo would be the end of the line for him. *Time to hit that road, old boy*, he said to himself, as he snuggled contentedly against his wife.

CHAPTER TWENTY-THREE

Early Sunday morning in Kinshasa was like early Sunday morning in the cities and towns of any country where Christianity was the dominant religion. The world seemed to sigh and turn inward, as if observing a welcome truce. The only stirring in the town were the goings-on of market women preparing to leave their homes. Sunday was no different from any other day in the contract they had with life.

Shayna and Amina sat in the living room of Amina's apartment, looking glum and sleepy. They were never up this early on a Sunday. And fully dressed at that, albeit casually. They had been up since dawn and had already had a light breakfast. They hardly slept. In fact, Shayna spent the night in Amina's room, stretched out on the bed beside her. They talked for hours, recounting the incredulous turn the day had taken. They fell asleep about two hours before dawn.

Saturday had been the usual grocery shopping and visits with some of Amina's friends. They just returned home when Tom Miller called to say he would be dropping by around seven that evening. He would love to have dinner with them, he said, sounding as cheerful as if they were old friends and it was perfectly normal for him to invite himself over for dinner on a Saturday night. The call puzzled Shayna and Amina. But they soon agreed that it had something to do with Janice McWright's death and the alleged assassin roaming around the country. Miller was the melodramatic type, Shayna said to Amina.

They were totally unprepared for Miller's announcement that they both had to leave the country the next morning, orders from Washington. It was all arranged, he said before they could protest. They were to pack their things immediately and he would take them with him that very night. A car would come for them at seven in the morning. They were to dress casually as if they were going into the country for the day. They would be flown to Italy and from there to United States. An armed agent would be on both flights. No, the agent's identity would not be disclosed. They would be met at the airport, of course.

"I'm afraid you are not to tell anyone you're leaving. You can contact anyone you need to contact once you're back in the States," Miller said, almost apologetically.

"What's happening, Tom?" Shayna said quietly.

Miller nodded appreciatively at the use of his first name. He had hoped they would part on good terms after their meeting in Ambassador DeGrasses's office. He felt she at least respected him. He would settle for that. She didn't have to like him, though he himself liked her. He liked her a whole lot, in fact.

His face felt warm as she faced him squarely. There was no sign of hostility in her eyes or in her voice.

He spoke candidly. U.S. intelligence had located the suspect in Kinshasa and were about to have him picked up by the Congolese security police, he said. While they had no evidence of a plot to harm Shayna, they were not taking any chances. Amina was equally vulnerable because she was so often in Shayna's company.

Shayna and Amina protested in vain.

How could he expect her to drop everything and run, without a word to anyone, Amina demanded. She had patients waiting to see her. What will they do? The doctor who took over when she was in America would not be there for another two weeks. She couldn't just walk out like that! It was unconscionable.

Miller shrugged. "I'm sorry, Dr. Milenga. We have our orders. I don't mean to sound callous, but if you're killed, your patients would not be seeing you anyway."

"But you have no proof of anything. This is insane!" Amina said, knowing already that she would be in New York the next day.

Shayna held out a bit longer. "Tom, we went over this already. I'm here on a mission and I haven't accomplished it yet. I promised I would leave soon, but not this soon. And certainly not this way," she said, trying to make her voice agreeable.

"It's not up to me, Ms. McWright. Perhaps you should start packing now. It will be a long day for you tomorrow. You'll need a good night's sleep." His eyes smiled at her.

Amina stood up.

You came to dinner, Mr. Miller. We'll dine first," she said wearily.

As they waited for the car to arrive, Shayna thought of the nearly three months she spent in Kinshasa, a city she was beginning to understand and accept in a way she never would have believed possible. Somehow, at some point, she did not know when, she had dropped her defenses—"shed the crap," as Amina would say—and opened herself to the city. Amina and Gaston made her see herself as an integral part of it. She was no less or no more a "kinois" than either of them.

A few weeks after her disastrous visit to the court, she started walking around the city on her own. She hoped her walks would jog her memory, or that the sight of her would jog someone else's memory. They were anxious walks at first. She would peer into the faces of the people around her with an intensity that puzzled most of the passers-by. A few even stopped to greet her, asking apologetically if they met before.

But no memories were jogged. So she abandoned the pursuit of recognition and concentrated on discovering this maddening but seductive city that was her birthplace. It was foolish to go on pretending that Kinshasa was an intrusion in her life, she told herself.

The more she walked or rode around with Gaston, the more she wanted to know the city in the most carnal sense of the word. She wanted every nerve in her to respond to its rhythms. Now and then, a certain fragrance or smell would make her stop abruptly, and she would struggle to connect the smell to something she knew was part of her past. But the connection would elude her, leaving her with the feeling of having lost something precious, but with the comfort of knowing she had walked this way before.

Once, when Gaston took her on a tour of the cîtés, she thought she heard someone call out "Shayna Yasmin!" She clutched at Gaston, looking around wildly.

"Did you hear that, Gaston? Someone called me! I could swear someone called me!"

But there was no one.

Then there was the time she and Amina went shopping in the Grand Marché. She wandered away from Amina and stumbled upon a scene that horrified her. A soldier was hitting a young man with the butt of his rifle. The young man's face was bloody. A small crowd gathered, but no one was trying to intervene. In fact, they seemed to be cheering on the soldier. Shayna glared around in indignation and was about to step up to the soldier when a smartly dressed man standing beside her touched her arm gently but firmly and put his mouth to her ear.

"We're all kinois, aren't we, my sister? Let it be. We both know what is happening here," he said in Lingala, keeping his eyes on the soldier.

Shayna turned to him. She did not understand every word, but she got the gist of it. But the man had already stepped back into the crowd and was gone. Shayna caught up with Amina and told her what happened. Amina did not seem at all surprised.

"The soldier was probably beating a thief or a spy for the rebels.

Sometimes when you see such things you just have to let them be. There is a certain kind of justice in Africa that is hard for many people to accept," she said. "I hope you realize he saved you from being arrested and thrown into jail."

After dinner that night, as they talked about the market episode, Amina had said to her, "You see how well you blend into Kinshasa? That man didn't think twice about your being one of us. That's what I mean when I say you're waging a war with yourself that has nothing to do with the rest of us. For the rest of us, you belong."

Maybe that's when I really started to feel I belong here, Shayna said to herself. She stretched and slumped down into the chair, looking at her watch.

"They should be here any moment now," she said dejectedly.

Amina did not reply. She sat in the same spot Crispin sat in just a week ago, her legs stretched out under the coffee table as his had been. Her eyes were closed. She emptied her mind and was focused solely on her breathing. She didn't want to think of where she would be before the day was over. She didn't want to dwell on the fact that she would not be here when Crispin came back, that he might think she had "run away" from becoming involved with him the way he wanted her to. For the first time since she started coming back to Kinshasa, she was sad to leave. She had always been happy to leave, knowing that she was going back to so much that she loved…knowing, too, that she would be returning soon.

"I'm so sorry, Amina, so sorry to have gotten you into this."

Amina opened her eyes. Shayna was kneeling before her, looking at her anxiously. Amina smiled. She reached out and rubbed Shayna's head. "Don't worry about it, Shayna. What difference will a few days make?"

"But you're not ready to leave yet. Crispin…"

"Crispin wouldn't have been back before I left, anyway. I got an e-mail from him on Friday saying he would be away for another week at least," she lied.

Crispin's e-mail said he was returning that very Sunday, but only for a few days, as he had to be in Brazil later in the week.

"I don't believe you. You look heartbroken," Shayna said.

"I'm not heartbroken," Amina said, forcing a laugh. "I guess I'm just overwhelmed. It's all so sudden, so unreal. It's like we're in some low-budget Cold War movie."

"I know what you mean. I still get these feelings that I'll wake up one day and Hilton will be holding me and telling me that I've been having a bad dream. That I was saying all sorts of crazy things in my sleep about my mother being assassinated in Brussels, about being half-Congolese and going to Kinshasa to find my birth mother. But even as I think that, I know it isn't a dream. There's no waking up to the life I knew before that day in April. It's all real, Amina."

She laid her head on Amina's lap and Amina stroked her hair.

"I was supposed to go with Gaston to see the Reverend Mother again," Shayna continued. "I guess I'll have to come back when they've caught whoever it is they're looking for. I want to find her so bad, Amina."

"I know. We won't give up," Amina said gently, still stroking her hair.

The knock on the door made them jump at the same time. They looked at each other. Amina shrugged.

"This is it, I guess," she said, trying to sound cheerful.

She stood up, picked up a small bag and moved toward the door. Shayna picked up her pocketbook and an overnight bag. She looked around with a sigh.

"I'll be back," she said, mimicking Arnold Schwarzenegger's heavy Austrian accent from his line in the movie "Terminator."

A black Lincoln town car with darkened windows and an American flag on the bonnet whisked them through the still sleeping Kinshasa to the airport. Ambassador DeGrasse himself was accompanying them so he could "get them through that nightmare at the airport without any headaches," he explained to Miller and the consul general. Actually, either the consul general or Miller would have served just as well. But the ambassador insisted on going himself. He shared a special kinship with Shayna, he told his wife.

Shayna and Amina were flown directly to Rome, where they boarded an American Airlines flight for New York an hour or so later. They slept most of the way, waking up to have a meal, to chat a bit, or to think about how the recent past would shape their future. Huddled against the window, a blanket covering her from head to toe, Amina cried silently to herself part of the way.

#

He was the first person Shayna saw when she emerged from Customs and Immigration at JFK. He was standing there with a broad grin on his face, a bouquet of yellow roses in his hands. He stretched out his arms to her. She uttered a cry of joy and ran toward him. Hilton picked her up and swung her around. When he set her down, they clung to each other for a long time, oblivious of the stares and smiles cast in their direction. Finally, Hilton held her away from him and looked at her with so much love that Shayna's eyes filled with tears. She opened her mouth to speak, but he put a finger on her lips.

"Shhhh," he said. "Someone called your Aunt Fiona and she called me. Even before you left New York, I was miserable. I called her one night just to talk about you. She was so understanding, so comforting. We spoke often after that. So when the FBI called to say you were coming home and knowing how I feel about you, she thought it was right for me to be here. So here I am, asking you again to marry me."

"Yes. Oh yes, Hilton. I do want to marry you. But I still don't know who I am," Shayna said, looking up at him anxiously.

"Yes you do, Shayna. You know who you are. You just don't know who your mother is. It's you I want to marry, not your mother," Hilton said.

Shayna's eyes brimmed again.

"I'll have to go back," she said.

"I know. May I tag along?"

"I'm not so sure you're ready for Kinshasa, Hilton," she said seriously.

"I said the same thing about you in April, my pet."

Shayna laughed. "I love you so much, Hilton. I've never been so sure of anything as I am of that," she said.

#

Merry and Jamillah glanced worriedly at each other when they saw Amina's face. She had not yet seen them. They had already seen Shayna "flying past everybody like a mad woman and literally flinging herself at Hilton," Jamillah was to say later. Amina walked with her usual slow, graceful stride, scanning the crowd. Her face seemed so sad and so drained that Merry gasped. Jamillah scowled. Normally, when Amina returned from Kinshasa, she was as bouncy as a woman reborn.

"What has happened to her, for God's sake?" Merry said, clutching at Jamillah.

"We'll soon find out. But I hope that Crispy Creme guy or whatever the hell his name is did not hurt her, because if he did, I swear to God I'll find a way to hurt him back," Jamillah said grimly.

Amina spotted them just then and her face lit up, pushing the sadness out her eyes. She strode quickly toward them. Merry and

Jamillah ran to her. They fell into each other's arms and hugged all at once, Merry's hard, protruding stomach getting in the way.

Amina spoke first. "It's so good to see the two of you. Christ, Merry, you're huge! Sure you're not carrying twins? How did you know I was coming?"

"Your mother called me from Los Angeles. She's attending some conference there. You know your mother. Grass doesn't grow under her feet," Jamillah said. "Anyway, she said everybody else was out of town as well. Nobody was expecting you until next week, of course. So here we are."

Merry could not contain herself. She put her arms around Amina again and pressed her cheek against hers.

"Oh, Amina. What's wrong? Why did you look so sad when you came through the doors?"

"Did I look sad? I didn't know I looked sad?" Amina sounded evasive.

"Well, you did and it's got us worried sick," Jamillah said gruffly. "What happened with you and that Crispy guy?" she demanded.

"It's Crispin, Jammy," Amina giggled. She took a deep breath and looked at them with resignation. "I guess it's useless trying to hide my feelings from the two of you," she said. The sparkle in her eyes died.

"Yes it is and you know it. So it has to do with him, doesn't it?"

"I don't want to talk about it. Not yet."

"Come on, let's go. We'll talk about it later," Merry said quickly, slipping her arm through Amina's.

Amina had that stubborn set to her mouth that they knew so well. Normally, they would ignore it and press on with whatever they were challenging her about. But this was different ground—too sensitive.

The three of them started walking toward Shayna and Hilton. Jamillah carried Amina's bag. They were all smiles by the time they reached Shayna and Hilton.

Shayna hugged Merry and Jamillah. Her face glowed. She introduced them all to Hilton, calling him her boyfriend.

"Fiancé. She just agreed to marry me, finally," Hilton said, sounding more relieved than overjoyed.

Everybody hugged everybody again, the women squealing, Hilton looking proud as he accepted their congratulations.

"Well," said Jamillah, "What a day! I'm sure Shayna and Amina are pooped. Let's all go home. See you soon, Shayna. You'll have to join us for the usual post mortem on Amina's stay in Kinshasa. We've got to add your experience to the mix."

"You bet," Shayna said. She put her arms around Amina.

"I can't thank you enough, Amina. I may not have found my mother, but I found so much more of me, with a lot of help from you," she said. Putting her mouth against Amina's ear, she whispered, "Crispin will come to you, you know," she whispered.

Amina smiled at her. "Maybe, maybe not…but I really enjoyed having you with me in Kinshasa, Shayna. You were good company. And though you may not know it, you helped me resolve a lot of my own issues. Thank you for your strength. We'll see each other soon. It's hard to believe we'll wake up in New York tomorrow, isn't it?"

"I know. But I'm glad to be home. See you soon."

They hugged each other again and parted company. Shayna and Hilton headed for the limousine Hilton rode in to meet his bride-to-be. Merry, Jamillah, and Amina trundled toward the parking lot to pick up Black Magic, Jamillah's eight-year-old Volvo.

"We're sleeping over at your place tonight as usual," Jamillah announced as they got into the car.

"You'd better," Amina said, settling herself in the front passenger seat.

Jamillah put the key into the ignition. She started to turn it and stopped. She sat motionless, her hand on the key. After a moment, she turned to Amina.

"Just answer me this right now. Did he hurt you?" she demanded.

"You call this 'later?'" Amina said incredulously.

"Yes. Answer her. Did he hurt you?" Merry piped up from the back.

Amina sighed and shook her head, appreciating, nevertheless, the depth of their concern for her.

"No he didn't. He's in love with me," she said cheerlessly.

"And that makes you sad?"

"No. It's just that I had to leave before I could sort out how I really feel about him," Amina said.

"He came up against your wall," Jamillah said gently.

"Yep, my famous wall," Amina said with some annoyance.

"So you'll sort out how you feel right here in New York, then let him know. What's the big rush? You have every right to take it slow after what you went through with that dog Michael," Merry declared. Her legs were stretched out on the seat and her back against the door. "Besides, he'll find his way to you soon enough if he really loves you," she added.

"I'm not so sure, Merry. He may think that I left because I decided that I could not love him. He would respect that and stay away," Amina said.

"Without a fight? Without even trying to find out for sure? Well, if it were me I'd come running!" Merry said.

"So you'll tell him the truth about why you left. Call him. Send him an e-mail," Jamillah said.

Amina said nothing. Jamillah knitted her brow.

"Amina, you *will* let him know why you left so suddenly, right?" she said.

"No, she won't. She'll just sit there loving him to death as we all know she does already and moping because she wants him to come to her no matter why she left. And he'll sit there loving her to death and waiting for her to come to him as proof that she loves him. So both of them will sit there on opposite sides of the damn ocean, miserable as hell in their proof prisons, like some cheap romance novel. Tchuh," Merry said, sucking her teeth in disgust. "Tell mi mi wrang, Amina."

"Yeah, tell her she's wrong, Amina," Jamillah said, turning around and staring coldly at Merry.

"Please, you two. Let's just go home," Amina said wearily.

"Yes, Jamillah, start Black Magic and mek we go before mi ha fi pee in this parking lot," Merry grumbled.

Jamillah and Amina burst out laughing. Merry grumbled some more about proof prisons and peeing then started laughing herself.

#

On his way home from Ndjili airport, Crispin was excited at the thought of seeing Amina. He preferred not to call her from the car. Instead, he would call her the moment he got home. Who was he trying to kid? It was obvious that she cared for him. Wasn't that enough? Did he have to demand her whole soul? Who was he to demand such a thing, anyway? He would take what she could give right now. The rest will come in time. And if it doesn't? He'll take his chances. He needed her in his life.

"*Patron*, had a good trip?" Mizele's voice broke into his thoughts.

Crispin raised his eyes to the rearview mirror and met Mizele's. "Yes. It was a good trip. Very good," he said curtly. He did not feel like talking. He went back to his thoughts. Amina hadn't responded to his e-mail. He didn't make a big deal of it. He figured she simply had not signed on. It was the weekend, after all. She probably never signed-on on the weekend. He glanced up again and saw Mizele still looking at him in the rearview mirror, as if waiting for him to say something. It was the first time Mizele came to meet him at the airport. In fact, it was the first time Mizele drove him anywhere. He knew Mizele said something about Moussa, his regular driver, being suddenly called away, but he could not recall if he had given any details.

Mizele insisted on learning to drive a few months ago.

"You never know when I may be called upon to use such a skill, *patron.* Life is very unpredictable in Kinshasa these days," he argued.

Crispin gave in without a fight. Mizele would have worn him down anyway, raising the subject morning, noon, and night until it drove him crazy. That was standard Mizele procedure. Not that he regretted conceding. Mizele's reasoning was very much on point. In Kinshasa, you had to be prepared for every emergency. So he asked Moussa to teach him to drive.

"And don't even think of putting God out of your thoughts to ask me for a car," he warned Mizele.

Aw, *patron.* Could I be that presumptuous?"

"Absolutely."

Seeing the eager expression in Mizele's eyes now, it dawned on him that he ought to say something about his driving. Decked out in sunglasses and a shirt and trousers Crispin discarded, Mizele looked like he owned the Mercedes. Crispin studied the image Mizele projected, trying to hide a smile.

"You drive well, Mizele," he said.

Mizele grinned with pleasure.

"Oh no, *patron.* Far from it. I'm still learning," he said bashfully.

"Cut the crap, Mizele. You drive damn well and you know it."

Mizele sighed.

"Ah, *patron.* You should allow me some modesty."

"You don't know the meaning of the word. Where did you say Moussa was?

"Your father sent him on an errand."

"Okay. Who called me while I was away?"

"Your Chinese brother called just this morning to say he was on for the meeting."

"Good. Anyone else?"

"Many others. I logged them all into my computer. I have the printout at home," Mizele said importantly.

Crispin rolled his eyes. Installing a computer and printer in his room had been another one of Mizele's recommendations.

"*Patron*, I strongly recommend you provide me with a computer. I can use it to prepare my reports on the situation at home, especially when you travel. You can study them at your leisure," Mizele told him with a straight face one morning.

Still, he had to admit that getting him the computer was worth it. Many times he returned to Mizele's one-page reports and phone call summaries for information he could not find anywhere else or to verify a phone number. He found out later that Mizele was accessing the Internet to research market conditions and prices for traders—for a fee, of course. Mizele defended his actions on the grounds of national interest.

"But, *patron,* my information gives our traders an edge over those gangsters across the river. I am performing a valuable service to our country."

Crispin chased him away, thinking for the umpteenth time that Mizele's gifts of gab and hustle will make him a very wealthy or very dead man one day. He did not stop Mizele's research business. The truth was, he respected Mizele's enterprising mind.

Crispin's thoughts turned to the message from ET. Glaucio wanted the group to meet in Brazil that very week. He stressed that they needed to take some heavy-duty action in Sao Paulo right away, if they wanted to win the bid for the shipping line. Whatever they did, it had to be a show of force, carried out in person; that meant money, *and* calling in some big names. All the old assumptions were out the window, Glaucio said in an urgent call to Crispin. His inside sources were telling him that a particular bidder—he would name names when they met, he told Crispin—was taking major steps to ensure that they won the bid themselves.

Crispin was not surprised. It didn't even matter who upped the ante. It wasn't the first time that a winning bid would be determined by the attractiveness of its offsets and ancillary perks, rather than mushy stuff like Third World pride and dealing a blow to the global power structure. Brazil was in a win-win situation whichever way the chips fell. All the bidders were topnotch names. The country would get a huge chunk of the global shipping business no matter who won the bid. So what harm would it do if one or two members of the deciding committee managed to set up educational funds for their children in the process?

Crispin understood that reasoning.

"I'm ready to get down and dirty if that's what it's going to take, Glaucio. I know you are too," he told Glaucio.

"I thought you would be...any news from the peninsula?" Glaucio asked, referring to Crispin's meetings with the Emirati.

"Very good news indeed: they're in. They've agreed to take a minority position in our consortium and to make some investments in Brazil's maritime sector, which is something they've been talking about with your folks for a while, apparently. They'll also put some money into upgrading the Matadi infrastructure, of course. *And*, they're going public with the news right away. They'll probably leak it to *The Journal of Commerce*. I'll fill everyone in on the details when we meet."

"Great! That's a huge plus for us, Crispin, especially with the new turn of events. We'll also have to let the word out. Oh man! This is just great!"

"Who's left to contact for the meeting?"

"Just ET. You deal with him. You always know where to reach him."

Crispin roused himself from his thoughts as Mizele turned into his driveway.

"Well, at least you kept us standing, Mizele," he said as he got out of the car.

Mizele beamed. "I try my best, *patron.* Welcome home, *patron.*" He picked up Crispin's bags and headed toward the back door.

Crispin stayed to chat for a few minutes with the watchman, and then went inside. He dropped his briefcase on a couch, picked up the phone, and dialed Amina's number. Her recording came on after four rings. Crispin hung up without leaving a message. He looked at his watch and knitted his brow. He dialed again. This time, he left a message. "Amina, this is Crispin. I'm back in Kinshasa. I'd like to see you. Please call."

"Excuse me, *patron*," Mizele said. He came into the room in time to hear Crispin leave a message in English for the American doctor.

"What is it, Mizele?" Crispin asked irritably.

"I saw your two American lady friends at the airport while I was waiting for you. I think they have left, sir."

"Left?"

"Yes, *patron.* They have left the country. I saw them get on the plane. A white man walked with them right up to the steps. He stayed on the tarmac until the plane took off. I think he was the American ambassador because the car he left in had the American flag on it."

"Are you sure it was the same ladies who were here? Both of them?"

"I would know them from any angle, *patron.*"

Crispin gave him a threatening look.

"What I mean is, they stand out from everyone else, *patron.* It would be easy for anyone who has seen them once to recognize them again, *patron*," Mizele said quickly.

"Thank you, Mizele."

"Will you have your meal now, *patron*?"

"Later. And there were no calls from Dr. Milenga?"

"No, *patron*. None."

Crispin felt hollow inside. Amina could not have left like that. She would have told him, sent an e-mail, left word on his phone, or with Mizele. She would have let him know somehow. Surely she would...or would she? He went into the study and turned on his computer, tapping his foot impatiently as he waited to connect to his e-mail. There was nothing from her. He logged off and hurried out to his car. The watchman sprang to open the gate. Crispin sped all the way to Amina's building and pulled into the driveway. He stopped just beyond the entrance to the building, jumped out and ran into the lobby.

"Dr. Milenga is not here, *patron.* She and Ms. McWright left early this morning. They have not returned," the doorman said.

"Did she leave a message for me?"

"I'm afraid not, *patron.*"

Crispin started to walk away. Abruptly, he turned back to the doorman.

"You have no idea if they..." he stopped. "Never mind," he said and walked slowly out to his car.

The doorman watched him leave. *A man can never hide the fact that he is in love*, he thought. He came out from behind his desk and walked casually to the entrance. The car was still there. *Patron* Abeli was sitting behind the wheel staring ahead of him. His expression was unreadable behind his sunglasses.

The doorman walked up to the car. "Excuse me, *patron*," he said.

Crispin turned to him and waited for him to continue.

"Forgive me, *patron*, but I just thought of something."

"Yes?"

"I think Dr. Milenga has left the country, *patron*. It was something she said. She is a very nice lady, *patron*, very kind and considerate. She never passes me without greeting me or asking about my family. Today was no different. She waved to me as she was leaving with Ms. McWright and said 'Stay strong, warrior Masumu.' That's what she said."

"Stay strong, warrior Masumu."

"Yes, *patron.* Masumu is my name. Dr. Milenga said 'stay strong, warrior Masumu.' That's what she always says when she's returning to America. It's the only time she says that to me."

Crispin turned away from the doorman and looked into the distance. The doorman stepped back from the car and waited, studying the face of a man who has just learned that the woman he loves left without saying goodbye. There wasn't much to see. Not a muscle moved his face. *This man's love is like steel*, the doorman thought.

Crispin took a deep breath. "Thank you for that information, Masumu. In any case, if she does return, please tell her that I came by.

"You are welcome, *patron*. I will do that, *patron*."

Crispin pulled away from the curb and drove out to the wide boulevard that would take him home. The doorman went back to his desk.

Crispin took the road that ran along the Congo River. Not far from his home, he parked the car and got out. He walked over to the railing along the promenade and leaned on it, looking at the river. This pain that tore through every fiber of his being he had never known. This is the pain she had spoken of at her apartment that night. He understood, now, her fear of feeling that pain again. He loved her more now than he had loved her the day before. He knew he would love her always, even though she may be gone from him forever.

CHAPTER TWENTY-FOUR

In terms of attendance by heads of state, the annual World Bank and International Monetary Fund meetings in Washington, D.C., would rate as the world's second most elite gathering after the United Nations General Assembly in New York. In terms of impact, the Bank-IMF meetings arguably are far more important, for it is here that the world's monetary and business matters—and, as a consequence, the economic fate of many nations—are decided.

America's mainstream media gave much more coverage to the goings-on in Washington than to the General Assembly. The excuse they gave was that the GA was largely an occasion for flowery, often anti-American oratory. No major decisions affecting America's or the rest of the world's money and economy were made there, they said. On the other hand, the United States and its allies in Europe pretty much controlled the pace and direction of economic development through the World Bank and in the IMF.

Time and again the foreign press proved this notion wrong, with reports on the UN's work and agreements that had far-reaching impact on world stability. Most American news editors shrugged it all off and took what they needed from wire service reports. The American public cared mostly about what Americans said and did in America, the editors contended.

Furthermore, unlike the General Assembly, where the United Nations itself is host and the United States stands on equal footing with all other nations, the U.S. government played a huge role in hosting the World Bank-IMF meetings in Washington. That made it practically an American show. Americans matter most at American shows.

The Bank-IMF meetings were held in Washington for two years in a row, and in another member country in the third year. Augmented by a series of related events, the meetings lasted for eight to ten days, beginning late September. Activities were split between the headquarters of the Bank and the IMF and Washington's largest convention hotels, the Omni Shoreham and the Marriott Wardman Park Hotel.

The official attendance list carried about ten thousand names. Attendance was a privilege, not a right. It was reserved for heads of state and their delegations, business and banking executives, heads of NGOs and their delegations, and top journalists from around the world. Over the eight or so days, the boards of governors of the Bank and the IMF discussed their work, addressed international monetary issues, and released their much-awaited outlooks for the world economy. Member countries got a chance to vent about World Bank and IMF policies, global economics, and finance issues that impacted their national economies.

Bank and IMF staff were at their public relations best. This was their biggest opportunity to fill the public in on what their often misunderstood organizations did, what their goals were, and what the outcome was of the poverty-eradicating commitments they made around the world. The main objective of the meetings, Bank and IMF officials stressed, was to foster creative dialogue among the private sector, government delegates, and senior Bank and IMF officials, with a view to constructing effective solutions to issues the institutions addressed.

It was a heady time in Washington, with parties and receptions and shopping galore. Deals were struck quietly between countries, between countries and corporations, and between corporations and corporations. Deserving heads of state were hauled on the carpet—behind closed doors, of course—for steps taken nationally that disrupt, or risk disrupting, global or regional stability. News was leaked to the most influential journalists in lobbies and hallways, in private suites and over drinks, or over a meal.

There were cliques everywhere. There was the clique of rich countries and the clique of poor countries. And within each of these cliques there were smaller cliques. Each had its own agenda within the broader agenda of the meetings.

There were seminars and consultations and press conferences and special briefings. There were private meetings, public meetings, formal meetings, and informal meetings. There were meetings arranged according to pecking orders that did not officially exist, but which everyone knew existed.

Every year, tens of thousands of protesters from around the world protest gathered in the streets. They were concerned, not only with the standard Bank-IMF issues of poverty reduction, economic development, and finance, but also with a host of other issues, ranging from the protection of the environment to xenophobia. Some came simply to denounce the "twin tyranny" of the institutions that wielded so much power over the social and economic development of poor countries, sometimes with tragic consequences.

A delegation from the African Business Roundtable was among the invited guests each year. The ABR was the acknowledged representative of Africa's private sector. Made up of Africa's leading business owners, the group worked with governments, multilateral organizations, and with the wider business community to improve Africa's trade and investment climate. It also strove to raise global awareness of the potential of Africa's economic development. More than any other African group, the ABR had the ear of national governments across the continent. It used this privilege to convey the concerns of the international and African business sectors of those governments.

Crispin Abeli was this year's chairman of the ABR. In his first meeting as chairman, he announced that the top item on his agenda was securing broader and faster debt relief for Africa. Everyone agreed that this kind of relief would free up badly needed funds to finance national economic rehabilitation programs. But creditor nations were balking, reluctant to leave their banks out on a limb like that.

Crispin's second objective was greeted warily by his fellow ABR members. He announced it solemnly to the members. He would persuade the World Bank's powerful Development Committee to insert into its final communiqué at the annual meeting in Washington a commitment to incorporate nationally designed economic development strategies in the formulation of the Bank's poverty-reduction programs. Incorporating strategies with regional or continent-wide reach was even more crucial, if the Bank's programs were to be truly relevant and effective, he insisted.

"In the final analysis, our concern is for the development of the continent as a whole, not a few favored countries," he told skeptics.

No one was surprised that Crispin chose this battle. He had harped on the subject for years. The Bank was wreaking economic havoc in the developing world, and would continue to do so, as long as its specialists and consultants stuck to a formula that was too abstract, he argued.

"I have no doubt that the intentions of these specialists and consultants are honest and good. Unfortunately, they go into their assigned country, diagnose the situation within the parameters of their one-size-fits-all formula, and then come up with a prescription that tragically ignores the priorities and realities on the ground. A prescription that ignores the fact that the country has relationships with an entire region that may have collectively decided to move in a certain direction, toward certain goals," he said.

Crispin conceded that getting the committee to include his statement would be an uphill battle. "But if we could get rid of apartheid, this we can certainly do," he declared. The ABR membership approved his agenda on the spot. If anyone could pull it off, Crispin Abeli could, they said.

Crispin embarked on an aggressive lobbying campaign before the week was out. He arranged private meetings with the president of the World Bank, who was also the chairman of the Development Committee, with influential U.S. and German individuals, and with the finance ministers and central bankers of the Group of Twenty Four. The Group of Twenty Four was the developing world's de facto front against the Group of Seven: the seven richest nations that jointly set the world's monetary and finance policies. Comprising the governments of the twenty-four leading developing nations, it coordinated the positions of Africa, Asia, Latin America, and the Caribbean on those policies and other global monetary and finance issues.

As ABR chairman, Crispin was the head of the group's delegation to the Bank-IMF meetings. Even before his departure from Kinshasa, he received word—leaked separately to him by Committee insiders—that his lobbying paid off. His language was inserted into the communiqué. The press reported long ago that these kinds of communiqués were written in advance and were rubberstamped at the meetings themselves with little, if any, changes.

At 10 a.m. on the eve of the last day of the meetings, Crispin was caucusing with his delegation in his hotel suite when a Bank staffer brought him an official copy of the communiqué. It was identical to the one being read to the press at that very moment by the chairman of the Committee, the staffer said. The copy he gave to Crispin confirmed what Crispin was told in Kinshasa. Crispin let out a resounding whoop and did a few steps of his tribal dance. The jubilant delegation poured a libation for their ancestral spirits, and then proceeded to drink several toasts themselves. They drank to Crispin, "the leopard who leads us." To friends and supporters "who walked on pointed stones with us." To the "saner" minds on the Development Committee "who were not too proud to see beyond themselves." To an Africa soon to be free—well, *considerably* free, a lone voice said, from the yoke of external debt. And finally, to the African Business Roundtable, "whose name will forever ring out at gatherings of big affairs."

Word flew around that the ABR was celebrating "a major victory." Soon, Crispin's suite was jammed with well-wishers from nearly every country represented at the meetings. Each new arrival insisted on giving at least three toasts: to Africa, to the ABR, and to Crispin, the leader of the coup.

By the time they felt they had paid sufficient homage to everyone and everything remotely related to "our victory here in the capital of the most powerful nation on earth, hah!" most of the ABR delegation and their well-wishers were too inebriated to keep appointments, or to attend the remaining official events of the day. They retired to their suites and made the necessary cancellation phone calls.

Newspapers and broadcast commentaries reported in all seriousness on a wave of malaise that suddenly and mysteriously hit a number of delegations immediately after the reading of the Development Committee's final communiqué. The malaise, they said, caused several key individuals to miss important sessions. Some reporters went so far as to suggest that the sickout was an unprecedented, collective "action." It did not matter that they were hard-pressed to come up with a credible reason for such action, given the diverse interests of the no-show delegates.

The coup celebration took place on the same day that the American Business Council on Africa was holding a dinner-dance in honor of the ABR delegation. ABCA was a group of some 200 multinational corporations that did business in Africa. Its sole mission was to facilitate and strengthen commercial ties between the United States and Africa.

Crispin was in fine fettle at the event. Following the raucous celebration earlier in the day, he spent half an hour on the treadmill and another forty minutes or so doing tai chi and qi gong. He was one of the few who consumed fewer than four glasses of champagne.

While he dressed for the evening's event, he telephoned the other members of the ABR delegation to make sure they "recovered" and would be attending the event.

"Take a cold shower. It would be unforgivable if even one of us did not show up. Let's not forget that the Council is one of Africa's best friends in Washington. We cannot afford not to be there en masse," he told the ones who begged to be allowed to stay in bed.

#

"Crispin!"

Crispin looked around and saw Shayna hurrying toward him. He smiled broadly and waited for her to catch up to him. They were in the hallway leading to the Grand Ballroom of the Marriott Wardman.

"Shayna! I was delighted when I heard you were mistress of ceremonies. How are you?" he said as they embraced.

"I'm fine. I should congratulate you on that wonderful coup you pulled in the Development Committee. Getting that line about collaboration with the poverty-reduction strategies of national authorities into the final communiqué was just brilliant!" Shayna said.

Crispin laughed. "Yes, I must say we are enjoying the victory, though they managed to wrap the statement in all kinds of language to give themselves an escape hatch; but we'll deal with that when the time comes. The best part is the confirmation, that we can reshape international policy using the tactics of the very institutions that make such policy. That's what those protesters outside should learn to do: manage the system to get what they want," he said. "And who is this man chasing you?" he asked in the same breath, as Hilton just caught up with Shayna.

"Oh!" Shayna giggled. "This is Hilton. Hilton Pierce, my fiancé. Hilton, this is..."

"Oh you don't have to tell me who he is, Shayna. Mr. Abeli it is an honor to meet you," Hilton said, pumping Crispin's hand vigorously.

"Don't take his arm off, Hilton. He's human just like us," Shayna laughed. "You promised me a story, Crispin. I heard the deal is about to go down in Brazil."

"Well. Congratulations are in order. Congratulations, Hilton," Crispin said, shaking Hilton's hand again. "And congratulations to you, too, Shayna." He kissed her on the cheek again.

"Thank you, Crispin, but don't try to change the subject. What about the story you promised me?"

"Hilton, is she this persistent when she's not being a journalist?" Crispin asked with amusement.

"You can't imagine how much," Hilton said, putting his arm lovingly around Shayna's waist.

"So when do I get my story?"

"Tell you what. I'll be in New York after all this is over. Let's meet on, say, Wednesday and I'll tell you whatever you want to know then."

Won't everything be public by then?"

"Everything like what?"

"Oh Crispin, you're so difficult," Shayna sighed.

"Not really. I *am* offering to sit down with you for an interview, aren't I? That would be the second time I've agreed to do something so foolish. And both times it's been with you. You should consider yourself privileged," Crispin grinned.

"Okay, okay. I'll take it. Next Wednesday, then. Where? At The Baobab?" She looked at him mischievously.

"No. Not there," he said seriously.

Shayna looked at him closely, surprised at the sudden change in his mood.

"Have you seen Amina yet?" she asked.

"Actually, I haven't," he said quietly. "I hope she is well."

Shayna did not like what she was hearing.

"Excuse us for a minute, Hilton," she said. She took Crispin's arm and led him a few feet away from where they were standing with Hilton.

"Crispin, when is the last time you spoke to Amina?" she asked when they were out of Hilton's earshot.

"The last night I saw you."

Shayna's mouth fell open in surprise, but she recovered quickly.

"And when were you supposed to get back to Kinshasa from your trip to the UAE?" She asked the question very slowly.

"Well, let's see. I left the day after the dinner for the UAE delegation, so that makes it two Sundays after that. That's when I got back to Kinshasa. I found out that you left the country that very day. Where is this leading, Shayna?"

"So you don't know why we left before you got back? Amina never told you?" She heard the shrillness of her own voice and looked around self-consciously. She saw Hilton frowning at her and she gave him a sheepish smile.

"Never told me what, Shayna? What is it that I don't know?" Crispin said.

Shayna marveled that he could sound so calm when his eyes were blazing with excitement. She told him all of it, beginning with the phone call from Tom Miller. He looked intently at her as he listened, one hand folded across his waist, propping up the elbow of the other. He stroked his chin with his thumb and index finger as he listened.

"She's here with her two best friends and Hilton and me," Shayna said as she finished her story.

Before Crispin could respond, a man they both recognized as their host organization's senior vice president of public relations swooped down on them.

"Oh, good! There you are. I've been looking all over for you two. We're assembling for the procession now. Everyone's there except the two of you. Shall we go?" he said fussily, motioning them toward a small room off the Grand Ballroom.

"Terribly sorry, Jason. Ms. McWright and I got a bit carried away. We hadn't seen each other for sometime," Crispin said.

Hilton hurried over and kissed Shayna lightly on the cheek.

"Break a leg, sweetheart. I'll go join Amina and the others," he said. "I look forward to meeting you again, Mr. Abeli," he said, extending a hand to Crispin.

"It's Crispin. Yes, I'll see you again I'm sure," Crispin said, shaking Hilton's hand.

They entered the small room where the others who would be sitting on the dais had already gathered. Crispin turned to Shayna.

"Thank you for telling me, Shayna," he said.

"Were you planning to see her when you were in New York?"

"It was my sole reason for going there," he said.

#

Jamillah kicked Merry hard under the table. Merry turned to protest but clamped her mouth shut when she saw Jamillah's face. She followed Jamillah's eyes. They were moving back and forth frantically between Amina and the dais. Specifically, between Amina and the man Amina was staring at with a strange expression on her face. The man seemed to be looking back at her, too. It was hard to tell with the lighting in the room. He sat to the very right of the chair vacated by the woman at the podium. The woman introduced herself as president of the American Business Council on Africa, "the organization that had the foresight to throw this marvelous affair in honor of the African Business Roundtable on the very day that the world learned of its coup at the World Bank."

Merry turned back to Jamillah with a look of utter delight. She pursed her mouth as if she were about to say something, but Jamillah cut her off.

"Shhhhh!" Jamillah mouthed, frowning.

Merry had to say it anyway. She leaned close to Jamillah.

"Jamillah, I love my Phillip with all my heart, but that is the finest, sexiest black man I have *ever* laid my eyes on," she whispered.

Jamillah squeezed Merry's hand under the table, nodding in agreement. Merry continued whispering to her.

"Just look at that god. Mmmph! Mmmph! Mmmmmmph! No wonder Amina has been going crazy."

Jamillah squeezed her hand again and nodded again. Amina

turned around suddenly. "What's with all the whispering and head bobbing, you two?" she asked suspiciously.

Merry straightened up guiltily. Jamillah decided to come clean.

"We were just commenting on Crispin Abeli's exceedingly fine looks. That *is* Crispin Abeli, isn't it? The one next to the president's chair? The one who's looking this way?" she asked innocently.

Amina blushed.

One of the women at the table spoke up before Amina could respond. "It sure is and I was just thinking the same thing about him," she said.

She was sitting across from them. The moment the words were out of her mouth, she turned to the man sitting beside her and touched his cheek reassuringly.

"That's the only thought I had, dear. That he was fine-looking…honest," she said.

Everyone at the table laughed, including the man the woman addressed.

Amina avoided Jamillah's and Merry's eyes. She turned her back deliberately to them when Crispin rose to give the keynote speech.

"Jammy, this is going to be one steamy night. This baby better stay put," Merry whispered to Jamillah.

#

Crispin spoke extemporaneously for half an hour. His passion filled the room and held the audience in its giddy grasp. He spoke about where Africa stood right now in the global scheme of things, of where it should have been, and why it was not yet there. He spoke of what African leaders themselves, with the help of the local private sector, were doing to make the continent get where it needed to be, even as they coped with the ravages of wars and droughts and diseases like malaria and HIV/AIDS that were ravaging the continent. He spoke with sincere appreciation of the assistance that came from institutions like the United Nations, the World Bank, and the IMF, and from creditor countries like the United States.

"We may not always see eye to eye with those who assist us on how things should be done, but it is *our* duty and no one else's—the duty of Africa's leaders and its people—to manage our relationships with them so that *we* benefit," he said.

"Globalization is not new to Africa. For us, globalization began the day the first foreigners stepped on our continent. Their agenda has not changed since. They want what we have and they want it for little or nothing. After all these centuries, why can't—why shouldn't we learn to play their game, use their rules and their institutions to get what we want from them? It is the ancient notion of using the energy of your opponent to overcome that opponent.

"Yes, we need to build our own systems, our own institutions. And yes, these should be based on our unique needs and our unique traditions, our unique historical experience. But our history is one that mixes with that of others. Inevitably, our systems and institutions will reflect that mixing."

Crispin paused and the room stood in a prolonged applause. When Crispin continued, he gave thanks for the NGOs whose work made a difference in the health and welfare of African people.

"But most important of all," he said, are "the many unsung contributions made by so many children of the vast African Diaspora."

He looked directly at Amina as he said this. Jamillah and Merry dug into each other's ribs.

One of his greatest wishes now, Crispin said, was to see far more and far stronger commercial ties between businesses on the continent and those in the Diaspora.

"We can do so well by each other and so much for each other. But the level of commerce that exists between us now is—well, when you consider what others are doing and how fat they are growing—disgraceful."

The room erupted in a thunderous applause.

"I take it you are agreeing with me, not celebrating, that it is disgraceful, and that something will be done about it, beginning tonight, with so many CEOs in the room," Crispin said when the applause died down.

Laughter and more applause filled the room.

"And on that note of concurrence, let me extend, on behalf of my colleagues in the African Business Roundtable, my deepest thanks to the American Business Council on America for this wonderful coming together. Your hospitality, as always, is touching. Thank you."

He acknowledged the standing ovation with a bow. Shayna embraced him as he went back to his seat and stood at the podium, waiting for the applause to end.

Merry and Jamillah were cheering wildly, whooping and carrying on with the sizable contingent of young entrepreneurs and MBA students in the room. The woman across the table was fanning herself. She bared her feelings to Jamillah in a single look.

Merry leaned across Jamillah and tugged at Amina.

"Amina, I will divorce Phillip, do you hear me, *divorce* him, and throw myself at that man if you don't want him!" she whispered hoarsely.

"Not with that belly you won't," Jamillah said.

Amina's eyes shone. "He's wonderful, isn't he?" she said.

Shayna's voice rang deep with emotion and pride as the room grew quiet.

"Ladies and gentlemen, I think we now have a better idea why Crispin Abeli is who he is, and why Africa is going to be okay," she said, to another round of cheers.

"And now, ladies and gentlemen, it is truly, *truly,* my privilege to announce the winner of this year's Entrepreneur of the Year award: Madame Sukaina Tshiala—Suke to many of you—founder and chief executive officer of ShaYaSu Enterprises in Kinshasa, Democratic Republic of Congo!"

The entire Grand Ballroom was on its feet in a thundering ovation, Shayna herself joining in.

"As you know, as you know, ladies and gentlemen, this award is given to one of Africa's leading business owners who not only embodies entrepreneurship at its best, but also whose life itself is a testimony to the ideals of compassion, of charity, of service to humanity," Shayna continued when the applause subsided. "Ladies and gentlemen, I am truly humbled by what I have come to learn about the life of Madame Tshiala. Thanks to her adoring colleagues, close friends, and employees, for she refused to talk to our researchers about herself, we were able to put together what we know is only the broadest brush of what this great lady is all about.

"Some of those who helped us are in this room with us tonight, like her best friend Dr. Dominique Yamungu, who also is the wife of the vice president of Congo."

Shayna gestured to Dominique's table and led the cheer as Dominique stood in acknowledgement.

"Others are with us via videocast," Shayna continued, turning to one of the two huge screens suspended from the ceiling.

A picture of exuberant workers at ShaYaSu Enterprises in Kinshasa appeared on the screen. Dressed in their ShaYaSu uniforms, the workers waved and cheered, some of the women ululating in high-pitched voices.

When the cheering on both sides of the Atlantic died down, Shayna gave a brief history of ShaYaSu, of how Suke ventured out on her own after learning everything she thought she needed at Musana

Import-Export, precursor of the empire built by none other than Crispin Abeli, esteemed chairman of the African Business Roundtable.

The room erupted in applause again.

"Of course Mr. Abeli was a mere boy then, if he ever really was such a thing," she joked.

Laughter and more cheers filled the room.

"Honestly, that man is the bane of every journalist I know. What *is* it with these Congolese?" Shayna said, feigning frustration.

"You tell us, Shayna!" Amina, Merry and Jamillah shouted in unison above the laughter.

Shayna pointed at them laughing. For the first time since her wild dancing with Gaston in Matonge, she was having the time of her life.

Shayna told them about the hostel Suke had built for AIDS-stricken women and their babies; about a garment production company called "Tala Mwasi," Lingala for "See, Woman," a division of ShaYaSu employed and run by former prostitutes; about the refuse-recycling project she started just last year in one of Kinshasa's poorest communities that helped address the worsening pollution problem while bringing income to the community.

And in a somber voice that hushed the room and made even the waiters stand still, she told of Suke's incarceration in Kinshasa when she was just in her twenties on trumped up charges that she would not dignify by mentioning them.

"Suffice it to say, her innocence prevailed. She was released after the intervention of several influential businessmen and women, but only after she spent six months in conditions most of us cannot imagine," Shayna said.

Her statement on Suke's personal life said only that she had been married at a very young age and had a daughter, a son and four grandchildren.

"Ladies and gentlemen, please put your hands together for Madame Sukaina Tshiala!"

Suke rose to another standing ovation and moved to the podium. She bowed graciously and turned to accept her award from Shayna. Cameras flashed.

"Thank you, Shayna Yasmin," she said softly, embracing Shayna and kissed her on the cheek.

Shayna froze. Suke looked into her eyes for a brief moment, and then stepped away from her. She stood at the podium.

"Thank you. Thank you so much," she began in English as the applause died down. "If only you knew what an honor it is for me to receive this award and from—from…" she turned to look at Shayna. Shayna had not moved. Her eyes, wide with fear, were fixed on Suke's face.

Suke's eyes met hers and Shayna stood transfixed.

"…from this very beautiful young woman who has made us all so proud," she said in a voice that seemed to speak only to Shayna.

She turned back to the audience.

#

It was time to party.

The first band had already struck up its opening sequence. A second band, a local Congolese group, would come in later when things got hot.

Shayna came over briefly to make sure everyone was all right and to get the verdict on her performance. She was greeted by boisterous whoops and cheers from the squad at Table No. 3. Despite the convivial atmosphere, Shayna seemed tense. Amina noticed it, but chalked it up to the long evening in the limelight. Shayna left a few minutes later, dragging Hilton with her.

Amina, Merry and Jamillah watched them disappear into the crowd.

"Bwoy, we've come a long way, haven't we," Merry said contentedly. "Who would have thought…" she didn't complete the sentence. She shook her head.

"Don't go getting emotional, Merry. You're too close to delivery and you've already gone crazy enough for tonight. Let's just take it easy 'till we get back to New York. I want to enjoy the rest of this night with all these beautiful people," Jamillah said.

"You mean you would not enjoy being with me if I had the baby tonight?" Merry demanded.

Jamillah kissed her on the cheek. "That's a different kind of enjoyment, love. You know exactly what I mean," she said.

Merry looked at her suspiciously.

Amina giggled. "Is dancing too emotional for her?"

"Don't you start, Amina. Merry is not going anywhere near that dance floor. I promised Phillip I would restrain her."

"Just you try," Merry threatened.

Amina looked around and stood up. "I'm afraid duty calls. I see a lot of people who would be offended if I did not greet them. Mind if I leave you for a while?"

"Not at all," Merry and Jamillah said in unison.

Be sure to bring him over," Merry added with a straight face.

"I'll ignore that," Amina said.

"Sit back down for a sec," Jamillah said, pulling Amina's hand.

Amina sat down and the three of them leaned their heads together. Jamillah spoke in a low voice.

"Amina, please know that you don't have to come back to tell us good night if you have to leave with you-know-who," she said.

"That's right, Amina. Just call us tomorrow sometime, when you're ready, and we'll run up with some clothes," Merry added, ignoring Amina's open mouth.

"Run up? How do you know he's staying here?" Amina said.

Merry and Jamillah looked at each other.

"Well, we assume he is," Jamillah said carefully.

"I don't believe it! I don't believe you actually checked that out!" Amina exclaimed.

"Shhhh. Don't shout. We're only looking out for your interests," Merry said.

"Amina, be real. He had his eyes on you all night. And you weren't exactly looking away, you know," Jamillah said.

Amina sighed and shook her head. "Well, what can I say? I'm off," she said. She stood up again to leave.

"Okay. But just remember what Jamillah said. Keep straight. You can introduce him to us later," Merry said.

Amina laughed and left them. The truth is, she was too nervous to remain sitting at the table. Crispin would find her. She knew that. Or she would find him. She would tell him right away that she loved him. That she was sorry she had not contacted him before. That she had been afraid to do so, but she was no longer afraid.

She had been surprised to see his name on the program as the keynote speaker. When Shayna invited her to the event, it did not dawn on her that Crispin would be part of it. *I should have known*, she thought now. After all, business delegations from all over the world attend the World Bank and IMF meetings. She knew that. Of course Crispin Abeli would be among them.

But she did not put two and two together at the time. In fact, after a month went by since her return to New York and she heard no word from Crispin, she tried to put him out of her mind by immersing herself in work at her clinic and at the hospitals with which she was affiliated. At first, she told herself that she would contact him eventually to let him know why she left so suddenly. Several times she started to e-mail him and ended up canceling the e-mail.

She could not explain it. She knew she loved him. But the more the time passed, the more excuses she found not to contact him. And then, so much time passed that she thought he had surely put her out of his mind. What man would bear such silence? But here she was. And here he was, with all that longing in his eyes when he looked at her from the podium.

She looked up suddenly and her eyes met his across the room. She saw him excuse himself from the group he was speaking with and move toward her, his eyes never leaving her face. Amina stood still and watched him as he came toward her, praying that she would not make a fool of herself and shake or cry or both.

He was just a few feet from her when a woman in a tall, cylindrical brown hat with a thin strand of black elastic holding it in place under her chin planted herself in front of him. Her demeanor, even seeing her from the back as Amina did, was beguiling.

"Crispin, that was such a wonderful speech," the woman said in a voice loud enough to let everyone around her know that she was on first-name terms with the famous, handsome, sexy Crispin Abeli. She placed a hand on his arm. "I would love to have you as the keynote speaker at my organization's dinner. How long are you around? We need to get together to discuss it."

The hat looked ridiculous, more so because it was cocked to one side of her head. It was a statement of Afrocentric high fashion that had come out very wrong. Amina put her hand over her mouth to suppress a giggle. She saw Crispin knit his brow but smile politely as he stopped to address the woman. She didn't hear what he said, but it must have been dismissive for he was moving toward her again in no time.

The woman, meanwhile, was sashaying in the opposite direction toward the bar. Everyone she passed took one look at the hat and looked away quickly, lowering their heads to hide the twitching at the corner of their mouths. A group of young Caribbean and West African diplomats who played soccer together on Sundays laughed outright but managed to make it seem as if they were laughing at something they had been discussing all along.

The woman seemed oblivious to them all.

Amina smiled nervously as Crispin stood in front of her.

"I have missed you so, Amina," he said, taking both her hands in his.

Amina felt her hands tremble in his. Her lips quivered as she started to speak.

"Crispin, I'm..."

He thought she was going to say she was not ready yet.

"Don't say anything. Right now I just want to hold you. Will you dance with me?"

She nodded and he guided her to the open space in front of the band. They danced in silence as the band rolled from one soulful instrumental into another: from Nina Simone's "If You Knew" to Percy Sledge's "When A Man Loves a Woman" to Roberta Flack's "The First Time." Crispin held her closer and she felt herself relax. She sighed and abandoned herself to the music and to the sweetness of being in his arms. The smell of his cologne heightened her desire for him. Unconsciously, she brushed her lips against his neck and murmured his name. She felt a tremor go through his body. He stopped dancing and held her a little away from him.

"What are you saying to me, Amina?" he asked, searching her eyes.

"I love you, Crispin," she said in a rush. "I love you with all my heart and with all my mind. I love you so very much."

Crispin swallowed hard. He drew her back to him, closer than before, and they resumed dancing, foolishly believing they could control what was fast welling in each of them.

"Let's get out of here," Crispin said when he could stand it no longer.

#

The elevator stopped at the tenth floor and an elderly woman in formal eveningwear stepped in. She smiled and uttered a cheery greeting to the gorgeously attired, handsome young man and woman standing at the back of the car. They were obviously together, though they were standing apart: he in one corner, she in another. They were gazing at each other. Neither acknowledged her greeting. The elderly woman was offended. She drew herself up and looked from the man to the woman, her eyebrows raised in indignation at their breach of common courtesy. *And they seem to be people of good breeding*, she huffed to herself.

She turned her back to them with a haughty sniff and faced the open door, waiting for the elevator to begin its ascent to the Wardman suite, where she was attending a small reception hosted by the Russian ambassador and his wife. The elevator stood there. The elderly woman waited patiently, back erect, her face a mask of contempt. The door did not close. Nothing moved. No one spoke. The elderly woman's eyes drifted to one of the mirrored panels. She could see the man and the woman still gazing at each other.

She looked away with a sharp twist of her head, hoping they would see her contempt. But they didn't acknowledgement her. The elderly woman's eyes slid back to the mirror and stayed there. She focused on the couple more closely, squinting at their reflection in the mirror. Slowly, it dawned on her that the two were locked in "an optical embrace," she would later tell the sister. She saw in their embrace a passion so raw that it made her blush and look away.

She opened her purse, withdrew a slender black and gold case and flicked it open with a deft movement of her wrist. Her gold bracelets jingled, and a lace-trimmed black and gold fan spread open on a waft of Elizabeth Arden's Bluegrass.

The elderly woman fanned herself vigorously, her eyes determinedly avoiding the mirrors. She could have sworn they were fogging up anyway. She was beginning to grow impatient. The elevator still had not budged.

She squinted at the button panel, and zeroed in on "Wardman Suite." She aimed her finger at the button and stabbed it with an impatient sound. The doors slid shut noiselessly. She glanced at the couple through the mirror.

The man was smiling now. The woman was too. They smiled at each other like two people who were on their way to making love. The woman blushed again and looked away quickly. The elevator still had not moved.

"What is the matter with this ridiculous elevator?" she said aloud.

She fixed her eyes on the button panel again. This time, "Door Close" stood out in bright green. She stabbed at it. The elevator began its ascent.

#

The hallway was deserted when Crispin and Amina stepped out of the elevator. They were in each other's arms the minute the door closed behind them, releasing in a crushing kiss some of the passion they kept in check for so very long. His mouth still locked on hers, Crispin backed Amina against the wall and leaned his full weight into her. She responded with equal fervor, wrapping her arms around his neck and thrusting her hips hard against him.

"Say it again, Amina. Say you love me. I want to hear you say it again," Crispin said, covering her face with kisses.

"I love you, Crispin," Amina said. "And I want you so much."

Crispin could hardly control himself. He moaned. "I'm so hungry for you I can take you right here," he said hoarsely.

"Oh darling, please don't. I may not be able to resist," Amina said weakly. "And there may be cameras."

Crispin eased himself away from her reluctantly and led her quickly down the hallway. He pulled her to him the moment they entered his suite, kicking the door shut.

"Know this, Amina Milenga. I love you as I never imagined a man could love a woman," he said, his voice laden with emotion.

Amina raised her lips to his. She wanted to give herself to him completely. Their kiss grew more urgent. Soon they were both groaning with the need for release. Amina fumbled frantically with the front of his trousers. She felt him unzip her gown.

Clothing and underwear fell to the floor. Crispin covered her naked body with kisses, kneeling as he moved lower and massaging her flesh with insistent, circular motions that made her legs go weak. She shuddered as he rose again and held her tight against him, whispering her name. She took his swollen manhood in her hands, gasping as she felt him grow harder. Her touch drove him to heights he could not endure.

He swung her around so that she was braced against the door. He lifted her leg and drove himself into her, throwing his head back with a guttural sound as she too cried out in ecstasy. Their bodies heaved and dipped as they climaxed together, again and again.

"That was disgraceful," Amina said, clinging to him breathless and spent.

"Disgraceful indeed," Crispin agreed. "Absolutely, deliciously disgraceful."

They were still pressed against the door, their arms wrapped around each other. Beads of sweat rolled down their bodies and formed tiny puddles where their bodies joined.

"As disgraceful as that day at The Baobab, Amina murmured.

"Even worse," Crispin replied.

"I wanted you so much, Crispin."

"You have me now. You have me always. Do you know I have loved you from that first day?"

She buried her head into his chest. "Is that possible?"

"It was for me. I will enjoy having you in my life," he said, kissing her on the forehead.

"And I having you in mine," Amina said.

"Do you think we can make it to the bedroom and do this again in a more civilized way?"

Amina giggled. "Maybe we can make it to the bedroom, but we definitely can't do the civilized part," she said. "Not yet."

#

Next to the walk from the limousine to the freshly dug grave for Janice McWright on that terrible day in April, this was the longest walk of Shayna's life. Hilton stood at the elevator and watched her. Halfway down the hallway, she stopped and looked back at him. He smiled and gave her a thumbs-up sign, and then stepped quickly into the elevator. Shayna saw the door close.

She continued hesitantly down the hallway, her gown trailing behind her with a soft "swoosh, swoosh." Her steps slowed even more as she drew closer to the room she was seeking. She stood at the door, her heart thumping wildly. She raised her hand, but it fell back to her side before she could press the buzzer. She tried again and failed again. She wanted to run away as much as she wanted to enter the room. She knew she would not run away.

She covered her face with her hands and then slid her fingers down, just enough to uncover her eyes. She stared at the door, trembling uncontrollably. Then, with a resolute move she thrust her hand out and pressed the buzzer.

"It is open. Come in."

It was the same voice that had said her name.

So many people remarked throughout the night on how much she resembled Sukaina Tshiala. She was flattered, but thought little of it. *Pure coincidence*, she said flippantly to some of them. "Aren't we all supposed to look alike anyway?"

But how strange it was when Dominique Yamungu embraced her when they met again tonight. Dominique touched her face and looked at her in that wondering way, just as she did at Crispin's dinner in Kinshasa. Shayna thought she had seen tears in Dominique's eyes tonight. But Dominique rushed away as she had that night, leaving her standing there with a scary feeling.

It was at that moment that she finally acknowledged the gut alerts she had felt all day. She pushed them away, not wanting to remember the last time she felt them.

And then Sukaina Tshiala planted herself into her life, calling her by her birth name in a way that reminded her of the way Janice had spoken her name sometimes, although she never called her Yasmin. As she stood there, scarcely daring to breathe because she felt so very afraid, Suke slipped her a card with her room number written on it.

She stood before the room now, her hand on the doorknob. She opened the door slowly and stepped inside. She stood just inside the door. The room was one of those magnificent executive suites, with a living room big enough to hold a small reception. Beyond the open curtains, Washington fell away on a carpet of twinkling lights.

Suke stood erect in the middle of the living room, her face loving and strong.

They looked at each other for a long moment.

"You called me Shayna Yasmin," Shayna said in a low, unsteady voice.

She moved just a few inches into the room.

"Yes, I did," Suke said quietly.

"How did you know my name? It was not written on the program or anything."

"I know it because I gave it to you."

Shayna uttered a cry and covered her face with her hands.

She crumpled to the floor sobbing. Suke ran to her and sank down beside her, gathering her into her arms. She rocked Shayna back and forth.

"Pasi! Pasi! Motema na ngai-o," Suke began to sing softly.

Shayna jerked herself away and stared wide-eyed into Suke's face. Suddenly she laughed. Suke laughed with her.

"Do you know that's exactly what you did the first time I sang that song to you? You were crying and crying and you would not stop. Then I started to sing that song because you always liked to hear it. You would dance when Abeti sang it," she said.

Shayna pressed her palms against Suke's cheeks.

"I don't know you. But I can feel you. In my heart," she said.

Suke smiled. "It is enough. It is more than I hoped for."

Shayna caressed her face. "Look where I found you," she said and laid her head on Suke's breast.

Suke wrapped her arms around her daughter. They remained like that for a long time.

#

Merry started to say to Jamillah that it was high time they left the party when she felt the pain. She gasped and placed both hands under her stomach. Jamillah grasped her by the shoulders.

"What is it, Merry? For God's sake, what is it?" The fear in her voice was unmistakable.

Merry raised a hand. "Wait a minute. Just let this one pass," she said.

"Here. Sit down, Merry. Come on, sweetheart, sit down." Jamillah pulled out a chair from the nearest table.

They had been on the dance floor for fifteen minutes nonstop. Jamillah warned Merry repeatedly that she risked going into labor if she did not sit down. But Merry paid her no mind. The Congolese band drew the whole room onto the dance floor and trapped them there with its rhythms.

Merry eased herself into the chair, still holding her stomach.

"I think this baby will come tonight, Jammy," she said, shaking her head. "I really think this baby coming tonight."

A few women who saw what was happening came over. "Is it the baby? Should we get her to the hospital?" asked the woman from their table who had been lusting after Crispin all night.

Merry shook her head.

"No, please. Not yet. I'd like to go to my room first. I'll be all right. It's not time yet."

"Are you sure?" another woman asked. "You look very pale."

"She'll be all right. She's a gynecologist herself. I'll take her upstairs. Thanks all of you," Jamillah said quickly.

Merry stood up and leaned heavily on Jamillah's arm. They began to move toward the exit.

"Need any help?" a man asked as they passed him.

"No thanks. We can manage. Jammy, let's get upstairs quickly. I hate to make a scene."

"You're not kidding, right, Merry? You're not kidding that the baby is coming, are you?" Jamillah said when they were in their suite.

Merry burst out laughing. "You should hear yourself, Jamillah. Calm down. No, I'm not kidding. I've been having slight contractions for a while now but I ignored them," she said.

"*What*! Are you crazy? Why the hell didn't you say something?"

"And poop on such a good party? Naaah! Besides, they were too faint and too far apart to do anything. Who wants to be laid up in a hospital bed doing absolutely nothing when all this action is going on here? Did you see Amina leave with Crispin? And something's going on with Shayna and that woman Sukaina Tshiala. Did you notice that?"

Jamillah threw up her hands. "Okay, Merry. Let's leave everybody else's drama alone for now and concentrate on yours. The contractions are closer and stronger now, right?"

"Yes, Mummy."

Jamillah rolled her eyes at her. "Okay. I know you're serious because you've been calling me Jammy. I'll call the hospital and have them send an ambulance. Or should I call the police for the ambulance? I've got all the numbers right here."

She was digging around in her pocketbook. "They're right here. Don't worry. Everything will be all right. We got in touch with the hospital as soon as we got to D.C., so they know about us. You said we should do that just in case. That was smart. Everything's going to be all right, Merry. I'll call..."

"Stop talking and call a taxi, Jamillah! I don't want no ambulance. Too much damn noise and fuss. It's not that bad yet."

"...Phillip too. Don't worry. I'll..."

"Call the taxi now, Jamillah! And don't bother about Phillip. I called him a long time ago, when the contractions started."

Jamillah sprang across the room and reached for the telephone. She was so nervous that she knocked it to the floor. Merry started laughing. Jamillah sucked her teeth, picked up the phone and dialed the concierge to arrange for a taxi. She made a few more calls while Merry changed into a casual dress. Just before they left the room, Merry ran a final check of the small bag she packed since New York to take to the hospital if the time came. Fifteen minutes later, they were on their way to the hospital.

#

Merry's son came into the world four hours later at Georgetown University Hospital. The birth was witnessed and cheered on by Jamillah, Amina, Shayna, and Suke, all of whom still wore their evening gowns.

Shayna and Suke arrived minutes after Amina. The sight of them coming in together brought tears to everyone's eyes. Shayna did not have to tell them that Suke was her mother. They guessed it right away. Standing side by side, they were the spitting image of each other. When Shayna formally introduced Suke as "my mother," her arm around Suke's waist and her eyes shining, Amina, Merry and Jamillah could not contain themselves. Tears flowed down their faces and they made no move to wipe them away. Amina and Jamillah hugged them both. Merry insisted on hearing the whole story of how they finally came together.

"You'll just have to stop every now and then so unnu kyan help me deal with these contractions. But nobody's going to mind that, right? This is my show," she warned.

Crispin and Hilton were in the waiting outside. Hilton was still in his tuxedo, but his bowtie hung loose and his shirt was open at the neck. Crispin was wearing his abacos, but he had unbuttoned the jacket all the way down.

Two bottles of champagne and a stack of paper cups sat on the table in front of them. The bottles were chilling in plastic tubs of ice Hilton got from a small eat-in kitchen next to the waiting room. Crispin grabbed the champagne just as he and Amina dashed out of the room minutes after Jamillah called.

Oblivious to the admiring glances of the nurses, he and Hilton spoke with amazement of the meeting between Shayna and Suke.

"But Suke is my aunt. I knew where she was all the time that Shayna was Kinshasa. This is absolutely incredible," Crispin said.

The elevator ding-donged and a wild-looking Phillip rushed out, his long dreadlocks swinging as he looked this way and that. When he spotted Hilton, his face broke into a relieved grin and he hurried toward him.

"Hilton! Good to see you, man. Thanks for being here. Is she okay? Has the baby come yet?" He kept shaking Hilton's hands as he spoke.

"The baby's not here yet. Should be here any time now, though. Merry's all right. She's got a room full of women dressed to the nines around her. Your kid's coming into the world like royalty, man," Hilton laughed. He introduced Crispin.

Phillip knew who he was. "Heard something about you going after that shipping line in Brazil. That's a nasty fight. But everyone I know is rooting for you, man. You can count on my business when you lock it up," he said, pumping Crispin's hand as he had done with Hilton's.

Crispin's cell phone rang before he could respond. Hilton signaled he would take Phillip to Merry's room while Crispin took the call. Crispin nodded and the two men hurried down the hallway, Hilton's arm firmly around Phillip's shoulders.

Crispin's eyes followed them as he spoke into his cell phone. "Glaucio. What's the word?"

A smile spread slowly across his face as he listened to Glaucio's response. "Yes!" he shouted, shooting his fist into the air. Hilton and Phillip heard him and turned around. Crispin grinned at them and punched the air with a thumbs-up sign. Understanding immediately, they raised their fists in a "Power!" sign and turned back toward Merry's room.

Crispin spoke into the phone again. "Get some sleep, old man. It's been a long, hard fight," he said finally, then hung up.

He picked up the bottles of champagne and the stack of cups and hurried down the hallway behind Hilton and Phillip.

EPILOGUE

Agent Bryan Parkins sat behind his desk, absently throwing darts at the red and black target board on the wall across the room. It was an old-fashioned bristle board, made with sisal from east Africa—a collector's item. Agent Parkins thought about its previous owner. Had he lived, he would have been seventy today.

Agent Parkins' aim, even from that distance, and even with his attention divided, was remarkably accurate. All but one of the darts he threw hit the bull's eye. The other was less than half an inch off. He threw the last dart.

Happy birthday, Major Jenkins," he said quietly, as the dart struck the bull's eye.

Agent Parkins' office at CIA headquarters in Langley, Virginia, was located on one of the upper floors on the northeast side of the building. The office was plain, except for the intricately carved mahogany desk and matching chair angled in a corner and facing the door. Agent Parkins brought them back to the United States after his last Peace Corps tour in Africa about twenty-five years ago. A local carpenter in the rural town where he was based made the set for a Belgian diplomat who never showed up to claim it. Agent Parkins paid fifty U.S. dollars for it, but he figured the desk alone was worth at least two-thousand dollars in the United States today. He never had the set formally appraised and had no intention of doing so. But he knew enough about quality woodwork and the prices it fetched to have a pretty good idea what his desk and chair were worth.

The only other item that stood out in the office was a custom-made political map of the world from Oxford Cartographers in England. The map took up an entire wall. It had taken the company two attempts to get it exactly the way Agent Parkins wanted it, with all the border and transportation network details he requested. Agent Parkins positioned himself in front of the map first thing every morning to listen to reports coming in from around the world. As the report on a particular country came in, he would move his fingers slowly over that country on the map, as if willing them to memorize every inch of the territory. He had done this for so many years that he could draw the map of any country from memory, locating its main cities, towns and industrial sites.

Everything else in the office was pretty mundane. Two very ordinary armchairs faced his desk for those who stopped in to discuss matters of importance. No one ever stopped by to simply shoot the breeze. There was a built-in closet, built-in bookshelves, two metal file cabinets, a computer station with printer, scanner, and fax in separate units—Agent Parkins detested the all-in-ones—and a shredder." Video, audio, and telecommunications gadgetry took up the spaces of a wall unit. A strange-looking telephone with two rows of buttons and red and green lights, the latest model Quotron for up-to-the-minute financial market data and related world news, a television with video and DVD attachments, a tape recorder, a short-wave radio and a state-of-the-art digital camera.

There were no pictures of a wife—Agent Parkins was long divorced; children—his son and daughter had families of their own and he rarely saw or heard from them; parents, dead; siblings, he maintained only a birthday and Christmas card relationship with his brother and sister who lived on the West Coast.

There were no pictures of himself either.

"I already know what I look like and what the people I've met look like," he told an assistant who dared to ask him why he never displayed any of the pictures that had been taken of himself in the company of some of the world's intelligence icons.

The office was meticulously organized. Except for the dartboard, the only items that did not directly relate to Agent Parkins' work were a CD player and a CD collection of the works of Wilhelm Richard Wagner, the nineteenth-century German composer.

"Wagner?" the director of the agency asked in surprise when he dropped by to discuss a particularly nettlesome operation with Parkins. It was his first visit to Parkins' office. Parkins had joined the agency less than a month before.

"Yep, Wagner. I happen to like opera and I happen to like the way Wagner approached it," Agent Parkins replied.

Not wanting to show his ignorance of the life of one of the most influential cultural figures of the nineteenth century, the director immediately changed the subject. But he was curious enough about Agent Parkins' likes and dislikes to start reading up on Wagner. It did not take him long to figure out why Agent Parkins was drawn to the composer. Wagner was a revolutionary when it came to the concept and structure of opera, just as Agent Parkins was a revolutionary when it came to the concept and structure of intelligence gathering. Wagner thought of himself as "the most German being" and "the embodiment of the German spirit." Agent Parkins saw himself as the embodiment of the agency.

Agent Parkins was the proverbial loner. He fraternized with his colleagues only when it was unavoidable, which was when the director himself ordered him to attend some Agency function or the other. He spent much of his spare time in the gym and it showed. Many in the agency saw him as the resident weirdo; but no one denied his brilliance. Inside the Agency and within the wider intelligence community, he was referred to almost reverently as "The Tactician," the man who single-handedly could design the most complex covert operation, down to its finest details, without leaving room for scrutiny of any kind. He saw twists and turns and probabilities that no one else did.

Agent Parkins wrote controversial pieces on intelligence gathering and operations tactics for the prestigious *Studies in Intelligence*, which was published by the Agency's Center for the Studies of Intelligence. He taught at Georgetown University as an Officer in Residence, a program sponsored by the Agency and administered by the Center for the Studies of Intelligence. Among America's allies, he was highly sought after to lecture at intelligence institutions and at various elite gatherings where intelligence was revered.

His personnel file showed that he became hooked on intelligence when he attended a lecture in boot camp. He kept as close as he could to the young black officer who gave the lecture, bombarding him with all sorts of questions about intelligence gathering and about covert operations strategies. A year later, the officer was critically wounded during an undercover assignment in Vietnam. He left his dartboard and matching set of darts to Sergeant Parkins.

An authoritative knock on the door aroused Agent Parkins from his thoughts.

"Come in," he said, pleasantly. Wagner's "Die Gotterdammerung" (The Twilight of the Gods) played low in the background.

He was expecting them. David Billings, director of the Agency, and Tom Miller, a.k.a. "The Ferret," Agent Parkins' own protégé. Agent Parkins appreciated the fact that they waited until this late in the day to come. The building was almost empty.

He rose as they entered his office. Billings came in first. Miller closed the door quietly but firmly.

"Please have a seat," Agent Parkins said, motioning to the two guest chairs.

There would be no greetings, no small talk. The director's shoulders were hunched. Tom Miller's mouth was set. He avoided Agent Parkins' eyes.

The director got straight to the point as soon as he sat down.

"You know why we're here, don't you, Bryan?" he said, his voice formal, but heavy and sad.

"Yes I do, sir," Agent Parkins said. His face was impassive, his voice neutral. He sat with his arms folded and looked directly at Billings.

The director sighed deeply and shook his head. He took a sheet of paper from an envelope and handed it to Agent Parkins.

"This drawing…this is you, isn't it?"

Agent Parkins studied the drawing for a while. "Not bad. Not bad at all," he said, handing the sheet of paper back to the director. "Yes. That's me all right," he said.

"Did you do it, Bryan?"

"Yes, sir. I did it. You know that already, thanks to Agent Miller."

"But why, Bryan? Why? Why in God's name did you commit such a diabolical act? How could you?"

Agent Parkins shrugged. "She was an encumbrance."

"That's it? An *encumbrance?* Christ, that's callous, Bryan. It's almost—almost…" He struggled with the word.

"Insane?" Bryan said helpfully. "I disagree, sir. My actions had nothing to do with insanity or devilry. They were purely tactical."

Director Billings stared at the man before him as if he were seeing him for the first time. He studied every detail of his face, lingering on his eyes and his mouth. Agent Parkins did not flinch. Director Billings pondered the notion that Parkins *was* insane. How could he not be insane? How else could he be so clinical in a situation like this? The director bowed his head.

No, he told himself firmly. Agent Parkins was not insane. When he looked up again, his eyes were like ice. He sat erect as he addressed Agent Parkins.

"I want to go over with you the facts as we have them," he said coldly.

He turned to Tom Miller. "Read your report, Agent Miller."

Bryan shifted his gaze to Tom Miller. Of his three protégés at the Agency, this one made him the most proud. They were very much alike, he and Miller. He recognized that the first day he met Miller at a lecture he was giving to the Agency's newest batch of recruits. Miller had not asked any questions. He sat silently through the lecture, taking notes, screwing up his face and biting his lower lip from time to time as he pondered Bryan's words.

Bryan watched him surreptitiously, waiting almost impatiently for the moment when he would reveal the nature of his mind. That moment came just as he was about to dismiss the group; Tom Miller raised his hand and asked permission to make two observations. Bryan was impressed, though not surprised, by those observations. Miller approached him after class, just as he, Bryan, approached Major Jenkins so long ago in the Army.

I should have known he would be the one, Bryan thought, watching Miller lift his briefcase to his lap and deftly roll in the security combination with his thumbs. Bryan almost smiled.

He could not help feeling a little smug, knowing the kind of brainwork it took to bring about this meeting in his office.

Tom Miller's eyes suddenly met his and Bryan saw the flicker of hurt in them before they became steel. Bryan nodded at him. He was grateful to know that Miller cared enough to be hurt. He knew that because of that emotional investment, this meeting would be the most difficult assignment the young man ever undertook in his career with the Agency. He imagined the turmoil Miller must have experienced as his investigation led him closer and closer to the truth.

Miller lowered his eyes and began to square the edges of the sheaf of papers he had taken from his briefcase.

"Let's hear what you have, Agent Miller," Parkins said.

He nodded several times as Agent Miller read the detailed report he had prepared on what took place from the time the Congolese suspect was taken from his home in Kinshasa. It included a transcript of his own interrogation of the suspect.

The report revealed that Miller accompanied the Congolese security police when they went to pick up the suspect. The man had not resisted. Miller did not let him out of his sight from the time he was picked up. He rode in the same car with him to security headquarters and stayed with him all through the chief of the security police's interrogation.

But after half an hour of drilling by the security chief, he began to doubt that the suspect had anything to do with the death of Ambassador McWright. The man was scared witless, but he kept insisting that he was innocent, that he had been set up by a black American man from the Embassy whom he did not know. Frustrated, the chief of the security police whacked him across the back with a club and threatened to crack his balls and stretch his penis to the length of an elephant's trunk if he did not stop lying. Even then the suspect did not change his story.

By then Miller, was convinced that the suspect was telling the truth. There was absolutely no discernible motive. Besides, the man had not exactly burrowed himself into the underground, as a guilty man would have done. It had been fairly easy to find him once they started looking in earnest. Not only that, Miller himself picked up bits of information from various sources. And in the context of that information, the Congolese suspect's story was not all that odd.

Miller got the security chief and his officers to leave the room, using the excuse that he wanted to try out a new psychological technique on the suspect. He was still in the process of perfecting the technique and preferred not to let anyone see it just yet, he explained. With the security chief gone, Miller calmed the suspect and got him to speak more coherently. He did not show up for work the day of the accident, the man said, because a black American forced him to leave the country. The American came to his house the night before and told him that if he did not leave Belgium by the next day, he would tell the Belgian authorities that he had been caught passing counterfeit notes around to the Congolese staff at the American Embassy. He even showed him some fake notes that he said he would use as evidence and said that his compatriots were prepared to testify against him.

He said he thought the American was joking because he had never been involved with that kind of thing, although he knew people who were. Then the American asked him who did he think the Belgians would believe, an American Embassy official or a futureless Congolese whom the ambassador took pity on out of her sentimental attachment to his country and put in a low-level maintenance job. He knew the American was right, that the Belgian police would never believe him, so he took the train to France that very night and stayed with some friends.

When he saw on television the next day what happened to Ambassador McWright, he took the first plane he could get on back to Congo. Where else could he go? He knew suspicion would fall on him after his sudden disappearance from the Embassy. He thought he would be better off among his own people when they came for him.

Miller kept on probing. Was he sure the man was American? Yes, he was sure, the Congolese said, because he had "that same way," like the other Americans he had seen around the Embassy. And he spoke French with that same American accent. Had he seen him before? Yes.

Only once. He was the same man he had seen talking angrily to Madame l'ambassadrice earlier that same week. No, he did not hear what he was saying, because they were a little distance away, but he could tell by his face and his gestures that he was angry. And anyway, even if he heard every word, he would not have understood for they must have been speaking in English.

Miller pressed him further. What day was it that he saw the American and the ambassador speaking? What was the exact time of the day? Where were they speaking? Did Madame McWright also speak angrily? How did you come to see them? Was anyone else with them? Did anyone else hear them or see them? The Congolese responded without hesitation to all these questions. Finally, Miller asked, "Did the American man see you?"

"Yes, he did. I was not trying to hide. I was doing my work. But I remember glancing up after a while and seeing him there alone staring at me. Then he turned and walked away. I tell you he was the very one who came to see me, *patron.*"

Miller called for an artist. One came in almost immediately, along with the chief of police, his deputy and two other officers. Miller recognized the face that finally emerged from the artist's drawing as that of Agent Parkins, but he said nothing to the Congolese officials. Instead, he asked that the suspect be kept in protective custody, without any harm being done to him, while he sent off his report to Washington and awaited a response. Miller was summoned to Washington a few days later. The man was still in protective custody in Kinshasa. He would remain there until Washington ordered his release.

"I want you to tell me why, Bryan," Director Billings said harshly when Miller concluded his report.

Bryan nodded to Tom Miller. "Tell him why, Agent Miller."

The director turned sharply to Miller.

"What more do you know, Tom?" he demanded.

"I have only a theory, sir. Something I pieced together on the way here from Kinshasa. Agent Parkins will have to say whether I am right or wrong."

"Go on," Billings said.

"Agent Parkins was a Peace Corps volunteer in what was then Zaire at the same time that Ambassador McWright was consul general there. We know that Ambassador McWright adopted her daughter Shayna in Zaire. We also know that the natural mother insisted that the child's father was an American. She must have revealed his name to Ambassador McWright because Ambassador McWright privately tracked him down. But the man denied it when she confronted him, although he did not deny knowing the woman. Ambassador McWright was convinced he was the father.

It would not have been difficult for her to find out the extent of his relations with the woman. Still, she never disclosed his name to anyone. Apparently, he was so vicious and threatening in his denial that she wrote him off as dead. All this I found out from someone in whom the ambassador confided at the time, the mother superior at the Franciscan convent in Kinshasa. I went to see the Mother Superior after I found out that Shayna McWright visited her while she was in Kinshasa looking for her birth mother."

Tom Miller paused and looked away, as if to hide the expression on his face. Then he sat forward in his chair and clasped his hands. He did not look at Agent Parkins. He addressed the director again.

"As you know, sir, Agent Parkins' name is on the short list of candidates to head the task force on modernizing the Agency. It seemed certain that he would be chosen, especially in light of your endorsement. But for reasons that no one understood, Ambassador McWright objected strongly to Agent Parkins' being considered for the position. All she would say was that while Agent Parkins was a brilliant man with an outstanding record of service both in the military and in intelligence, she did not think he was the right person for such a sensitive office. None of this is public knowledge, of course.

When Ambassador McWright learned that you would be in Paris, she made an appointment to meet with you. You yourself informed me of that appointment, sir, when you told me that our own meeting had to be delayed. I recall you said it was an unusual request. It is my belief, sir, that Ambassador McWright planned to disclose to you the reason or reasons why she objected so strongly to Agent Parkins. Agent Parkins accompanied you on that trip to Paris, but, you may recall, he went to Brussels for a few days. As protocol dictated, he called on Ambassador McWright at the Embassy. That must have been when he found out that she was going to meet you in Paris. The rest, well..."

Miller left the sentence hanging and shrugged. Agent Parkins looked at him with open admiration and pride.

"I had you pegged from the first day I saw you, Tom. You have never disappointed me. To follow up with the Mother Superior was brilliant," he said.

Tom Miller remained silent. It was the director who spoke.

"For chrissake, Bryan! Don't you feel anything for what you have done? You killed that woman in cold blood and set up an innocent man to take the blame. You even got some of the hawks around here all riled up ready to take action against Congo. Why, some of those jerks on the Hill were even talking about withholding aid to Africa, period, as a warning that we would not tolerate anti-American actions in any form from that continent. Do you know what that would have done? Don't you feel anything, man? *Anything*?"

Director Billings rose to his feet and leaned across the mahogany desk, his face shoved as close to Agent Parkins' as he could get it. Agent Parkins leaned back on the hind legs of his chair and clasped his hands behind his head. His face was expressionless. When he spoke, his voice was quiet and polite.

"As I said, sir, Ambassador McWright was an encumbrance. As head of the modernization task force, I would have been better able to influence the way the Agency operates, introduce new thinking, new tactics that are needed for a twenty-first century environment and a more sophisticated enemy. My agenda would have been good for the Agency. It would have been good for the country. Janice McWright wanted to derail all that. I made a tactical move."

He brought his chair forward again and turned to Tom Miller, looking at him with a mixture of admiration and regret.

"But I did not factor in Agent Miller's personal feelings for Shayna McWright." He looked intently at Tom. You like her, don't you, Tom? But that's not so surprising, when you come to think of it. A Pulitzer Prize-winning journalist: that means she's got the kind of mind you admire, a mind like yours. And she *is* very attractive."

Tom Miller's face grew red. The muscle at his temple twitched. He stared at Agent Parkins in steely silence. Agent Parkins returned his gaze with a look of sympathy.

Still leaning across the desk, David Billings marveled at the balls of Bryan Parkins. Never in his life had he felt such a strong urge to choke the life out of a human being. Even so, he was devastated. He had quietly godfathered Parkins' career at the Agency, positioning him to play a leading role in the restructuring of the Agency. Choosing him over that Texas asshole to head the revamp team ticked off many of his senior staff. But Parkins was the best he had seen in a long time. Exactly what the Agency needed. He, Billings, had more or less convinced the President of that and was prepared to go to the mat with the racists and visionless idiots in the Agency and anybody else who had any say in the matter.

Billings was one of the very few who knew that the favorite Texas son was a closet alcoholic. As far as Billings was concerned, that took him out of the running. How in God's name could you trust the judgment of a man who needed liquor to see him through the day? Parkins would head the revamp team even if it meant leaking the information about the Texas boy's drinking problem.

Billings swallowed hard, straightened up and walked over to the window. From there he could see the "Kryptos" sculpture in the courtyard. The sculptor, James Sanborn, used Native American materials to depict the theme of information gathering and cryptography. Billings liked its clean lines, the way it rose dramatically from the ground. Looking at the sculpture, Billings wondered what had gone so wrong with the world. *Is it something that we're doing or not doing that causes us to create the Parkins of our world? How can we live so closely with, even extol, a mind such as this and not see its demonic side? Or is it that we see the demonic side and choose not to pay attention to it because it's...what's his word? An encumbrance*, he thought to himself.

"Couldn't you have talked things over with her, reached some sort of compromise? I mean, she had no problems with your technical qualifications for the job. What's so bad about admitting you're the father of that girl?" he asked aloud, still staring at the "Kryptos."

Agent Parkins' response was swift and unequivocal.

"I could never do that, sir. Even if she *is* my child biologically, she was conceived against my wishes. That would make her, her mother's child and hers alone. No. There can be no compromise there."

The director walked back from the window and stood in front of him.

"You're a heartless son of a bitch, Parkins. Janice McWright was right. In the end, you would have been a disaster for the country."

He turned to Tom Miller.

"It's over, Agent Miller. Let's get Agent Parkins out of here," he said.

"I'm ready," Bryan said, rising from his chair and reaching for his jacket.

He turned to Agent Miller. "She must never know," he said.

The director flew into a rage. How dare he think he had the right to make requests?

"Damn right, she'll never know, you goddamn lunatic! You'll never enter her thoughts, you have my word on that!" he shouted before Tom Miller could respond. "Come on, Agent Miller. Let's get him out of here!"

Bryan smiled and put on his jacket.

Neither Director Billings nor Agent Miller saw it coming. Before either of them could grasp what was happening, Bryan had already popped the pill into his mouth.

"Cyanide," he said to them pleasantly.

ABOUT THE AUTHOR

Rosalind Kilkenny McLymont is the editor in chief of *The Network Journal*, a magazine for Black professionals and business owners, and a partner in McLymont, Kunda & Co., international trade and business development strategists. An award-winning journalist, she has a master's degree in journalism from New York University, a bachelor's in French from the City College of New York, a certificate in Spanish language and literature from the University of Madrid, and a black belt in Tai Chi from Ming's Tai Chi Academy. Born in Guyana on March 15, 1951, she migrated to the United States in 1965 and lived in Uganda and the Democratic Republic of Congo from 1973 to 1980. She lives in Valley Cottage, N.Y., with her husband and three of their children.

Printed in the United States
69806LV00001B/100-171

9 780931 7611